VERA KURIAN

Ver........ is a W~~ashi~~~~ngt~~on D.C.-based writer
w......................................who has
st...~~V~~ONA
a..rize.

@vera_kurian
www.verakurian.com

VERA KURIAN

Never Saw Me Coming

Coming

VINTAGE

1 3 5 7 9 10 8 6 4 2

Vintage is part of the Penguin Random House group of companies
whose addresses can be found at global.penguinrandomhouse.com

Penguin
Random House
UK

Copyright © Albi Literary, Inc. 2021

Vera Kurian has asserted her right to be identified as the author
of this Work in accordance with the Copyright,
Designs and Patents Act 1988

First published in Vintage in 2022
First published in hardback by Harvill Secker in 2021

penguin.co.uk/vintage

A CIP catalogue record for this book is available from the British Library

ISBN 9781529114669 (B format)

Printed and bound in Great Britain by Clays Ltd, Elcograf S.p.A.

The authorised representative in the EEA is Penguin Random House Ireland,
Morrison Chambers, 32 Nassau Street, Dublin D02 YH68

Penguin Random House is committed to a sustainable future
for our business, our readers and our planet. This book is made
from Forest Stewardship Council® certified paper.

For Katie.

NEVER
SAW
ME
COMING

1

Day 60

As soon as the door to my new dorm room closed, I went to the window, scanning across the quad for him. It wasn't like there was any possibility he would just happen to be out there among the families lugging moving boxes or the handful of students sprawled in the grass.

But there! A head of dirty-blond waves. Will. My mouth opened. Then the person turned and I saw it was only a girl with an unfortunate haircut. Seriously, you'd think she'd put in more of an effort for move-in day.

I turned and faced my empty dorm room with its sad linoleum floors, mentally going through my to-do list. 1. Get rid of Mom. Check. She had already left and was probably speeding up the I-95, popping open a bottle of champagne now that she was finally rid of me. 2. Claim the most advantageous space before my roommate, Yessica, arrived. 3. Make six to eight friends before 4. My mandatory check-in appointment at the psychology department. 5. Find Will.

We had a double with two bedrooms, one clearly larger than the other. While my normal instinct was to claim the larger one, I immediately saw the problem with that. The larger bedroom had windows that overlooked the quad. What if I wanted to crawl in or out of my window in the middle of the night? People will record anything even remotely interesting on their phones these days, and I could be easily seen from the other dorms and academic halls that lined the quad—too much of an audience for my liking.

I took the smaller room. My generosity would score me points with my new roomie, but more importantly, the room had a view of the brick wall of the building next to us and there was a metal fire escape attached directly to the window. Easy access in and out of my room without detection—perfect. I dumped some of my boxes into the room and made the bed, placing my stuffed plushie whale on top to clearly stake my claim. The voices inside the dorm were calling me and I had to establish myself quickly.

I gave myself a brief once-over before leaving the room, reapplying my lip gloss and fixing my hair. The hair had to be just right—a loose, effortless side French braid that actually wasn't effortless. You have to be the kind of girl who "doesn't put any effort in" but naturally rolls out of bed looking like a horny but somehow demure starlet. If you meet some standard of objective attractiveness, people think you're better than you actually are—smarter, more interesting, worthier of existing. Combined with the right personality, this can be powerful.

Brewser had one long hallway with rooms shooting off on either side. I peeked into the room next door where two brunettes were wrestling a duvet out of a plastic package. "Hi!" I chirped. "I'm Chloe!" I could be whatever they wanted me to be. A fun girl, a potential best friend, someone to tell secrets to over midnight snacks. This type of socializing was just me playing little roles for a few moments, but when I need to go all in, I can. I can make myself younger when I want to, opting for looser clothes that hide my body and making my eyes shiny with dumbness—a whole costume of innocence. I can look older with makeup and carefully selected clothes, showing skin when necessary. It's easy because people tend to see what they want to.

I went door to door. Room 202. "Omigod I *love* your hair," I said to a bubbly blonde I suspect will end up popular.

Room 206. "You're not brothers, are you?" I said shyly to two boys on the crew team (nice bodies but baby faces—not my taste). They grinned at me, looked at my boobs, and each vied to say something clever. Neither was clever.

Room 212 was a pair of awkward girls. I was friendly to them but didn't linger long because I knew they would never be key players.

While I met a few more people, I was simultaneously assessing who seemed like they were going to be part of Greek life. Will was in a frat—SAE—and one of my first orders of business was to get in with that frat. The crew boys were already in the hallway loudly talking about going out to a club that night. That was good—an outing, and the crew boys seemed like they would be the type to pledge a frat. "I love dancing," I said to what's-his-name, the taller of the two, fingering the end of my braid. "It's the best way to get to know people." He smiled down at me, his eyes crinkling. If high school taught me anything, it's that social life is a game that revolves around navigating hierarchies. Be someone guys want to fuck or you will be invisible to them. Be someone the girls want firmly tucked into their inner circles, whether as friend or enemy, or die the death of being totally irrelevant.

Even from our brief interactions, I could tell no one in this dorm was in my program. I've never met someone like me, but when I do eventually, I think it will be like two wolves meeting in the night, sniffing and recognizing a fellow hunter. But I doubt they would put two of us in the same dorm—there were only seven and they probably had to spread us out to prevent a war from breaking out.

I had to go then, leaving my new friends behind, to check in with the program.

The psychology department was diagonally across the quad, visible from the windows of the common area of my room. The quad was lush grass crisscrossed with brick paths, with each brick having the name of an alumnus engraved into it—John Smith, class of '03. Funny—Will was never going to get a brick, but I was. One of the larger dorms, Tyler Hall, had a massive banner hung on it that said WELCOME FRESHMEN!!! I stopped to take a selfie with the banner in the background: here's a girl excited for her first day of college, busy doing college things!

It's practically destiny that I ended up at John Adams University. I knew I had to be in DC, which meant applying to Georgetown, American University, George Washington University, John Adams, Catholic University, and Trinity College—all of which are inside the District. As safeties, I also applied to reasonably close places like George Mason and the University of Maryland. I got into all of them except for Georgetown. Seriously, fuck them. My application was golden: I have an IQ of 135—five points short of genius—solid SATs and grades. I paid for most of my wardrobe with a business I set up writing papers for other students. Who knows how many of them got into college with a heartfelt essay about the dead cancer grandmother they didn't actually have.

I had been offered scholarship money at various schools, but nothing like what Adams had offered. Even if I had turned down the psychology study, I still could have gotten generous scholarships given to students with my pedigree to entice them to a Tier 2 liberal arts school. But I didn't care—Adams was always my first choice because of Will. Another bonus was the school's placement in DC: a busy city with a relatively high murder rate. The campus was in the gentrifying neighborhood of Shaw, just east of bougie Logan Circle, and south of U Street, a popular going-out destination. A neighborhood that, despite the presence of nice restaurants, was also a place where drunk people occasionally got into fights and stabbed each other and pedestrians got mugged. Law enforcement was busy with the constant parade of protests, conferences, and visiting diplomats—they probably gave two shits about what was going on in the mind of a random eighteen-year-old girl with an iPhone in her hand and a benign look on her face.

I liked the somber castle look of the psychology department. Its dark red bricks were covered with ivy and the windows, edged with black iron, were warbled like they had old glass in them. The inside was dimly lit by a hanging chandelier with flickering amber bulbs, and the cavernous foyer smelled like old books. When I walked through it, I imagined a camera following me, viewers worried about what dangerous things might come my way. I would be the one they would root for.

I went up the curving staircase to the sixth floor where I was supposed to check in with my program. Room 615 was tucked at the end of the hallway, secluded. A placard on the door said Leonard Wyman, PhD, and Elena Torres, Doctoral Candidate. I recognized the names from my paperwork.

I knocked and a few seconds later a woman flung open the door. "You must be Chloe Sevre!"

She stuck out her hand. They probably had a whole dossier on me. I had had a bunch of phone interviews with a couple of screeners, then one with Wyman himself, and they had also interviewed my mother and high school counselor.

The woman's hand was bony, but warm and dry, and her eyes were chocolate brown and unafraid. "I'm Elena, one of Dr. Wyman's grad students." She smiled and gestured for me to come inside. She led me past a messy reception area, a desk cluttered with papers and three laptops, and down a hallway to a smaller office, hers presumably.

She closed the door behind us. "We'll get you all settled. Everything was fine with the financial aid office before you got here?" As one of the seven students in the study, I was granted a free ride to John Adams University. All I had to give in exchange was my willingness to be a full-time guinea pig in their Multimethod Psychopathy Panel Study.

I nodded, looking around. Her shelves were crammed with books and stacks of printed-out articles. Three different versions of the *Diagnostic and Statistical Manual of Mental Disorders*. Tomes on "abnormal" psychology. Robert Hare's book *Without Conscience*, which I had read.

"Great," Elena said. She pulled something up on her computer. She took a bite of the scone resting on her mousepad and chewed loudly. She was pretty in a grad student sort of way. Olive skin and a nice collarbone. You could picture her falling in love with some reedy nerd and trying to have children too late. "Here you are!" She clicked a few times and her printer came to life. When she stood up to retrieve the paper, I leaned over, trying to see her computer screen, but she had a privacy shield. I didn't know if it was supposed to be a secret or something, but I had found out how many students were in the program when one of the administrators had been working out my financial aid package. I was dying of curiosity about the other six students. The bizarre elite.

Elena handed me a bunch of paper-clipped documents. They were consent forms for the study, assurances that my data would be kept private, that there was minimal risk associated with computer-based surveys, that blood drawings would be performed by a licensed phlebotomist, blah blah blah. A lot more about privacy, location tracking—which I paid closer attention to—and what their legal obligations were to report it if I threatened to either harm myself or others. Oh, please. I wasn't planning on making any of my threats known.

When I finished signing the documents, I saw that Elena was withdrawing a small package from a safe. She pulled something shiny out of a small box. "And here's your smartwatch." I liked it immediately. It was sleek and black, like something you'd see in a spy movie. "You're to wear it at all times, as stipulated. It tracks your heart rate and sleep rhythms—oh, it's waterproof, by the way, so don't worry about taking it off in the shower. You can even swim with it." I held out my arm, and like a jeweler with a tennis bracelet she fastened it around my left wrist. "If it cramps your style, you can also take off the wristband and wear it as pendant under your shirt. When there's a mood log for you to take, you'll get an icon like this." She did something on her computer and a little red exclamation point appeared on the black screen of the smartwatch. She gestured for me to touch it. When I did, the exclamation point disappeared and was replaced by text asking me what activity I was doing right then, and then the question *How happy do you feel right now? 1 2 3 4 5 6 7.* "The mood logs are pretty short," she explained. "They won't take more than a couple minutes. You're supposed to take them as soon as you get the notice—this is to try to measure how people actually feel throughout the day, not in artificial lab settings. But it's okay to wait if you're taking a test—I wouldn't want a professor to think you were cheating or something."

"Do the professors at Adams know I'm in the study?"

"No, your participation and diagnosis are entirely confidential."

"And the watch tracks where I am all the time?"

"No. I mean, a satellite probably does somewhere, but no, the only time we retain location data is when you submit a mood log because we want to understand the context of where you were and what you were feeling. I think you'll be interested to see how this can help you understand your own emotions." She smiled at me widely, showing one snaggletooth. I was relieved about the location tracking. I had a backup plan, of course— taking off the smartwatch and leaving it in my room, or maybe hiding it in Yessica's stuff so that it tracked her, not me, if I was up to no good. A liability turned into an alibi: the watch says I was at home studying and drinking a glass of milk!

"How often am I coming in for the other experiments?"

"They're not necessarily experiments. Some of them are just surveys. But it won't be more than one or two a week, and the MRIs we schedule weeks in advance."

I admired my new watch. When I touched the blank face it woke up, showing an array of clever icons. "What about the other six students? Will I meet them?"

"Not face-to-face, really, but you might interact with them down the line."

It sounded interesting actually. Sure, I was there for the free scholarship to be in the city where Will was, but let's be honest. People love psychology because people are narcissistic. And as a psychopath I'm particularly narcissistic.

Elena stacked some papers together and rapped them against the desk, lining them all up. "You'll have an intake meeting with Dr. Wyman this week, but there isn't anything else we need from you today, so welcome to the study!"

With my new toy adorning my wrist, I headed back across the quad to the dorm, hoping Yessica had shown up. Yessica was my biggest wild card—someone who could intentionally or not make my life and plans very difficult, and I wanted to suss out what sort of roommate she would be. If she was cool, we could be a power couple at Brewser. If she was nosy, I would have yet another problem to deal with.

I heard movement inside the room just before I went in. A lanky, nut-brown girl with massive dark waves was shoving a box into the corner. "Chloe!" she shouted. She came over, a big grin on her face, and we shook hands. "I'm Yessica!" She had huge dark eyes framed with thick, possibly fake eyelashes. Points for good skin and the flat, elf-style boots. Double points for the minifridge. "I just got here! I feel so bad—are you sure you want the smaller room?"

"I'm okay—I prefer to face in that direction." We helped each other unpack, yammering on in the way girls do, deciding what should go where as I assessed her. I decided she was more of a positive than a negative addition. She was pretty, funny, and seemed laid-back—not someone who would snoop through my computer or raise an eyebrow if I brought a guy home. After we put our stuff away we went into the noisy hallway to meet more people. There was more talk of going out.

I was impatient. I knew this was the right thing to be doing—forming alliances, making a good impression—but I wanted to get things going. It was August 24, the start of Freshman Orientation, sixty days until October 23. This was a date I had carefully selected—it gave me enough time to maneuver, but more importantly there was going to be a massive protest in DC that day, centering on the National Mall. It was a convergence of several different demonstrations: a pro-free speech rally, an anti-racism rally that was protesting the pro-free speech rally, a pro-impeachment rally, and a March for the Earth demonstration. Based on social media postings, Airbnb rentals in the city, and bus ticket sales, pundits were predicting that the convergence of political fervor was going to lead to a turnout that would tax every city resource. The timing was auspicious. The news had previously covered how such massive events often led to cell phone networks being overburdened. The police would have their hands full with protestors and skirmishes breaking out, as they have had for the past few years. It was going to be chaos.

It was the perfect day to kill Will Bachman.

2

Here is what I know about Will Bachman.

He lives at 1530 Marion Street NW, exactly 1,675 feet from my dorm. The nearest police station to his house is a five-minute drive away. The house is a rowhouse, attached on either side to other rowhouses. The first-floor windows and front door have iron bars welded over them. Within the past year, there have been thirty-three violent crimes near that house, most of which were armed robberies.

Here is what I've derived from any number of his online accounts.

Will Bachman is in the Sigma Alpha Epsilon fraternity—SAE—whose frat house is a few blocks away. His roommate is Cordy, also in SAE. Will Bachman is a junior majoring in political science and deciding if he wants to minor in econ. He's on the lacrosse team, but also likes swimming. I used to swim with him when we were kids. He likes house music and smoking weed. He owns a black Volkswagen Jetta that some asshole dinged in the parking lot of the Giant supermarket. He reads the Drudge Report and thinks that all snowflakes need to be melted. He has a mother who wears pearls and volunteers for the Red Cross and a younger brother. They live at 235 Hopper Street, Toms River, NJ, 08754.

I would guess Will shops at the Giant in Shaw, because that's where his car was dinged and he also reported that the closest Safeway to 1530 Marion Street was "filled with cunts who never get the line moving." I know he frequents Buttercream Bakery because he posted about getting his tenth coffee for free. He once lost his cell phone between P and S Streets on 14th Street, stumbling home drunk, so it was probable he often hung out in that vicinity. He did not like to go east of 7th Street because of "the locals." There was a muffin shop with a direct line of sight of Will's front door. The sort of place where you could camp out with a cup of coffee for a few hours and no one would notice that you were staring at the house across the street, scheming.

I would estimate that Will Bachman is about six-one. Adams has a decent lacrosse team, so he's no doubt athletic and physically stronger than me—this is something I should never forget. He has thick blond hair and a thin upper lip. He prefers to wear polo shirts and khakis. He wears a white necklace made from small seashells.

His friends are a predictable array of frat bros and lacrosse players: mostly white, faces flushed with beer, pointing at things in bleary pictures. They drink beer and have themed parties and sail on boats in the Potomac River. It isn't a party until someone is hospitalized with alcohol poisoning. #YOLO

There's Cordy, who posts a lot about video games and the NFL. Cordy and his girlfriend, Miranda Yee, appear to be on and off again, but when they are on again, he often sleeps at her apartment in Dupont Circle and not at home, leaving Will alone. Also part of the crew is Mike Arie, also on the lacrosse team and a member of SAE. Mike appears in pictures with an array of girls on his arm sticking their tongues out. This is the sort of girl I could easily be, someone who could slip in and out of someone's life unnoticed. Will, Cordy, and Mike have recently attended an event thrown by someone named Charles Portmont. Charles is also in SAE and his Instagram is clogged with posts of people partying. One of the latest showed Will and his friends dressed in white, attending a fundraiser. A quick internet search shows that Charles Portmont's father, Luke Portmont, is the Virginia state chairman for the Republican National Committee. The event included lobsters and craft cocktails. #ClassicCharles.

Will Bachman does not have a girlfriend because bros before hos and because never trust a skank.

Will Bachman probably does not have a gun because of the strict gun control laws in DC.

Will Bachman posts enough about his classes that any intelligent person such as myself could easily figure out his schedule. The hashtag #SAElife is used often enough that one could tell what the brothers are up to on any particular weekend. Where they're going, and who with, and how inebriated they'll be.

Will Bachman drinks too much and hangs out with people who don't look after him.

Will Bachman has made some mistakes.

Will Bachman has sixty days to live.

3

Leonard opened the door and welcomed Chloe Sevre inside. "I'm Dr. Wyman, the program director, but you can call me Leonard." The girl came inside, her eyes casting about his office curiously. "Sit wherever you like," he said, gesturing to the variety of chairs that faced his desk. She was about five-five with clear skin, a bit on the pale side. Large blue eyes. She wore leggings and an oversize tunic, her dark brown hair in a ponytail. She looked younger than eighteen, or at least she did right now. He had seen other versions of her on her social media. Dramatic makeup and little dresses and high heels. Her accounts were carefully curated, the "spontaneous" and "carefree" shots much too perfect to be either.

She selected a large armchair and tucked her legs under her. "Does this just work like a normal therapy session?" she asked.

"More or less, although we do work on your diagnosis and teach you methods of dealing with it. How has your first week been so far?"

"A blur," she said, bringing her hand up to her mouth to nibble at a nail. "I've been meeting so many people I can hardly keep their names straight. I got all the classes I wanted, though."

"Did you make any friends?"

She nodded. "My roommate is cool, and there are some kids in my hall. We went dancing. You haven't sent any quizzes yet, right?"

"They're not quizzes, they're logs. No right answer, just a re-cord of what you're feeling at that particular moment."

Chloe nodded, her eyes scanning the volumes on the shelf behind him. "When will I meet the others?"

"It's not a playgroup!" he joked.

She pointed to her watch. "Do you use this with the univer-sity police or something? To know where we are?"

Leonard had to answer the question carefully. "Of course not. Chloe, it's not illegal to have this diagnosis."

She shrugged, sullen. "People act like we're monsters. My old guidance counselor, my mom."

"You're not a monster."

"Then why did you diagnose me with something worse than what they gave me in high school?"

"Psychopathy is not 'worse' than Antisocial Personality Disorder—they're different, and people unfortunately use the terms interchangeably. I think you, along with many others, are part of that subset that got diagnosed with ASPD when it should have been psychopathy, which I'm not convinced is a 'personality disorder' in our classical understanding of the word. Unfortunately, the word *psychopath* has been tainted with a stain of criminality, mainly because one of the foundational researchers on the topic—Robert Hare—started and focused his research on criminals. I'd like for us to reclaim the term as something more useful."

"So you don't think I'm dangerous?"

Leonard was used to his patients arriving with a misunder-standing about their diagnosis, probably half informed by lurid police procedurals and horror movies. Most had been diagnosed and referred to him by clinicians who were in over their heads, but only a select few were appropriate for the Multimethod Psychopathy Panel Study. They had to be young, they had to be smart and they had to be willing to try. "That's a popular misconception. My own estimate is that about two or three percent of the American population is psychopathic—can you imagine the chaos if they were all dangerous? I'm unusual compared to most clinicians—well, for one, because I study it while so few do, but also because I don't view it as that different from other biologically based disorders, like schizophrenia."

"Like a mental illness, then." She said it flatly, as if displeased.

"Okay, then, let's say it's more like a biologically based limited capacity to understand and feel the full range of human emotion or manage impulse control."

"You make it sound like dyslexia or something. My mom says it's pathological selfishness."

"I wouldn't use the word *pathological*. You lack empathy because of the way your brain functions. Because you don't feel fear the same way, you end up seeking excitement. There's this affective dimension to the disease—the lack of empathy, manipulativeness, superficial charm and an antisocial dimension—that is the part more associated with criminality. Impulse control, attraction to risky behavior and the like. But much of it ties back to biology."

"If it's biological, why can't you just give me a drug?"

"That's the perennial American question, isn't it? There's never been a successful protocol for treading psychopathy. I'm hoping to change that, and how people see the disease. And the nomenclature—any time there's a mentally ill serial killer or a mass shooter, everyone calls them a psychopath."

"But don't a lot of us end up in prison?" she countered. She didn't defer to him right away. That said something interesting about her. She was testing him.

"Prison is disproportionately populated with psychopaths but that says more about a lack of impulse control than anything else. Most psychopaths don't end up in prison and, with the right direction, can lead productive lives without destroying the relationships around them."

"What if they don't get the right direction? What if they don't think there's anything wrong with them?"

"If they can't figure out how to live in the world on their own, yes, they can make bad decisions and end up in prison, or they take advantage of one person after another until they have to skip town and end up alone."

She chewed her lower lip. "And you think I won't end up that way?"

"I'm sure of it. You have excellent grades, which shows that you *do* have impulse control when you want it. You had friends and extracurriculars and no criminal record."

"That's only because I never got caught," she joked. She, like many psychopaths, had an easy confidence around her. None of the awkwardness one often saw in young adults, still gawky in their own bodies. "What's the difference, then, between a psychopath like me and the ones that end up on death row because they have a collection of heads?"

"Well, for one, they lack your skills of evasion," he joked, and she laughed loudly. "It's not something you need to worry about—people like that often have a constellation of other issues. Traumatic brain injuries as kids, a tendency toward sadism. But you can lack empathy without being sadistic."

"Oh," she said, averting her eyes to stare out the window, frowning. "What if that's me, though? What if my mom dropped me when I was a baby and I hit my head?"

"There are a lot of factors that make people end up that way. Have you ever wanted to hurt someone else physically?"

"I mean, it's a trick question. Everyone gets mad sometimes, and you think, *God, I'd like to slap them!*"

"But you've never wanted to hurt someone, really hurt them, just so you could watch them be in pain?"

She shrugged, chewing at her nail again. "Only in my imagination."

"Have you ever hurt or killed an animal?"

"No," she said.

Not what your mother told me, he thought, silently making a note of the exact time. She had said it with such a straight face, no hesitation. He would check with the data from her smartwatch later, checking to see if her pulse had changed. It was hardly a lie detector—not as if he believed in those, anyhow—but the physiological intricacies of psychopaths had long fascinated him.

"I just want a regular life. I want to be a doctor and have a boyfriend and lots of friends and maybe a vlog."

"And many people like you do just that. You've probably met a few in your day-to-day life—journalists, doctors, teachers, even CEOs."

She smiled shyly. Leonard was reminded of why he loved his job—the possibilities. "So I could still become a doctor?"

"As long as you learn and practice the techniques we teach you, and follow the law, why not? You can be anything."

4

Andre headed downstairs to leave a plastic bin of his stuff by the front door, the smell of waffles hitting him. Normally the smell made him hungry, but this morning a ball of nervousness sat in his stomach. He and his mother had formed a habit his last two years of high school: he would get up early so he could eat breakfast with her before he headed to school and she went to work. He liked this private time between him and his mother. His father often worked night shifts, and it wasn't like Isaiah, Andre's brother, ever got up before noon.

"You have everything?" she asked as he entered the kitchen. She was wearing the light blue scrubs she wore for work and pouring him a glass of juice.

"I think so, and I'll come back when I need to," he said, sitting down. His parents had assumed that they would be helping him move, but Andre had begged them off, saying there was no need for a big to-do when they lived in Brookland, in the northeast quadrant of DC, and John Adams University was only a half an hour bus ride away. The disappointment they had expressed at not getting to help him move in had made him want to die inside, but it was really critical that his parents spend as little time as possible at Adams, so he had played it off as if they would embarrass him.

They ate breakfast, watching the news on the small TV in the kitchen, which was showing hurricane flooding in North Carolina. This, followed by a story about nuclear weapons, was enough to elicit a disapproving noise from his mother. "Andre, you better graduate before the world ends." They laughed, a little bitterly, the helpless way people had been in the past few years of school shootings and politicians screaming at each other.

After breakfast, Andre picked up his bin and walked out with his mother, where they would part ways for separate bus stops. She stopped to hug him. His mother was thin—all the Jensens were thin—no matter what she ate she never gained weight. Her thinness worried him, as if it correlated with bad health, but her hugs were fierce. "You sure you don't need help? I can take off from work…" Andre shook his head. "Text me when you get there," she said, as if he was going across the ocean.

Andre nodded, then headed for the bus stop. The houses on Lawrence Street were mostly detached, small single-family homes with carefully kept yards. Andre's house, like most on his street, had a front porch where people often gathered to socialize.

He boarded the bus and sat down, resting the plastic bin in his lap. He took a deep breath. *Okay*, he thought as the bus began to lumber forward, *I got this far, so the rest will be fine.*

The bus rolled to a stop, then gave its pneumatic wheeze as it lowered to accommodate whoever it was who couldn't make the steps. A short woman boarded and when Andre saw her he raised a hand to wave. Ms. Baker went to his mother's church and had much to say about everything.

"Andre Jensen," she crooned as she sat in the seat across the aisle from him. Clearly she saw the bin filled with fresh note-books at the top, clothes on the bottom. "Off to college? What are you majoring in?"

"I haven't even had a class yet!"

"You have to have some idea these days."

"Journalism, I guess." He felt a little silly saying it—two years ago the idea of getting into college had seemed like a pipe dream.

"Well, you better bring home the A's!" Ms. Baker gave his shoulder an affectionate pat and settled down to her knitting; above the soft clacking sound of her needles, Andre wondered what she would report back to the church ladies about him. Just about everyone in the neighborhood had opinions about the Jensens. A middle-class family that had been buffeted by a bizarre tragedy. But the Jensens soldiered on, a family of five now a family of four. This was the great act they all put on— waffles for breakfast, much commotion over Andre's heading off to college—a smile stretched tight across a chasm of sadness. Kiara should have been the first in their family to go to college.

The bus trundled forward, crossing 13th Street. He tried not to think about Kiara, but like the nub on the inside of his cheek he chewed sometimes, he kept returning to it painfully. He had been twelve that day when his mom had shown up at school in her scrubs to pull him out of class. She *never* missed work, so he knew something had happened. As they walked down the street, toward home, she explained. "Your sister had an asthma attack."

"Okay?" he said.

"At dance class. It was very bad." The look on his mother's face was strange. Ashen, frozen.

"Is she at the hospital?"

"She died, Andre," his mother replied. A motorcycle roared past them, its sound half drowning her out, assuring him that he had heard her wrong.

"What?" His mother was staring straight ahead, set on some horizon as if everything would be better once they got there. "She was having an asthma attack, a bad one. They called an ambulance. It took forty minutes to come." She spoke quietly. Around them, no one seemed to notice the gravity of what she was saying. A man walking an old dog. A woman playing with her phone, not even looking up as she passed them. Andre's mother wouldn't look at him as they hurried home, and in the moment this hurt, but later on he knew it was because if she looked at him she would cry. Which she did, once they were safely in the confines of their house, surrounded by stunned family members.

And now, with him just scraping his way into college, he was an article of pride for the tragic family. A kid who turned his life around after a bout of terrible misfortune. Kiara had been a straight-A student. She probably would have gone to law school. Another Black life lost, and no one was keeping count.

Andre's phone buzzed with a notification. He shoved his earbuds into his ears eagerly. A new episode of *Cruel and Unusual* had dropped, the latest true-crime podcast that he had become obsessed with. This month it was featuring a ten-part series on the Zodiac Killer—he had already listened to each of the first six parts more than once.

The host's scratchy voice became a strange soundtrack as the city became increasingly whiter as the bus moved west—fewer houses and more coffee shops and restaurants. Andre couldn't help but feel a wave of excitement despite everything, rolling his head around to pop his neck in a few places, like a fighter about to enter the ring. The bus pulled up to the stop in Shaw that was closest to Adams.

He found Tyler Hall, which was to be his home for the next nine months. It was a wide building that took up half the block, brick with neat rows of windows sporting various items: flags of different countries, more than one *Impeach!* sign, *Refugees Welcome* and *Black Lives Matter*.

He walked into Tyler where three bubbly white girls were manning a foldout table, checking people in. "Andre Jensen?" he said.

"Jensen, Jensen, ah, here we are," the girl said, riffling through manila envelopes. She checked him off a list, then handed the envelope to him. "There's a bunch of orientation stuff in there— maps, useful places, et cetera. The card is your student ID— you'll use it basically for everything. It's how you get in the dorm. Normally there's a student just inside the door who will make you swipe to get in. Your keys are in here, too, and just so you know, if you get locked out it's a ten-dollar fee each time after the third lockout. It looks like your roommate hasn't checked in yet. If you have any questions, your RA, Devon, will be on your floor."

Andre tucked the envelope under his arm and took the stairs to Room 203. The room was a rectangle with two twin beds flush against opposite sides. To the left was a small bathroom that was clean with white tile.

From the bottom of his bin he removed a parcel carefully wrapped in two sweatshirts in addition to its own soft case: the camera his parents had given him for his birthday. According to his father, who had researched on the internet about cameras, looking carefully through his bifocals, it was a solid upgrade to the one Andre had previously bought used on eBay. A good DSLR for serious beginning photographers. Andre had only taken a couple photography classes at the community center before he graduated high school, figuring that wherever life took him—journalism, blogging, podcasting—being able to take good pictures was a skill set he needed to develop.

He had a few hours of free time before he had to check in with the psychology department. He had confirmed via a series of phone calls with the financial aid office that, indeed, he would be coming to John Adams University and his tuition and fees were in fact paid in full. No, it wasn't a joke.

Andre heard another key in the lock. A guy came in and looked at him. He was short, his head shaved, and he sported a blue sweater and a red bow tie despite the fading heat of summer. "Do you think they put all the Black kids together?" he said.

Andre laughed—he had been thinking the same thing.

He introduced himself as Sean and they talked as they un-packed. Sean was from PG County, Maryland. (*Murralind* was how he said it.) He was the salutatorian of his high school class. He insisted that Andre stand as far back as possible so Sean could hang an enormous movie poster, which, Andre was pleased to see, was for *Aliens*. "Greatest horror movie ever made!" Sean said.

"Oh, I don't know about that." They argued good-naturedly about horror movies, Andre feeling a flush of pleasure that they had something in common.

They headed to the school store together, talking the whole way. *I kind of like this guy,* Andre realized. He came to his first decision point about his whole college scheme: Should he tell Sean that the roommate he was about to live with for the next year was a diagnosed psychopath?

The first overt lie came easily: Andre said he had to go to the financial aid office when really it was time for him to check in at the psychology department. Sean accepted the lie readily and Andre consulted his campus map. As if he didn't have enough to feel nervous about, the psychology department was creepy look-ing. Gothic somehow despite being plopped in the middle of a modern campus. He wondered, as he crept up the stairs one at a time, if the entire game would be up the second Dr. Leonard Wyman laid eyes on him. He had a PhD, after all.

Andre knocked on the open door of 615 and an older white man, maybe seventy-something, held up his hands apologeti-cally. He was eating an enormous, tempting-looking pastrami sandwich. Embarrassed, he pointed to his mouth and gestured for Andre to follow him to a more private office. Andre sat and watched as Wyman, still chewing, gathered a stack of papers. "Sorry, I knew you were coming but I hadn't had anything to eat all day!" he exclaimed at last.

Andre felt a strange feeling wash over him as he accepted the man's hand.

"Andre... Jensen... Jensen," Wyman murmured, searching for something on his computer. "Ah, here we go."

Andre then realized what it was that bothered him, although it didn't make sense. He had never met Wyman before—they hadn't even talked on the phone—and Andre knew this to be one hundred percent true. But if that was the case, why was this complete stranger so familiar?

5

Billy the Crew was one of the two baby-faced crew boys on my floor in Brewser. Luck, or fate, whatever you want to call it, was on my side. That first night when my floor went out dancing, I heard him mention that his older brother was in SAE. I flirted with him, knowing this would mean invitations to parties or whatever other late-night shenanigans possibly affiliated with Will Bachman's friends. Billy mentioned offhand where the SAE house was and said he could take me there when they had their Welcome Week party.

The party wasn't till the weekend, and I was impatient for it. Every time I walked through the crowded campus streets between classes, part of me was searching for Will. I didn't know what I would do if I saw him and was almost scared that I would lash out without thinking. I didn't know if he would recognize me—it had been years since he had last seen me. Each time I arrived at a new class—Biology, Physics—I scanned over the other students, looking for his blond hair. Of course he wasn't there. He was a junior and probably wasn't taking freshman-level premed prereqs.

Once I could establish that he wasn't in my classroom, I'd relax and settle in, scoping out the territory. I'm an auditory learner and don't need to take that many notes, so I spent much of those first classes sniffing out my fellow classmates. It took me all of a day to figure out that any time I saw a sleek black smartwatch, this wasn't necessarily interesting. A lot of people were wearing them, not just students in my program. But these people would be my competition for med school and my future friends and enemies. They could be accomplices or obstacles. Lovers, even. I had been having an itch for sex lately. I eyed one boy in the front row who had broad shoulders, but when he half turned around I saw his horse face. Bummer.

I did make it a point to take the long way back to my dorm after class, passing in front of the SAE house. It stood at the intersection of two tree-lined streets, a corner lot containing a large, three-story Victorian house of dark orange brick with a black shingled roof. It had a yard that was littered with beer cans, deflated footballs, and a couple of beat-up-looking grills. Sometimes the frat brothers would sit outside in patio chairs, drinking beer as they watched the students—girls, specifically—go by.

I walked past each time, holding my laptop bag at my side, assessing the house. Its doors (two, front and back), how close the neighbors were (throwing distance) and if there was a discreet way of leaving it quickly (yes, the alley out back, which was dark and didn't have surveillance cameras). I never saw Will when I cased the house—I had to find out how often he hung out there. But on the third day of classes, I was walking by and saw three boys sitting outside. One made eye contact with me and I gave him the quick sort of shy smile that implied I was easily impressed. "Hey," he said, sitting up. "What's your name?" Even the tone of his voice had the slight air of making fun of me.

"Chloe," I said, edging closer. My eyes flicked to the right and my heart jumped. I instantly recognized one of the other guys from my internet investigations—Cordy, Will's roommate.

I was going to make them like me, which wouldn't be hard. Be attractive, don't disagree, and mostly just listen—you could not say a word and a guy would still compliment you on what a great conversationalist you were.

"Wanna beer?" the first one offered.

"Sure," I said. I climbed over the low wrought-iron fence that lined their lot, feeling their eyes on me. They introduced themselves and offered a lawn chair that felt damp when I sat on it. The one who offered me the beer was Chris, a sophomore. Cordy was Cordy, and the third boy was Derek, a junior. They proceeded to ask me teasing questions and I flirted appropriately, laughing as if they were brilliant.

I dropped a mention of lacrosse, but no one took the bait. For a while we drank beer and made colorful commentary about the people walking by, and I tried to slow down, telling myself that information-gathering takes patience, and that everything they said could prove useful at some point. What I wanted was an invitation inside the house so I could do some reconnaissance, but it seemed too suspicious to try to worm one all of twenty minutes after meeting them. Not at least if I didn't want to deal with one trying to paw his way inside me.

Silently, I filed away the names of other brothers they mentioned. How close were the brothers? If Will went missing, would they form a search party or just go back to plying freshmen with cheap beer? They talked about the protests. "Oh, hell yeah," Cordy said. "I've been going down there and livestreaming everything. Just wait until the riots break out." I made a mental note of this—any activity Cordy did could be something Will might tag along to.

"I think there's another one this weekend. I'm getting the hell out of town for that October one, though. I don't want to deal with crowds that big—buncha wannabe anarchists," Derek said. He chucked his chin at me. "What about you, premed?" They had started calling me premed. Like there was something funny about a girl knowing her major on the first week of school. I'm sure this is in no way related to the statistical fact that women are less likely to drop out of college than men are.

"I haven't decided," I said.

Chris looked at his phone. "Terrible Charles is having a thing at the lake house again. Open bar."

The conversation paused when a blast of screeching feedback burst out of a window on the third floor. "Bogey!" two of them screamed in unison.

The screen door at the back of the house opened and a boy emerged. My breath caught. It wasn't Will, but whoever he was distracted me from the task at hand. He was a little older and was looking down at his iPhone. He was maybe six feet tall and had the body type I liked—narrow hipped, some muscle tone, but not too much. Unlike the other boys, he was well dressed in designer jeans and a thin, dark green sweater. When he looked up I was pleased. The face he revealed was nothing short of classically handsome—striking cheekbones, a fine straight nose, and eyes that looked green even from across the yard. A sensuous mouth. His hair was light brown with the sort of stylish quiff that guys were sporting of late.

"Speak of the devil!" Cordy said.

The boy finished with his phone and slipped it into his pocket, coming over to take a beer from the cooler.

"Terrible Charles, this is our new friend Chloe. She's a freshman," Cordy said.

Good, then, Cordy liked me. I looked at Terrible Charles sharply, trying to convey everything I admired about him with my eyes.

He barely acknowledged me with a nod. "Welcome to Adams. Try to steer clear of assholes like these three."

They hooted in protest. Terrible Charles grinned—more at them than at me—showing perfect white teeth, and popped his beer. "I gotta take care of election stuff—see you guys later."

I was disappointed, but with his exit I could think again. "Wait, Charles? Was that Charles Portmont?"

Chris nodded.

Charles Portmont of Will's Instagram! With another member of Will's entourage within my sights, I was getting closer, a vulture flying careful circles.

An exclamation point appeared on my smartwatch. I figured I had made my appearance at SAE and, not wanting to waste any more time if Will wasn't going to show up, said goodbye. Leave on a high note. Leave with them wanting more.

I was curious about what these mood logs were. I walked halfway down the street, not wanting to be geolocated near the SAE house. The street was lined with trees thick with autumn leaves—it was almost Golden Hour, the hour just before sunset with the most perfect light for selfies. I paused at one of the wooden benches that were dedicated to alumni, snapped a photo, then turned to my smartwatch.

I tapped the screen. It displayed the time at the top, which faded, then the screen said: *On a scale of 1 to 7, with 7 being the most you could possibly feel an emotion, and 1 being not at all, please answer how much you feel each of the following emotions right now.*

I touched the screen to advance the program.

Happy.

2, I said.

Anxious.

1

Excited.

5

Angry.

6

6

Day 53

Yessica and I hit the bookstore with a gaggle of girls from our dorm and then trudged home with heavy bags filled with over-priced textbooks. "I don't understand why I have to get Edition 10 when it's fifty bucks more expensive than Edition 9," she complained, dropping her bags on the floor of our dorm room. Everyone had their doors open and was yelling agreement across the hallway.

"It's a racket!" someone shouted.

"Did anyone buy sticky putty? To hang posters?" called someone else.

I paused after I arranged my new books on my desk. There was the FOMO part of me that wanted to stay and hang out and do what everyone else was doing their first week of college. But then there was that other part of me. My only consolation was that once I was done with Will, I could throw myself body and soul into what college is supposed to be: romantic intrigue, baiting girls into stupid fights for fun, having affairs with professors.

I took my laptop bag, claiming that my job at the psychology department was calling. Saying I had a part-time job there was a decent cover for Yessica rather than telling her I had a series of appointments and experiments associated with the diagnosis of psychopathy. Anyone with a less sophisticated understanding of my psyche would probably object to rooming with a "psycho," let alone one who was getting a free ride when she had to take out a Stafford Loan.

I headed up to Marion Street and was happy to see that there were only a couple of people in the muffin shop, in addition to the two young girls working the cashier station who kept saying, "Oh, *heeeeelll* no," to each other before lapsing into what was either Arabic or Amharic. I selected a small table facing the window that provided a direct and clear view to Will Bachman's house. I opened my laptop and my biology textbook, arranging my set of highlighters. I read half a chapter, glancing up to observe and mark with a tick every time someone crossed in front of the house. I wanted to get a sense of how much foot traffic there was on the street.

Idly, I woke up my laptop and perused Will's latest Instagram posts. He had a picture of himself and another brother trying to load a keg into a hatchback. #WelcomeWeekPartay.

I whirled my cursor around the Google homepage. "Charles Portmont," I typed. A webpage immediately popped up. Apparently, Terrible Charles was running for student council president. There was a picture of him, but not a very pleasing one, because it was taken from behind him, showing the outline of his back as he delivered a speech to a crowd. He had endorsements from the school newspaper, the *Daily Owl* (which actually only came out once a week), in addition to two student union organizations. Damn, people took politics serious in DC. Who cared who the student body president was, anyway?

There was a form box where you could submit an anonymous question. *Have a question for our candidate?* Are you a soulless asshole like your frat brothers?

I looked back up at Will's house and felt a compulsion seize me. Why don't I go over there, just to check it out? I knew, in the smart part of my brain, that this wasn't a good idea—it was broad daylight and there were too many people around. But sometimes the snaky, reptile part of my brain that's impatient and impulsive wins out. The snake wanted to break windows, snoop through his bedroom, open the fridge and spit into his milk. I shoved all my stuff into my backpack and left the shop, crossing the street.

The trick to undetected mischief is to have a look on your face like you're just heading home to do laundry. I looked carefully at Will's front door, which had two locks on it. I had bought a lock-picking kit online, but the YouTube videos I had watched made it look easier than it really was. I had practiced at home and on one or two of the neighbors' houses, but was hardly a pro.

To get to the back of the house, I had to walk half a block, then turn into the alley that provided access to the back of the row of attached houses. I walked toward Will's house while rooting through my bag as if looking for something, maybe a set of keys. I did this a lot when shoplifting—occupying myself with some task so it didn't seem that I was actually doing some other task, such as stealing. A tension built in me like a spring getting compressed as I got closer to 1530 Marion Street. There were two construction guys at the house next door, cutting bricks with a loud machine. The noise could provide cover, but also—there were two guys standing there. Will's house had a rotten-looking deck that led to a sliding glass door. Half a dozen moldy bricks led down to an English basement, its windows black. I slowed my walk, pretending I was distracted with my phone, hoping the construction guys wouldn't notice me.

As I looked up at the house with its dirty yellow siding, the smart part of me said that I should go, that I could get caught. The snake part was pointing out that while there were bars on the first-floor windows, maybe the sliding glass door could be pried open, or if not, there was a pipe that led down from the gutter that looked sturdy enough to climb.

He could be inside, I thought. But no, now wasn't the time for any kind of confrontation.

I mean, unless it was.

Or he might not even be home.

But maybe I could leave a bear trap in his bed.

The glass door would be hard to get past. But there was that pipe leading up to the roof, and there, a window that looked pretty old. The roof wasn't that far up. I was decent at climbing, not afraid of heights, and given my general lifestyle, the ability to sneak quietly, to climb, to find my way into places, was a skill I had developed. I had always been the girl who climbed the tree, jumped off the roof into the pool, got back up when she got scraped.

I could already feel my muscles tensing to move forward, but then a noise distracted me. One of the construction guys was cat-calling me. I gave him a look of disgust and walked off quickly, almost more annoyed at myself for being careless than I was at him. I get carried away like this sometimes. I know revenge is supposed to be a dish best served cold, but no one ever told me what it was like to wait those last few moments when the dish is on the cart right next to the table, steaming. I wanted Will perfectly in my grasp, squirming. I wanted it to be perfect. I would have to wait.

Besides, the SAE party was tomorrow night, and he would definitely be there, prime and ready to be plucked.

I headed to the psychology department for my first experiment, my last official homework for the day. When I pried open the heavy wooden double doors of the castle, it was quiet, motes of dust floating in the rays of light coming in from the big windows behind the curving staircase. Something about the building reminded me of a haunted church. I climbed up to the sixth floor, but went to the other side of the building from Dr. Wyman's office.

The hallway got darker as I walked down it, one of the fluorescent lights blinking intermittently. I found Room 654a, which had a door with a keypad. I entered the code my smartwatch had given me and opened the door. The lights turned on automatically, revealing more of a cubicle than a room. It was sterile, with no decorations other than a blank whiteboard, and the only thing in it was a singular computer and a desk. The watch must have sensed that I was in the room: *Please take a seat and the computer will provide you with instructions*, it said.

I sat down and woke the computer up by moving the mouse. I had to click through some consent forms before the experiment started.

This experiment is about decision making and money. The money used in this experiment is real. This means if by the end of the experiment you are left with $15 from the activity, you will be given $15 in cash.

Not bad! I clicked to the next page.

A picture of a five-dollar bill filled the top half of the screen.

You are playing with one other person. You each have two choices— share the money, or keep all of it. If you both choose share, you each get half. If you both choose keep all of it, you both get no money. If one player chooses to keep all while the other chooses to share, keep all gets all the money, and share gets none.

Then I was presented with two buttons at the bottom: Share and Keep All. Was this a joke?

A chat box opened on the right side of the screen. I was identified by an icon that said Player A, and a Player B was beneath me. Neither of us said anything.

Begin.

I clicked Keep All.

You have $0, the computer told me. I wrinkled my nose.

Trial two. Keep All.

You have $0. Selfish bastard!

The same thing happened on round three. Player B was typing, ellipses indicating the keyboard was in use. If we want to walk out of here with anything we have to both share.

Do they actually give money? I typed.

Yes. I like money.

So whoever I was playing with had done this before. Were they one of the other six, or just a random research subject?

Round four began. I clicked Keep All.

You have $0.

You said you would share! they wrote.

You said you would, too.

Liar.

The fifth round was no better.

Do a cost benefit analysis here, they wrote. We're wasting time not getting anything. If we cooperate we each get money.

But if we don't, I get all of it, I thought.

Stupid Player B—I didn't get any money from that experiment.

7

Day 52

"Pleeeease!" I pleaded with Yessica. She had her arms folded across her chest, one hip stuck out, objecting to the idea of going to a frat party. "It's a quintessential part of college life—you have to go at least once before you write an article about the poison that is Greek life for some alt lit mag," I reasoned. She pressed her lips together and nodded, then we both laughed. A few other people on our floor were going, Billy the Crew and his roommate Jed or Ted leading the horde.

I picked through several outfits on my bed. I didn't want to attract too much attention, but then again there may be certain beautiful boys there. It was August, so I opted for jean shorts that were short, but not what's-wrong-with-you short, and my scoop-neck silver top. I put on my silver necklace with a little lobster charm and messed with my hair. Yessica was one of those girls who could pop on a simple black jersey dress and look ready to go. (Her lashes, it turned out, were real.)

Our group exited the dorm and headed up the street. We turned toward the SAE house and I felt the hair on the back of my neck stand up. I could already see the people streaming into and out of the house, partyers all over the lawn. Music blasted from a speaker perched in the third-floor window and a bonfire burned in the yard. I wasn't even sure if the bonfire was allowed. Then again, neither was underage drinking, but the university police looked the other way as long as nothing got too crazy. Their view was that getting into minor trouble on campus was better than getting into major trouble off campus.

Yessica wiggled an eyebrow at me as we squished through the front door. Two boys were playing beer pong in the "dining room," and everyone seemed to be shouting louder than they needed to. In the living room people danced in the cramped space surrounding a leather couch and a coffee table speckled with beer cans, Solo cups, and an occasional bong. Some guy with greasy bangs was sitting on the edge of the coffee table, blowing vapor everywhere while he pontificated about the protests that were scattered across the country, often converging upon DC. "This country is descending into chaos!"

Billy the Crew led us to the kitchen where one sad little pledge had been forced to man the keg all night. He said hi, handing me a foamy beer. "Let's do a lap," I shouted into Yessica's ear.

"Looking for anyone in particular?" she asked sweetly.

Well, who should make fun of who, because half a lap in, a guy in a Dodgers T-shirt bumped into her, then they started talking about baseball. I let them be and continued scanning the crowd. I saw one guy so drunk that he stumbled in place, dazed. I saw two girls having a fight and several couples making out. My prospects lit up when I saw Cordy now seated on the leather couch with a bunch of other people, taking a huge hit off a water bong. He waved vigorously when he saw me. "You made it!"

I said something noncommittal and observed him take another hit. He was out of it—drunk and high at the same time. He must have been talking to the girl beside him, but she had turned away, leaving him sitting awkwardly alone. He scooted over, patting the leather beside him. I squished in and smiled. "Is your roommate coming?" I asked.

He blinked slowly. "Will? He's here somewhere." He made a vague gesture—his head was bobbing. Then he seemed surprised suddenly by how close I was to him, which was strange considering that I was pressed against his side. "You're pretty cute—anyone ever tell you that?"

"Is he an awful person?"

"Will, yeah, he can be a douche."

"Do you ever just want to fuck him up?"

"Totally," he said, picking up the bong again.

I decided I liked Cordy.

I heard laugher suddenly and looked over my shoulder. A group of the SAE brothers were standing around—I guess the more senior ones because Derek and Charles were there. Charles was wearing a nicely fitted white button-down, which I approved of, and a pin that said Portmont for President. There was a girl hanging on him—literally, hanging onto his arm, laughing up at him. God. So desperate. Another girl was immediately to her left making cow eyes at him. He wasn't necessarily not flirting back. I was just about to get up and do something about it when a blonde girl slipped across the clog of people and Charles put his arm out, tucking her into his side. The other girls fluttered away like injured sparrows, and he kissed the blonde girl on the top of the head in a way that did not say "frat party." It did not say, "I'm going to get you drunk and try to have sex with you upstairs on a dank, NFL-themed duvet."

"Who's that?" I asked, nudging Cordy.

"Kristen? Charles's girlfriend. They've been going out for like ever."

"There's no 'like ever' in college."

He hiccupped. "Yeah, there is. You know who his dad is, right? He's like big in the fracking world. Her mom is the heir to GenCo Media. What a waste," he said, shaking his head.

Indeed, what a waste.

"Hey, man," a new voice said, reaching across me to fist-bump Cordy. "Who's your lady friend?"

I looked up and suddenly I couldn't hear the music that was pumping through the house, the laughter or the screeches, the pinging of beer pong balls. It was like time froze. Will Bachman was literally leaning over the couch, grinning down at us. I felt a steely calmness come over me.

I smiled at him, reminding myself that for it to look real the smile had to reach my eyes. "I'm Chloe," I said. I waited to see if he would recognize me—it had been years. Everything I did in the next fifty-two days would depend on if he recognized me, and how my calculus would have to change if he did. But I was betting on him not recognizing me. I grew up. I changed my name. But I never forgot.

His face was flushed with alcohol. In person, I could better see how his facial features had aged from our childhood, but the shape of his upper lip was the same and he had the same sandy eyebrows. Will Bachman. I thought about taking out the mechanical pencil in my purse and inserting it into his left eye.

"Chloe," he said, smiling. "You don't hear that name very often."

"No," I said. "Not really." Even less frequently do you hear the last name Sevre, which is why I never put my real last name on my social media accounts. My plan would go so much smoother if he never figured out who I was.

Will perched on the arm of the couch and we quickly dispensed with formalities: our years, where we lived (of course I had prepared a fake background of being from Connecticut). "Where you from?" I asked, pretending to take a sip of my beer.

"Toms River, New Jersey, but spare me the Jersey jokes."

There is not a lot I will spare you, Will. Not now, since I've found you.

8

Phase One complete: Will Bachman was my buddy now. I had been tempted at the party to try and lure him away, but I told myself to concentrate on Phase Two: Interrogation. But now he knew me and trusted me, and it seemed like it would be pretty easy to get him alone. He followed me on Instagram but I didn't follow him back. I didn't want too many links between us that people could find once he was worm food.

Both Will and Cordy were insisting that I simply *had* to come down to Terrible Charles's party that weekend. I had already mulled over this possibility. I wasn't sure how I felt about conducting Phase Two at Charles's party. For one, I had no idea about the location, so I would have little control over it. I also didn't have a car. On the other hand, the isolated locale was appealing. The house—estate, rather—was about a forty-minute drive away at Fort Hunt, not too far from George Washington's Mount Vernon estate. From what public property records and Google Maps could tell me, the Portmont estate was right on the Potomac River in Virginia, with Maryland on the other side of the river. I also wasn't sure about showing up at a party at

Charles's house without him having expressly invited me. Technically it wasn't his party—his parents were throwing a benefit to provide CEOs with manicures in white-collar prison or something. Showing up as an uninvited and unwelcome guest might only draw attention to myself.

I zoomed in on a campus map on my computer. If not at the Portmont estate, where would be a good place for the interrogation? It wouldn't at all be hard to get Will drunk and corner him in a private room at the SAE house, or maybe his own house, but the problem with either of those is that they were his territory, and his friends could be in the vicinity. Another possibility was partying with him somewhere, then inviting him back to my dorm room only to lead him through a labyrinth of academic buildings, finding an isolated study room somewhere and using it as my staging grounds.

"Roomie," I heard Yessica say from directly behind me. I didn't jump. "What're you up to?"

"Trying to find where this discussion section is meeting."

"Do you want to go to Starbucks?"

"Do I have to put a bra on?" I said. I was wearing plaid pajama bottoms and my crop-top that said *obvi* on it.

"Hell no!" She was also wearing pajamas.

I donned my fuzzy slippers and she slid into her flip-flops. We only lived one block away from the massive Student Activities Center, where there was a Starbucks in the basement along with a million other things. There was a shortcut at the corner of the block, where you could duck into one of the academic buildings, Albertson Hall, and move through the ground floor rather than walking outside in your PJs. Albertson housed the music department and little practice rooms for music students lined the narrow hallway. It was cold down there, and smelled like concrete, but I liked to walk down the hallway and hear different instruments. I peeked in one window and saw a girl working a French horn. In another, four people were singing a cappella. When I looked into the third room—Terrible Charles! He was in profile, sitting at an upright piano, his fingers pouring over the keys. The music was dark, complicated rippling up and down in a tense tempo.

"What?" I heard Yessica whisper loudly. She peered over my shoulder, digging her chin into it. "Rachmaninov."

"He's good, right?" I whispered.

Charles stopped playing abruptly—we both jumped—but apparently he had made an error. He leaned forward and looked more closely at his sheet music, then flipped it back. We pulled away from the window before we could be spotted.

"Do you want a tissue?" Yessica asked. "To clean up all that drool."

"Oh, come on. He's beautiful. Piano players are the best type of musicians—all the brooding without any of the douchiness of guitar players."

She giggled. We continued on to the SAC and waited in a long line for coffee. She got an Americano and I got a mocha because I needed to come up with a list of at least ten potential interrogation sites tonight. Also, I had half a novel to read for my lit class.

We headed back to the dorm, but as soon as we opened the door that lead into Albertson, we ran smack into Charles and his girlfriend. He had his sheet music tucked under his arm and she held a bunch of his campaign posters and a roll of masking tape. God, she was so basic it was painful to see them together. She was pretty, but not *that* pretty, like a third-tier character on a CW TV show. "Oh, hey," he said, "You're, uh…" He did that politician thing like my name was on the tip of his tongue when it probably wasn't.

"Chloe."

He reached to shake my hand, revealing a Jaeger-LeCoultre watch. Not bad. "This is Kristen, my girlfriend slash campaign manager." She smiled. Her eyes were baby blue and she had on the most innocuous shade of pink lipstick. I introduced Yessica. "You all were invited to my party, right? It's not an *election* party," he said, smiling. "Technically an election party would be illegal according to our student bylaws. My parents are having a fundraising thing, but we can party adjacent to it."

"I was thinking about it," I said.

"Definitely come!" Kristen chirped.

"Open bar," he said brightly. "My parents don't mind if I bring whoever as long as we're dressed appropriately and mainly stay outside."

I wondered what he wore to dress appropriately. A toga and a golden laurel halo.

"As you know," he said, adopting a formal tone and pressing his hands together. "We're having an upcoming election. I hope we can count on your vote."

"Where do you stand on funding for student groups?" Yessica asked coolly.

"I think all funding for student groups should be cut," he said, not missing a beat. She frowned. "That money is coming from increasingly rising student fees, which disproportionately affect our neediest students. Student fees are my number one concern." It was comical how conflicted Yessica looked. I laughed, but so did Charles even though he was sort of laughing at himself.

We said our goodbyes and continued to our dorm, exiting Albertson into the muggy night. "Will you go to the party if we can get a ride?" I asked, careful. If I went, I didn't want Yessica there. The less people who knew me at the party, the better—no one would be checking up on me.

She wrinkled her nose. "Chlo, the guys at that party were total bros."

"Oh. Yeah. But they're not all like that—like that gentleman you were talking to for two hours."

"He was just there because of his roommate, like me! And if Terrible Charles turns out to be an alt-righter, he is not coming into our room."

"I wouldn't worry about it." I had no idea about Charles's actual political values, and as hot as I thought he was, he had a girlfriend. At least for now, anyway. Add that to my to-do list after the more pressing issues.

9

Andre had been hanging out with Sean, Marcus, and Dee the first time he received a mood log. Marcus was a junior who had quickly sought out Andre and his roommate the first week of school, bringing them welcome packages from the Black Students' Union. He took the two freshmen under his wing, introducing them around and inviting them to the regular cookouts he held in the backyard of his rowhouse. He was so politically involved that Andre felt embarrassed around him; he was always bringing up names of people that Andre got the sense he was supposed to know but didn't, and it seemed like everyone else knew those names.

At the moment, they were hanging out in Marcus's backyard, drinking sweet tea mixed with cheap rum, talking about the protests—not just the big October one, but the one coming up that weekend. "You guys should come," Marcus said, opening a box of Cheez-Its. Andre tried to steal a glance at Dee, the girl sitting directly across from him who hovered in the same circle of friends. She was a sophomore with an acerbic wit and eyes that reminded him of a deer—probably way out of his league, but what was the harm in trying.

"I'll go if you guys are there," he said. He opened his mouth, trying to find a nonawkward segue. Dee had mentioned working at the *Daily Owl* and that they were always looking for photographers—specifically that they wanted more minority representation on the staff. He wasn't sure how people schmoozed like this—did they just come out and ask for jobs? Did working at the *Owl* pay anything, and was it crass to ask? He needed a job.

Just then, he felt the vibration from his smartwatch. Furtively, he excused himself to use the bathroom. The watch asked him what activity he was currently engaged in. *Socializing*, he selected. The watch asked him to rate how much he felt of each of the following emotions: happy, anxious, angry, excited. How happy *was* he right now? Andre puzzled over this.

How would a psychopath answer this question?

Well, they were probably hardly ever happy. Or maybe they were only happy during the exact moments when they were getting what they wanted. He said that he was not very happy, and figured that he shouldn't be anxious, either, even though he was in real life, because he had somehow found himself almost accidentally committing fraud via smartwatch, and because of the presence of hot girls and upperclassmen who were cooler than he was. He said he was not angry, then paused when he was asked if he was excited. No, he should make it seem like very little ever made him excited. His finger shook a little when he pressed on Submit. His smartwatch vibrated, but nothing exploded and no alarms went off. But he did realize how late it was.

He popped back outside. "Guys, I have to head out," Andre said.

"Hot date?" Sean called after him.

"Nah, I was supposed to get something done by 10 p.m. and forgot." Well, he hadn't forgot so much as he didn't want to leave the party, in particular because he wasn't sure what awaited him at the psychology department. It would be his first experiment or survey.

Andre headed toward that part of campus, not pausing when his phone rang. It was his mother. "What'd you call for, Pooh?" she asked.

"Oh, yeah," he said, trying to sound casual. "I wanted to know if maybe you knew a professor here. Dr. Leonard Wyman? He teaches psychology, and I met him, and he seemed so familiar. I wondered if he had been to our house or something." It wasn't that far-fetched. His mother was a nurse, and his dad an EMT, so the variety of friends who cycled in and out of their house for social events were often affiliated with the medical field.

"Mmm, don't think so. Let me ask your father." There was some muffled talking, then his mother said that the name didn't sound familiar to either of them. But then she wanted to ask about his classes, his dorm, his friends; he felt bad about it, but had to cut her short because he had found his way to the psychology building, which looked eerie from the yellow cast of nearby streetlights. The whole concept of talking to his mom about college stressed him out. He always felt she was one question away from figuring out what he had done.

The few years after Kiara had died, he spiraled. He would cut class to watch TV or hang out with friends his parents disapproved of. Fistfights led to vandalism, which led to joyriding in "borrowed cars." And even as he did all these things, he knew they were wrong—he was just so *angry*. Angry at Kiara, which made no sense. Angry at his parents. His flirtation with juvenile delinquency landed him in a special school, a behavioral rehabilitation program, and he was diagnosed with Conduct Disorder. Conduct Disorder was diagnosed in children when they exhibited persistent antisocial behaviors that often took the form of violating social or legal norms; it was often a precursor to a later diagnosis of Antisocial Personality Disorder. When Andre was a junior and first received a packet from a program that was interested in recruiting him, the Multi-method Psychopathy Panel Study, he had laughed it off, showing it to his brother. His brother, rolling an enormous blunt, thought it was hysterical, because of course Lil Pooh didn't really have Conduct Disorder, and of course there was no chance he was a psychopath. *You should fake out their asses.* So that's what it started as: a game.

Andre participated in a number of phone interviews and questionnaires that he answered with the help of the internet. It wasn't like there was a blood test that could tell you were a psychopath. It was diagnosed off questionnaires, interviews, and therapists' assessments. And fuck that counselor who diagnosed him with Conduct Disorder not a year after the death of his sister. He didn't feel bad the day the program called for the parental interview and Isaiah, taking on a formal tone, completed the entire interview pretending to be their father, embellishing stories so ridiculous that Andre cried silently from laughter, his face stuffed into a pillow.

The program stopped calling and Andre forgot about it for months until things got *real*. He came home to find that his mother had opened a thick envelope addressed to him. His first reaction was to be mad at her, but she turned to him with tears shining in her eyes and he realized that the letter must have been something upsetting about him. Silently she handed him the letter. He had been admitted to John Adams University. He had been given a full scholarship, covering all four years. "Baby, how did you do it?" she had asked. "Raim, get down here!" His grades had been in a tailspin for the past few years, but he had decently salvaged what he could his junior year. But not enough for anything but the University of the District of Columbia. And with their financial situation, he would probably be working and attending part-time while racking up student loans.

In a flash, his father was there, also skimming the letter. They were both looking at him expectantly. It was surprising how readily the lie came: "It's...part of their Ancestor Scholarship," Andre said. "Remember that project I did on family trees? Anyway, Adams has some program where if you can trace your ancestry back to any of John Adams's slaves, and you write an essay and everything, you can win the scholarship."

His mother was holding her hands together over her face in prayer position, tears brimming over her eyes. "Oh God, Andre, this is—we've been so stressed about college, with your father's back surgery and everything—this is...this is like a gift from God."

When she pulled him into a hug, Andre, horrified, thought, *Wait, Mom, wait!* But then he looked over and saw that Raim Jensen, his stoic father, had fully teared up. That was what did it. He had only ever seen his father cry once—about Kiara.

And so began a little snowball of a lie that kept rolling into a bigger one. It ran from complex machinations (intercepting any packets or phone calls that came from the program), to difficult ones (getting Isaiah to comply), to ridiculous ones (hoping and praying that his parents never bothered to Google and find out that John Adams never actually had slaves).

This was why he approached the first assessment with trepidation. Andre climbed up to the sixth floor, hearing voices very faintly. It sounded like they were coming from downstairs, at the north end of the building. He went down a tiny hallway with flickering lights and walked past two experiment rooms until he found his, the last one. The little room was as clinically white and blank as a lab in a science fiction movie. He set down his book bag and locked the door. The building gave him the creeps.

On the computer, he clicked through some consent forms and demographics. Then came a long survey, or perhaps it was a series of surveys, because some of the items seemed to be grouped together. The more he clicked, the more the tension left his shoulders. Some of the content clusters he could answer honestly—others gave him more pause about how he should be answering them. *Women should be protected by men.* Was he supposed to agree with that, or disagree?

But then a noise from outside his little room pierced across the air, muted but still incredibly sharp. It was a scream that made Andre's entire body freeze, his pulse jack up in his chest, his ears perk. It was like the scream of an animal caught in another animal's sharp jaws.

There—another scream, then a loud thud. He thought he heard the word *help.* Andre scrambled from the office, poking his head out into the hallway. Maybe someone was watching a movie?

But then it came again—another scream, a bang that was clearly coming from a few doors down, from another one of the little experiment rooms. There was a light coming from beneath the door—something that definitely hadn't been there when Andre had arrived. He heard a miserable cry, then a scraping sound moving up the door—someone was lying on the ground, trying to unlock the door. Maybe another research subject had had a seizure or something.

"I'm here!" Andre cried, pulling the door open. Beneath the garish fluorescent lights of the little room was a young man struggling and gurgling on the ground, blood pumping from his neck at a violent rhythm. Blood was pooled on the ground making him slip, and sprays and jagged pops of it littered the walls.

Andre didn't even have time for a cohesive thought, just a general sense of *Oh shit!* as the guy—a student?—made eye contact with him, his mouth opening as he reached out.

"Help!" Andre screamed. He ran forward, pulling his sweatshirt off. Why had it been so long ago that he took first aid? When had that been—fourth grade?

The guy gasped as Andre pressed the sweatshirt to his neck. It was the cause of most of the bleeding, but there were several other stab wounds—two just under his collarbone, one straight through his ear. *"Is anyone here!? Help!"* Andre screamed.

Shit, shit. Andre fumbled for his phone, trying to keep the pressure on the wounds (even now he could feel the blood soaking through the thick cloth of the sweatshirt). His bloody thumb slipped over the smooth surface of the phone and it clattered onto the floor. Andre reached for it, then realized that someone was standing just outside the hallway. Thank God. "Help me—I think he's bleeding to death!" Andre shouted.

Two things happened at once, their simultaneity somehow terrifying. Andre realized that the man in the hallway might have been the one who did this, and at that same moment, the man raised his hands into the air, smiling a little wryly as if to say, *Good luck with that.* Then he turned and walked down the hallway, apparently not in a hurry.

Stunned, Andre scrabbled for his phone and managed to call 911.

"Nine-one-one, what is your emergency?"

"I'm in the psychology department at Adams! There's a guy here who's been stabbed."

"You said he's been stabbed?"

"Yes, he's bleeding everywhere. Tell me what to do!"

"Can you tell me your exact location?"

"Sixth floor, um, turn right when you get up the stairwell. Am I supposed to elevate his head?"

"Can the victim talk?" the operator asked.

"Hey, man," Andre said, shaking him gently. "Can you see me? They're coming." Helpless, Andre looked behind him through the doorway, wondering if EMTs could possibly arrive in time. The guy's eyes had started to take on a glazed look.

"Did you see what happened?"

"No, I heard it. I heard someone scream for help and then some thudding noises."

"Can you tell me your name?"

"Andre. What should I do!"

"Andre, you're doing great—just hang in there. Help is on the way."

10

"Hey," the cop said, setting a Coke down in front of Andre. "This might make you feel better."

When Andre reached for it, his hand was shaking. He had said he felt like throwing up, and they had provided him with a trash can. Andre was sitting in an office chair, one cop crouched in front of him, buddy-style, another one standing up, a notepad out. "I'm Detective Bentley," the buddy one said, "and this is Detective Deever. We'd just like to get your statement so we can figure out what went on here."

Andre took a tentative sip, but the second the sweetness touched his tongue, he thought of the terrible gurgling noises the guy had made just before the EMTs had shown up. Zombielike, he had agreed to go back with the police to have his statement taken. This also involved one of the forensic techs taking samples from him: the blood on his arms, his hands. They had taken his shoes and his shirt and given him a faded MPD T-shirt to wear instead.

Now he sat in the Homicide Office. Homicide: as soon as he saw the words on the door, he realized that there was no way that gurgling man could have survived. That guy was dead, and it wasn't until then that it truly hit him that here he was in front of the police, a Black kid who happened to be a diagnosed psychopath, or actually *faking* that he was a psychopath—not that that made it any better—who just happened to be within throwing distance of a violent stabbing. *Oh dear God, what I have I gotten myself into*, he thought, imagining desperately, for a moment, calling his parents. But what could he even say?

"It would really help us out if you told us everything you saw or heard—start from the beginning."

"I was on the sixth floor of the psych department—"

"And you were…?" Deever interrupted.

Andre wondered if this was the sort of thing he should insist on having a lawyer for. But wouldn't insisting on a lawyer make him look suspicious? "I was doing an exercise for one of my classes." He contemplated how much he was willing to lie. Maybe they wouldn't care about the stupid program. Maybe they would only care about the stabbing. Maybe all they wanted was the information and then they would leave him alone. Bentley had kind eyes—Deever did not. "I pretty much know exactly what time it was when he first screamed. I know because I looked at my phone probably two minutes before—9:48." Bentley nodded. He was white, with muscular, hairy forearms. "The scream was coming from that room. He screamed a few more times and I think he was trying to get out of that room, but couldn't turn the knob."

"He couldn't open the door?"

"I think—" Andre's mouth felt dry. "I think he had too much blood on his hands. But I thought maybe someone had a heart attack, so I opened the door and he was in there bleeding everywhere. I put my sweatshirt folded up on his neck to apply pressure."

"What was the state of the room?"

"Normal. Like a desk and a chair and a computer, and a whiteboard. Actually, wait, there's a window."

"Right when you got there was it open or closed? Did you touch the window?"

"I didn't." He tried to imagine it. "It couldn't have been open the whole way because I saw my reflection. Maybe it was open, I don't know. There was blood everywhere."

"Did the victim say anything?"

Andre shook his head. "No, other than when I heard him scream."

"When you say you heard him scream, was he just making a noise, or did it sound like he was screaming at someone?"

Andre pursed his lips together. "I'm pretty sure it was just sounds. Like pain. So right before I called 911, there was a guy there."

"Another guy?"

"Yeah, I saw him, and I was like relieved someone could help me because I don't really know first aid. I said, help call 911 or whatever and he…"

"He…"

"He made this gesture." Andre got up to act out what he could only call a shrug—nothing else could do justice to how weird it had been. The cops looked at each other and frowned.

He felt a tiny grain of relief when it became apparent from their facial expressions that they, too, thought this was bizarre. "Can you describe him?" Bentley asked.

Andre sat back down. "He was white. Maybe like somewhere between my age and…thirty-five?"

"What was he wearing?"

Andre chewed his lower lip. He shook his head.

"Can you describe his face?"

"Uh… Just like…normal?"

"Anything distinctive? Hair, eyes?"

"He definitely didn't have red hair. Black or brown, I don't know, maybe it could have been dark blond."

"How tall was he?"

The more Andre tried to think of who he had seen, the less clearly he could see him in his mind's eye. "I was on the ground, so…" Andre got off his chair and sat on the floor, then looked up at Deever, who was starting to look annoyed at Andre's failure to be the perfect witness. "Maybe your height."

"Any tattoos, piercings?"

Andre exhaled slowly. "I can't remember, but that doesn't mean he didn't. I just saw him for a split second."

"You said he was white," Bentley said. "White like me or white like Deever?"

Andre's eyes went from one man to another. Bentley was closer to what white people called "swarthy"; Deever looked like he sunburned. "Uh…somewhere in between?" What if he just gave them a description? Any description, a detailed one, whether it was true or not. Wouldn't that lead them to someone else, away from him? He felt a wave of nausea. "I'm sorry. If you had a picture of him I think I could say yes or no."

"What kind of feeling did you get from him?" Bentley asked. "What kind of presence did he have? Did he seem angry?"

Andre blinked. He understood what Bentley was asking, but he hesitated about saying what he was thinking. "If he had just looked at me and walked away, I would have thought it was really weird. But that gesture he made, it like… It makes my skin crawl."

When Andre finally returned to his dorm room, exhausted, his heart felt even heavier when he realized Sean wasn't home. He hadn't been sure how he was going to begin telling the story of what had just happened, but now it wasn't an issue. He was alone in an empty dorm room and suddenly had a terrible urge to turn tail and head back to Northeast to his parents' house.

What the hell had just happened? And *now* what would happen? Would the police question him again? Would they start poking into his background just because he happened to be there? Why not just leave Adams, head home and never pick up the phone?

Andre rubbed his temples and opened his laptop. His head was swimming with emotions, but the one thing he couldn't stop thinking about was the fact that this had happened in Wyman's experiment room, not ten yards from his office. Was it too much of a coincidence that a guy got stabbed to death right next to an office that had a special program studying psychopaths? And what was it about Wyman that was so weirdly familiar?

Andre skimmed through the search results for "Leonard Wyman psychologist" on Google, some part of him dimly aware that he was only doing this to distract himself from the images that kept repeating in his mind—the man slipping on the bloody floor, the gurgling sound his throat made—and the temptation to call his parents. Most of the results were articles Wyman had written with long, complicated titles. Others were blurbs about conference presentations. One link about Elena winning a dissertation scholarship.

But then Andre saw two words that made him freeze. *Forensic Files*. Suddenly he knew exactly why Wyman had sounded familiar.

In the two years that followed Kiara's death, Andre cut class often, sometimes to hang out with his friends, but sometimes to simply return home and be there alone. He would lie on the couch eating Cheezy Poofs, watching old episodes of *Forensic Files* and *48 Hours*. A true-crime rabbit hole appeared, and Andre fell into it, the darkness of the material matching his macabre mood. He watched old documentaries, subscribed to podcasts, and even poked through message boards online of self-described sleuths.

There were two cases in particular he became obsessed with because they were local: the DC Sniper and the CRD Killer.

The former was actually two men who had randomly gone around shooting people with no rhyme or reason, Zodiac-style. But their shooting spree was dwarfed by the activities of Gregory Ripley—CRD or the Rock Creek Killer. From the mid-nineties to the early 2000s, a series of murders dotted across the mid-Atlantic, concentrated in Virginia, Maryland, and DC. The repeated MO led to the killer's moniker: CRD, choke, rape, dismember. When he was finally caught, he admitted to twenty-two killings, and was given the death penalty based on the solid physical evidence from nine of those killings.

Andre clicked around, finally finding a sketchy website that would allow him to watch the old episode of *Forensic Files* about the CRD Killer that he had already seen before. He skipped past all the stuff about the hunt for CRD and got to his arrest. A voice-over said that the one person who understood CRD was a psychologist, the only person who had extensively interviewed him and who had testified during the trial. That psychologist had been Dr. Leonard Wyman. Then there was the grainy video of him behind a desk—he had aged a lot since then, but this voice was the same. Andre had forgotten one other peculiar aspect of the case. After the jury reached its verdict, Wyman had rushed out of the courthouse while reporters shouted at him—he had argued for clemency when the entire nation was screaming to put Greg Ripley to death. Greg Ripley, who smiled at the jury during his trial and doodled during gory testimony. "I do not think that Gregory Ripley deserves to die," Wyman said to the camera, making the hairs on Andre's arms stand up. Wyman's own hair had had almost no gray in it back then. "He's not the monster you think he is."

What exactly, Andre wanted to know, was this fucking program for *psychopaths* at John Adams University that he had gotten himself into? It was run by a man who defended the CRD serial killer. If he could defend CRD, what else would he defend?

11

I was in a car heading to Charles Portmont's estate. Billy the Crew's brother was driving and Billy rode shotgun, messing with the radio. I was sandwiched between two Kappa Delta girls, one of whom I surmised was fucking Billy's brother. Another guy, a pledge they called Reek, was squished against the far window, not even accorded a seat belt.

Me and Reek were the only ones who had never been to one of Charles's parties. "It's sooooo open bar," one of the girls said. "Like I asked the bartender to make me a Manhattan and he knew what it was. It was gross but I drank it anyway."

Clumped together in the trunk were our personal effects—the boys' clothes were stuffed into a couple of plastic Safeway bags. I had a book bag with a number of items: a cocktail dress, some toiletries, and two vials of a liquid Rohypnol solution. "I'm going to land a sugar daddy who will pay off my student debt," said Kappa 1.

"Yeah, if you're into jowls," said Kappa 2.

The drive down was pleasant. It was mostly one highway the entire way down, the sides of the road thickly lined with trees, their leaves just starting to turn. We turned onto a smaller local road and then a narrow street with a Private Property sign. The woods had been dispensed with, replaced with an expansive green yard leading up to a sprawling Tudor-style estate. Ahead of us I could see Charles getting out of his Jaguar and Kristen getting out on her side.

We piled out of the car. "We're the first ones here," Charles said. "But I'm only giving one tour because I'm going to be too plastered later." There were supposed to be about thirty of us coming, but the others were still trapped in traffic.

We followed Charles inside, and as soon as the double front doors were open, I could see the bustle of activity to prepare for the charity event. People in catering uniforms were scurrying about with chairs, and one woman was on a dangerously high ladder so she could dust the massive chandelier. A double staircase curved up behind it.

"Charlie!" came a voice. An older woman—his mother, I presumed—entered the foyer and held her arms out to hug him. She was the type of extremely well-put-together that can only exist among wealthy women with little else to care about. "My Charlie Bear, look at you." She went on to hug Kristen next. Charles refused to be embarrassed by being called Charlie Bear.

He introduced us as his friends and then took us on a brief tour of the house. I mentally cataloged all the rooms: a library, a dining room, a formal dining room, his father's study, which had animal heads in it, and a kitchen so massive it made me want to learn how to make pie crusts. Huge windows in the kitchen overlooked the backyard. There was a substantial patio, a covered pool, more yard, then a dock leading directly out onto the river. I considered each of the places for my interrogation.

I had researched all I could about truth serums. Unfortunately, there is no such thing as a real truth serum. I needed the next best thing: something that would make Will's mouth loosen, lower his inhibitions, but also something that would make him forget it the next day. Alcohol had many of those characteristics, but wasn't entirely reliable. I definitely needed alcohol to be involved, because getting drunk and blacking out presented an obvious explanation to the question "What happened last night?" Rohypnol is illegal in the US, but enterprising people can still obtain it online. Back in high school, I had experimented with creating a concentrated liquid form of it. I selected boys I estimated were about the same size as Will, cornering them at various house parties and bonfires, leading them away to the woods. Of course they thought they were going to get laid, but in reality I just held bizarre conversations with them, extracting private information and seeding them with strange stories so I could question them the next day to see if they remembered.

"I have to make some rounds—meet me back here in an hour. We can eat and drink whatever we want, but just stay out of people's hair," Charles said.

"What exactly is this benefit for?" Billy asked.

"Conservation."

"Isn't your dad in fracking?" I couldn't help asking.

"He's also a hunter," he replied. This also didn't make sense to me, but I accepted it.

We dispersed to get ready upstairs, where Charlie Bear said we could take any room that didn't have a closed door. Although the house was huge, it didn't have thirty bedrooms, so I imagine there were some shenanigans of bed sharing anticipated for tonight. The machinations that would probably be taking place very late at night were critical: I needed to be well-placed with Will already wrapped around my finger, drunk but not too drunk. (The last thing I needed was for him to have a bout of uncontrollable vomiting, which would make it hard to question him.)

Myself and the two Kappa girls took a bedroom that overlooked the backyard. While they tried to steam their dresses in the adjoining bathroom, I peered out at the landscape. It would be dark out at the river soon. In the long expanse leading out to the river, there were two small, detached guesthouses.

Not too far away, but fairly isolated, the guesthouses seemed ideal. I couldn't one hundred percent count on Will being docile—things could get violent. I had taken a bunch of self-defense classes, but it wasn't like there wasn't risk involved. On TV, the good guy always wins; in real life, if someone outweighs you, they can easily overpower you. The key thing was to stay levelheaded so I would have the upper hand.

"Shouldn't you be getting dressed?" Kappa 2 asked, looking at me with her lips outlined in lip liner.

I wriggled into my dress. It was a short, formfitting Sue Wong cocktail dress with an art deco flapper feel to it, blush-colored with black lace accents and black ostrich-feather trim. I had no jewelry other than a black cuff-style bangle I had brought to cover over my smartwatch, which didn't really go with the outfit. The Kappas futzed over their hair for a while, while I left mine in loose waves.

I was standing outside the door to the bedroom, slipping into my heels, when several of the upperclassmen appeared from a room down the hall. Sigh. Here was Charles in a slim-fitting dark gray suit, his pocket square perfectly folded into three points. Kristen was beside him in an emerald dress that made the color of Charles's eyes pop. "You look nice!" he said in the same exact bland tone one uses on one's sister.

I didn't want him to think I looked "nice." There were times I wanted to be invisible, usually for practical purposes, but not right now. Seriously, Kristen in her plain sequined green dress? Vom.

Guests had started to arrive since we had shown up. I followed Charles and Kristen down the curving staircase. He shook the hands of several people who must have been friends of his parents.

The first floor of the house was now crowded with older people in cocktail attire. Waiters circled with trays of champagne and hors d'oeuvres. In the kitchen, Charles snatched a tray of canapés in one hand and three bottles of champagne with the other. Separate from the main party, we sat on the patio and drank the champagne directly from the bottles until a waiter appeared with some glasses. I kept a glass that always had some champagne in it, but only mimed drinking, pretending to get progressively sillier.

By the time the others showed up, it was already dark, the patio lit by strings of small globe lights. Here was Cordy with Will in tow. Bottle after bottle of champagne appeared, but also the occasional waiter delivering a cocktail someone had requested. I cawed the way a drunken girl would, laughing helplessly when people made stupid jokes. I made sure I was in the vicinity of Will, monitoring how much he drank while showing my drunkenness like a peacock spreading its plumage. I could feel him looking at me.

I ate a miniquiche, then pronounced it an awesome idea when someone suggested we go check out the dock. The girls walked carefully in the grass, their heels sinking into the sod. It was dark on the dock, the water looking black. There was lighting, but no one had turned it on. I leaned at the edge of the dock as far as I dared and looked to the left. The estate was isolated enough that you could not see any neighbors. "You and Derek are totally vibing," one of the girls observed.

The other giggled. "I mean, what if I want something to happen, you know?"

I looked back toward the house. We were about as far away as I would be if I were in the northernmost guesthouse, and from where I stood I couldn't hear the rest of our group talking even though I knew they were being loud.

Just as we got back to the patio, Charles produced a baggie of cocaine. Not everyone did it—I noticed that Kristen never did, and that her eyes lingered on her boyfriend when he did (you bet I filed that nugget away!) although he only did one line. I pretended to do some, smearing the line of powder with my finger as I pretended to snort. A couple of the SAE brothers were on the lawn, shoeless, arguing, and started hitting each other. A few girls were dancing. Charles was laughing, holding a bottle of champagne, while Kristen cried, "Noooo, that's not what I said!"

People were very drunk. One girl headed for the woods to throw up, another coming to hold her hair. I was amazed at the brothers' ability to consume alcohol. The girls couldn't keep up in terms of volume. A few pairs of people disappeared into the house, possibly to hook up somewhere. The benefit, whatever it was for, was winding down, and now there were only staff cleaning up.

I was the only one with my wits about me.

I started to make moves. My hovering near Will became more direct. I touched him on the arm and laughed wildly at anything he said resembling a joke. He teased me about my name, saying it was a hippie name, and I pretended to pout. We sat at the end of one of the patio tables, picking at some appetizers, talking about lacrosse. God, did he really think I wanted to talk about *lacrosse*? I leaned forward, hanging on every word, at one point putting my hand directly on his knee.

Our crowd was thinning as people had turned in or been taken upstairs to lie down and drink water at their friends' urging. Only a handful remained, and I had to outlast them and make sure that Will had enough of an idea in his head about getting laid that he would stick it out with me. Charles had loosened his tie and he and Kristen were making out so hard I could see their tongues. She was mussing up his hair and they, too, no doubt, would disappear into the house to have sex. Perfect Charles and his perfect girlfriend—please go away and leave me to my business.

Derek then headed inside with one other brother and two girls, leaving the four of us.

"We're gonna head in," Charles mumbled, his hand on Kristen's ass as they left to go upstairs.

Will and I sat on the patio alone. I stood up slowly. "I guess we should turn in, too," I said, trying to sound reluctant. Will stood up, wavering on his drunken feet. "I feel so bad leaving such a mess," I said, gesturing to the discarded plates and glasses. I started to stack them.

"Yeaahh," Will said, clumsily helping me. Charles and Kristen were good and gone by then. No staff in the kitchen. I looked at Will directly.

"Do you want to check out one of those guesthouses?" I asked.

"Sure!"

I made sure to squirrel away half a cup each of a mixed drink in two glasses. I carried them carefully as we walked across the grass toward the houses. I was barefoot, having shed my heels to have better purchase just in case I needed to run or kick. My purse was tucked snugly against my side, the vials and a switchblade inside. Will was bigger than me, but I was smarter. I was ready.

I led Will to the guesthouse that was closer to the water and farther from the house. He peered in the window. "It's a little house!" he exclaimed.

Charles had said the guesthouses would be unlocked for us to use. I turned on the lights, but then used the dimmer to take them down. The guesthouse had a small open kitchen, which led out to a living room. A half wall divided the living room from the bedroom. Just to the right of the TV was a fireplace.

"Sit down," I said, gesturing to the fluffy sheepskin rug that lay on the ground between the fireplace and a leather couch. "I'll fix us some drinks." I heard him flop down heavily as I headed to the kitchen. I set the cups on the counter, then carefully poured out the entire contents of one vial. "Drink up!" I said, walking back into the room and handing him the glass. He was lounging on the sheepskin rug.

I stood over him, watching as he tipped up the cup into his mouth, and I couldn't help a shiver of excitement. Everything was going according to plan. The drug would take effect soon. Will was right within my grasp. He smiled at me with his dumb mouth. "Why don't you sit down?"

"Hold on, I need to use the girls' room." I left him there, heading to the bathroom that adjoined the bedroom. I didn't really have to go to the bathroom, but rearranged my hair, plucked a stray eyelash from my cheek and tugged my dress up. I peered behind my bangle to look at my smartwatch. The drug needed a couple minutes to work.

I sat next to Will and examined him. His eyes looked glazed and his face was flushed, his lower lip looking wet. He was sitting far too close to me. The coffee table had a book about caverns on it, topped with an agate geode. I picked it up, looking at the layers of bright blue agate that had been formed by the earth. "Where's your phone?" I asked. "Let's take a selfie!"

He cringed. "I don't have it. I dropped it and it's getting fixed." Will put his hand on my knee and squeezed, then ran his hand up a few inches. "You're really hot—anyone ever tell you that." He blinked slowly.

I put my hand over his. I realized he hadn't finished the drink and propelled the cup toward his mouth. He took a sloppy sip, but there was still some left. He leaned forward to kiss me, his mouth open. I deterred him with two fingers to the forehead. "Not so fast." The push, even with just my fingers, had an outsize effect. If he wanted to, if he were fully sober, he could have easily overpowered that push. "Let's have a chat first."

"A chat?" Even with no *S*, somehow he slurred the word. He fell back on his elbows, his head lolling, nearly spilling the drink, which I saved.

"I just wanted to ask you some questions," I said, waving the cup around enticingly.

"You don't remember me, do you?" he said suddenly.

I froze. "What?"

He pulled himself back up to an upright position. "You don't... We used to know each other. I thought maybe you didn't—don't you recognize me?"

"Recognize you from where?"

"New Jersey," he said with some urgency, or at least as much urgency as you can gather while on Rohypnol and alcohol. Had I been wrong? Had he recognized me the second he saw me at the SAE house? I had kept telling myself that I looked so different, that puberty had hit me hard, that changing my name to Chloe would probably be enough to fool someone as dull as Will. He looked at me with wide eyes, his pupils hugely dilated. The look on his face was almost vulnerable. "You know...about what happened that night."

I was stunned, which immediately made me angry. He had flipped the tables on me and I had to be the one in control. "Will, do you have the video?"

"Things got out of hand that night...they got out of hand and they shouldn't have."

"Where is the video? Who else has it?"

"But you liked me though, I know you did."

"I did like you."

"You liked me," he said, louder this time. He was drooling a little.

"I liked you. I drew your name in bubble letters because I was twelve, and you raped me."

"Whoa—wait," he said very slowly, leaning toward me. "You *liked* me."

I blinked, pressing my fingers against the jagged outside of the geode I was holding; it felt cold in my hands, one side perfectly smooth and polished, the rest of it rough. I studied his face, my heart beating evenly: his pale eyebrows, the beginnings of stubble starting to push out of his face. "You held me down and Brett Miller filmed it with your phone and I was twelve.

Where is the phone? Where is the video?" Phase Three was Get the Video. I had to have it.

He stared at me—I couldn't tell if his face was in shock, or if the drugs had washed any sensible expression off him. I watched with disbelief as his eyes filled with tears. "Michelle... I'm sorry."

I lashed out with the geode, cracking him in the forehead. Blood burst out and he gave a scream of surprise and pain as he fell to the ground, then lay still. How dare he. How dare he say my name. Try to apologize. After what he did. After humiliating me.

When the heat faded, I realized what I had just done and, dismayed, I watched as blood began to matt the pristine whiteness of the sheepskin rug.

Shit!

Goddammit, Chloe, why can't you control yourself! I popped up on my knees, holding my hands over the lower half of my face, thinking at a thousand miles per hour. He was lying perfectly still—how hurt was he? The grand irony: I needed to kill Will, but *not now*. Not before I had that video.

Shit, shit, shit. I went over to him and turned his head. I couldn't tell how bad the wound was, because head wounds tend to bleed so freely. Soon his blood got all over my hands. I sat back on my haunches, thinking.

But then I heard something that made me freeze. A step. From the entrance of the guesthouse. I turned.

Charles stood just inside the doorway, his face pale, his mouth open in shock. His eyes moved across the living room, taking in Will's body and the bright red blood that marred the snowy rug. No. Not Charles. The absolute last person I wanted to see this.

"He attacked me!" I sobbed. "Oh God, call 911. I don't know what happened." I buried my face in my hands, smearing blood onto my cheek, and wailed hysterically. I had the vague sense that Charles was coming over to help me. "He hit me. Oh God,

I thought he was going to kill me. Call the police!" I chanced to look up, tears streaming down my face.

Charles was crouched beside me, his mouth now closed. His expression was devoid of emotion and the look in his eyes was stern, seeming to say, *Stop.* I stopped crying, for the second time tonight uncertain what was happening, or what to do. Charles reached for his pocket square slowly and pulled it out. He snapped his wrist to unfold it, then used it to wipe the blood and tears from my face. "My, my, what a mess you've made," he said mildly.

12

I stared at him, wide-eyed.

He reached out and gripped my wrist, pushing down the black bangle to reveal my watch. I was stunned, mesmerized by the look in his eyes, which had a blank hardness to it mixed with something like amusement. He reached under his shirt—the top two buttons were undone—and pulled out something small and back. His own smartwatch, the wristband removed.

"You're…" I couldn't even articulate my surprise.

Charles let go of my wrist. "I would have never guessed about you," he said.

Just then, Will emitted a low moan, and I felt relief rush over my body. He brought his hands up to his head. He was alive. Okay, I hadn't ruined everything. The only thing was—

I turned and realized that Charles was staring at *me*, not his injured friend. "What exactly were you doing here?" he asked in the smooth tone of a teacher who had walked in on students divvying up stolen goods.

"We were just talking."

"About what?"

His eyes were on me, steady. I said nothing—I had no idea how much he had overheard. There was something crafty about how his pretty eyes slipped from me to Will's body. "Well, I guess we should get him to the hospital," he said.

"No!" He looked at me, an eyebrow raised. I understood he was threatening me, in a way. "We can't go to a hospital. I drugged him," I admitted.

"With what?"

"Rohypnol."

"I hardly think you need any such aid for male company," he said, smiling.

I pretended I thought he was flattering me and blushed. "He'll be fine, but the last thing we need is someone finding out—"

"We?"

I looked at him beseechingly, with big eyes. You can argue with men but it's far more powerful to appeal to their most basic instincts. Latch on to that part of their Y chromosome that likes explaining things to women, the part of them that likes to help because it makes them feel bigger. "He's fine, Charles. I think he just needs to lie down and sleep it off."

"He could have a serious brain injury."

I said nothing. I wasn't exactly sure how much trouble I was in.

Charles sighed, giving me a look like I was being mischievous. He dropped the pocket square and stood up, surveying the now-messy guesthouse. He walked over to Will and crouched in front of his body. "Will? You awake?" Will moaned. "My dad has guys," Charles said, turning to me, "like bodyguards. One of them was in the military and probably knows some serious first aid. He's helped me before."

"With what?"

"I've never brained anyone with a geode if that's what you're asking, but I've crashed a car or two and wanted to hide it from my dad. I'll give him a call and we can make sure Will's okay. You go back to the house," he said, gesturing with his head in that direction. "Take the first car you can out of here in the morning and I'll keep an eye on Will."

"I don't know if he'll remember anything—he didn't finish the drink."

"I guess you'll find out," he said unsympathetically.

I hesitated. "Why should I trust you?"

"Because I'm not calling the police when I could have. Go wash up—you have blood all over your dress."

I padded to the bathroom silently, my mind racing with the strange turn of events. I was furious with myself for losing control at the worst possible time—it was something I talked about with Dr. Wyman about wanting to improve. But also, even though this new situation was perilous, being around Charles excited me. Suddenly he was not just a cute boy whose relationship I was planning on destroying: he was so much more. He was *dangerous*. And I knew exactly why he was helping me: it gave him power over me. The only question was what he planned to do with that power.

When I looked at myself in the mirror I groaned. There was blood smeared all over my beautiful dress. I wriggled out of it, then washed my face. It wasn't the sort of dress you could wear a bra or underwear with, so I wrapped myself in a fluffy white towel, then picked up the soiled dress and stuffed it into the clean trash bag. I didn't want to leave any evidence behind.

Charles was finishing a quiet phone call when I went back into the living area. "He's coming—let's go."

"In a towel?" I teased. "People will wonder what you were doing with me."

He sighed, then took off his jacket, resting it on the back of the couch. He unbuttoned his white dress shirt, pulling it off, revealing a plain white T-shirt. He handed me the dress shirt, then turned his back to me. I took the towel off and put on the shirt. It was soft and warm and smelled like him.

He turned around and for a split second looked at me. He had never really looked at me that way before, his eyes flicking below my face to my body. His shirt came to midthigh on me.

Charles poked his head out the door of the guesthouse, then edged around to the front. I followed him, my bare feet sinking into the cool grass. Back at the house, the kitchen lights were still on, but the upper half of the house was dark.

"I can't see," I whispered. I felt his hand grasp mine. It was warm and his fingers seemed elegant. He led us back to the double doors where we had been partying. "Go up," he whispered. "I'll take care of everything else and call you after I talk to Will." He slid open one of the glass doors.

"If you plan on blackmailing me, you should know that I'm piss poor."

"Do I look like I need money?" he asked quietly. That hint of darkness in his eyes—a reminder that there would be some kind of price to pay. "Get back in your room without anyone seeing you. Give me your phone number." I recited it. Maybe I had fantasized Charles putting my phone number into his cell, but not like this.

As he closed the door my mind flew through contingency scenarios, stories I could make up to cover my tracks. I had never gotten the sense that Charles had a particular liking for Will—just because they were frat brothers doesn't mean they were friends. And there was something boorish about Will that made me think they wouldn't be close. More like Charles tolerated him as a beta-level orbiter.

I snuck back to my room, feeling my way through the dark. I shoved one of the Kappa girls nearly off the bed and wriggled under the covers. I brought Charles's shirt up to my nose and inhaled, already sleepy. It had been a long night. The geode and Charles had complicated my Will plan, but once the sun was up I would do what I had always done—adapt, regroup, and make my next move.

13

Kristen was pulling her blond hair into a ponytail and was left defenseless when Charles buried his face in the tickly part of her neck. She cringed, laughing. "It's a tax on being too slow," he said.

"Charlie Bear, I'm going to tell your mother," she crooned, and they laughed at the awful nickname. Somehow, miraculously, Kristen understood his family. The sunlight streamed through the windows of his bedroom, hitting her hair in a way that made it seem to float like golden strands. To any casual observer they would look like a normal, handsome young couple. He hugged her from behind, looking at their reflection in his mirror. Moments like these were times where his darkness should have felt stark in contrast to everything about Kristen that was airy and carefree, but something about their relationship made him feel like he could be just like her. When she smiled, she always smiled with her eyes.

He leaned forward and kissed her. He wanted to kiss her more but there wasn't time for that. "Can you head downstairs and oversee breakfast? I want to make sure Will's alive," he said.

"Did he get too wild last night?"

"He fell and cracked his head against the stone steps. I just want to make sure he's okay. Save me a bear claw."

Kristen kissed his cheek, then left the room, moving with the posture of someone entirely at home in her own body, something he had always liked about her. But with her absence it was almost like he could hear something click: the slight easing in his mind that occurred when Kristen wasn't around, like a tiny, subtle muscle that had been almost involuntarily flexed finally getting to relax.

Charles had put Will in the bedroom next to his own—the one his brother, Eric, used when he visited. He figured that if Will was going to throw up in anyone's room, it should be Eric's.

Charles knocked on the door and let himself in. Will was just beginning to stir from under a tangle of sheets. He groaned and held his head. Mercer, his father's bodyguard and jack-of-all-trades, had dutifully examined Will, stayed with him for several hours and then vanished like a ghost, leaving behind nothing but a glass of water and a bottle of Advil. Like many of the men who worked for his father, he did as he was told without asking questions. "You feeling all right?" He affected the tone one uses when making fun of people the night after they had acted a fool.

"My head is killing me." Will managed to sit up, wincing, then seemed surprised when he touched his forehead and found a bandage.

Charles crouched to his level and studied his face. "You remember anything from last night?"

Will frowned, looking down. "I remember we were doing shots..." He reached for the Advil and dry swallowed a few. "Mmm... I don't know after that."

"You got plastered and fell and smacked your head on the stone steps outside."

"Ughhh."

"Come downstairs and have a Bloody Mary," Charles said loudly.

Will cringed. "I'm never drinking again."

"Famous last words. Why don't you sleep it off for a while, then?"

"No," Will said quickly. "I'm gonna take off actually. I've got stuff for lacrosse."

Good. He didn't want Will and Chloe to cross paths.

Charles waited until Will had gathered his things and followed him into the foyer to watch the door shut behind him. Only then did he feel it was okay to join the group, who were moaning through their own hangovers as they picked over a spread of pastries and cheese soufflé. As he filled his plate he could tell that Chloe was trying to make eye contact with him, but he avoided her. At least until Kristen left the room to bring down her overnight bag. He flicked his eyes to Chloe's, silently saying: *Everything's fine so far.*

What a strange convergence of events! He hadn't even noticed the girl before—just one of the flock of never-ending coeds. Charles thought himself good at reading people. Dr. Wyman said that for a psychopath he was above average at recognizing emotions in others. If a person was smart, Wyman had once said, one could use the ability to read and understand others to their advantage, to make their way through a confusing world, to make a successful life. On the other hand, they could also use this same ability to manipulate others and get in trouble.

What exactly had he walked in on? Funny that Chloe had immediately thought he would blackmail her. He wasn't sure what he would do with the information but he knew one thing: it was at least something novel and intriguing in a world filled with so few novel and intriguing things.

"You seen Will?" someone asked. Annoyed, Charles looked to his right into the dumb, earnest face of Chad, the president of SAE. His arms were so ropey with muscle that there wasn't a shirt on earth that didn't look tight on him.

"He left early," Charles said.

The group divided into the cars and headed back to campus. Kristen tended to fall asleep during car rides, which left him with some privacy to think. His Jaguar purred comfortably as he wound back toward DC. Had he heard Chloe right? Did she say the word *rape* or *tape*? She definitely mentioned a video. The reference to being twelve? And the white-hot rage as she lashed out with the geode. Charles had seen the violence just when it was at its precipice—he could have stopped her by calling out, but had been too interested to see what would happen next. She had hit Will hard with an extremely dense object— someone stronger, someone like Chad, could have easily killed a person with a single blow with that rock. She could very well have killed him.

But why?

Did Will *rape* her? Charles glanced over at Kristen, as if the thought alone would wake her. But she was nestled against the car window, the rainbow of autumn-colored leaves blurring with movement behind her. Charles didn't know Will well. He was friends, in a generic sense, with a lot of the brothers, but his only close friend from SAE was Derek. They had been friends since freshman year when they had both pledged. He hadn't wanted to, but it had been his father's frat. Charles had overlapped in the frat house with Will for one year, but had then moved out of the disgusting house and off campus to an apartment more his style as soon as he was able to.

Will was a nondescript bro, not even interesting enough to be as unlikable as Chad. He drank beer and said dumb shit, and would probably end up working in finance and marrying someone he called a whore behind her back. *Do I think he raped a twelve-year-old?* Charles considered the question.

Would Will get a girl drunk and have sex with her? Yes,

Charles thought, he probably would, although he had no specific evidence to suggest Will ever had. Would Will get a girl drunk and have sex with her even if she were saying no or trying to fight him off? Maybe? And if either of those hypotheses were true, was it that far-fetched that he would have raped a twelve-year-old?

What he really wanted to do was ask Dr. Wyman. Of course, it would be phrased all in hypotheticals. It seemed very Chad-like—embarrassingly earnest and well-intentioned—to be honestly engaged at something as woo-woo as therapy, but Wyman was the only person he could have this sort of conversation with in-depth. No judgment that Charles didn't understand something he was supposed to understand. A genuine interest in reframing the question in a way Charles could grasp.

When they got back to DC, he dropped Kristen at her house and then headed to the psychology department. It was Sunday and Wyman wouldn't be there, but Charles had to complete an exercise by Monday at noon and he'd rather get it done now.

The exercise was part of a series using virtual reality. The VR felt surprisingly immersive. In the virtual world he would sometimes interact with one or two other people in a conversation, or they tried to solve a problem, or they would talk about something personal. Then something would shift—the perspective would change, and he would be the other person, looking back at the avatar he had just been. The experiment then measured his emotional responses. Wyman told him this trained him in the skill of perspective taking. That if he could start by seeing *himself* through others' perspectives, that this could train him in the art of switching to see things from others' perspectives. Charles was not sure he was getting any better at it, but it would be a good skill to master. That was the sort of stuff that got him in trouble with Kristen.

He parked in the space reserved for the Dean of Social Sciences (he could almost always get away with this) but then met a strange sight once he got out of his car. The double doors to the psychology department were locked with an oversize padlock and chain. Bright yellow crime scene tape crossed the doors.

Annoyed, Charles pulled out his phone. With the psychology department off-limits, Charles figured he would instead check up on Will again, then text Chloe the results. As he headed to the house Will shared, he flipped through the Metro section of the *Washington Post* on his phone to see if there was anything to explain the crime tape he had seen—nothing. On Twitter there was one post of the chained doors with a bunch of question marks around it. Several people commented with questions, but one person said, I heard a guy got brained to death.

At Will's house, Charles was once again stymied—the door was locked and no one was home. Given that it was Sunday, it wasn't unreasonable that Will would be over at the SAE house. He headed there next, returning the nervous smiles from two girls walking in the opposite direction. "No, he was totally like *bled* to death—everyone's talking about it," one of them was saying.

The SAE house was its standard self: messy, odorous, filled with people who should have something better to do. Two guys were trying to figure out if they could play Ping-Pong but with the ball on fire. Charles thought this a questionable endeavor.

When he got midway up the stairs he could see Will halfsticking out of the hall closet. He was rooting around, throwing stuff, flustered. "Hey, I just wanted to see if you were all right," he called.

Will froze. "I'm good," he said, looking at Charles pointedly. It was the sort of look that said, *Go away*.

Charles jogged down the steps, helped himself to a bottle of beer from the fridge and went outside to sit on one of the lawn chairs. He opened WhatsApp and texted Chloe, I talked to him in the morning and he acted like he couldn't remember anything.

But just now spotted him at the frat house looking for something pretty hard. (he doesn't live here anymore)

Almost instantly, the little ellipses that indicated the other person was typing appeared. Whatever she was, Chloe typed slow. Charles leaned forward, hunched over the phone.

Ok, was all she wrote. He cocked his head to one side. That's it?

☺ she added.

"Dude!" someone called loudly. Charles looked up and saw Derek jogging toward him, his fuzzy black hair looking extra fuzzy—he had clearly not showered. "Did you hear?"

"Hear what?"

Derek climbed into the chair beside him. "Some guy got *killed* last night! In the psychology department!"

"I was just there! *That's* why there's police tape everywhere?"

Derek nodded. "No one knows the whole story, but apparently some freshman was there and tried to save him."

"Who died? Anyone we know?"

"Michael Boonark?"

"Doesn't sound familiar," Charles said. How tawdry. He wondered how fast everything would be cleaned up. He still had that assignment to do.

14

Leonard answered the door almost as soon as Detective Bentley rang the bell. He had not seen Bentley for some time, and so it didn't seem strange for the two men to embrace. He had known Bentley's father and remembered when the detective had been a child zooming all over Leonard's Foggy Bottom rowhouse. Decades later Bentley would follow in his father's footsteps to become a police officer, then a detective.

Another man, presumably Bentley's partner, gave them a look of impatience. "Please come in," Leonard said, leading them to the living room. Bentley stood in front of the leather recliner, which faced the fireplace, and shook his head with amusement.

"Damn, you still have this chair. I remember climbing up on it."

"Good things last the test of time," Leonard said, smiling sadly as he sat on the couch. The circumstances of them meeting again were not happy.

Leonard had consulted with the MPD for the past thirty years, starting with the elder Detective Bentley, and this relationship had helped him get approval from the school and its IRB—institutional review board—to host the Multimethod Psychopathy Panel Study at Adams. Catch the ones who could be saved while they're young, he had argued, and they would never live a life of crime. MPD had already referred several young people to the program—ne'er-do-wells in their eyes—but kids who Leonard recognized were clearly bright and not a risk to other students. Several had gone through the program to become productive members of society: husbands and wives and parents, a lawyer and a CPA, even the owner of a small business.

"This is my partner, Deever."

Leonard nodded and gestured for them to sit. Normally they would have met in his office, but now his intellectual sanctuary was a crime scene. "I'm absolutely devastated," he said, rubbing at his tired eyes. "I don't understand who would do this."

"We were hoping you might have some idea," Bentley said. "Did Michael talk about having problems with anyone lately? Did he have money issues? Drugs?"

"Michael drank as much as your typical college student. Came from a middle-class family and had no secret gambling addiction or anything. I can't see why anyone would want to harm him."

"Who has keys to these experiment rooms?"

"Only me, my graduate student—Elena, I understand you talked to her already—and our more senior research assistants. Students in the program can only get inside when they have an experiment scheduled—their smartwatch can unlock the door."

"So with Michael's diagnosis, did he act out in ways that made him enemies? People he's crossed?" Bentley asked.

Leonard shook his head, for the first time in two decades suddenly craving a cigarette. "Michael had actually improved quite a bit since he started the program. A couple of quibbles with his roommate over dishes and whatnot—nothing serious. Kirby Gurganus," he said, anticipating the next question. "That's the roommate. Also a junior."

"This program Bentley tells me you're running," Deever said.

Leonard instantly didn't like his tone. "You invite a bunch of psychopaths to the same school so they can wreak havoc on a bunch of innocent undergrads? How does this make sense?"

"Funny, it seems that someone has wreaked havoc upon one of my psychopaths. These are students who we are teaching to adopt moral codes and to manage their maladaptive behavior."

"Still—why bring them here?"

"These students are in intensive treatment. If there are eight thousand undergraduates here, about three hundred of them are probably psychopathic—they just never got diagnosed. My kids are students who want a better life and whose families are invested in their improvement." Deever looked unimpressed.

"So, he's been in this study for three years," Deever said, starting a new thread. "You must know a lot about his psychology." Deever, Leonard realized, was exactly the sort of man who, when he found out you were a psychologist, smirked and asked if you were *psychoanalyzing* him. "What's going on in inside his head? What can you tell us about his character?"

Leonard hesitated, feeling a strange pull to respect Michael's privacy, but then remembering that Michael was no longer alive, and that the boy had been murdered. "He was misanthropic, but not in a way that wasn't social. He read a lot, fancied himself a poet. He wanted to dazzle people but... My patients are often drawn toward manipulative behavior, and maybe Michael would have preferred to be that way, but his attempts at manipulation were pretty heavy-handed... They didn't always work."

"There's something else we should probably talk about," Bentley said. "There was an eyewitness to the attack, another student who called 911 and tried to administer first aid. He was on the list of names you gave me."

Leonard was stunned. Buried within the pages and pages of consent forms was a small clause that indicated that students in the program who had criminal records would have their names turned over to the police. It had been a concession and a goodwill gesture he had had to make in convincing the school to host the panel study. "Andre or Kellen?" he asked.

"Andre Jensen."

The poor boy—after already having seen so much death at a young age. Andre in his first session had been incredibly reticent, giving sullen one-word answers and asking about Leonard's background as if he didn't believe that he had the proper training. "How did he respond?"

"Kid's pretty shook up. He tried to stop the bleeding when it happened, and when we got him to the station to get a statement, he kept implying that maybe it wouldn't have happened if he knew better first aid."

Leonard could barely digest this nugget of information before Deever interrupted his partner. "Big coincidence that another one of your students just happened to be in the same area at the same time. What can you tell us about this guy?"

"How is it a coincidence at all? Two students in the same program hosted at the psychology department would repeatedly visit that location," he replied, trying to keep the annoyance out of his voice. "I can't see Andre doing something like this, if that's what you're asking. He got mixed up with some foolishness when he was fourteen or fifteen, but nothing like a precursor to murder."

"Anything violent?"

"Technically assault, but more the 'I'm going to beat you up after school' variety. Joyriding, vandalism." Deever was writing furiously. To Leonard, it was clear that joyriding and the occasional fight were not at all in the same class as murder. "Detective, why would he help Michael and call 911 if he did it?"

Deever shrugged. "With half a dozen sociopaths running around here, you can't think I'm going to overlook that fact when there's a murder."

"Psychopath," Leonard corrected. "And I *hope* you don't overlook anything because my student was murdered."

"The smartwatches they wear—you collect location data on them?" Deever pressed.

"The smartwatches log location data all the time much the way a smartphone does, but in accordance with our privacy rules, we only keep locational data for the moments when they submit a mood log and discard the rest." Leonard checked on his computer. "Andre submitted one at eight-thirty from around this location," he said, writing down the geocoordinates, which he pointedly handed to Bentley.

Bentley said they would probably be in contact again and both men stood up to leave. Deever left the room first, heading out the door toward their unmarked car, which was parked illegally on the street. Foggy Bottom's tiny historic district was sandwiched between the Watergate Complex and the sprawling campus of the George Washington University. Strange to think that all the chaos and anger toward the government during those Watergate years seemed to be happening all over again. Bentley touched Leonard's arm gently. "You all right?"

Leonard shook his head. "I know it isn't rational, but it's like history repeating itself. Me, you as a stand-in for your father, the crime scene tape." He blinked, looking out into the night where an ambulance siren was warbling. "I don't like to think back to those days."

"It's just one murder. And we're going to nail this guy. Trust me."

15

Reek seemed surprised when I made a beeline for him when we were told to pick Bio lab partners. "Hi," he said nervously, tucking his ash-colored hair behind his ears as I claimed the lab stool next to him. "I don't want to do this."

"Come on, this is pure biology." In front of us was a dissection kit, complete with a pan, scalpel, forceps, and scissors. I had been looking forward to lab—dissections are the best part of the class.

"It's just…that *smell*," he added, looking pale.

The smell was formaldehyde. But also, it may have been Reek, because SAE was not allowing him to shower for the next week. I didn't mind either smell, because I'm going to be a doctor, and because Reek might have useful information about Will.

The TA came around and gave us each a plastic bag with a fetal pig inside. Even with surgical gloves on, Reek was squeamish. I cut open our bag and drained the formaldehyde. Our piggy was cute with its little face, mouth open and tongue sticking out.

The lab stations were far enough apart that I could go on

a fishing expedition with Reek without anyone noticing. He seemed happy to let me take the lead on the dissection while I made mild gossip with him about the party. He knew who had hooked up with who, was impressed with Charles's house and his hot girlfriend (oh, please), but never made any mention of Will and his little accident. Good—his presence and absence hadn't really been noted, then.

"Who's Charles's girlfriend, again?" I asked, making a long incision down Babe's belly. Key to getting the Charles situation under control was knowing as much about him as possible.

"Kristen Wenner?"

"How long have they been going out?" I asked. The inside of the pig was all different shades of gray. Dead-looking pinkish gray, sodden-intestine gray. I would be great coming up with the names for shades of paint.

"Two years."

Two years? Didn't he want to test the waters and play the field a little?

I fished some more, both literally and figuratively, removing the baby pig's organs one by one, pulling from Reek all the information he had. He had been pretty drunk, too, and had limited observations about the party.

"Chad was giving you the eye," Reek said as he watched me remove the pig's liver.

"I didn't meet a Chad."

"You know, SAE Chad."

"Sorry, my mind's drawing a blank."

He seemed surprised. "He said something about your dress."

I concentrated on the gray organs in front of me. I poked the pig's tongue with my scalpel, thinking about the flecks of blood on my pink cocktail dress, now long gone after being stuffed into a dumpster outside a Popeye's. "About my dress?" That dress hadn't been cheap, and I looked good in it. What a waste.

I chanced a look at Reek. He was flushing. "Uh, that you looked good in it."

"Oh."

I couldn't get any more information out of him. I wanted to ask him about what Charles had told me—that Will had been looking for something at SAE—but there was no way to ask that without drawing unwanted attention to myself. But as soon as Charles had texted me that, I had mentally celebrated. Will had the video somewhere—he wouldn't look for something he didn't still have. Soon it would be mine.

We washed our hands and I scrubbed professionally, pretending I was a surgeon. "I'm starving. Do you want to go to All Purpose for pizza? Some of us are meeting in a couple hours."

"No, thanks," he said, glancing at the biohazard bag where we had deposited the remains of our piglet.

"Your loss," I said, popping my earbuds in.

I had one last task to complete before dinner. I headed to Hallbreck, a sophomore dorm on the south end of campus. It was easy to just slip in because there was a crowd outside talking about some murder TV show.

I lingered outside the communal bathroom, pretending to text, until two girls exited. I waited till they were back in their rooms before I went in, jamming a rubber wedge underneath the door so no one would walk in on me.

Indeed, the communal showers were heavily decorated with scraggly hairs: long hair, pubes, coils of all colors. I put on the disposable surgical gloves I had stolen from Bio lab and took out a clean Ziploc. With a pair of new tweezers, I carefully picked out a dozen or so hairs and sealed them into the bag for safekeeping. I then went to Thresher, another dorm, the men's locker room at the gym, and a local YMCA to repeat the process. In the YMCA I nabbed not only some hair but an even bigger prize: a used tampon. DNA city—and none of it mine.

That was for Phase Four, which involved a lot of moving pieces, but the main thing I had to concentrate on was Phase Three: Get the Video. And from what Charles has said, Will was already in the process of locating it.

16

There was a moment that day, for a period of about two hours, where Andre Jensen entirely forgot that he had held his hands over a hemorrhaging neck wound as a man died before his eyes. He forgot about the police and their questions, weird thoughts of Wyman and the CRD Killer and all the things that made him not a normal college student, and for a moment he was hardly an individual at all.

He was an eye. He was someone documenting the course of history. His new camera felt warm in his hands from being tightly gripped. The huge crowd of protestors moved down Pennsylvania Avenue like a swarm of humming bees. Andre, perched on top of a mailbox, snapped away, hoping that somewhere within the bunch was the shot that could land him on the front page of the *Daily Owl*. Too skittish to directly ask Dee, Marcus had brought it up for him, and he was told sure, send anything along, and if it was good it would get published. Here was a shot of a girl with her mouth wide open, her fist in the air. Dozens of shots of clever signs. It was the biggest protest Andre had ever seen in person and it was astounding to think that it would be dwarfed in size by the one coming up in October.

He snapped a picture of a toddler being carried on his father's shoulders, the child holding a sign that said Civil Rights Are Human Rights! What had sparked this particular protest was the announcement that the Justice Department was going to roll back investigations into mortgage companies and landlords that discriminated against minorities. Andre held on to his camera carefully as he jumped down from the mailbox. He snapped a few more pictures as he walked toward campus, heading to where his friends said they would meet afterward. He felt *good* being in a huge crowd even though they were all strangers—it felt safe and entirely separate from his day-to-day life.

A dozen or so people were already at the Black Students' Union, descending upon a snack table that had been set up. Marcus, a bright red bandanna tied around his neck (in case of tear gas, although this protest seemed to be pretty mild), nodded in his direction. Parched, Andre took a Coke, but the moment the soda hit his tongue, he remembered the Homicide Office and a wave of nausea hit him. Suddenly the good feeling was gone and he did not want to be around anyone, friends or no.

For the past few days, the attention the murder had drawn had made him feel even worse. Everyone wanted to be sympathetic while also hearing the juicy story, and some wanted to give unqualified legal advice, including dire warnings that the police would pin it on him—as if he hadn't thought of that himself. Deep down, some irrational part of him wondered if his being a witness wasn't some terrible payback for the fraud he was committing. He imagined himself getting carted away in cuffs, a phone call to his mother that made her collapse. He imagined an alternative scenario of the true murderer getting caught, Andre exonerated, only to have a grim group of administrators show up at his door with questions about how he had gotten into Adams. What would happen then? Was what he had done technically illegal? How could anyone prove whether or not he had answered any of those questionnaires honestly?

Andre slipped out the side door of the Union, and without thinking dialed his parents' landline, just wanting to hear their voices, the boring sameness of their home life. His father picked up almost immediately. "Pooh! They said on the news some boy got murdered at Adams!"

Hello to you, too. "Uh, yeah."

"That school isn't safe!"

"Come on, people get murdered in DC every day. It was some meth thing."

"A drug deal?"

How did he get trapped in this conversation when what he had wanted was the soothing sound of his father laughing at some dumb dad joke, Isaiah somewhere in the background being a jackass, the soft chastising of his mother? Instead, he was cutting the call as short as possible, saying he was about to lose reception as he headed up the elevator in his dorm.

He pretended to be asleep when Sean came home, ignoring Sean's sighing and complaining about the soreness of his feet, then his loudly eating Crunch 'n Munch before he finally fell asleep. If Sean got kicked out of Adams, Andre reasoned, he would "take a gap year" and then somehow be at a place like James Madison or UVA once things were arranged. He wasn't annoying about it, but Sean had been his high school salutatorian and little things, small things, like the fact that Sean knew how to ski and that he had a brand-new PlayStation, made it clear that Sean's life contained more possibilities.

When it became apparent that Andre was too buzzed to doze off himself, he got up, went to his desk and opened his laptop. Watching that student—Michael—die had become a bone stuck in his throat, something that irritated and couldn't be removed. He had been following the news and not heard anything about the culprit being caught. Was it just a coincidence, or did the murder have something to do with the psychopathy program? Exactly how dangerous were the other students in the panel study, and how likely was Andre to run into them? If he hadn't already, that is. Something had been gnawing at Andre. Wyman seemed like a nice, well-intentioned man. He was interpersonally warm every time Andre interacted with him, but the murder on top of the CRD connection had begun to make him have doubts.

What if Wyman was all in on this program, something that brought him professional success and grant money, and he had everything staked on proving that the students who went through his program walked out the other side as model citizens. What if he was wrong and, worse still, what if he knew he was wrong?

Wyman's official Adams webpage was terse. *Leonard Wyman, subfields: abnormal psychology, psychopathy and antisocial personality disorder, cognitive behavioral therapy*. Nothing about the Multimethod Psychopathy Panel Study. Why was there nothing about the program? Yet when Andre searched the archives of the National Institutes for Health grant database, Wyman was listed as having a massive multiyear grant—clearly this had to be the panel study.

Andre went to the top of his browser and typed in "scholar. google.com." Wyman had publications listed, but none of them gave any hint of "I am running a secret program for psychopaths" or "I've defended a truly unredeemable madman for some inexplicable reason." His articles had titles like "Recidivism and Moral Reasoning in Psychopathic Populations: An Exploration of the Stress-Diathesis Model" and "The Neurosemantics and Moral Reasoning of At-Risk Populations."

Andre searched for criminal records and came up with nothing. He tried every combination of Wyman + CRD—the killer's real name and other monikers—but that didn't come up with anything he hadn't seen already.

"Whatcha doing?"

"Agh!" Andre slammed his hand on his desk. "Sean! Do not do that to someone who just—who just—"

"Oh, right, sorry. I was worried about you." He sat on the end of Andre's bed. "I mean, you have to worry about your roommate when he's up late at night after witnessing a murder, looking up shit about serial killers."

Andre rubbed at his eyes. "Can I tell you something crazy if you promise to keep it a secret?"

"Hold on." Sean left, then returned with his box of Crunch 'n Munch. "Proceed."

"You've heard of the CRD serial killer?"

"Obviously. I've seen that TV movie four times."

"He has something to do with this school. There's this psychologist at Adams who was part of the case. He's the only person who ever interviewed CRD, but he's *never* talked about it—I've looked."

"He's at Adams?"

"He's a full professor in the psychology department. You know—ten feet from where I saw that guy get murdered."

Crunch. "You think a tenured professor murdered an undergrad steps from his office?"

"What difference does it make if he has tenure?"

"I mean, you can't get fired if you have tenure."

"No, he doesn't seem like a *murderer*, but it's a big coincidence. I think he's hiding something." Andre hesitated—he wasn't about to start telling Sean about the panel study. But it wasn't hard to imagine how things could have gotten out of control. Wyman trying to manage one of his psychopaths, a current or former student, only to have them kill someone. Would he report them to the police or be in such denial about his own program's success that he couldn't see the possibility? Or would he instead want to protect the student or program? "Here's the thing I don't get—this guy is ostensibly an expert on studying psychopaths. Like people that don't have a conscience or empathy. During CRD's trial he argued for clemency. He kept saying, 'This guy isn't a monster. He shouldn't get the death penalty.'"

"Huh…" Sean thought about it. "I mean, the justice system is just so fucked with racism and classism, but Christ, CRD…"

"The one time I'm like, *All right, that guy should get fried*, is when you hear about guys like CRD or Ted Bundy or John Wayne Gacy," Andre added.

"So why don't you just ask him about it?"

"Are you crazy? Like 'Remember this really high-profile case that you never talk about…can you just go into detail about it with me, a complete stranger?'"

Sean shrugged. "You'll never get answers if you don't ask questions."

A week ago, it had seemed like he was running a scheme with potentially serious consequences: losing his scholarship, maybe getting kicked out of school. But now, after seeing that guy die in his arms, it felt a lot more like a life-or-death situation. It could have been him who had been stabbed. Was he safe participating in the study? What if the culprit knew he was a witness, or even got mad that Andre had tried to save Michael's life? He had read in an article once that psychopaths sometimes got fixated on real or perceived grievances and could hold grudges for *years*. "I don't know. I might work up the nerve. I'm trying to find out as much as I can about his connection to CRD. It feels connected to this murder somehow."

Sean peered over his shoulder. "Maybe he wrote a case study about it or something?"

"So far I haven't found anything. Maybe he signed a gag order or something?"

Sean shook his head. "Maybe Wyman never published any-thing about it, but you can still look for the next best thing. Who would have been talking about it nonstop at the time? His graduate students."

17

As soon as the elevator doors opened on Floor G2, Elena frowned. The lights were off. In front of her, the linoleum floor of the second-level basement reflected back the pale red light from the emergency exit sign down the hallway. Why was the power out?

She sighed. Time on the MRI didn't come cheap—it cost close to two million dollars and was shared between the Psychology Department, the Neuroscience Consortium, and the Biology Department. She walked down the hallway, her Toms making soft sounds that seemed amplified in the darkness. Her eyes adjusted to the dimness, making out the familiar doorways of offices and supply rooms.

Hopefully Kellen was able to finish his session before the power cut out. He had been scheduled for a scan an hour ago and the RA running him, Belle, was smart enough to know to call if something went wrong.

She turned a corner and paused, looking down a long hallway at the flickering beam of an emergency light starting to die. Something was wrong, but she couldn't put her finger on it.

"Hello!" a voice near shouted.

She gave a short scream, nearly dropping the laptop she was carrying under her arm. Charles was behind her, his grin white in the darkness. "Not funny!" she chastised him, annoyed.

Charles seemed to find her response amusing. "I forgot you're scared of the dark. Peace offering?" He propelled a Starbucks cup toward her.

She slurped suspiciously. "How many pumps of hazelnut is in this, four?"

His smile got bigger. Clearly he wanted something. "I'm early for my session *and* I brought coffee, and you can't even put the lights on?"

She sighed. "Come on. Let's see what happened." They began to walk toward the room where the scanner was.

"Well, everyone's talking about the murder," Charles said. Elena looked at him in her peripheral vision. Sometimes Charles had a strange affectation, like he had watched too many movies about how WASP-y rich kids were supposed to behave. Why was he wearing a button-down and a vest in the middle of the day? He had his hands clasped behind his back.

"Yes," she said simply. She was not supposed to talk about Michael—not with anyone, especially not with any of the other patients. She had been advised this both by the police and by Leonard. Elena herself was still in denial—it couldn't possibly be that less than thirty feet from her office a boy who wasn't even old enough to drink legally had been stabbed to death. Right on campus. A patient she had known for three years!

"It's so awful," he baited. For a split second, Elena wondered if Charles could possibly know that Michael was also in the program. Was he just being gossipy, or did he actually know?

They rounded a corner and Elena stopped short. Charles bumped into her. "It's definitely off," she said, realizing what was missing. The MRI was normally a constant hum of noise—

when you got closer to it you could hear a steady *wooo-wooo-wooo* sound. Charles strained to hear something, his head cocked to one side.

Then Elena heard something else.

A muffled cry. A moaning sound. A cold chill wrapped around her stomach. She knew she should walk toward the sound—someone could be hurt—but she really didn't want to see.

Charles cut in front of her. *Of course*, she thought, *he doesn't know better.* He was heading toward the L-shaped room they called the Control Room, the place where she or the RAs would sit manning the scanner. A glass pane separated it from the MRI room itself.

She didn't want to know what was in that control room, but she forced her feet to move. When she got there, Charles was leaning forward, hands on knees, talking to someone.

Belle sat on the floor, under the desk, grasping her knees to her chest. She was shaking, eyes glazed, face wet with tears. "Are you cold?" Charles asked. "What's wrong with you?"

Belle pointed with one wavering hand behind them.

Elena looked through the glass into the MRI room and saw someone on the ground. She could see only their feet. She pushed past Charles, stepping into the room.

At first, she couldn't fathom the scene. Someone lay on the ground in a pool of blood, their body contorted at strange angles. Several bloody bits were on the floor, and when she looked up, she saw spots of blood on the scanner.

She looked back at the body, her heart jumping. "Oh my God, it's Kellen." She reached for him, ignoring Charles, who had come up behind her and shouted for Elena not to touch the body. She pressed her finger against Kellen's neck—and felt nothing.

"Oh my God."

Charles crouched down, his expensive loafers carefully positioned away from the blood. He looked from the MRI machine to the bits scattered on the ground.

"What—what are those?" Elena asked.

"Buckshot. The little metal bits they put in shotgun shells."

Images flashed through Elena's mind. The active shooter situations were so common on the news that she couldn't even keep them straight. Adams even had an active shooter alert that went to the cell phones of the entire student body.

Charles stood up, his hands on his hips. He didn't look upset so much as interested.

"Act normal!" Elena snapped, unable to help herself.

Charles started, realizing the impression he was giving. "It sounds like you're upset."

Elena nearly screamed at him. That was verbatim something Leonard had taught him. Repeat people's emotions back to them as if you understood. Fake it till you make it. His stupid lack of fear could have deadly consequences.

"He—he was like that when I got here. The power was off." Belle was standing at the entryway.

Elena popped to her feet. "Did you call 911? How many shooters were there?"

Belle nodded, but then looked confused. "You mean, you think they could still be around?"

Elena pictured a shooter prowling, a figure in black combat gear carrying a suicide note to a girl who had rejected him.

"He wasn't shot," Charles said suddenly. He gestured for her to hunker down and look with him. He pointed to the body, which had bled heavily from the chest and stomach area. He pointed to the base of the MRI where bloody buckshot lay. "The buckshot didn't go into him. It came *out* of him."

"I'm going to be sick," Elena muttered, stumbling out into the hallway. The police were on their way, but there was one other phone call that was just as important. Of course Leonard wasn't picking up—he was probably *meditating* or something. "You need to get down here," she hissed into his voicemail. "The police are on their way. Oh, it's awful. It's *Kellen*. He's been murdered. Leonard, it's the second student in the program in weeks—what the hell is going on?"

18

Charles caught a cab to Old Ebbitt Grill. The police had kept him so long for questioning that he was now significantly late for dinner, not to mention that his head was reeling with new information. Poor sweet Elena—she was book smart but sometimes lacked the sort of common sense that would tell you to be far away from a psychopath when having a private conversation. And what Charles had heard was critical: that body was the *second* student from the program who had been killed in less than a month. He wasn't even sure what to think.

Old Ebbitt was downtown, closer to all the touristy stuff, frequently stuffed with these tourists because it was the oldest restaurant in DC. It was typically dark inside, accented with polished wood. It was one of the places his father had arbitrarily decided to take a liking to. They mixed a good cocktail—that was probably the reason.

He pushed past the tourists and spotted Kristen from behind. She wore a pink silk blouse tucked into a pencil skirt, her straw-colored hair tumbling in waves past her collarbone. He came up behind her, placing his hand on her lower back. She jumped, then laughed, realizing it was him. His older brother, Eric, was supposed to be here, which probably put her on high alert. Eric had come on to her at the last Portmont family Christmas party. "What took you so long?" she asked.

"I saw a car accident. A hit-and-run. The police had to interview me as a witness and it took forever." The lies came simply, and there really wasn't another option. The last thing he wanted was the drama of a family dinner when what he really needed to do was *think*. Two students in the program killed. What was the probability of that being random? Best not to say anything to Kristen until he knew the entire story and there wasn't anything for her to worry about. She already worried about him too much.

"God, were they okay?"

"No," he said, "they weren't." Kristen probably assumed that he was concerned about his father being mad about his lateness, which at least provided some cover for the furrow in his brow. She was the only person who understood the complicated knot that was his family. Sure, he talked about it sometimes with Dr. Wyman, but hearing it was one thing—seeing it another.

A waiter who recognized Charles led them to a table in the back of the restaurant where his family was already seated. Luke Portmont was opening a lobster claw, sitting at the head of the table. He was apparently annoyed about some political squabbling in Congress. Luke, silver-haired, had passed on his handsomeness to his son, but not his eyes, or the mouth that was somehow cruel-looking. Eric, the elder brother, sat at his right side. Both were drunk already. Charles's sister, Julia, was in town, and popped to her feet to hug them both. She was six feet tall and unapologetically wore her body with the presence of an Amazon. His mother, Lynn, a petite, soft-spoken woman, followed suit.

The conversation about politics continued, Luke not even acknowledging Charles, nor his tardiness. Charles wisely said nothing, unfolding a napkin onto his lap, a vapid, polite look on his face not unlike the one his mother wore. Two people in the program had been killed. Luke gestured for a man in all black to come over and ordered a Manhattan as if he hadn't already drunk all the five boroughs. The man, clearly a busboy and not a waiter, said he would let the waiter know. If two people had been killed, did that mean *Charles* was in danger? He had recognized the guy in the MRI room—Kellen, Elena had called him. Not a friend or an acquaintance, but someone he had run into at a party or two.

Charles's wandering attention snapped back when he realized the focus of conversation had turned to him. Being late was bad—not paying attention was even worse. Charles's father cracked another lobster claw, shaking his head. "Now why the hell you would want to be the president of some no-name school when you could have gone to Georgetown." His fresh drink arrived, which he sipped, then used to point at Kristen. "Did you know this? I pay to high hell to get my idiot son into Georgetown on legacy and he decides not to go."

"Well, then he wouldn't have met Kristen," his mother said, trying to turn this into a kind moment.

"Plenty of Kristens at Georgetown," Eric said, not even looking in her direction.

"It really doesn't matter where you go to college," Julia said.

"It matters because of the connections you make," his father said. "Prestige matters. Our name matters. You think you could get on in this world without our name? Where do you think you'd be?"

"I think I'd manage to get by," Charles said.

He almost couldn't comprehend what happened next. He looked up from his beet salad because there was a blur of movement. Then wetness hit his face with an intense sting to his eyes. Something heavy cracked against his forehead. There were audible gasps and not just from their table. The sickly sweet smell of bourbon and cherry covered Charles's face, dripping down onto his shirt. His eyes were screaming, his contacts like films of acid sticking to his eyes. "I can't see," he said.

"Come on," Kristen whispered urgently, grabbing his arm and standing him up, leading him through the restaurant.

Charles held his hands over his eyes, blinking constantly. "Is he all right?" someone, a stranger, asked. He heard hushed voices. Kristen led him to what must have been a bathroom and ran the water. He reached at it blindly, trying to flush his contacts out.

"Wait, I have eye drops." Charles pulled himself up onto the counter. Kristen tilted his head back, used the drops and swiped at his eyes a few times, retrieving the contacts. The drops soothed his eyes, but only a little. The bathroom door opened— Charles tensed—but it was only their waitress, looking morti-fied, and the busboy his father had barked his drink order at. The latter held a towel filled with ice, which he gestured with. The waitress nodded sagely.

Kristen pressed it to Charles's forehead.

"Should we...?" The waitress trailed off. "If you have a con-cussion, you shouldn't go to sleep," she said. "I read that once." The busboy nodded in agreement.

Kristen touched his arm. "Let's just leave," she whispered. "We can go out the back."

God, he loved this woman. Charles got to his feet, then took out his wallet. He handed three crisp hundreds over to the wait-ress, who looked confused.

They rode home in a cab silently, but the moment they got inside Kristen's house she made Charles a bag of ice. She perched at her computer and started looking up the symptoms for con-cussions. "You have to tell me if your headache gets worse. Or if you throw up or lose consciousness."

"I don't have a concussion," he said.

"Do you want to go to Urgent Care?"

"No."

"Let me find you some more drops."

"Come here," he said quietly. Kristen climbed onto the couch and embraced him. She cried silently, but Charles quickly noticed. "Hey, come on, I'm fine. It's no big deal. I'll probably just have a bump for a day or two."

"I hate him," she cried into his chest.

"It's okay," Charles said, balancing the ice on his head so he could hold her with both arms. They lay still for a while, Charles stroking her hair.

"Do you think they'll call?" she whispered.

"Let it go to voicemail if they do. I've gotten you sticky. Let me take a shower."

She went back to her internet medical sleuthing and he went into the bathroom and shed his clothes. The shower was tiled with glazed, striated tiles in a blue-gray color, and had several showerheads at different levels. A steam bath, as well, which you could also use simultaneously if you really felt like wasting water. Which he did. He washed the bourbon off, then touched at his wound again. It stung.

Something bothered him. Why had he given that money to the waitress and the busboy? He had done it without thinking. Well, it was a tip, some part of him replied quickly. Yes, a tip—a tip for checking on him. No, not so much a tip. The money had been a compensation somehow. For what? Well, because he had been embarrassed. His father had thrown a glass at his face, emasculating him, and what would make up for it was flashing a bunch of cash to people who lived off tips. Was that it? Or because they would have to put up with his father and his brother for the rest of the night. What was that, that grain of feeling in him? Was this what guilt was? Maybe—maybe not.

Charles blinked, realizing that there were blank spots and jagged lines on the tiled wall. He turned off the water quickly and wrapped a towel around himself, not caring that he dripped water onto the floor and out into the hallway. "K, I'm having an aura."

Kristen popped to her feet immediately. They kept Excedrin at both their places and Charles always carried two capsules in his wallet in case he felt an aura coming on. He typically had an aura before he had a migraine, either visual abnormalities or the hallucination of smells that weren't actually there. Once he got one, there was only a small window of opportunity to stave off the debilitating pain.

Kristen pushed two white pills past his lips and handed him a glass of Coke (caffeine helped the medicine hit faster). "Just lie down—I'll put the TV on," she said. He nodded silently.

With his eyes half-open, he watched Kristen look for the remote. She had left her laptop open on the coffee table. The little green light on the webcam was on. Something about that bothered him—it had been broken for weeks and she hadn't been able to use FaceTime—but thinking was getting increasingly hard as the migraine rolled in, like a dense carpet that snuffed away any rational thought.

19

Day 40

Charles was very much not being helpful by ignoring my texts asking if he had seen or heard from Will again. Will hadn't posted anything on social media since Charles's party and I hadn't seen him. I started to worry that he had skipped town. I hovered in the hallway outside of his poli-sci lecture, intermittently peering through the window to see if he was there.

I fucked up: he hadn't had enough Rohypnol and I shouldn't have hit him. If it was the video Charles had caught him desperately searching for and not something else, then he probably remembered some stuff from the night of the party. Contingency 1: Will didn't remember. I could continue getting closer to him, maybe interrogate him again. Get him to admit to me where he keeps all his secret things. Contingency 2: he remembered. Then I would have to escalate, because why would he willingly hand it over?

For six years, I have obsessed about the video. What happened to it, who had access to it. Will doesn't strike me as someone who is strategic or meticulous about covering his tracks, so I was pretty sure he still had it somewhere. Either Will was so fucked up that he kept it because he liked to watch it, or Will was so fucked up that the video meant nothing more to him than the endless party selfies and family photos that he never got around to deleting.

I eyed every student who trickled out of the lecture, becoming increasingly angry as each one wasn't Will. Everything was taking too long. I had missed the discussion section for my Ethics class to look for Will and was now becoming dangerously hangry. I sulked all the way to the main dining hall, my boots making clomping noises on the sidewalk. They better have the good pizza today. Then I had to fucking wait in line only to have some bitch take the last pineapple pizza. I jammed the business end of a slice into my mouth as I sat by the window, chewing viciously.

My eyes skipped over the students, then my teeth clenched. Will must have skipped class because there he was, eating pizza like an asshole. I dumped my half-eaten slice in the trash and prepared my face with an innocuous look. Friendly eyes, hair tucked behind ears. I approached his table from the side so he wouldn't notice me until I was right beside him.

"Will! How are you?" I said brightly. His jaw twitched when he saw me. I instantly had a bad feeling.

"Hi," he said.

"I haven't seen you since the party." I smiled, but I knew it was too late. There was no charming this snake.

He stared at up at me. He remembered something from that night, although how much? But then I knew, because he said, "You need to get away from me and leave me alone."

I wasn't going to waste any time. "Where is the video, Will?" I asked quietly. I stepped toward him, leaning down, trying to make myself seem menacing.

"I don't have the stupid video. You'd better leave me the fuck alone."

"I know you have it."

He snorted. From across the cafeteria a bunch of guys—lacrosse players—entered and Will waved them over. "I threw out that phone years ago."

"Then why were you looking for it after I mentioned it? You found it. Give it to me. Did you upload it anywhere?"

"Why would I literally hand you something that incriminates me?" The boys were closing in, coming closer. The corner of his mouth went up into a smirk. "Besides," he said, standing up, looking down at me. He folded his arms across his chest and leaned down too close to my face. He was reminding me that he was bigger, stronger. "What are *you* going to do about it?"

He turned to walk away, not even in a hurry. Halfway across the cafeteria, surrounded by his bros, he half turned back at me with one of those looks that's supposed to make you feel small.

I stood rooted to where I was, rage washing over me, the exact same feeling I had just before I hit him with the geode. He doesn't understand just who I am. He doesn't understand how patient I can be. That his days are numbered.

Will is like every man who has ever kicked a dog. When they kick a dog, they forget that the dog cries and puts its tail between its legs only because of thousands of years of domestication and training. They forget, every time they kick, that every now and then they're going to come upon a dog with teeth.

20

Can you meet me at the Bean at 11? Charles texted Chloe. It's urgent. He stared at his phone, waiting for her to respond. It was 8 a.m. Kristen was still curled up, asleep, and the only evidence of last night was the bottle of Excedrin on the nightstand. He ignored the plying text from his mother, the one that acknowledged that Charles probably "wasn't feeling well," but didn't acknowledge that it was because her husband had thrown a glass at his head.

It was only a matter of time before rumors would start swirling about the two students murdered on campus, and of course Kristen would hear about it. But there wasn't any way she would find out that they were both in the program, was there? The only way she could was if he told her, Charles reasoned, and he didn't plan to. What was he supposed to say, that now she had to worry someone might be hunting down students in Wyman's study, one by one? And that suddenly these things started happening with the appearance of a certain female psychopath, Chloe Sevre? And the fact that he had colluded with said highly flirtatious female psychopath to cover up an assault at his own house, and that the aforementioned psychopath might also be an MRI-using serial killer? He didn't know what the hell was going on, but he hoped to get it sorted out today.

His phone pinged: Okay, she wrote. I have a present for you lol.

Bean and Nothingness was the second coffee shop in the SAC, located on the top floor. It was large, its windows overlooking campus, but most importantly, day or night it was always filled with students studying and talking. It was a public place.

Charles arrived at the Bean early to position himself with his back to the window, facing the entire coffee shop. He watched for Chloe and observed closely as she came in. Chloe did not look like a girl who had just stabbed a guy to death and killed another—one who was almost a foot taller than her—using an MRI machine. She looked like the sprightly spokesperson for mint-scented face wash. She had one of those infinity scarves in autumn colors all the girls were wearing that reminded Charles of lions' manes. She sat down and pushed a packet wrapped in a Safeway bag across the table. "It's your shirt. I washed it," she said, then waited as if expecting applause. "So…?" she asked. She evidenced no fear on her face. "Have you seen Will?"

"I haven't seen him since I told you."

She leaned forward. "*I* did. He *threatened* me."

"What did you expect? You almost killed him."

A look crossed over her eyes. Humor? "What I did was an accident. I just want my property back."

"Ah, yes, the mystery video." She ignored the comment and smiled idly at one of the waiters, inviting him to come over. He made an "in a minute" gesture.

Chloe leaned back, her eyes taking him in. "You're not going to tell anyone, right? If you're trying to blackmail me, you're barking up the wrong poverty tree."

"Maybe I'm helping you out of the kindness of my own heart."

The waiter came over and Chloe ordered a slice of death by chocolate. "Do me another favor, then. I want that video." She held up her hands when she saw the skeptical look taking over his face. "I'm not asking for anything big—just give me a heads-up if you know he'll be out for the night so I can search his house."

"I might be willing to do that," he replied. Might as well get on her good side if she was dangerous. While having information gave him power over her, it also made him a target.

The waiter returned with her slice of cake, holding the little card reader that students used to charge their food. "Do you mind?" she asked Charles.

Smiling ruefully, he swiped his card to pay. "May I ask, what were you doing yesterday afternoon?"

She shrugged, taking a bite. "Classes. Yessica and I went to yogalates."

"I'm sure you heard about the student who was killed on the sixth? The day before my party."

"Yeah," she said, her face registering nothing more than interest in idle gossip. "I heard it was a robbery?"

"It wasn't," Charles said. "And did you know that someone died yesterday? Guy named Kellen?"

"Yesterday?"

"Did you know that both the people killed were in our program?"

Chloe paused with a forkful of cake halfway to her mouth, then put it down. "What?" The look on her face was genuine surprise, or at least something that looked like it. She had already proved herself a good actress.

"The first was stabbed to death in one of the experiment rooms in the psych department. The second, I don't know—basically someone injected him with metal and it got ripped out of him in the MRI machine."

"*What?* They were both in *our* program?" He stared at her.

A slow realization dawned on Chloe's face. She leaned forward, indignant. "You think *I* had something to do with it?"

"Did you?" he asked, trying to sound casual.

"*No.* Ever occur to you that I've been *busy*?"

"Busy with what exactly?"

"But why would I…? I don't even know who the other people in the program are!"

"I don't know what you know," Charles said.

She seemed upset, but her reaction struck him as strange. More disappointed than angry at the accusation. She looked down at her plate. "I swear to you, I had nothing to do with it."

"Considering I saw you brain my fraternity brother with a geode, you lack credibility."

"You don't understand."

"I liked that geode—I got it in Switzerland."

Chloe put her fork down and met his gaze. The look on her face, in her eyes, was different. Less guarded—ostensibly. Oh, she was good—very good. He could easily picture her getting out of tickets when cops pulled her over, pleading to turn in papers late for class. "Okay. I'll level with you," she said. "I came to Adams for Will. The only reason I know you is because I had to get in with your frat to get close to Will—it's all I care about."

"Did he rape you?"

Her eyes hardened. "That's private. But if you're going to be morally outraged about anything *I* do, you should be more careful about the company you keep."

He tried a different tact, smiling, leaning forward, tasting the frosting of her cake with his index finger. "Chloe, I'm not going to tell on you if you snuffed some guy in an MRI. I just want to know. Because if two people in the program are dead and it's *not* you, someone could very well be hunting down all of us. Me, for example."

"I'm not like that," Chloe said, wide-eyed. "I'm like a good psychopath."

"And I'm supposed to take your word on that?"

She reached across the table—he restrained himself from pulling back—and put one of her hands over his. "I swear to you." She turned back to her cake. "Besides," she said, now cheerful. "For all I know *you* did it."

"Shouldn't you be more worried?" The wound on his forehead itched—without thinking he reached to touch it and cringed involuntarily. Her eyes flicked to his hairline with interest. Shit. He had carefully arranged his hair to cover the small bump and the livid red line on it, but he was always touching his hair without thinking about it.

Her eyes flicked back to his and she smiled. "Hmm," Chloe said, licking the back of her fork. "Nobody is hunting us. That stuff only happens in movies."

If she were doing this, killing people in the program, wouldn't she be putting on a big show about being scared? Talking about how they should find who did it? Or would her calculus include thinking about how he would think she would act? He frowned. "Chloe, I think you should take this seriously. I'm the one who found the second body—me and Elena. They used a fucking MRI."

She snorted. "If someone is actually capable of hunting and killing me, they deserve a genius award. I can look out for myself." The look on her face became crafty. "And if you're nice to me, I'll look out for you, too."

21

I had to face it: Charles Portmont was becoming a problem. He knew far, far too much. At this point, I was sure he knew exactly what the video was. Enough so that if Will was found dead, he could tell the police I had a good motive. And this bizarre accusation that I was killing people in the program! What was that, a veiled threat? I quickly checked the news—yes, there had been two students killed on campus within the space of two weeks. That *was* pretty bizarre, but what proof did I even have that either of them were actually in the program? For all I know, Charles was lying, playing some messed-up game with me.

I absolutely could not have Charles stand in the way of my plan, which included a smooth endgame of not getting caught. I had to consider the worst-case scenario—killing him if I thought he would blab about Will. The problem with this was twofold, no, threefold: for one, he's really hot and *what a waste*. Also, the Will project had been strictly limited to those who had been involved that night. I was righting a wrong, which makes me right. And lastly, I got the feeling that if Charlie Bear went missing, his billionaire parents would stop at nothing to find the culprit.

Maybe there was an easier way out: I could ensnare him. Games aside, he was halfway there already—I could tell from the way he looked at me at the guesthouse. While a normie might run straight to the police if they thought someone killed Will, Charles was a psychopath like me. There's no telling what he would do—it would depend entirely on what suited him. This would be my way out.

Everyone in the dorm was talking about the murders, but more so the second one. The MRI-as-murder-weapon was just too juicy a story to resist. All we heard from the college officially was that these were tragic events, blah blah blah, thoughts and prayers, we are cooperating with the investigation.

"You guys, I'm legit scared," said my friend Apoorva. We were sitting in a circle on her dorm room floor drinking triple sec because it was the only thing we could get our hands on. "So now on top of mass shootings, everyone being rape-y, and the world ending, we have to be worried about a serial killer."

"I couldn't sleep last night," Yessica admitted.

My mouth puckered as I scrolled through news results on my laptop. Molly was rubbing a hot oil treatment into my hair. "Two people isn't a serial killer. I think you need three to qualify," she said. I felt a tiny bud of an idea appear.

I looked at the coverage of the murders in the *Daily Owl*. One op-ed blamed it on Greek life, saying that the second guy, Kellen, had probably died in a hazing incident—what other reason could there be for him swallowing a bunch of buckshot? The most recent op-ed, the one that came out today, refuted this.

"This was a tragic, horrifying thing that happened," said Chad Harrity, President of both the Interfraternity Council at Adams and SAE. "But it has nothing to do with Greek life. Kellen wasn't in a fraternity and it wasn't a hazing. Fraternities have been the cause of some bad behavior over the years, but this generation is trying to change that."

Suddenly it hit me like a geode. I didn't think that someone was actually trying to kill all the panel students. I think I would know if someone were trying to kill me. So, I would keep an eye out—and how is that different than everyday life worried that Will would catch me alone? Maybe the same person killed Michael and Kellen, maybe not. What mattered was that people *thought* it was a serial killer targeting Adams students. What better way to deflect attention from myself! I could dispose of Will and pin it on our mystery hunter. If there actually was a serial killer, they had done me a huge favor.

Charles must have believed me when I said the video was my endgame, because two days later he texted me that SAE was having a pledge event, which meant that Will's house would be unoccupied. I donned my cat burglar outfit: black running tights and a matching top, tight ponytail, a small knapsack worn close to my body. I had a knife tucked into a holster above my right boot. Will and his roommate wouldn't be there, but I had to be prepared if either came home early and found me.

I walked to Will's house looking like I was heading to yoga and didn't don my gloves until I was in his carport. After a quick look around, I climbed up the drainpipe I had spotted before and got up on the flat roof. From there, I was able to edge my body over to examine the second-floor window with the tips of my fingers. It was half latched, open a couple centimeters. I jiggled it repeatedly with focused patience. It took about ten minutes, but slowly the latch moved and then I was able to get the window open. I climbed down.

I was in.

I perked my ears. I snuck through the house, stepping over piles of clothes and lacrosse junk to make sure it was empty. Which bedroom was Will's? Both had lacrosse stuff, and neither had family photos. I had no time to waste, and I wanted the search to be extensive. They each had a PC tower in their rooms. With my small tool set, I opened each tower and removed the hard drives. Now for the phone. If he was smart to begin with, he would have just destroyed his old phone or deleted the video, but if Charles saw him looking for it, maybe he still hadn't found it. I rifled through drawers, looked under the mattresses. I poked through closets and behind furniture. I turned up a jockstrap, a melted candy bar, and an old phone charger, but no old iPhone. Nuts. At least I had the hard drives.

I checked my watch. How long would a pledge event be? There was also the basement, but I wasn't sure if Will and Cordy actually had access to it. Many basements in DC are English basements—independent apartments separate from the rest of the house that people often rented out. Unless I was missing it, there was no way into the basement from inside of the house. I climbed back out and down the drainpipe. I checked the street carefully, then crouched at the back door to the English basement. Lock-picking involves jimmying around slim pieces of metal—it takes patience, which is not one of my many virtues. I worked diligently for what felt like an eternity but finally something clicked into place and I creaked the door open.

The basement was pitch-black, but I was prepared. I kept the door half open to provide some light and pulled out my miniheadlamp. The lamp shone in a bubble of light across the cramped space. I felt my heart sink. There was so much stuff—how could I possibly have enough time to search it? There were bureaus and boxes of crap. I might have to break in here more than once to do a thorough job. I saw what looked like a water-damaged grandfather clock. It smelled musty—the basement had definitely flooded at some point and it felt damp under my feet. I wedged my way between stacks of boxes and wondered where to start.

I opened a cardboard box and pulled up some musty clothes. A gingham dress. Women's clothes. Water dripped in the darkness. I opened another box and found books. Were they books that college students would read? Upon closer inspection they appeared to be in Cyrillic.

I turned, easing my body around an overfilled coatrack, and came face-to-face with bright eyes and a maniacal grin. My fist clenched—but it was only a toy. A clown sitting on a metal shelf with some other toys. Wait a minute, toys? I examined that shelf more closely: there were dolls, dusty board games I had never heard of, one of those plastic cars that toddlers pedal around in. No way this was Will and Cordy's stuff—it probably belonged to the people who owned the house.

Even though I didn't find the phone, I was relieved—searching this entire basement would have been a time suck. I maneuvered around the coatrack again and started to head toward the door, the light from my headlamp illuminating it in the dark. Then I froze. The door was shut, and I definitely hadn't shut it. I stood so still I think my heart stopped beating.

Then I heard it. A very soft sound—like the sound of brushing against cardboard.

I snapped off the headlamp. There was someone in the basement with me. Unless they had night-vision goggles or something, using the headlamp made me a sitting duck. Slowly, I reached down and freed my knife from its holster. I needed to leave the spot where they had last seen me. Crouching, I felt with my hands for empty space, moving so slowly and carefully to make as little sound as possible.

I heard a muted noise—they had knocked something over. Where had the sound been? Behind me, to the left, moving closer. How far had I moved from my original spot—three feet, four? Did they know where I was? This cannot end this way. This cannot end with Will coming home early from some frat party, drunk, killing me in a basement. Then I remembered: I had shoved the lock-picking kit in my pocket rather than returning it to my knapsack. But the stupid kit had a flap that closed with Velcro.

Will didn't move. He was waiting to hear where I moved first.

Using both hands, I held the flap of the lock-picking kit and, with excruciating slowness, began to pull the Velcro apart, muting the sound by pressing my thumb into the space where the fuzzy and hooked parts of the Velcro met. I felt sweat move down my neck, tickling me, and ignored it. Patience. Come on. One hook at a time. If this takes a hundred years, I will not let Will win.

Finally, I had four or five of the metal lock-picking tools in my hand. I flung them as hard as I could against the wall farthest from me, the metal pinging off various objects. There was a roar of noise as something moved with violent speed in that direction, crashing into things and knocking them over. I vaulted toward the door, bumping into objects, feeling something scrape painfully against my leg but not stopping or crying out. My hand was six inches from the door when I felt someone grab me by the knapsack.

Fights are not the way you see them on TV, men taking turns. Real fights are ugly, scrabbling messes. I jerked back my elbow, knocking into something hard—someone's head? I heard someone taking a breath, then something heavy hit the side of my head and my shoulder. I refused to scream, instead gritting my teeth and lashing out with the knife. I clawed blindly, then felt something slam into me, almost knocking the air out of me and sending out a shock of pain as the doorknob jammed into my back. I stabbed again—this time hearing a grunt of pain.

I have never moved quicker—I turned, grabbed the doorknob, jumped up the stairs, and ran like hell because my life depended on it. My back was aching, my lungs screaming for breath, but I had practiced for things like this—high-intensity interval training and all those self-defense classes. *Run hard. Don't stop. Don't trip like the dumb girls in movies. Get somewhere public.* I didn't feel safe until I was five blocks away where there were a ton of people in the street. Three rowhouses were throwing a joint party, blasting hip-hop. I felt blood in my mouth.

The computers! Not caring how crazy I looked, I groped at my own back, confirming that the knapsack was still there. Had it torn? I unslung it, and shoved my hands inside for the hard drives.

Thank God.

Thank God they were still there.

It was then that it hit me. How much pain I was in. My back hurt the worst. My shoulder and face already felt bruised. My legs burned from running. Suddenly an older girl stood right in front of me. "Hey, are you okay?"

God, I must look like shit. I forced a smile but didn't show my teeth, afraid there would be blood. "Oh, just karate class." I waved her off and jogged away as if I wasn't in pain. It seemed to take forever to get back to my dorm. I didn't want anyone to see me, so I snuck up the fire escape. My window was so old that the lock had been painted over a dozen times. I slid it open, cringing, and crawled inside, not resting until I found something that was the right size to jam between the top of the closed window and the window frame, forming a makeshift lock. One of the slats from the bed did the job just fine, but I almost cried out in pain from the effort it took to move the mattress.

I opened the door to my room and stared at Yessica's closed door. I could hear her talking inside in Spanish, probably to her mother. I wanted to go over there and say, *Look at me, look what happened to me. Look at my injuries.* I wanted the look of shocked concern on her face, the tending to my wounds, the embrace of her skinny arms. But there would be so many questions. And even if I lied and said I was mugged, there would be an expectation that I report it. I stared woefully at her door, then closed mine. I took half a dozen Advil and crawled into bed.

Every time I started to doze off, reaching for the reparative sleep I knew my body needed, I kept seeing the smirk on Will's face when I confronted him at the cafeteria. I didn't want to think about it, but the image kept coming back. But I would regroup in the morning. I would heal—I always did.

22

Day 37

I awoke to a cloud of pain. I stared at the ceiling, not quite believing all that happened yesterday. I jerked my head to the left—
feeling a sharp protest in my back—then with relief saw that my
knapsack was still there. My makeshift window lock was still in
place. Yessica was blasting music.

What the hell happened last night?

Either Will had come home early, or Charles had been right—
someone *was* hunting us. Most importantly, hunting *me*. I got
on my phone and searched for any evidence that Will either was
or wasn't at the frat last night. Nobody had posted anything. I
texted Charles. It is 1000% critical for you to find out if he was
actually at the frat event last night, and if so during what hours
specifically.

I braced myself, then got up, carefully moving over to my
mirror to assess the damage. I had a black eye, and a purple
bruise stood out lividly on my shoulder. Crying out, I lifted
my shirt and examined my back. A worse bruise speckled across
my right side. I dry swallowed some Advil and took out my
makeup. I am very good at makeup. It wasn't hard to hide the

black eye with a combination of cream concealer, foundation, and highlighter. I had already seen YouTube videos on how to do this before.

I stared at my reflection, verifying that my work was good. A quiet rage was simmering in my stomach. I wanted to scream and break the mirror and throw it out the window. *But no, calm down. Anger never got you anywhere. Count to ten backward, like Dr. Wyman taught you.*

I sat at my desk and took out my bullet journal. I never journaled about Will—God that would be stupid—but there was no harm in considering my own security. I had just picked up my pen when Charles texted back. I don't know for certain because I didn't go, but I can check with Chad who would know.

Thanks, I replied.

Was it Will or the mystery hunter? If it was Will, it didn't change my endgame, only how the rest of it would play out. I would know that he was willing to use violence to quiet me. He had no idea I was planning to kill him—maybe he thought just a few punches would scare me away. Yes, I could work with that and pretend that I'd been scared off.

But what if it wasn't Will? What if someone actually was hunting me? Why? What did *I* ever do to *them*? Whoever it was knew that I had broken into someone's house and was snooping around. They would wonder why. Beyond having the audacity to think they could kill *me*, whoever it was thought they could stand in the way between me and my plan.

With grim determination I began to list out all my security concerns and how I could tackle them. I needed a real lock for the window. And, if it was feasible, better locks for my dorm room—ones that no one else had keys to. Having regularly scheduled classes was a liability. I didn't want my grades to suffer, but I could switch around which discussion sections I went to and vary my routes each day. *Social media*, I wrote, underlining the words. I had gathered so much information about Will via social media—someone could easily try to do the same to me. But I wasn't stupid like him. Instagram has a feature where you can preschedule posts. I made a note to scattershot a bunch of posts, tagging myself in locations where I never actually went to make it seem like they were my regular hangouts. Dorm security was not that great—you were supposed to swipe your card when you came in the building, but sometimes the work-study student on duty didn't give a rat's ass.

Well, maybe there was something I could do about that. I dressed carefully, then threw makeup and a few makeup-removing towelettes into my purse. I skated by Yessica's door and headed for the Office of Security, which was on the third floor of the SAC. As I walked, I scanned everyone in my vicinity, looking for sudden movements. One of my weaknesses is that I don't feel fear the same way other people do. I guess they get a spidey sense or something, but I can't comprehend what it is. Like ESP or something? If Yessica had been in that basement, would she have somehow psychically known that she was in danger before she heard them? Or would she have known to not go into the basement at all? Once I read about psychopaths not feeling fear, I wondered if a normal girl would have known there was something wrong with Will. If she would have never gone over to his place that day.

Okay, I can still beat this. How would I hunt Chloe if I wasn't Chloe? What were her weaknesses? For one, she's small. Well, there's nothing I can do about that. I can carry weapons with me and I can travel with other people as much as possible. Class security was an issue—literally any crazy person could walk into an Adams class and just sit down. Didn't they worry about mass shooters? Then again, sitting in class gave me safety in numbers.

Suddenly I had a thought that made me stop in my tracks. I actually had a huge, glaring liability. Worse than my lack of size and muscles, worse than shitty dorm security. Chloe Sevre had a little hobby. A hobby that necessitated her sneaking around, alone, doing things in secret, going to isolated locations. Hunting Will was my biggest liability.

Fuck.

Furious, I entered the SAC and pounded up the stairs. Even now, was it safe to walk up the stairs alone? Who was this person, and who the fuck did they think they were, standing between me and a goal I'd been working toward since I was *twelve*? How long had *they* been working on *their* stupid plan?

I got onto the third floor, then slipped into the bathroom. I wiped my face with the makeup-removing towelettes, leaving my skin looking raw. I had dressed appropriately, too—khakis that weren't tight, a cardigan over a white shirt with a Peter Pan collar, a never-been-fucked headband in my hair. Because there's only two types of women who make the sort of complaints I was about to—virgins and whores—and only one will be listened to.

I walked into the security office and feigned nervousness as a surprised secretary took in my face. "Hi," I said mousily. "Um, can I talk to someone? Security?"

I was quickly ushered into an office where a man with a mustache sat. He was dad-aged—perfect. "Oh my," he said when he saw me.

"I was wondering if you could help me?" I pointed, embarrassed, at my face. "I already reported this. This is...my ex-boyfriend. He sort of followed me to college."

He sat up, alarmed.

"Mr. Tedesco," I said, reading his nameplate. "He violated his restraining order. He always finds out where I am." I started to cry, making it look like I was desperately trying not to. His face crinkled and he pushed a box of tissues to me. "I already reported this, you know, to the police and talked with them about everything."

"That's the right thing to do."

I blew my nose. "Yeah, I know. The one thing I was thinking...

I can't really control what happens in the dorm? I live in Brewser. Like yesterday, right after I got home from the police, all these people were just coming in, you know? I know they're Adams students but it's so easy for anyone to just walk in."

"Oh, honey, we don't want that to happen. The security personnel—"

"The security personnel are work-study students who watch Neflix and play Dog Dash on their phones," I said, hoping my tone wasn't too harsh for my character. I teared up more. "Sorry. Could you put out a special notice or something so they really make sure to do security in Brewser?"

He leaned across the table, his brown eyes big and sympathetic. "Absolutely, I will do everything in my power to make you feel safe."

What I wanted, desperately, was to have time to start going through Will's computers, but all that security stuff ate up time, then I had to put my makeup back on, then I had an experiment, and I still hadn't had a chance to eat anything. There was a shop that specialized in pastrami not far from the psychology department. I got myself a sandwich and headed over there, not having any time to sit and eat. *I'm walking alone*, I realized, then picked up my pace to glom on to a group of students heading in the same direction. Every time I looked around me, my back ached.

You couldn't even tell that anyone had been murdered in the psych department. The floor was squeaky clean and I wondered if my little experiment room was the same one it had happened in. I locked the door and looked around, as if there would be a clue floating in the air.

Of course there was no such thing, just my aching body and grumbling stomach. This experiment was boring and I was already in a bad mood. It consisted of a bunch of scenarios where I had to write out responses. I took out my sandwich and started working, my greasy fingers making the keyboard shiny.

You are standing by train tracks and a train is coming. There are four people tied to the tracks who will be hit by the train and killed. Your hand is on a rail switch. If you move the rail switch, the train will switch to another set of tracks. However, that set of tracks has one person tied to them who will be killed if you divert the train. What do you do?

A glop of pastrami fat landed on the keyboard.

Look for the person who tied them down, I wrote. Why are they tying all these people to train tracks?

I was moving to the next page when I heard a click, then a rattle. I looked up. This side of the hallway where the small experiment rooms were had been quiet when I had entered, although I had heard voices faintly on Dr. Wyman's end. I looked at the L-shaped metal door handle as it slowly moved back and forth.

I got my knife out and edged around my chair. I could see the shadow of two feet in front of the door. Then they walked away. I put my ear to the door, but could hear nothing but a mysterious humming that ran throughout the building. Was that whoever attacked me? Or a student who came to the wrong room? An RA? Or a murderer?

I took a bite of my sandwich, the meat now cold. I was angry. Cold sandwich. Some dumb asshole trying to kill me, fucking up my plans. I didn't know what was going on, but if it got in my way, heads were going to roll. I did some quick research on my phone. I then opened WhatsApp and pulled up Charles's message. I pressed his number to call him. After six rings, he picked up and said quietly, "Why are you calling me?" I had big things on my mind and resented myself a little, but *God*, the sound of his voice. Like butter melting on a biscuit. "I was going to text you when I found out about what you asked."

Why was he being so cryptic? WhatsApp is encrypted. Maybe his girlfriend was in the room. "I think we have a problem," I said.

"What problem?"

"Can I borrow your car?"

"For what?"

"So I can go to a gun show. I don't have a car and it's too far for an Uber."

"Am I going to lend my rather expensive car to a girl who doesn't have a license so she can go to a gun show?"

"How do you know I don't have a license?"

"Because I looked through your purse that night when you were cleaning up."

Shit, he's smarter than he looks. My mother had not let me get a license. She thought making me mobile would turn me into "terror on wheels." Probably the same reason I'm eighteen and have never been on a plane. I had been meaning to get a license, but it would require signing up for driving lessons, and I was busy with school and everything else.

"I need to protect myself." An idea occurred to me. "Your dad's a hunter. Don't you have a gun I could borrow?"

"Borrow? They aren't library books. Do you even know—never mind. Why this all of a sudden?"

"I shouldn't have blown you off before—I think someone *is* hunting us." I needed Charles to believe that I was genuinely scared and fully on board with his theory.

There was a pause. "Why do you say that?"

I told him what had happened with the door, but made it sound more dramatic and unambiguous. I sure as hell wasn't going to tell him that someone had beaten the shit out of me. And I left out the part about how a gun would be super convenient to have now that Will knew I might be a problem.

"I'll take you to get something," he said finally. I brightened. Far better than tooling around in Charles's car—Charles himself. "But if you think someone's lurking around, you should call the campus escort service."

"Those boobs? It's daylight."

"It might not be safe."

"I thought I was the one who was dangerous."

"Maybe," he said. "Can you be ready at four?" I agreed and he said he'd text me with where to meet up.

I called the escort service, curious to see who or what would show up. If the service was good, it could be a decent way of getting around campus. I can't always go it alone, even though I'm young and in shape, and a Krav Maga teacher once told me I'm special. Although once Charles mentioned it, it occurred to me that the escorts probably had easy access to all campus buildings. A few minutes later, a university cop arrived, looking a little bewildered to be called during the daytime. I didn't tell him about the door, just gave him a smile and said, "Better safe than sorry," as I got in his car.

"Especially these days," he added, grinning. He was thirty-something. "Where to?" I gave him the intersection. He proceeded to ask me basic questions and kept up the chitchat like he thought we were on a date.

"Do you guys get a lot of escort calls?"

"Sometimes." He shrugged, palming the wheel. "But also sometimes I'm driving around at two or three in the morning and you see these girls walking home holding their shoes." He shook his head. "I mean, it's not a safe world out there—you girls have to know that." He pulled up to the curb and then, seemingly out of nowhere, produced a business card. "You ever need anything, you can call me directly, okay, Chloe?"

I was confused about how he knew my name, then I remembered that I had to give my student ID number when I called for the escort service. "Sure thing," I said, tucking the card away in the garbage pocket of my purse, where I kept wads of chewed gum wrapped in old tissues.

Charles showed up at four on the dot at the corner of P and 6th in a silver Porsche. He was sporting a pair of sunglasses I wish he wasn't. They made it harder to tell what he was thinking and I needed to be on the top of my game despite all my distracting aches and pains. "Full disclosure," he said as, wincing internally, I got into the car. "I'm not taking you to get a gun—that doesn't sit right with me. But I know a place where we can get a stun gun."

I pouted.

He glanced at me, but all I could see was my reflection in his sunglasses, then he began to drive down P Street.

"Someone was definitely trying to get into that room to get to me," I said.

"There's no chance it was just someone trying the door?"

"No, they were definitely after me. I think you're right about the murders." I couldn't let on that I had a vested interest in everyone thinking it was a serial killer. Everyone needed to believe the killing was going to continue. Ideally, Will would be next, which would break the pattern, because if a third person in the program got killed, Will would stand out as a different MO. Two dead psychopaths could be a coincidence—three could not.

"Suddenly you're a convert to my theory?" he asked, his pleasant tone belying the suspicion I knew he felt. He turned onto Rhode Island Avenue.

"Not a full convert—it could just be a serial killer who's after college students. It's not like there's a public list of people in the program floating out there."

"Yeah, there is. Dr. Wyman, and Elena, and all their research assistants know all our names. The financial aid office, too," he said.

"Do you seriously think Wyman or one of his minions could have done it?" I couldn't help asking. "Isn't he a vegan?"

"So was Hitler."

"It could be Elena. A Jekyll and Hyde thing."

He laughed in response, then I giggled, which is something I only do ironically. It made my insides hurt. "Aren't you going in the wrong direction?" We were heading east, not southwest toward Virginia.

"I need to pick something up first," he said, turning onto Q Street. "A provision."

I felt some tension in my stomach, thinking about how when you are in someone's car you're their captive. But a few minutes later we pulled into Wendy's and I was confused. Was this an innocuous place for him to meet a shady guy who would sell me a stun gun? We got out of the car and headed into the restaurant, which smelled like fries. I waited for something unusual to happen, but instead he went to the counter and ordered a large Frostee.

"Really?" I asked.

"Do you want anything?"

"No."

"You better mean that because I don't share," Charles said.

"We could have gone through the drive-through."

He looked disgusted. "Portmonts don't go through *drive-*throughs."

I had to laugh at that, which made a weird feeling in my bladder. "BRB," I said, heading for the bathroom. There was no one else in the restaurant so the bathroom was blissfully empty. I wanted to double-check my makeup after I peed. I didn't want Charles to know that someone attacked me because then he would know that I'm capable of being attacked.

I finished peeing, but then froze after I folded up some toilet paper. The water in the bowl was pink—and I was nowhere near my period. My hands were shaking as I cleaned myself up. I stared at my fingers as they shook, resting on my knees. *A kidney injury.* I had been hit so hard that my kidney was injured. *It's okay*, I told myself. *Get up before Charles thinks you're taking too long. Injuries heal. If you don't feel better in a few days, go to Student Health and make up a story.* But for some reason I couldn't get up. My head hurt, my shoulder ached, my back throbbed.

I heard the door opening, then Charles's droll voice. "Did you fall in?"

"This is the ladies' room," I shouted, standing furiously and pulling my underwear and pants back up.

"Gender is a social construct. Besides, I have news."

"What news?" I said, busting out of the stall.

His smile faded when he saw me. He was holding a Frostee in one hand, his phone in the other. "Chad texted me back," he said, his eyes searching my face. "He said Will was at the pledge thing all night. Like till three or four in the morning."

I stared at him. Then it couldn't have been Will who attacked me.

"Why did you ask me about that? Did something happen last night?"

I said nothing.

He shoved his phone into his pocket, balanced the Frostee on the trash can and stepped forward to examine my face before I could move away. "Are you wearing cover-up?"

"Someone beat the shit out of me," I admitted, too exhausted to think of a lie. I thought about Yessica's closed door. His eyes widened. "I assumed it was Will, but it can't be, not if he was at the pledge thing. But whoever it was, look for a guy with a stab wound."

"Are you being serious?"

"There's blood in my pee."

"What?" I turned around and pulled up my shirt, exposing my back. The bruise had deepened to a livid purple color. Water dripped into the sink. I almost cried out when he touched me— the injury was tender and his hand was cold from the Frostee. He moved his hand up the bruise and I closed my eyes, holding on to the stall door. I hate to admit it, but somewhere between the pain and sensitivity, I felt a jolt of interest between my legs. I thought of the way he looked when he played the piano.

I heard him step back and I pulled my shirt down and turned around. "Then this is really happening," he said grimly. I washed my hands, nodding. "Then let's get you a stun gun."

We got back into the car and headed out on the highway. He took off his sunglasses and drove too fast. I closed my eyes, loving how the open windows made the wind whip through my hair. The air had that autumn smell of creosote.

"I've never been to a Wendy's," I said over the wind, wanting to change the subject.

"What?!" He took a slug of his Frostee, the hollows that appeared in his cheeks suggesting that it was thick.

"My parents hated that place for some reason. They had a thing against it, so we never went there."

"What a strange thing to have a hatred for."

"What's the big deal about Frostees? Everyone's always talking about them."

"I already said I'm not sharing."

I made eyes at him for a good stretch of the 395 where traffic had slowed to a near stop.

Then he looked at me, laughed, and handed over the waxy cup. As I took a sip I couldn't help but think about how my lips were now wrapped around the same straw his own lips had just been touching—a kiss by association. For a split second he looked right into my eyes as I sipped from it. The wind fluttered a lock of my hair, getting into my face. Charles leaned over, smiling, and tucked the hair behind my ear.

23

Andre stood at the landing halfway up the stairs to the sixth floor. A knot stood in his throat. It was quiet in the psychology department—almost 11 p.m.—and he hadn't meant for it to get this late. He was supposed to turn in some forms to Wyman's office, but there were classes and discussion sessions and it felt like he was already falling behind...but also he hadn't been there since the incident. *It's fine*, he told himself. *They cleaned everything up. The police haven't contacted me again, so they probably already made an arrest.* In truth, no one seemed to know what was actually going on with the investigation, but this didn't stop students from spreading various "facts" he heard from students with supposed connections to MPD, Adams, or even the FBI.

Andre hooked his thumbs under the straps of his book bag and slowly moved up the remainder of the stairs, edging toward Wyman's office. As he slid the packet into the slip of darkness under the door, he imagined something terrible going on inside. But the packet was delivered with no drama. He had just turned to leave, pulling his cell phone out of his pocket, when the phone slipped from his hand and clattered to the floor. As he stooped to pick it up, something caught his eye. Halfway down the hall, there was a door he hadn't noticed before. On the ground in front of it sat something small and white—upon closer inspection it was a fat little rectangle of paper. He picked it up, then contemplated the door. If you were inside an office and didn't have a key, but wanted to leave the door unlocked for yourself, one way of doing that would be to block the lock with a little packet of paper like this. Curious, he put his hand on the knob and discovered that the door was not fully embedded in the jamb, but only closed enough to look closed.

He hesitated, his heart pounding. In a movie, this would be exactly the part where he and Sean would be yelling at the screen. He edged his head in, trying to allow his eyes to adjust to the darkness. He had seen this back part of Wyman's office from the inside before—a jungle of filing cabinets and a mess of stacks of books and old journals. Did someone break into the office? Who had jammed up the door?

Andre stepped inside silently, pulling the door closed behind him. Then he heard a sound—someone shuffling through papers from somewhere inside the office. He crouched slightly, then edged his head around the corner to look down the main throughway of the office.

"Freeze," said a stern voice, and a blinding white light shone on his face.

Andre's stomach jumped. He immediately thought of the police, Deever's smug face. He held his hands up.

"Keep your hands up."

The bright light turned off. Andre blinked, for a moment seeing green instead of what was actually in front of him. Slowly an image materialized. A girl, not a cop. A girl about his age, dressed all in black. She was holding not a gun but either a Taser or a stun gun—Andre never knew the difference. He put his hand on his chest and told himself to breathe.

The girl gestured at him with the weapon. "You're in the program," she said matter-of-factly.

Stunned, he saw then that she, too, had a smartwatch on. Not an unreasonable assumption, considering they were both breaking into the same office, although really Andre hadn't meant to. Andre had feared this moment—meeting one of these real psychopaths. They could be dangerous, or see straight through his bravado. But Wyman hadn't. This gave him a modicum of confidence.

He assumed a more relaxed posture and looked at her as if almost bored. "You, too?" They regarded each other, cagey. If what he understood about psychopaths was right, either she wouldn't care that he was technically doing something wrong, or she would use it against him.

"What're you doing in here?" she asked.

"You left the back door open."

"No, I didn't," she said defensively.

He held up the nub of paper. "Cute trick."

She cocked her head. She was probably here because she wanted to look at her own file, or steal smartwatches or money. No harm, no foul—they could both promise to keep a secret and part ways. Suddenly she raised the stun gun and it emitted a frightening zapping sound as a bolt of electricity appeared between the two prongs. "Let me ask you a question," she said, stepping forward.

Andre willed himself to not step back. To focus his eyes calmly on her face. "Yeah?"

"Michael Boonark—that name familiar to you?"

He was shocked, but he bit back any expression. "Absolutely. I almost saved his life, did you hear?"

"What?" she asked suspiciously.

"Someone skewered him like a fondue shrimp. I found him and was practically saving his life, but then these EMTs showed up and fucked it up."

"You're the guy who was the witness?"

"Yup. I didn't even get a reward or anything."

Wyman's computer behind her made a noise—she barely glanced at it. "What about the night of the thirteenth?"

"The thirteenth?"

"Two people from our program have been killed in the past month. Michael on the sixth, and another guy, Kellen, on the thirteenth."

Holy shit. Andre had heard some story—apparently not a true one—that the MRI death had been a frat prank gone horribly wrong. All sorts of stories were flying around. Then he realized the suspicious way she was looking at him. "Wait—you think it was *me*?"

"If there are seven psychopaths on campus, and only a small number of people who know who they are, the list of suspects isn't that long," she said impatiently.

"I'm the key *witness* to Michael's murder. I tried to save him!"

Her eyes narrowed. "Sure—you 'helped' him. That happens to put you at the right place at the right time."

"You think the police aren't interested in arresting a Black guy who's in the wrong place at the wrong time? They took all this forensic stuff off me—they already know I'm innocent." She blinked. "What was the other one—the thirteenth? I need my phone, but I can prove where I was."

He reached slowly for his phone while keeping an eye on her, then quickly began opening apps. There were Snapchats galore of him at a party at Marcus's house that day, straight through the night, all the way till 7 a.m. breakfast plates at the Florida Avenue Grill.

She didn't lower the stun gun. "You could have taken those at some other time and just posted them. Gives you a nice alibi." She stepped forward again.

This girl had a blank look in her eyes. A look that made him think of a child idly pulling the wings off a fly. *Sweet Jesus.*

He opened his photo album. "Except they're all time and date stamped here." Thank God for the shallow documentation of life required by social media. She snatched his phone and looked through it, then seemed conflicted.

"Get undressed. If it wasn't you, you won't have a stab wound anywhere on your body."

This made fuck-all sense, but Andre was not going to disobey a batshit crazy girl holding a deadly weapon. He pulled off his sweatshirt, T-shirt and jeans, and tried not to shiver as she shined her flashlight over his body. It felt like the world's weirdest doctor's appointment.

Finally, the bright light disappeared and she handed back his phone, tucking the stun gun into the back of her jeans. He forced himself to laugh as he pulled his clothes back on. "Is that what you're doing here, investigating these murders or whatever?" he asked.

She hesitated, then said yes. "I'm Chloe," she said.

"Andre," he said.

"We should help each other," she whispered, her tone entirely different, now conspiratorial. "There's seven of us," she said, holding up seven of her fingers. Then she put two down. "Two dead. Then me and you." Three fingers remained. "This one," she said, pointing to her middle finger, "I sort of know and I'm not sure about him. We could work together."

Oh, hell no, was his immediate thought. He wanted nothing to do with this girl—but then he hesitated. For all he knew, maybe she already had a wealth of information. Hell, she had already gotten into Wyman's office on her own. While she could prove useful, he was also frightened. With all his research, he knew just how dangerous psychopaths could be, and being in her proximity risked her finding out that he wasn't one.

"What should I help you for? I got my own problems," he said. Andre wondered when the night watchman would be making his rounds.

"You're not thinking straight—your problems are the same as my problems. Wyman's students are being killed," she said. "Whoever is hunting us, I got into a knife fight with them. They could have killed me. I'm pretty sure I stabbed them, though."

Suddenly the bodily inspection made sense. Someone was trying to kill the panel students? Now there was a whole new layer to the how-far-in-over-his-head thing for Andre. He hadn't even yet hit the part where he had fully comprehended that he had watched a man get murdered, and now he was supposed to contemplate that the same thing might happen to him. And here was this psychopath girl looking at him, expecting him to make rapid-fire decisions with the same impulsivity that she would. "Why are you here, then, exactly?" he whispered.

"I'm trying to pull patient files," she said, gesturing with her head back toward Wyman's desk.

She was already steps ahead of him, and this wasn't something he could figure out on his own. "We share all information," he said finally.

She nodded. "Are you good with computers by any chance? I was hoping his password would be something stupid like his birthday, but it's not." They both stood behind Wyman's desktop, the monitor throwing a pale blue light over everything as the computer rejected a few more password attempts.

"He probably knows he has patients who would do this sort of thing," Andre realized.

"See if you can find anything written down, or maybe he's old-fashioned and has hard-copy files." Chloe sat at the office chair and Andre worked around her, looking at what seemed like good hiding places for passwords: behind a framed photo of a beach, under the mousepad. Using the flashlight on his cell phone, he peered inside the desk drawers, looking for files, but mostly there were just office supplies and old journals. The top right drawer, though, held a notepad and there was some messy handwriting on the top page. Numbers mostly, but it looked more like someone doing a math problem and scratching things out than someone neatly writing down a password. Andre snapped a picture just in case and handed the pad to Chloe. "Try this, maybe?" He then moved on to the filing cabinet behind the desk. He wasn't sure what he was looking for—maybe Wyman kept hard-copy notes of old patients. Maybe—

They both started at an abrupt sound—a peal of laughter. Voices. Elena? Then came the sound of keys jangling. Chloe shoved the notepad back into the top drawer and turned the monitor off. They both hurried toward the back of the office, squeezing outside the door just as the lights inside the office turned on.

They paused in the garish light of the hallway before hustling toward the back staircase. They didn't stop until they burst outside in a blast of cold air. "Shit," Chloe muttered. "He's got better security than I thought."

"You didn't get anything before I got there?"

She seemed a little miffed at his asking. "You interrupted me!"

"That office has two pieces of information that we need. Who's in the program, and who has access to all that information."

"We can get it if we put our heads together," she insisted. "You know what they say—two psychopaths are better than one."

24

The closest thing to a perfect subject in the Multimethod Psychopathy Panel Study was Charles Portmont. Leonard had observed him to be an intelligent young man whose narcissism worked in his favor—he liked thinking about himself, thus giving him the capacity to have insight into his own behaviors. Patients could have the best of intentions, but if they lacked insight or self-awareness, there were limitations to therapy and behavior modification programs. All the better if the client was actually motivated to change.

The Portmont family had the kind of money where the free tuition to Adams hadn't been an incentive to come. Charles had gotten into better colleges, but had chosen Adams because of the panel study. He had admitted this in therapy, detailing how his decision to attend a third-tier liberal arts school instead of Georgetown had rendered his father apoplectic.

If a child lacked empathy, one could hardly appeal to him by saying not to hit others because it hurt them—the psychopathic child simply did not care. Wyman's neuroscience research had even demonstrated what occurred inside their brains when they struggled to process other people's points of view. When they were shown pictures that elicited strong emotional responses in the control population—pity, sadness—their brains indicated that they were not feeling emotion so much as thinking about how they were supposed to be feeling it, and perhaps even imitating it.

But some of Charles's impulsiveness had successfully been curbed by his learning to apply the program's principles. Every decision was not described in terms of its morality, but how his self-interest could be affected by the consequences. Charles wants his sister to love him because he craves affection; when Charles does things that his sister thinks are selfish (regardless of whether or not Charles *agrees* they are selfish), that supply of affection is put at risk.

He had grown from a selfish boy who burned through his family's money, wrecked cars, and indulged in controlled substances to having a relatively stable life—all because he had applied what he had learned in the program. He used his charm and ability to manipulate to find socially acceptable and legal ways to feed his needs. If he wanted to assure people of his intellectual superiority, he had better do well in school. If he wanted to avoid being disinherited, he better find constructive ways of dealing with his father. If he wanted adulation and attention, he could seek the limelight of student council president, not by acting out.

Leonard hunted for his favorite fountain pen—it was normally resting by his banker's lamp—before finding it on the floor. He turned his notebook to a fresh page after reading his last therapy notes and looked toward the door just as Charles entered. Right on time. If you would like to talk about yourself for an hour—and what narcissist doesn't?—you must show up on time.

Today Charles was leaning forward eagerly. "How are you doing with everything that's been going on?" Leonard asked. They had had emergency therapy sessions for both Charles and Andre after what they both had witnessed. The first had blunted affect for the entire session; the latter seemed entirely detached. "This is an enormous amount of stress for everyone to go through, and I hope you know you can always stop by to talk."

"It feels really...surreal. I almost can't believe it happened even though I saw it with my own eyes." He put his hand over his heart. "Basically his chest was *open*. The buckshot—what do you think happened?"

There was a hiccup, a pause in Leonard's reaction. "If we could just have a process comment for a moment, I want to point out that your tone is inappropriate."

"It is?"

"When someone dies, when someone finds a dead body, they would be upset. You sound more curious. Like someone sharing a gory detail from a horror movie." More horrible than Charles even knew. Leonard certainly wasn't going to pass on what Bentley had told him: that Kellen had had Rohypnol in his system, probably to render him compliant as he was force-fed buckshot.

"Oh."

"What has Kristen said?" The blank look on his face told Leonard what he wanted to know. A nonpsychopathic person would have cringed or looked sheepish or guilty. "Charles, you didn't tell your girlfriend that you discovered a dead body?"

"How could I! She would just do what you did now and..."

"And what?"

Charles looked down at his shoes. "Maybe she'd be like grossed out if I didn't have the right response. I mean, I don't *care* about the murders. Am I supposed to pretend I do?"

"What do you find more upsetting, having this conversation with Kristen, or the death itself?"

"It depends—are the killings connected? People are saying all kinds of things."

"I'm not really at a liberty to talk about it."

"Why, are the police talking to you?"

"I'm not really at a liberty to discuss that, either."

Charles sighed, sinking down into his chair and tilting his head to the ceiling. "I don't know... I'm avoiding her a little because she's talking about it like everyone else is."

"Kristen has shown an incredible amount of understanding about your diagnosis."

"Right, but I'd have to lie to her, and lying is bad. So first, I have to fake my feelings, and then I have to pretend that I don't know something that I do—that both those guys were in the program."

Leonard's pen froze over his paper. How could Charles possibly know that? Had he been snooping? Flirting with an RA— who would most definitely have to be fired. Or was he simply making a guess based on proximity? And now trying to confirm it based on Leonard's reaction to the accusation. It was also entirely possible that the accusation was an intended red herring to move away from a topic that made Charles uncomfortable. "You and Kristen have told each other than you love each other. Do you think her love for you is conditional upon meeting some standard of 'normal'?"

His brow furrowed and Leonard could practically see the thoughts churning through his mind. Kristen had been an important development in Charles's life, a key curb on his bad behavior. He had been so excited when he had met her, an attractive, interesting girl he had great chemistry with—and yet he had been so fearful that he would do something to screw it up. It was true that Kristen had been patient, but there was a limit to everyone's patience. "I don't want her seeing that side of my life." Charles shifted in his chair. "I was thinking, if I did tell her, how would she respond?"

"What do you think that would look like, Charles?"

"She might get...mad or disgusted. And then it would be a whole thing because she'd be scared. If two people in the program were killed, and *I'm* in the program, then something could happen to me, and she'd be worried. She might think, *Why am I even dating this guy who has all these problems?*"

Leonard had to withhold any facial expressions. Sure, the topic was horrible, and again Charles was fishing for confirmation about the victims being in the program, but what was happening was remarkable. Charles had gotten increasingly better at perspective taking, imagining how Kristen would feel. Of course, in true psychopath form, for him it took shape like chess gamesmanship.

"I have no reason to believe it has anything to do with the program." The police had a more likely lead: both boys had dabbled in drugs, and there were only so many drug dealers with connections to campus. It was sad to consider, but Leonard had to admit that he had seen drugs destroy the lives of many people, often when they were young and seemed to have so much more living to do.

"Is that what the police said?"

"As I told you earlier, I can't discuss anything the police have said because of the active investigation. I understand you're upset—"

Charles sharply exhaled, a look of cold annoyance on his face, making it apparent that it was not Kristen that had made him upset, but that his manipulation of Leonard to get more information had failed.

He wasn't, after all, Leonard reminded himself, a perfect subject. There was no such thing.

25

Day 32

It was my third time searching Will's hard drive, and I still hadn't found anything. It was easy to connect each hard drive to my computer and access their files. I was quickly able to discern that the first hard drive was Cordy's. I then concentrated on Will's. First, I indexed everything by date, then searched every possible combination of file tags for videos. Of course there was a lot of porn. Dumb videos of animals and stupid internet challenges. Pictures of Will and his family on vacation. Their golden retriever, Mockey, who I remember. He's probably dead now.

I helped myself to one of Yessica's frozen Snickers and gnawed while I worked. Not only was I looking for my video, but I also wanted to make sure there weren't videos or pictures of other girls. I did see a few naked pics, but they looked to be my age and of course I couldn't tell how he had gotten them. I had no intention of doing anything but a complete search, but after a couple hours, I was happy to have a break.

Andre and I were meeting at the computer lab and he had insisted that the meeting would occur at 2 p.m. on the dot. My discovery of Andre had been an interesting and important development. For one, I knew with a high degree of certainty that he wasn't the killer. In comparison, my faith in Charles wasn't as high. He was, after all, the one who had told me that the coast was clear to go to Will's that night. I had already scoured the internet. Charles hadn't posted anything that night, but apparently he had gone to Zaytinya for dinner. Kristen had posted pictures of him and so had other friends who had been there. It seemed unlikely that Charles had convinced both his girlfriend and a bunch of her friends—including two he wasn't even friends with on social media—to pretend they had all gone out to dinner on the same night. He had seemed genuinely surprised at my injuries in the bathroom—maybe even angry. Surely he was thinking about the very real risk that he could be next.

Anyway—about Andre. I would get him firmly on my side. I needed allies, not that I should ever put my guard down. Andre had vaguely hinted that he had figured out information about the murders that he would tell me about at 2 p.m. Good—the more he already knew, the less work for me, and more time for me to devote to what I was supposed to be concentrating on in the first place. Will.

When I got to the computer lounge, I saw that Andre was already in there, his back to me. He wore a bright red shirt like a target and didn't notice me sneaking up behind him to see what he was doing. I got a good look at his screen to make sure it wasn't anything sketchy—it was. Apparently, he was a football fan. It was kind of crazy that he was a psychopath. He was young looking for a freshman, and when he smiled he had dimples. What kind of psychopath had *dimples*? But I had to remind myself that anyone could be one of us and just because I knew he wasn't the killer didn't mean I could actually trust him.

"Ready?" I said, sitting next to him. "What's your secret information?" Luckily there was only one other person in the lab, sleeping by one of the printers, so we had privacy.

"Tell me everything you know first," Andre said. Of course

he asked me to go first. I was going to refuse just based on principle, but then he withdrew a baggie of peanut-butter-filled pretzels from his book bag. He offered some, which I took, even though we weren't supposed to eat in the computer lab.

I related what I knew about Kellen's death, which was very little, then told a story about how I had been attacked in a dark alley rather than telling him that I was snooping in Will's basement—there's such a thing as being too honest.

"Who's the other guy in the program who you know?" he asked.

"Charles Portmont. He was with Elena when they discovered Kellen's body." I took out my phone to find a picture of him. "If you see him around campus, be careful."

"I thought you said it wasn't him."

"I'm almost certain…but he's a liar. Don't believe anything he tells you about me."

Andre stared at me evenly. "What would he tell me about you?"

"Lies. He just likes to mess with people."

"But he told you the two dead guys were in the program—what if that was him just fucking with you?"

Good—Andre was no fool. "I believed him because he seemed genuinely concerned for his own safety. He thought I did it. I don't know how he knew they were in the program, but he's a junior. It's possible he knows everyone in the study."

"Everyone but me," Andre added.

I shrugged. "Like I said, don't trust him until we figure this out." I pulled out my journal and pen set. "Tell me everything about Michael's murder, by the millisecond."

"What is that?" he asked.

"I'm really into bujo. Bullet journaling? It's a way of organizing information." I made a timeline of that evening and Andre helped me fill it out. He wasn't entirely organized in his recounting of the facts, but he could remember tons of details from that night. He just couldn't ID the face of who he had seen while Michael died. "It's definitely not him?" I said, tapping my cell phone where a picture of Charles's face was still up, taken from Kristen's Instagram.

"No, I'd know if it was him."

"So, what's your theory? What's the big deal about meeting at 2 p.m.?"

Andre checked his smartwatch. "It gives us an hour. I have an experiment at three and you're going to come with me."

"I am?"

"Here's the thing—I think Wyman is the missing link."

I frowned, my pen hesitating. "He's like seventy." There's no way that had been Wyman in the basement in that knock-down-drag-out fight with me. Whoever it had been was physically powerful.

"No, I'm not saying he did it." Andre had the light in his eyes of someone about to nerd out on you. He pulled up his email on the computer in front of him. He opened up a picture and tried to make it as large as possible. "This is the notepad we found in the office."

In front of me was a series of two-digit numbers, some of which were scratched out: "06" was circled, there was a "33" with a star next to it, and a few other numbers. "I tried every combination of those numbers—it wasn't his computer password. Maybe he has a combination lock somewhere in his office, or a lock on one of the filing cabinets?"

"It's not a password—it's math. He's trying to figure out the relationship between two years." Andre jabbed his finger at the screen at a "96." "Does this year mean anything to you?"

"What do I care about a year if it was before I was born?"

"Have you ever heard of the CRD Killer? From the nineties to the early 2000s?"

"Of course."

"Wyman was his therapist after he got caught, the only one

who ever talked to him. He argued for clemency and said all this stuff in court about how he wasn't a bad guy."

"What?"

Andre nodded. "Wyman was doing math about years. Ripley was thirty-three when he was executed by the state of Virginia, a little over ten years ago. Go back twenty years, to 1996, and to the month of September specifically—that was the first CRD murder we know about."

"I don't see how this has anything to do with us."

"Okay, we don't have all the pieces, but we know that at least *Wyman's* wondering about the dates. This September is the twenty-year anniversary of the start of CRD's killing spree. And someone just happened to start their own series of murders on the exact day, twenty years later. It's a *copycat.*"

"But CRD was a rapist and he mutilated people or whatever. These murders are just murder for the sake of murder."

"Think about it," Andre whispered, leaning forward. "Wyman's running this program that's supposed to make psychopaths functioning members of society. But maybe something's gone horribly wrong. What better way to get Wyman's attention than to mimic a serial killer he worked with? The first killing happens and it's a random, terrible tragedy. But when the second one hits, he can't help noticing the timing."

I leaned back, my mind churning. There were too few clues and too many dead bodies for my tastes. "That math could have been anything—he could have been thinking about his mortgage, or his wedding anniversary or something... Or maybe the killings are meant to punish Wyman. Maybe someone really, really hates him."

"Maybe he has a secret suspicion he can't tell the police about—he doesn't want his program and all his research to look bad. Maybe it's a former student who he's known for years and is covering for them. Or maybe it isn't a student at all—it's just a random crazy who's coming after Wyman because of his CRD connection," Andre said.

"I doubt he or the school wants to advertise that he worked with CRD. Especially if there are a bunch of Wyman psychopaths wandering around campus."

He laughed, but slapped the desk with frustration. "I just think it's weird he never talked about the CRD case, you know, in a true-crime documentary or an academic study. I'm in the process of figuring out who all his grad students were, and what years they were here. If we could find his students from the nineties, they might have more information."

"I think our best bet is finding out who else is in the program right now. There aren't that many people who even know about the program—Wyman, Elena, some other grad students. Let's face it, if there are seven psychopaths on campus and someone is killing people, odds are it's one of us. But we can't rule out that it could be one of his former students or someone who graduated from the program years ago." I sighed. "Although if we can't even figure out who's in the program now, how are we supposed to figure out who was in it years ago?"

"I have an idea of how we can figure out who else is in the program right now." Andre stood up, pulling his bag on, and gestured for me to follow. We left the computer lab.

"You know how some of the experiments are just like surveys or exercises, and in others you're interacting with someone else?" Andre said.

"Yeah, like the Share or Steal one. Did you make any money off that?"

"Didn't you? The way I figure, for the paired experiments, sometimes they probably pair us with control subjects, but other times we must get paired against each other."

"Psychopath versus psychopath!"

"Some of Wyman's published work is about stuff like that—

how psychopaths interact with each other—but clearly he doesn't want us to interact with each other in person."

"Somebody might get set on fire."

He snorted appreciatively, then opened the double doors to the psych department. "So, we do a stakeout every time one of us has an experiment. I go in and text you right before and right after I finish whatever interactive part with the other person. You wait on the landing and act like you're playing with your cell phone."

What he was suggesting dawned on me, and I was jealous that I hadn't thought of it first. "Snap a picture of them," I finished. "Upload it to Facebook and Mark Zuckerberg tells me who the new mysterious stranger is via facial recognition software. Pretty clever, Andre."

He sighed, staring up the curving staircase, a disturbed look on his face. He definitely didn't want to go up there.

"I know," I said sympathetically. He seemed startled. "I know what you're thinking—if this was the movies we'd do this once and figure out who it is, but in real life it'll be tedious and we might have to do it ten times before finding out anything useful. Real life's never that easy."

"Yeah," he murmured. "That's what I was thinking."

26

Day 31

"What're you doing?!" cried a dismayed voice. The girls and I were sprawled across the hallway of our dorm, plastic bags from Home Depot littering the floor.

Byron, our RA, who generally proved useless except for occasionally asking if everything was copacetic, stood in the hallway surveying us.

"We're taking matters into our own hands," Yessica said, holding up a new dead bolt.

"The university president sent out this bullshit email about 'the unfortunate death of two of our own,'" Apoorva said. "They're not even telling us what's going on!"

"You can't *destroy* university property."

I pointed the power drill I was holding at Byron and pressed the trigger. "Sure we can. If you people can't protect us, we're going to install our own locks."

"I'm going to talk to Mr. Michaels about this!" he exclaimed, then walked off, as if any of us knew who Mr. Michaels was.

Two of the crew boys had wandered out of their room to observe our work. Molly and Apoorva were sitting cross-legged, watching a how-to YouTube video about locks. I finished my drilling and leaned back to observe my handiwork. Only Yessica and I would have a key to the dead bolt. And I had already installed a new lock on my window, which I could lock from the inside and unlock from the outside with a key.

Yessica sat back on her heels, her dark eyes wide. "This girl in my Civilization class? Her brother is in the MPD and he said the second guy who got killed was apparently *force-fed* pieces of metal, then he got shoved into an MRI machine and his guts exploded!"

It struck me as an inelegant way of killing someone. Whoever this person was, they were a showman: this could be their downfall. "I heard it's like a secret society that dates back a century. Every thirty years, they start killing again," I said, then left them to mull over this idea.

I grabbed my book bag and headed to the SAC to get the final piece of my home security system. The school bookstore was located on the first floor of the SAC and you could buy anything from textbooks to snacks to bedding there. You could also buy a wireless webcam. I took three, figuring I could set up one pointing at the window in my bedroom, then two more for our common area. They were small enough that you probably wouldn't see them unless you were specifically looking for them. They were also innocuous enough that no one noticed me walking out the store without paying for them.

Just as I left the store and approached the campus post office, I saw two figures. Charles—I felt a little jump when I saw him—faced me and was talking to some guy whose back was to me. The other guy was massive, his broad, overly muscular shoulders and back pressing against his T-shirt. He had brown tousled hair and was nodding at whatever Charles was saying. As I moved closer, Charles's eyes flicked toward me—I got the immediate impression that he did not like whoever he was talking to. "Hello," I said.

The stranger turned around. He was handsome in a generic sort of way, and his blindingly white smile blazed at me. "Chloe!" he said.

"Have we met?"

Charles smiled like a Cheshire cat.

"At Charles's party," he said, not noticing Charles's facial expression.

"You must have made an impression," Charles said wryly. "This is Chad. SAE's president."

I smiled and extended my hand. Chad—the guy who had verified Will's location that night. His large, warm hand encompassed mine, and I held on a second longer than I normally would have. It was then I saw he had the same smartwatch as me. My eyes shot over to Charles, who looked back at me impassively.

"Shame I didn't get to talk to you more that night," Chad said.

"I'm sure I'll see you around."

"Maybe if you gave me your number," he said, grinning. I was seriously thinking of doing it just to annoy Charles, who I thought was acting cool toward me despite our outing, but Chad got a phone call. "Excuse me, it's my grandma." He walked away with his phone to his ear, trying to get better reception. Good— I needed a private moment to fill Charles in about Andre.

"It appears our dear president has taken a liking to you," Charles remarked.

"Is he one of us?" I whispered.

"Maybe," he replied.

"Huh? Is he or isn't he?"

"I'm not telling."

"What? Weren't you the one warning me? If there's anyone I should be on the lookout for it's the other people in the program."

"Maybe. I'm not going to tell you who they are."

"Do you know them all?" I pressed.

"No."

"Just tell me the ones you do know, then."

"Why?"

"You *still* don't trust me? After—" I made a gesture to my back. And here I was about to tell him about me finding Andre and narrowing down our suspect list by one!

"It occurred to me later that I took you to get a deadly weapon based off what? A story and bruises you could have faked? I just *believed* you when you told me there was blood in your urine."

"There was!" I said between my teeth. The way he said the word *believed*—as if he was disgusted at himself for trusting me.

Charles examined me. No one ever says "piercing green eyes," as if blue has a monopoly on piercing-ness, but his eyes were definitely piercing as he examined me, as if looking for cracks in my soul. He leaned forward, his face close to mine. "You think this is fun, don't you?" he whispered. "You're playing some mind game with me that somehow has to do with Will."

"Shut up about him," I whispered. Just when I thought he was within my grasp, he was turning on me.

"Just face it, we're never going to trust each other."

I softened the look in my eyes. "While you've been busy thinking the worst of me, I've been making progress on the case. Getting all the names of the people in the program."

"So you can make a kill list?"

I rolled my eyes.

He straightened the cuffs of his jacket. "You know I have a gun, right?" he said, barely looking in my direction.

"Good for you!" Down the hallway, Chad paced as he talked on the phone, just out of earshot. "At least tell me if *he's* one of us."

Charles shrugged, a hint of amusement in his eyes. "I'm not sure if I should be warning you about Chad, or Chad about you."

"Do I detect a hint of jealousy?"

"Why would I be jealous?"

"I haven't gotten laid in a while and he's kind of hot," I lied. Chad was objectively attractive, but too much of a Crossfit bro.

Charles wrinkled his nose. "If you're into that, good luck."

I stepped closer to him—maybe an inch too close for him to be comfortable. "Maybe I'm into something else," I said.

"Because I'm so interested in a crazy freshman with impulse issues."

"You're lying."

"I have a girlfriend," he said.

"You think she'll ever understand you?"

"I've election stuff to do," he said, annoyed.

I did give Chad my number when he got off the phone. If Charles wasn't going to be helpful, I would work with Andre. And Chad was increasingly starting to look like a good source of information on multiple fronts.

I was just coming up the stairs of the SAC basement when I got a barrage of notifications. Cell reception never worked down there for me. Two memes from Yessica, and someone had tagged me on Instagram. Curious, I paused on the sidewalk and tapped. The person who had tagged me was Pinprick52, an account I didn't recognize, but I often had random people follow me or guys trying to slide into my DMs. When Pinprick52's account loaded, the header picture was an extreme close-up of an animal's eye. Their pictures were stupid: the outside of a building. A not-particularly-well-composed picture of a bunch of students walking to class—no filter or anything. I tapped to get the picture I had been tagged in.

It was a picture of me. I was sitting in class. Whoever had taken it must have been standing outside the window, looking in. It was my French Lit class—I could make out the words on the whiteboard. But there I was, idly twirling my hair while the person who was stalking me was standing less than fifteen feet away. I stood still on the sidewalk, holding my phone to my chest as I looked around at the other students walking down the street, at the windows of the academic buildings peering down on me, and all the little places someone could be hiding. Were they watching me even now? I gave the middle finger just in case they were—come and get it, asshole.

27

"Come in," Leonard said, moving from behind his big desk to take one of the leather chairs in the front of his office. Andre came in and took the chair opposite him, slouching. "I'm glad we had an appointment today. These past few weeks have been incredibly stressful, I can imagine." Andre hadn't been forthcoming in the emergency therapy session Leonard and Elena scheduled for him right after the incident with Michael. It was hard to tell the difference between someone who had been stunned and someone who was indifferent to something dramatic. At least in person it was—Andre's mood logs since then had shown him to be stable, preoccupied by other things.

Andre shrugged. "I just want the police to leave me alone."

"You haven't been able to identify the man you saw?"

Andre shook his head.

"We didn't really get a chance to talk about it last time, because I wanted to process the trauma, but I wanted to say that I'm really impressed with your behavior that night. In a potentially dangerous situation, you ran to aid someone who was in need."

A thoughtful look came over Andre's face. "I guess I was thinking if I saved that guy's life I'd be like a hero and the story would go viral and stuff. I didn't realize he would die and I would never get my sweatshirt back. And now the police could be thinking it was me!"

"I told them not to worry about you. Still, I wanted to commend your behavior, regardless of why you did it."

"Thanks."

"Another interesting thing—I saw from your mood logs that you've had a lot of political activity recently. Have you been going down to the protests?"

Andre seemed wary. Leonard had seen that look before—a common one from psychopathic patients. They had to figure out why someone else was seeking information under the assumption that it would inevitably be used to manipulate them. Because that's what they would do. "I went to some. One a couple days ago, one the week before that. They're happening all the time now."

"Takes me back to the old days of the Vietnam protests and Watergate. I was here then, too."

"You protested?"

"Oh, yes, it was a turbulent time. I was there with my sign and my beads and my long hair, if you can picture it."

A hint of a smile, a tiny curl, appeared on Andre's lips, making his dimples appear. But then the smile disappeared and Andre simply stared back at him.

"Do you consider yourself an activist?" Leonard asked.

Andre shoved his hands into the kangaroo pouch of his sweatshirt and shook his head. "No, I just think it's interesting. Basically that's what Black folk are into now—being woke. You want to be cool, you walk the walk and talk about Audre Lorde or whatever. It's fun, I guess. My friends are cool."

"But the causes—what was the one last week, Black Lives Matter?"

Now Andre grinned, dimples in full effect. "My Life Matters. I'm just there to record things."

"To be a witness to history?"

Andre frowned. "No, to literally record things. I've been submitting pictures to the *Daily Owl*. It'll look good for internships."

"Why does journalism interest you?" Leonard asked. Andre had mentioned it in their first session as a possible major, then paused and suggested business or economics.

Andre hesitated, gazing at a paperweight on the table in front of them. "Information is power."

"And that appeals to you?" Andre nodded. "What topics would you like to cover?"

"Whatever gets the most clicks."

Leonard flipped through his notes, opting to shift gears. "Last time we talked, we chatted a little about that period of time when you were thirteen."

"Yeah."

"Your grades indicate you were doing pretty well until that time."

"School can be boring."

"And you started getting into trouble?"

"Everyone was getting into trouble. Kids running around. It's what you did."

"Who's everyone?"

"My brother. His friends. All my friends." Andre stopped talking, but Leonard waited him out. "I don't know. Sometimes I just felt like people were bored and would start tearing shit up."

"Is tearing shit up what got you in trouble with the police?"

"They sent me to the school counselor and she said I've got Conduct Disorder." Leonard didn't say anything. Andre tapped his foot. Looked at his smartwatch.

"Can you tell me about your family?"

"I don't want to talk about them."

"What do you want to talk about?"

"About this program. Does it even work?"

Naturally, he wasn't the first patient to question the validity of the program or its methods. Leonard had had more than one patient who felt like lecturing him on his own field of expertise. It was just a test, but for someone like Andre it might have even been a youthful cover for vulnerability—the fear of not being able to improve. "I would say we've had some significant success."

"How long as it been around?"

"Oh, close to ten years, if you count the time when I was getting grants. I'm happy to talk more about the research behind the behavioral modifications if you'd like—"

"Can we really change? Do people get better every year?"

"I wouldn't be doing this if I didn't think people could change. And I wouldn't say it's a straight line upward, but with hard work comes improvement."

"But do people fail out of the program?"

"No, I've never kicked anyone out of the program. It's a hard population to work with, so you have to be willing to work against a lot of resistance."

Andre was staring at his shoes. "Don't you think there are some people who are just irredeemable, though?"

Leonard hesitated. "That question is why I started the program." Andre's head snapped up—something had clearly caught his interest. "Some people are certainly called 'irredeemable' and I think of such situations with profound sadness. I think of all the forks in the road where that person's life could have gone in one direction, but it went in the other, and the things society could have done to help them make the right choice. I think the field of psychology has failed people like this."

"You feel sorry for them?"

"On a good day."

"I don't feel sorry for people like that. Like whoever stabbed that guy."

"You know, Andre." Leonard put his notebook down. "What you were witness to two weeks ago was traumatic and what you did was a form of altruism. I don't think it was entirely about you wanting to be seen as a hero."

"No, it's not about that at all."

"Is it about your sister? Being somewhere in time to save someone?"

Andre fell silent.

Leonard made a note of this. He had already refused discussion of his family at their first meeting. At this rate, it could take months to build rapport, and the traumatic event with Michael had probably set them back. After Andre had been diagnosed with Conduct Disorder when he was thirteen, it hadn't appeared that he had received substantial treatment. Andre's behaviors and problems at school continued for another two years, until they started to peter out. Something had straightened him out, made him graduate with not stellar but decent grades. It made him a particularly interesting case because it showed his capacity for self-control. Whatever it was, Leonard was going to find out, eventually.

28

The triumvirate is meeting. Meet @ Charles's in one hour, said Chloe's text, including a dropped pin showing the location. Andre shoved his phone into his pocket. Around him, his friends were sitting on the floor in Dee's dorm room, Sean reenacting how he had fallen down the escalator stairs at the Metro to hysterical laughter. They had been drinking rum and Coke, listening to music. He would have to leave soon, Andre knew, realizing that he both did and didn't want to go. Half of him wanted to sit here with his friends and mess around. This was the same half that felt guilty that he was lying to his roommate and all his friends about who he fundamentally was, how he had gotten into Adams, and what he was doing there. Telling Sean that half-truth of his interest in the case had only made it harder—Sean understood his interest, but not the stakes. He had to sit here and pretend he wasn't terrified of being hunted by some deranged killer, and he couldn't even tell his friends about it—what kind of person does that? The same kind of person who had that other half—the half who was going to get up and leave in forty minutes rather than hang out with a girl he was inter-

ested in. They got to sit here and have a normal college life—
he didn't. Andre begged off, responding good-naturedly to the
teasing that he either had a hot date or was going to take a shit.

Once he got into the cool night air, Andre frowned and
zipped up his coat. It was nine, which wasn't even that late,
and students were still in the streets. He wanted to pull up his
hood, because it made him feel strangely protected, but he didn't
because it also blocked his peripheral vision. Ever since Chloe
had told him about the murders being connected, Andre had
done his best to never walk anywhere alone. This wasn't hard
because Sean was codependent, and there was always someone
around that wanted to eat a meal or go do something. Even as
he tried to study for classes or interact with people at discussion sections, he wondered if someone in the room was watching him, waiting. Somehow they had known Michael would
be alone in that experiment room that night. They had known
when and where Kellen would have an MRI appointment. Did
this same person know where Andre lived? Or that he was walking alone right now?

Andre spotted a horde of sorority girls a third of a block away
from him heading the same direction, all dressed exactly the
same. Good, safety in numbers. He picked up his pace a little to
catch up with them, then like a gaggle of geese they surrounded
him, soothing his anxiety a little with their chatter about hair
straighteners. *Chloe looks exactly like these girls*, he reminded himself, then felt the muscles of his back tighten. A psychopath, it
turned out, did not look like some person with crazed googly
eyes. He had found her social media accounts, and they looked
the same as any girl her age (okay, maybe twenty percent more
selfies).

He found himself going over his reasoning again for why he
could trust Chloe. She couldn't be the killer because she could
have easily killed him the night they met. She was also dead
serious about doing the work to figure out whoever it was—he

had half expected her to not stay on the landing taking pictures the first time they did a stakeout. But she had. He had to trust her and it concerned him how easy it was to forget what she was. He had almost gotten comfortable working with her, but now she wanted him to walk straight into the lion's den, to meet some other psychopath that she straight out said she didn't trust.

Andre watched in dismay as the sorority girls turned away at a stoplight—one of them waved and made a kissy face at him. He hurried the last block by himself, relieved when he saw Chloe waiting by the callbox of a building. Charles's apartment was in one of those taller buildings with floor-to-ceiling windows, the ubiquitous luxury apartments that were multiplying across DC like rabbits. Chloe was dressed in workout clothes, her bullet journal tucked under her arm. "Be ready," she said, "don't believe a word he says, and I want to get an assessment from you later on what you think of him." The door made a buzzing noise and they went in. The concierge sitting behind a desk in front of the elevators eyed him, but Chloe smiled at him, disarming.

"Is he dangerous?" Andre whispered when they got into the elevator.

"Who, Charles?" Chloe smoothed her hair. "I don't know. You shouldn't see him without me there. He's hot and cold."

Andre chewed at the nub on the inside of his cheek. Given the apartment building, he was already picturing the guy from *American Psycho*. He had bought a small knife at a thrift store on 14th and it sat in its sheath hidden under his shirt. "Any matches?" Andre asked, trying to keep anxiety out of his voice. In between their schedules, they had only had the opportunity to do two stakeouts. One of the students they hadn't been able to identify with facial recognition software and the other turned out to be a football player named Orvel Hines, who had been out of town at a rehab clinic during the time of both murders. Chloe said she would keep trying with the unidentified photo.

She shook her head. "We shouldn't say anything about the

stakeouts in front of Charles. He knows more information than us about the program, the names of more senior people. We can get him to tell us, then verify it on our own. Also, you need to distract him for a couple minutes so I can snoop around his apartment."

It seemed like a lot of machinations to Andre, but he supposed he was supposed to love machinating. They took the elevator to the top floor, then walked to a closed door, behind which Andre could hear piano music. Chloe gave a shave-and-a-haircut knock, the piano music stopped, then a white guy flung the door open. He was surprisingly cheerful for someone who was supposed to be worried about being murdered. "Charles Portmont," he said, offering his hand. He seemed older to Andre, like a banker or something.

Andre introduced himself and tried to saunter in the same way Chloe did, but in a more masculine way. Charles's apartment was not standard college fare—the sad poster of a half-naked woman, empty beer cans. There was a spacious living room decorated with modern sensibilities, large enough to accommodate a black baby grand piano without making the room cramped. The overall look of the apartment was nice, but profoundly strange for someone their age.

Charles got beers from the fridge and glasses from the freezer. "I told Kristen my little friends were coming over and she made us a cheese plate."

Andre looked down at the thing on the coffee table. It was a piece of slate with chunks of different cheese, a smear of some sort of jelly, little toasts. "Who's Kristen?" he asked.

Charles came over, pointing to a framed photograph on the wall. Despite the fact that he was wearing jeans and a Choate Swimming T-shirt, something about him seem weirdly formal. In twenty years, he could easily play the evil businessman in a movie. "My girlfriend," he said smugly, pointing at the picture,

which featured him with his arm around a girl who was somewhere between hot and beautiful.

Chloe had come up behind them, silent as a snake. "Kristen
had that picture framed and hung it, didn't she?"

Charles frowned at her in a way that suggested she was right.
There was some tension buzzing between the two of them that
Andre didn't understand. "Beer?" Charles offered him. The
smile was a millimeter too wide. He opened the beer in front
of Andre and poured it into a glass—it had to be safe. Chloe
was already drinking hers. Andre took a tentative sip of the bitter brew.

Chloe wandered to the piano, resting her beer glass on the top.
Charles quickly moved to slip a coaster under the glass, frowning again. Chloe lifted the lid covering the keys to slowly eke
out "Mary Had a Little Lamb" an octave lower than it should
have been while Charles stared at her, perfectly still. Andre
watched them from across the room, the hair on the back of his
neck standing up. They were the charming white couple who
claimed their car broke down in front of your house in a home
invasion movie. Of course you let them in, because surely they
weren't dangerous...

"Yeah, that's not creepy at all," Charles said.

"Creepy? I'm the one who organized this as a goodwill gesture despite your being an ass." She turned to Andre. "I told
him about our run-in, and that I basically cleared you of the
murders. Which means I've effectively weaned down our suspect list." This she directed more at Charles. She sat on the sleek
leather couch, taking out her journal. "We have two main items
on the agenda," she said.

Charles sat, casting an amused glance from her to Andre. *He
wants me to like him*, Andre realized, *and for us to be against Chloe.*

"Wyman," Chloe said. "We have some *very interesting* revela-
tions about Wyman." *We?* Andre wondered. She had sounded
pretty skeptical the last time they spoke about it. He chose his

seat carefully, sitting on the floor across from Chloe and Charles, reasoning that made it seem like he was not intimidated by them at all. Was the cheese safe to eat? It looked good.

"You think that Wyman is a serial killer?" Charles asked, smiling. Why was he *smiling*? He took a leisurely sip of his beer, then rested an ankle on his opposite knee, wiggling his foot. "Well, we can move straight to number two on the agenda. I've done some research on Wyman and there's no need for you to harass him," Charles said.

"What research?" Andre asked.

"I've known Wyman for three years."

Chloe rolled her eyes. "I was thinking of following him home at the end of the day so we can find out where he lives. We—"

"I've already done that," Charles said, satisfied with himself. "Last year. I wanted to see what his wife looked like. He caught me, though. It was funny—he led me in a full block circle. I didn't realize it, then he confronted me."

"What did he say?" Andre asked, not being able to help being fascinated, despite the fact that Charles was putting on a show.

"He wasn't surprised. I got the impression that patients had tried to poke around his personal life before. But I found out he lives at Foggy Bottom. I had one of my dad's guys search his house for anything suspicious two days ago."

"Your dad has guys?" Andre asked.

"My dad is wealthy and has had death threats made on him by environmentalists. Anyhow, they went through his things while Wyman was at work."

"Prove it," Chloe said, agitated.

Charles turned to the side table next to the couch. He picked up a paperweight—a geode sliced in half—and retrieved a sheaf of papers that he handed to Chloe, who had her lips pressed together. Andre moved over to look at the report with Chloe. It cataloged things that were in Wyman's house, his IT setup, the contents of his garage and even what was inside his washing machine. But this person, Andre realized, wouldn't necessarily know to look for CRD stuff.

Chloe dropped the sheaf impatiently and Andre picked it up. "How do I know *you* didn't write this?"

Charles sighed. "I can show you the email." He opened up his laptop and showed her the email, adding personably, "His name is Mercer, my dad's guy. He does all kinds of stuff."

"Well, Andre and I aren't eliminating Wyman from the mix," Chloe said. She nodded to Andre, and he gave an abbreviated version of the Wyman-CRD connection. He watched Charles's expression carefully—there was a sort of blankness to him in general, and since they had arrived, his expression was somewhere between amused and smug. But the more Andre talked, the more Charles looked increasingly, genuinely, bewildered—this was a real expression of emotion; the amused patina was intentionally worn.

"Basically, Wyman was linked to a high-profile serial killer, and these murders just happen to start on the twentieth anniversary of CRD's killings," Andre finished. "So maybe it's a copycat killer, or one of the students in the program or something—"

"Or both," Chloe interrupted.

"I think Wyman knows more than he's saying and maybe he's worried that it's one of the students in the program."

"I've known Wyman for years and he's never mentioned anything about CRD," Charles said.

"Why would he, dum-dum?" Chloe retorted. "Why would he tell *you* anything about *his* life?"

"What I'm saying is, don't harass the man. I know—"

"You know a bunch of stuff you're not telling us," Chloe accused. "Just tell us the names of the other people in the program."

"I don't know anyone else in the program," Charles said, his eyes wide. She almost jumped out of her seat. "I never said I did," Charles said, bewildered. "I can try to find out." Here he flashed a smile. "Elena likes me."

Chloe ignored him and spoke to Andre. "We need to consider the alternative. That none of this has anything to do with the program. It might just be that random people are getting killed—"

"And two of them just happen to be in the program?" Charles interrupted.

"Because you're only looking at people who are like you. For all we know, there might have been a bunch of other people killed, but we're only focused on the Adams ones."

"Actually, that might be true," Andre agreed. "I can start making a database of unsolved murders for the past year."

"The other thing is that we each need to have a security plan," Chloe said.

Charles opened a little cabinet inside the coffee table and withdrew a black case. He opened it, showing off a pistol. *Of course he has a gun*, Andre thought. "Here's my security plan. What's yours?" he asked Chloe.

"Besides my collection of weapons," she said without a hint of humor, "I have my recently installed security system. What about you?" she asked, turning to Andre.

"I got stuff," Andre said shortly. His "stuff" was his knife, a baseball bat under his bed and mace he had bought at CVS. The safety-in-numbers lifestyle made it hard to get his schoolwork done because he was forced to socialize, but what was he supposed to do?

"What, exactly?" Chloe asked him.

"Why should he tell you?" Charles interrupted. "We're all adults—we can all take care of ourselves."

"I can't have one of us get killed, and it hardly helps that you won't tell me what you know."

"What do you care—so long as you don't get killed?" Charles was watching her carefully.

Chloe snorted. "How am I supposed to get into med school if Adams becomes famous for this?" She put her hands to her head, frustrated, and announced that she was using his bathroom.

Here, Andre realized, was supposed to be his time to distract Charles. But before he could even think of anything to say, Charles was leaning forward, the Cheshire cat look gone from his face, replaced with a more serious one as he looked intently at Andre. "Listen to me. You need to be careful with her. Don't tell her much about your life, don't let her find out where you live."

"Why?" Andre whispered back, his heart pounding. He had already mentioned which dorm was his in passing.

"Why do you think? She's dangerous."

29

Day 25

My problems were compounding. Stealing Will's hard drive had turned into a dead end. I was also no closer to ensnaring Charles to be obedient to my cause—he was still playing cat and mouse, trying to make it seem like I was crazy to Andre. Third, and most pressing, was the serial killer.

I found myself at my desk wondering, once again, if Charles was a murderer instead of getting my homework done. But he was the one who had warned me about the murders, he drove me to buy a weapon and, most importantly, he's protective of the other students in the program for no good reason—kind of bizarre for a psychopath. I couldn't picture him stabbing someone to death in a frenzy—he wouldn't want to get blood on his shirt—and I couldn't imagine him doing anything as deranged as feeding someone buckshot. And unless he was a very good actor, I knew he was at least a little afraid of me.

But one thing at a time. It was time to move forward with Will to a new tactic since the hard drive had been a bust. I turned over the steps that lay ahead of me in my head.

~~Search home.~~

~~Hard drive.~~

Social engineer—friends? Charles only knew so much—but Chad was another option. I took out my phone and shot off another flirty text to him. We had been back-and-forthing a little. He just might be the strange nexus between my two problems: Will and our little hunter. Chad lived in the frat house and probably knew a lot of what went on there. He could also be another student in the program who fit murders in between Crossfit sessions.

Phone. As in, Will's current phone, which I was about to go get. It was escalating things, but it was time to escalate, with the two other options being more extreme.

Execute hard ball. This part of the plan I had started over six months ago, but I definitely wanted to leave it as a last resort to get the video, and to set up as my final lure for Phase Four.

Let go. I was starting to face the fact that I might not get the video back. If Day 0 rolled around and it still wasn't mine, I was still going to kill Will. I worried that it would forever nag me, the video floating around somewhere in the bowels of the dark web, people laughing at my humiliation the way they did that night. But at some point you have to accept that you can't have it all.

When I left the dorm that morning, few people were up. Lacrosse practice was about to start on the far end of campus and would last for two hours. I jogged, my knapsack flapping against my back. The locker room for the lacrosse team was located in the Blagden Athletic Center, a separate gym that the rest of us plebes didn't have access to.

I made a sad look wash over my face as I opened the glass door. An older man was manning the front desk, watching ESPN.

I came up to him, my eyes brimming with tears. "Hi, I called earlier?"

"Hmm?" he said, looking at me. He sat up when he saw my face. "I didn't talk to anyone."

"I called earlier? Asking if anyone found an engagement ring?"

"Oh, no, sweetie, I don't think so."

The tears were threatening to burst out. "I looked every-where. I know I had it the last time I showered here. I remem-ber because I twisted it and wondered if it was *loose* and I should have—"

"Why don't you go ahead and look for it? I'll take your name down, in case someone finds it." Sniveling, I left a fake name and the number for the nearest Duccini's Pizza and, at his in-sistence, went back to look for it in the locker room.

Except it was the men's locker room I headed for. Luckily there was no one in there. It was a labyrinth but I found the sec-tion with several pennants for Adams Lacrosse hung up. Each player had their name affixed to their lockers. I withdrew my jumbo-size lock cutter ($29.95 at Home Depot) and snapped Will's lock and three others. Will would know soon that it was me, but at least this would give me a few hours to make the en-tire team think one of them was pranking the others.

It only took me a second to find what I was looking for: a sleek black iPhone, a full three models newer than his old phone but that didn't matter. I could get into his iCloud with it. I went out the back entrance and began to walk toward Will's house. His phone wasn't set to require a thumbprint. Was Will's pass-word the month and year of his birthday? Yes, of course it was. I paused at a street corner as I opened his photos. All neatly cata-loged by time. Everything that was synced to his iPhone went back two years, but not beyond.

Motherfucker. It wasn't there.

I bit the inside of my cheek and seethed as I continued walk-ing, still searching the phone. I wanted to know if he had any other victims, but his pictures were mainly dumb college things. There were some naked and seminaked girls but they appeared to be college-aged.

Will would go from practice to Economics class wondering who had stolen his phone. I went straight to his house, barely even checking around before I started to shimmy up the drain-pipe, my adrenaline surging. This time the window was closed and locked. I found a chunk of cement on the roof and smashed the window. There would be no doubt. Will would know I had been here. Will would know that I'm crazy. I almost wanted him to come home at that moment, because this time I was ready. In the back of my mind, I was mad at Will because I got attacked in his basement, even though I knew logically it hadn't been him. That person deserved to be punished. They deserved to feel threatened.

I swung inside, then kicked the broken glass in front of me as I walked to Will's room, now identifiable by a C Quiz I found on the floor. Will's bed was unmade, a sad thing with dingy sheets, the fitted sheet half torn off, no duvet. I drew a smiley face on the phone with lipstick and placed it on the center of the bed.

I wandered through the house, knocking shit over, turning the stereo on high volume, pouring orange juice out on the kitchen floor. I went out the front door, leaving it wide open. Sometimes you have an itch and you just have to scratch it. I bit the insides of my cheeks to keep a smile from sneaking out as I thought about what Will's dumb face would look like once he saw what I'd done.

All I wanted now was to be at home taking a shower, ridding myself of any of Will's dust mites that might have clung to me searching for a more desirable host.

He would be paranoid that I had done something to his phone, installed spyware or collected all his pictures or email. Making him crazy was good enough for now. I had considered actually installing spyware on his phone, but the last thing I needed was for the police to find it on his phone and then link it back to me.

Just as I crossed in front of the muffin shop by his house, my watch buzzed with a mood log. I sighed and ignored it, waiting until I was halfway across campus to do it so my location would be logged away from Will's house. I hoped that my contribution to science was deeply appreciated because the mood logs were starting to lose their novelty. I used the drop-down menu to indicate my current activity: *Research*.

How anxious do you feel right now?
2
How angry do you feel right now?
7

30

I'm dying to know your assessment of Charles, I texted. I was sitting on the landing halfway up to the sixth floor of the psych department. Andre was already locked inside one of the experiment rooms, doing the preliminary surveys before his planned experiment.

20 yr old used yacht salesmen, he wrote back. I laughed so hard my stomach hurt. Good, though—that meant he didn't trust Charles. I wasn't entirely sure if Andre trusted *me*, however. Just before we got here I tested the waters flirting with him, grabbing on to his arm affectionately as we walked over, but he seemed to never notice when I did stuff like that or to find it bewildering, like he thought I was a silly girl who used a lot of emojis. (As if emojis aren't a deliberate linguistic tactic!) I wondered if he was one of those Black guys who only likes Black girls, or if, perhaps, he knew exactly what I was doing.

But at least he was still willing to work with me. The stakeouts were actually boring—on my turns I just played with my phone or tried to get some homework done, but often it felt like a waste of an hour. I did French homework for the twenty minutes Andre was in the experiment, which was apparently some competitive task about allocating play money to different student groups. Ok, just answered the last question—get ready, he texted.

I stood up, positioning my phone as if I were taking a selfie when I was using the outfacing camera. There were some footsteps headed down the stairs. I recognized him the moment I snapped the picture. "Reek!"

"Oh, hi," he said, awkwardly readjusting his book bag.

"What are you doing here?"

"If you do these experiments for Intro Psych, you can get up to three points of extra credit for your final grade."

"Was it interesting?" I asked. He shook his head, making a dopey sort of expression, then mumbled a goodbye before moving past me on the stairs. Could Reek be the killer? He was a freshman, which for me put him in the "likely no" category—how could someone who just got here so quickly understand the ins and outs of campus to never be detected? Also, he was exceedingly awkward, but that could all be an act. I made a mental note to ask Charles or Chad about Reek, whose real name I didn't even know.

Come on slow poke, I texted Andre.

It's not over—I have to do some personal assessment.

I began to trudge up the stairs, wondering if the tasks we were assigned each session were staggered so the subjects left the area at different times. When I got to the top of the stairs my eyes lit up: the door to Wyman's lab was open and someone was sitting at the RA desk. When I came closer, I saw that he was pale and rabbity looking, his eyebrows so white they barely seemed to exist. He was typing on the computer and eating a bag of pork rinds. I had been hoping to run into the perfect RA to run a circle around, but a lot of them were super organized Elena types. *Girls*, specifically. And one thing I will tell you about girls—they don't think with their penises.

I smoothed my hair and walked right up to him. "Hi, I'm Becky?" I said, as if he should have been expecting me.

"Yeah?" His eyes were really pale blue.

"I talked to Elena Torres earlier about applying for an RA-ship?"

His pale brows knitted together. "I didn't think we were hiring any others."

Hmm. Maybe he was worried about someone else encroaching on his territory. "Well, I heard that what's-her-name, you know, with the hair?" Here I made a vague gesture to my head that could have really meant anything.

"Angela?"

"Yeah, Angela. I heard she was leaving, so I was going to apply for her slot."

"You know you have to be an upperclassmen to be an RA in this lab," he said. I already disliked him. Who was he to say I wasn't qualified? Elena would totally hire me!

"I am," I said, forcing the crispness out of my voice and aiming for dumbly nice. "We were going to have a meeting, and she said to pull together a CV and write a statement. A CV is like a résumé, right?" I was pretending to be so dumb that he could never see me as competition.

He smirked. "Yeah, it's like a résumé but longer, with stuff about your research and conference presentations."

"Conference presentations?"

He looked like he was withholding an eye roll but it seemed to take him off the defensive—I was not going to steal the limelight in his lab, after all. "I'm assuming you want this RAship so you can apply to doctoral programs in psych?" I nodded. "Well, you're going to need to get some conference presentations or maybe even publications if you want to be competitive. A PhD isn't just College 2.0."

He sure liked the sound of his own voice. I was already picturing myself weaseling into his dorm room and stealing his
keys—Hurricane Becky, here and gone within the space of a
night. "I think I could put together a decent one—I have all
the other stuff, but not so much conference presentations. Do
you think you could look at my draft when I have it? Maybe
give me a leg up?"

You have to ask in just the right way. And when you strike
just the right note, you always get what you want.

31

"We know this is a stressful time for everyone on campus," Leonard said, feeling a twinge of guilt. Of course, Chloe would have no way of knowing that the two students who had been murdered had been in the program. Handing over information like that to a psychopathic student was a bad idea. Leonard was already uneasy with Charles somehow finding out or at least suspecting, although maybe their two-year relationship was what made Charles feel comfortable attempting to pump him for information.

There had been an incident seven years ago where a student in the program, failing most of his classes, attempted to sue the school for exposing him to "dangerous characters" through the program—despite his knowing the exact parameters of the program when he signed up and not ever meeting the other panel members. Adams had placated him rather than going through with the lawsuit, allowing him to drop the failing semester and still graduate on time. Since then, Leonard had altered the consent forms to account for this kind of situation, but there were always risks.

Chloe nodded, her eyes wide. She was sitting cross-legged on the leather chair she typically picked for sessions. "I feel bad for their parents." Did she feel bad, or was she good at making it seem like she did? Chloe never said anything in therapy that didn't sound like it came from a can labeled Wholesome American Coed. She loved talking about herself, but there was a careful distance he had not yet broken through. She was unwilling to say anything truly vulnerable. "Do you think it was drugs?"

"Let's not talk about that, Chloe. Let's explore something about you."

"My life is boring! Can I ask you questions instead, so we can get to know each other?"

"Some people like to test me to deflect attention from themselves. It's understandable—therapy isn't for everyone. It takes an intelligent client with emotional sophistication to really be *good* at therapy." Wyman paused to take a sip of water. "So, do you want to talk about something that's been on your mind, or do you want to talk about me?"

She fidgeted. "Can we talk about a disturbing dream I had?"

"Sure."

She averted her eyes to the window. "In the dream I was in a public bathroom. I had this big bruise on my back. A man came into the bathroom and touched the bruise." She paused, flushing. "It was sort of erotic, in a weird way. What do you think it means?"

"I'm not a Freudian, I admit. I tend to think of dreams as just image salad. Was the man the same person who made the bruise?"

"I don't think so, but why would I react that way?"

"Well, what is a bruise?"

"Damaged blood cells under the skin."

"A bruise is a physical mark. It says, *Someone's hurt me.*"

She met his eyes head-on, a genuine, intense look of anger crossing over her face for only a moment, and then was gone.

Back to the sweet coed act. "I just make bad decisions a lot with romantic partners."

"Oh?"

"Well, I'm sure my mom or my last therapist told you about what happened with Alexei." Here she offered a nugget, a topic she had selected that would be good to talk about because the dream was too dangerous a territory. Was it to show her "emotional sophistication," to brag about some misdeed, to win him over with her cleverness?

"I know a little about that."

"It's not what people were saying," Chloe said coolly. "Everyone made it out to be like he was this predator but that's not what happened. He was this young teacher—all the girls had crushes on him. I wasn't some innocent virgin. My ride left me stranded at school one day and he drove me home and we talked the whole way. We had so much in common."

"Do you think a fifteen-year-old and a twenty-two-year-old can have a lot in common?"

"We were on the same wavelength. I had boyfriends before, but this was like the first time I felt real chemistry with someone. He just happened to be my teacher. The first time I kissed him he told me I shouldn't. I said, 'Why not?' and he said, 'Because of our ages.' I said, 'Why should we have to adhere to some arbitrary law that says what age you have to be to touch someone?'"

"Let's do an exercise right now—I think you'll be good at it." This, of course, piqued her interest. "Let's say that you don't agree with the age of consent laws. But there's the problem of living in the world where rules you don't agree with exist, yes?"

"Sure..." she said, her inflection indicating that she didn't see where he was headed.

"What happens if there are these rules and you get caught, regardless of whether or not you agree with them?"

"But I didn't think we'd get caught."

"Did you think about what the consequences would be for you or for him if you did?"

"I'm the one who got talked about!" Chloe exclaimed, scratching at her leather armrests with her nails. "Everyone talked about me and posted mean things. They wouldn't have even known if he hadn't been so stupid."

"What do you mean? I thought your mother found out and brought it to the school?"

"Is that what she told you?" She examined one of her nails, which was painted a bright shade of lilac. "It turned out that Alexei was seeing another girl. They were so stupid sneaking around, hooking up in the drama room—someone walked in on them." It was sly, the way she said the last part. She couldn't resist being proud of herself. "All the parents got into an uproar."

"What were the consequences?"

"He got fired. They wrote articles about him so I doubt he could be a teacher again. My mom tried to make me switch to a boarding school, which didn't even make sense because it's not like he was there anymore."

"Tried to?"

"I didn't want to go," Chloe said. "I didn't want to leave my town—I was busy with all my extracurriculars." You could almost mistake her for a dreamy girl, preoccupied with the same things that college students were preoccupied with. But Chloe's mother had told Leonard that she didn't end up sending Chloe to a different school because she was scared that Chloe would retaliate against her if she did.

She was swinging her legs now. "But everyone forgot the scandal within a week. Someone who graduated from our high school was visiting for Thanksgiving, one of the local golden boys. He got into a bad car accident, drove his car through a field straight into a tree. Apparently, a deadly car accident was much more interesting to the town gossips."

"Did you know him?"

"Sort of. Everyone was talking about it. The car exploded but no one knew for a while, so he burned. By the time they found him he was gone. A total crispy critter."

32

Day 20

The cell phone search has been a bust so I needed to take a more direct approach. Will had blocked me from all his social media accounts, not surprisingly after the mess I made at his place.

The next part of the plan was almost fun, something I could do on my phone while socializing with the girls as we experimented with new face masks and traded the latest campus gossip in Molly's room.

I downloaded the dating app I knew Will used to my burner phone. The phone had been a significant investment a couple years ago: I paid for it in cash and purchased a pay-as-you-go plan with a cash card, but never actually turned on the cell reception. I used the internet on it, but only after installing a VPN app.

I began making fake accounts on the dating app using pictures of random hot girls from Instagram, putting in one or two dumb sentences as descriptions, i.e., "Netflix and chill" and "I like hanging out." Then I downloaded MassSwipe and used it with every profile I had made. The app would automatically swipe yes on every man aged nineteen to twenty in the area, leaving me with a list of every guy who liked any of my harem of girls. I could then sort through the matches in case Will showed up.

Within minutes tons of matches started pouring in.

I leaned back, trying to parse facts from rumors as my friends talked about the murders.

"They're going to start a curfew on campus," Yessica said, spreading a rumor I had already heard before. Two dead students—parents were starting to talk.

But a curfew? I needed that like a hole in my head.

My phone pinged, and I looked down to see a mass text from Charles inviting me to some event. I clicked on the included link and saw the news: Charles had officially been elected student body president, apparently without the help of my vote. I send him an emoji of a champagne bottle and immediately started wondering if I should go.

It was a Thursday night and I had avocado smeared all over my face, and I needed to start going through all the matches on my dating profiles. Then again, I had just signed up, and what was the probability that Will would swipe me right away? Besides, currying favor with Charles was also something I needed to do. I stood up, announced that I was going to the party, who wanted to come with, and the coven helped me get dressed. An hour later, fresh-faced and wearing an eggplant-colored minidress and Yessica's borrowed silver necklace, I was ready.

Several of us met outside the dorm and headed to a nightclub called SAX. There were red brocade curtains everywhere, gold paint on ornate wooden trim, velvet walls. Employees circled in burlesque outfits and a strange mix of people danced. There were some young people, but also old dudes who looked like they worked at the World Bank accompanied by suspiciously good-looking Eastern European women.

The Adams party crowded the dance floor. Charles stood in the corner with Kristen and Derek. I huddled with a few girls, then spied Chad at the bar, who I figured was either twenty-one or had a fake ID because they had given him a wristband—score! Apparently, I could be social and productive on the same night. I went over to him and his white teeth nearly glowed in the dark. He shouted something and bought us vodka shots.

"What?" I said, leaning closer and putting my hand on his forearm. It was furry and veined. He repeated himself and I could hear him smiling. He didn't *look* like a killer. Then again, neither do I.

I danced with everyone except for Charles and Kristen. I pretended he wasn't there even though it was his party, because if I wanted to have fun, the center of gravity for fun was right in me. Chad expectedly danced in the typical style of large boys, barely nodding his head. I didn't see Will and he hadn't been on Charles's mass text.

We danced in the circle, with Derek in the middle being silly. We laughed hysterically and took sips of our watered-down appletinis and beers. The music pulsed, the beat seeming to vibrate all the liquid in my body. My hair was sweaty, but I didn't care because everyone was sweaty.

A group of strangers pushed across the dance floor, breaking up our circle and squishing us together. I found myself right up against Charles. The darkness and strobe lighting made his white V-neck T-shirt seem iridescently bright. He was only moving a little to the beat, holding a beer in one hand down by his hip, pushing his sweaty hair off his brow with his other hand. I looked up at him, aware that our bodies had never been closer and that his girlfriend was somewhere in the vicinity behind me, beyond the crush of strangers. A small smile curved his lips and I could see only a thin band of color around his dilated pupils.

"Dance!" I said, making fun of how he was barely moving. He laughed. We were practically touching, anyway, so it didn't feel like much of a stretch when I felt his hand at my lower back. I folded into him naturally, responding to the subtle direction of his hand. We moved in sync and I tilted my head down, feeling his shirt with my forehead. Then his beer was gone and then I felt both of his hands on my hips. I slipped an arm around his neck and pulled my hair away from my sticky skin with my other hand. I dared to look up at him for only a moment, our eyes locking across the darkness and flashing lights. A drunken headiness filled me.

There was only the music and Charles pressed against me. I closed my eyes, wanting to give in to all my other senses: the hypnotic beat of the music, the smell of him, the lower halves of our bodies locked together. He had one of his legs wedged between mine and the grinding friction between my legs was starting to make me crazy. He was hard and I could feel it through his pants. I can't think of another time when I danced with a boy like this and he didn't kiss me. I could already feel his breath warm against my neck and it seemed like only a matter of seconds before I would feel his lips on my skin.

Charles, I tried to call him psychically. I didn't care if it turned out that Kristen was right behind us. I didn't care because it was obvious that we wanted each other and that she was garbage.

Suddenly the lights went garishly bright and the crowd groaned. "That's closing time, folks!" the DJ called out. Charles pulled away from me and in the next moment he was turning aside, speaking to Derek. There was a clump of people heading out the door and I was carried out in the tide.

Everyone stood around, making arrangements to go home. I saw Charles slip his arm around Kristen and say something into her ear, making her laugh. I hated him.

Someone called a Lyft saying we could all share, but when the car came, people crowded inside, leaving me and Traci, a friend from my dorm, out in the cold. Traci was wearing stilettos she couldn't actually walk in and was wavering—eighty percent chance she would vom. "Chloeeeeeeee...they left."

I called a Lyft myself, calculating the cost that would go onto my terrible secret credit card that came with a free burrito when

I signed up for it. The car they assigned was fifteen minutes away. "We can walk closer at least."

She clutched my arm. "Nothing's safe anymore."

"I have this," I said, holding up a small can. "Wasp spray. Better than mace because it can't blow back on you."

"I've a cat key chain—" *hiccup* "—you can stab with the ears."

We stumbled along. It was 1:30 a.m., but I thought it seemed safe because cars were still driving up New York Avenue. Still, I looked around, trying to make it seem like I wasn't looking around. It wasn't until we got around the Convention Center that Traci gripped me tighter. The place is bustling during the day, but at night it's just this big hulking building with nothing and no one around it. This is the problem—sometimes things seem safe until they seem unsafe, and at that point it's too late. Traci took her shoes off and walked barefoot, suddenly seeming more sober.

They tell you to get a guy friend to walk you home, not realizing that guy friends can rape you. Take a cab—but the cabdriver could rape you! Take an Uber—but they're even more rape-y! Take the Metro—rapists ride free! What if everyone was like me, I wondered, and hunted down their respective Wills. Would the economy collapse?

When I got to my room, Yessica was zonked out in front of the TV. I still had her necklace and wondered if she would notice if I forgot to return it. I knelt to tuck it into the shoebox where I kept my jewelry but then had a sudden thought. Where was the bangle I had been wearing the night I brained Will with the geode? I hadn't worn it since. I started digging through my closet, searching for the little clutch purse I had used that night.

I found the bangle in my purse, but not everything that was supposed to be inside it. Irritated, I texted Charles. Did you take my brownies the night of your party? There were two in my purse. Hopefully he wasn't dumb enough to think that I was actually talking about brownies. What was missing was the remaining vial of Rohypnol, which had not been easy to come by. (It isn't just date rapists who buy it, but bodybuilders also use it as an anabolic steroid. I had acquired it as a powerlifter with the username Ripped69 online.)

Finally, he replied. You already ate one brownie, I thought you had enough.

Those were mine

Not anymore

33

"Shh," Chloe hissed. "You look suspicious."

Andre threw up his hands innocently. On a crowded street of pedestrians, they were walking down 7th Street like any other two preoccupied students—Chloe with her phone, Andre with the camera he wore around his neck. A full block ahead of them walked Leonard Wyman, wearing a long black coat and carrying a briefcase. Andre's stakeout idea hadn't led to any real developments, and neither, at least so far, had Chloe's befriending of one of the program's RAs. Investigations took time, but Chloe was impatient. Andre had only reluctantly agreed with her to follow Wyman after work; all it took was him turning around and they would be spotted.

"He's texting—I think he's going to meet someone," Andre said.

Chloe jabbed her elbow into his side—Wyman had abruptly slowed down, looking with confusion at the door to a restaurant. Andre huddled next to Chloe, pretending to adjust his camera, praying that the man wouldn't turn around. Charles had never said if there had been any consequences to his attempt at following Wyman home. "He's got the restaurant confused—look, he's going into that other one," Chloe said as she turned to him, the look on her face urgent. "Wait sixty seconds and go in there after him and take a picture of whoever he's with."

"What! He'll see me!"

"Then make up an excuse! I'll get them from the outside through the window." It was too late to try to refuse—she didn't understand that he couldn't make up excuses as glibly as her, that he was, understandably, reasonably scared, that the place was a wine and cheese and charcuterie place that he was wildly out of place in—let alone his being underage—but also considering that wine and cheese and charcuterie places were not intended for people like him. But then there he was, standing in one, aware that Wyman was to his left, thankfully his back to Andre. Andre edged to the bar, which was half-full of patrons—the bartender was busy giving a long-winded explanation to a couple at the end.

There was a girl sitting across from Wyman. His heart pounding, Andre tried to size her up without it looking like that's what he was doing. She was college-aged. She had nothing-color hair and an indistinct face and wore jeans and a pale sweater that was strangely too close in shade to her skin. She had her hands curled around a mug, her expression riveted on Wyman, who was talking. Who was she? One of his grad students?

Andre held up the wine menu, pretending to examine it as he fumbled to turn his camera on. People took pictures of menus, didn't they? He had to act quickly before anyone noticed. He zoomed in on the girl and opted to snap a short video rather than photos. He wondered if he could get close enough to hear what they were saying.

"Can I get you a taste of anything?"

Andre jumped. The bartender, clad in all black, was now directly in front of him, smiling. "Ah..." He pretended to peruse the menu. "I was hoping for something from Chile."

"We have a beautiful Syrah if you'd like to check that out."

"Sure."

"Great, if I can just see your ID."

Andre grinned, embarrassed. "It's in my car?"

"Right," the bartender said, wrapping his knuckles against the bar and smiling.

Andre scurried from the place, ducking his head, and then nearly skipped past Chloe. "I got a picture, too!" she cried, running after him. Andre didn't stop until they were around the block. His video turned out better than her pictures, which were in profile. "Do you know her?" Andre shook his head. "I've never seen her."

"Look how they're sitting," Andre said. "How close."

"Clearly they know each other. Do you think he's having an affair?"

"She's like our age."

Chloe snorted.

"Look," Andre said, zooming in so she could see one particular segment when Wyman appeared to put his hand on her arm in a reassuring way. "She could be a patient."

"Why would he meet a patient outside the office at a nice restaurant? That's completely inappropriate."

Good point. They both watched the video a few more times. He could not read the look on the girl's face, and apparently neither could Chloe. An idea formed in his head. "Wyman's, what, seventy or so?" he said. Chloe nodded. "She's about our age. What if she's his daughter?"

"I'm pretty sure he's never mentioned kids. And he's the type that would have a picture of them in his office."

"I wouldn't have a picture of my kids in my office if I worked with psychopaths," Andre pointed out. In the dim lighting, Chloe's pupils were huge, like the eyes of a cat. She didn't understand how other people might see her, how they might see straight through her, as if her looking at a picture of Wyman's kids or asking a question about them would ever be entirely innocent.

"Charles might know if he has kids," she said doubtfully.

"What if she's his *secret* daughter?"

"They seemed like they knew each other well. Maybe she's a graduate of the program. Or the most boring explanation— she's one of his graduate students."

"Upload her to Facebook, see what comes up," he said.

"I don't have it on my phone. I'd have to sign in the stupid mobile site."

"Ugh, let's just go to the computer lab," he suggested. They were only two blocks from one of the twenty-four-hour ones that consistently smelled like Cheetos. Andre was familiar with them all, because at a school this size they were always a place to go if you didn't want to be alone. He didn't feel alone or afraid when he was with Chloe, he realized, which didn't make sense because how on earth did standing next to a smallish white girl make him safer? It was just that Chloe was always *moving*, always thinking and scheming—it was easy to get caught up in her current. Maybe it was because if some dude in a hockey mask carrying a machete appeared in the computer lab, Chloe would not be cowering under the table, sobbing like some girl in a horror movie, and would expect him to not be, either. It was weirdly easy to slip into the role of someone with a huge ego and no fears because it wasn't that different than the person he was pretending to be in the years he was fucking up his life. He hadn't cared if anything bad would happen to him because the worst had already happened.

They each took a computer, Chloe signing into Facebook as Andre emailed her the video file. "Try a couple different stills and see if it says the same thing," Andre suggested.

Chloe did just this, taking two stills from his video, then one of her pictures of the girl, which had been in profile. She opened three separate tabs and quickly uploaded the three different photos. For all three, the same tag suggestion popped up: *Is this Megan Dufresne?* With rapidity that was almost frightening, Chloe was already opening up more tabs with Google and had Instagram pulled up.

Andre turned to his own computer to search for "Megan Dufresne Adams University." After a few clicks he found an account on Instagram. He looked over Chloe's shoulder and saw that she was looking at a Facebook profile for Megan Dufresne. Here she was laughing, her arms wrapped around a friend. Here she was smiling over a latte with a heart floating at the top. Andre felt the exhilaration of figuring something out before someone else. The girl on Chloe's Facebook—Megan Dufresne—had auburn hair, not the nothing color of the girl they had just seen.

"Chloe," he said, but was unable to get her attention, so he had to physically turn her head to look at his own computer, to the Instagram page he had found for Emma Dufresne. "They're twins."

34

Kristen bustled behind him, getting ready, and Charles was eager for her to leave her house. "Why aren't you dressed?" she asked.

She was wearing an autumn dress that showed off her long legs. "My head hurts," he said, massaging his temples.

"And this just happens to occur an hour before we're supposed to go to dinner with my sister?"

"Is that tonight?"

"I asked you weeks ago. She's only in town for one night."

"Do you mind if I don't go?" he asked.

"You're just sitting here staring into space."

"It's a migraine—I had to sit through a two-hour student council meeting, and I just want to lie down."

"I guess you didn't realize that winning the election means you might actually have to do some work." She exhaled air sharply. "Okay, good night."

Uh-oh. He would have to quell her annoyance later, have her chalk it up to his occasional selfishness rather than explaining what he was up to. The last thing she needed was a reminder that her perfect boyfriend was not in fact perfect, but had a variety of unsavory problems.

The door clicked shut and, relieved to be left alone, he looked at his watch. Mercer would be getting here soon, and true to his word, soon came a knock at the front door.

Mercer was tall and burly with salt-and-pepper hair, and behind him was a smaller man he introduced as Mal the Tech Guy. Charles led them to the living room and showed them Kristen's laptop, which was sitting beside his own. Charles had forgotten about seeing the webcam light on the night they had gone to Old Ebbitt Grill until Kristen mentioned that the computer was acting strangely. Charles had had a sudden, sickening realization of what was going on.

"The webcam's been broken for months, but then I saw it go on on its own," he explained. Mal sat and Charles gestured for Mercer to follow him to the kitchen.

"Is this related to the other stuff?" Mercer asked.

Ah, the other stuff. Covering up Will's accident, the request that he search Wyman's house, and the most recent request that he do a background check on Andre Jensen. "I'm not totally sure. There are people who don't like me, and I think spying on Kristen is a way to get under my skin." Mercer nodded, and Charles followed him around the house as he began his search.

He tested the window locks and the dead bolts on the front and back doors, both of which had wrought-iron safety doors, as well. Then he turned on a small gadget with a dial and began to sweep the house with it. "Radiofrequency detector," he explained. "To check for bugs. You can have a rest, Mr. Portmont. I don't think this will take long."

Charles went back upstairs and sat at the kitchen table, eyeing the tech guy as he worked on Kristen's laptop. He uncapped a pen and pulled a notebook toward him.

Michael. He made a list of people he thought hung out with

Michael, cobbled together based on what he could tell from social media.

Then he made a list of Kellen's crowd, but the only overlap between Michael and Kellen was that they were both in the program. Kellen, for all Charles knew, could have been the one who killed Michael, or maybe the same person could have killed them both. Charles began to list people from least likely to have done it to most likely.

Elena, he thought, was the least likely. Pleasant, friendly Elena, whose life was filled with grant applications. Killing the subjects in her own research study seemed awfully stupid from a career perspective. Elena was too smart to do something like that.

Dr. Wyman. Charles just couldn't see him committing such violent acts against—as Wyman would put it—*youngsters*. But with the calm, collected way he conducted therapy, Charles could almost picture him doing something questionable if he thought it was in the interests of science.

Slightly higher on the list—Wyman's research assistants. Charles didn't know them all because some stayed and some worked for only a semester. Some only did data entry but the more senior ones were directly involved in experiments. They made for good suspects because they knew about the program and likely had access to a list of all the participants. But he couldn't think of *why*—why them and why now?

Andre. The moment Chloe proudly unveiled her conclusion that Andre couldn't possibly have done it, Charles made a note to look into him. A scrawny freshman kid—how bad could he possibly be? Particularly if he had well-documented alibis for both murders. Well, that was the problem, wasn't it? The alibis were a little too good, almost as if they were made on purpose.

Charles had asked Mercer to dig up what he could and it turned out Andre had some history of "juvenile delinquency." But other than a few schoolyard fights, nothing seemed that violent or unusual. Charles himself had crashed a car or two when he was younger, and more than dabbled in drugs. Charles had spied Andre in the cafeteria with a baker's dozen of multiethnic friends having the most absurd conversation about politics and how everything was going to change. Andre had been carefully listening, not contributing much. That, Charles knew, was a sure sign of someone who was into political manipulation, someone who was guarded and cautious. He wouldn't kill someone and then fake an attempted rescue and call 911 himself. He wouldn't use an MRI machine.

Will, he wrote slowly. Nothing about Will seemed to fit the bill of a psychopath—he didn't seem a master manipulator and he didn't seem more impulsive than the average frat bro. But Charles officially knew three psychopaths other than himself, and they did not at all seem cut from the same cloth. If what Chloe had implied about Will was true, that Will was capable of attacking a prepubescent girl and filming it, it didn't seem statistically improbable that he *was* a psychopath. If he was behind these killings, it might make perfect sense to help Chloe.

But... *Chloe*. She had to be high on the list—he had already seen her bash someone in the head. But maybe what was happening between her and Will had nothing to do with the program, and she certainly seemed surprised when he suggested they were in danger. He had no idea of what her motive could be, and she put on a show about wanting a weapon to protect herself. But maybe she didn't need a motive—maybe she just enjoyed killing. Maybe she got a sexual thrill out of it the same way serial killers like the CRD and Richard Ramirez did. And no one would suspect her because she was a girl. Charles *liked* Chloe. He found her interesting. Possibly more interesting than anything that had happened to him for a while. Perhaps her flirting was a cat-and-mouse thing, her playing with her prey before she struck.

Charles took out his phone and Googled her. Social media accounts popped up. Her Instagram was populated by the standard stuff: pictures of food, selfies, random dogs. No glamor pics of knives or MRI machines. He paused on one selfie—her in a blood-colored tube dress looking none too coyly at the camera. Elsewhere on the internet, she was identified as a semifinalist for the National Merit Scholarship. Charles swam through a couple pages of junk ads for white page listings until he found a local newspaper article.

Merrifield Teacher Accused of Sex with Students Placed on Administrative Leave Pending Investigation

MERRIFIELD, NJ: Police are involved in an ongoing investigation into allegations that Alexei Kuznetsov (22), a history teacher at Merrifield High, was having a sexual relationship with at least two female students, aged 15. The abuse was revealed when Kuznetsov was discovered with one of the victims on school grounds.

The article went on, but didn't name Chloe as one of the female students. He scrolled down to the comments until her name caught his eye.

The student involved is Chloe Sevre and she is a #slutcunt.

Well, being a slutcunt wasn't proof that someone was a murderer.

"Sir?"

Startled, Charles looked up and both Mercer and Mal were looking at him. The latter was packing up. "You were right. I found malware on both computers. Someone had remotely accessed this laptop and had control of the webcam."

"For how long?" Charles asked, his mind flipping through everything Kristen might have said or done in front of the camera. They had sex in the living room just last week.

"It's hard to say. Everything's scraped clean now, and I installed new software, which should help." Charles thanked them and saw them out, feeling panic in his stomach, telling Mercer that, yes, he would call if there were any new developments. What if someone had recorded them? Listened in on their private conversations? How could this be happening again?

Cyberguy, he wrote. Last year, Charles had been attacked, but he had never seen or learned the identity of the culprit. He just woke up one bright sunny morning to a phone call from his bank that there were strange charges on his credit card: someone had purchased an ATV in Waco, Texas, a thousand dollars' worth of diapers, and a three-year subscription to a hardcore gay porn site. Crazy, but not outside the realm of normal credit card theft. He had just finished denying the charges when his cell phone service cut out. It took an hour to deal with this at Kristen's house because his account had been canceled, but they refused to accept his password and kept telling him that he, Charles Portmont, was not Charles Portmont. Then his student ID couldn't swipe him into the library—it had been wiped clean. Charles had been dropped from all his classes. He was just dealing with the dozen anchovy pizzas that arrived to his condo when his father called, infuriated by a series of charges on his own credit card that appeared to be made by his profligate son.

Nothing made sense until he finally got his cell service restored and he received a flurry of texts from Daisy. Daisy was a girl Charles hardly knew and here she was nonsensically begging *him* for help, which didn't make sense until he realized they were both being attacked at the same time.

She sent him screenshots of hundreds of texts pouring in from blocked numbers calling her a whore and a slut, angry texts from friends who were suddenly infuriated with her. Her social media accounts had been hijacked and were posting nudes of her—or ostensibly of her—along with offers of free rough sex followed by her phone number.

"I don't know who's doing this," she had sobbed into his voicemail. Charles deleted the voicemail immediately. As far as Kristen knew, someone was cyberattacking her boyfriend for no apparent reason—maybe political reasons attached to his dad, but she hadn't figured out what Charles already had because she didn't have all the information. Someone out there had a Thing for Daisy and Charles had made the drunken mistake of hooking up with her. Someone must have seen them and gotten really angry. Suddenly Daisy's problem had become Charles's problem. At a loss, he proposed the only solution he could think of: he opened a draft email and wrote out the words I will pay you to leave me alone. The next day the draft email was still there with a new line added under it by a stranger: 10,000$. This followed by instructions of how to convert money to a cryptocurrency and deposit it in an anonymous account. Once Charles did this the attacks stopped as quickly as they started.

When Charles had first heard of Michael's and Kellen's killings, his mind hadn't immediately jumped to the cyberattacker as a culprit, but now that he had time to think of it, he wasn't so sure. This person had tried to mess with his grades, get this family pissed at him and had mined Charles's texts and emails for unflattering things he had said about Kristen to send to her. This person had done *everything but* out him as a member of the psychopathy program. The attacker could have outed him to all of Adams, and also had no way of knowing that Charles had already told Kristen about his diagnosis. Why would that one fact be withheld when everything else had been used against him? He had assumed the attack had been about Daisy, but maybe it had actually been about *him*. Charles had done some poking around on Google Scholar about internet trolls and discovered one study that showed that not only did they score high on measures of psychopathy, but also sadism.

Charles chewed on the back of his pen, then reluctantly added one other name to the list. *Emma.* He withdrew his phone to look at the latest text from Chloe. A picture of Emma and the words Do you know this girl? He did know this girl. And she was in the program. How had Chloe and Andre managed to track her down?

Charles had not noticed Emma his freshman year when they were both in Intro Philosophy together. She had stringy hair and bad posture and was nothing to look at. She was in Charles's discussion group and sometimes he caught her staring at him. This happened sometimes; Charles knew he was good-looking. He never saw her talking to other students or at parties or campus events. He had once been walking across the area outside the SAC with picnic tables—all the tables were filled with talking, laughing students except for one. Emma, sitting alone, facing the wrong direction. She was not, as it appeared, staring into space, but observing an inchworm dangling from a nearby tree from a gossamer thread. The stupid worm was sad, too—a dumb small thing that would probably be dead by tomorrow.

On a whim, Charles sat with her and ate lunch, pretty sure now that that insignificant action back then had caused Emma to have a crush on him, which was sadder still. Then a week later, he was catching a quick practice session in one of the piano rooms in Albertson and he caught her peeping through the window at him. He opened the door, catching up with her as she attempted to flee, intending to set her straight.

"I'm in the program, too," she had said, startling him out of speaking. At first, he thought she was threatening him, but then he realized that she just wanted to share something in common with him. She had seen him talking to Wyman once, and seen him do a mood log on his smartwatch. Charles was too curious about meeting another psychopath to be annoyed. But Emma didn't fit the bill of what he thought they were supposed to be. He thought psychopaths were supposed to be…well, like him. Charming and charismatic and able to get what they wanted from people. She seemed more like someone had taken a mouse and dipped it into warm water to make tea.

But Emma didn't grasp the concepts of the program as well as Charles did and didn't seem to care. She wasn't interested in being taught how to read emotions or why her actions upset people. She was only interested in her major (philosophy) and her hobby (photography), the only things that seemed to animate her. She was a girl devoid of charm, but what was it about her that evoked a deep feeling of sadness in him? Even a feeling of protectiveness?

Emma was not his *friend*. She would never qualify as that. But she was a kindred soul of sorts, and he liked to think that Chloe and Andre were wrong, that Emma couldn't be a suspect. But he had to consider some facts that made him uncomfortable.

Emma had already proven herself capable of tracking down someone else in the program. He didn't know really anything about her other than her major and that she had a sister who went to American who she was very close with. But he knew one other thing—that Emma had a crush on him. That she had followed him at least once. Was it possible that Emma and the cyberattacker were one and the same? He was resistant to the idea, although he couldn't pinpoint a rational reason why.

A few hours later, Charles heard the distinct sound of Kristen dropping her keys at her front door. He ran to open it, putting a contrite look on his face. Kristen had clearly had a few glasses of wine with dinner. He followed her to the kitchen where she took off her jacket and wrenched off her heels. "You didn't walk home alone, did you? Look, I'm sorry," he said.

She looked at him carefully. He hugged her, kissed the top of her head. "I'm an asshole." He had to get the tone right—soft, just above a whisper.

Kristen pushed back, wanting to get a look at his face. "What exactly are you sorry about?"

"I'm sorry I didn't go to dinner with you and your sister when I said I would."

"Are you?" she asked. She was daring him to lie. She knew too much about the way he worked. "Did you actually have a migraine?"

He contemplated her, calculating. "No. I just didn't want to go."

"Then why did you say you would when I asked you in the first place?"

"Because that's what you wanted me to say."

"So, you're *not* sorry."

"I'm sorry I did something that hurt you."

It wasn't working. Most girls were easier than Kristen. Now with sad eyes he followed her around the kitchen. As she poured herself a glass of water, he put his arms around her from behind. "Can you forgive me?" he asked quietly, nuzzling her neck.

She put her glass down, setting her hands flat on the counter. "You know, every time you disappoint me I love you a little less." Kristen walked away from him, settling on the couch. The words stung in just the right way.

"I don't want you to be mad at me," he said, lingering around her like a satellite in orbit.

He sat next to her, pressing his leg to hers. She turned the TV on and loaded an old episode of *Who Wants to Marry a Soybean Farmer?*—a show he despised. Charles had a strange contradiction in his very core: he both did and didn't care about people's view of him. He wanted to do whatever he wanted, but at the same time he wanted to be adored. This sometimes led to fights with Kristen, but at the same time she loved him. How much of all this was even his fault? Had he been born this way and it was all genetics, or was it perhaps the result of growing up in his family? The incident at Old Ebbitt Grill was not surprising given that his dad had been a functioning alcoholic for years.

When Charles had originally told her about his diagnosis, she had been alarmed. The first two months of their relationship had been a whirlwind, but then he had come clean after much consultation with Wyman. *Psychopath* was just the word that made you think of an insane killer running around with an ax, not a fellow freshman from a well-respected boarding school who came from a family with money and had friends and interests and decent grades. To his surprise, she didn't respond with disgust, but read up about the diagnosis and asked him questions about it. They were just too good together to let this get between them.

Charles rested his arm on the back of the couch behind her. Soon came the little kiss on her ear. The stroking of her hair. He looked for a sign of approval. She flipped channels, watching the news coverage of the protests that continued to swamp Lafayette Park down by the White House. Charles leaned in and kissed behind her ear. His hand landed on her knee. His lips traveled down her neck. She closed her eyes momentarily— Charles knew exactly how to touch her. Kristen reached out, cupping his head in her hand. "Sweetie, you're def not getting any tonight. This is the doghouse and you're sitting in it."

35

Day 16

"Do you like M&Ms?" the RA asked me.

"Yes?" I answered.

"Sit." On the desk in front of me in the experiment room was a blue bowl with a red mark along the inside. The RA dumped a bag of mini M&Ms into the bowl, filling it up to the red line. "You can eat these candies if you want to, as much as you want. Hang out for an hour, play with your phone, read a magazine." There were some outdated issues of *Self* and *Psychology Today*. "But if you don't eat any candy, when I come back at the end of the hour, you can have everything in the bowl in addition to another whole bag. Got it?"

I got it. She left and I looked around for the hidden camera. There wasn't a two-way mirror and the door was safely locked, my wasp spray snugly nested in my jeans pocket. I put my feet up on the desk, liberally ate M&Ms and played Dog Dash on my phone. I opened my dating app and deleted guys—no Will yet. I read an article in *Self* about the ten steps to perfect makeup-free makeup.

What are you up to tonight? came a sudden text. Chad!

Not much lol. U?

When it was ten till, I rooted through my purse. I had a couple pieces of notebook paper, which I crumpled up, testing the size a couple times until I was able to bury them in the bowl of candy so that the candy still went up to the red line. When the RA came back, she exclaimed, "You did it! Some people can't!" She was awarding me with another bag of candy right when Chad texted again. Meet up for drinks?

I walked out of the building buried in my phone, working out the logistics with Chad. We had just settled on a restaurant when a notification popped up: one more match from the dating app. A certain lacrosse player! I hurried home to get dressed, but made myself wait before messaging Will. I only had about two more weeks until it was D-Day, but I didn't want to seem overeager because then he might be suspicious.

I was pondering what to write when a message from Will popped up.

Cute pic, he wrote.

Lol. Did you catch that fish yourself? (For some inexplicable reason, he had a picture of himself holding a fish, presumably taken during a fishing trip.)

No it jumped straight into my arms

Is it slutty to be messaging one boy when you are on the way to meet another? Maybe not if you're planning on killing one of them.

I was meeting Chad at a restaurant on 9th Street after he finished up with "a business meeting." The place was one of those dim affairs with almost no lighting other than a single tealight at each booth. Chad was perched at the bar, talking to the bartender. He smiled widely when he saw me. He reminded me of Gaston from *Beauty and the Beast* except with better hair.

"I know the bartender here," he said, leading me to a booth, opting to sit next to me instead of across.

I asked what sort of business meeting he had and he went on and on about hurricane relief and how the frat was going to raise all this money. Why bother? Another hurricane is going to come anyway—we should be teaching people to swim.

We got beers and I began probing. Any time I tried to subtly suss out whether or not he was in the program, Chad would change the subject—sandwiches, astronomy. He was either an evil genius or an innocuous himbo. I stepped up the flirting when we were midway through our second round of drinks.

"I like your watch," I said, playfully examining it, and in the process also touching one of his big hands.

"I saw a Groupon and figured I'd get one."

A lie? And why did Charles hate him? It made him more intriguing. "It's nice," I said. I looked up at him and our gazes locked. "So, what do you do when you're not saving the world?"

"Weightlifting mostly. Tough Mudders. I'm training for the Crossfit games."

"Crossfit has games?"

"It's very competitive!" he said, grinning. "But SAE takes up a lot of my time. There's a lot of stuff to organize, like the hurricane thing."

"You live in the house?" I asked, wrinkling my nose.

"Come on," he said, bumping my side jovially. "I mean, my room's neat, and basically I get to live with all my best friends."

"Some of the brothers don't live there?"

He shook his head. "When you first get in you're required to live there, but you can move out after that first year. I try to make sure everyone still feels included. We're at the house every day—it's like a family. We've all been helping with Charles's election. Marty did the design for his posters, I helped with the rally, Will got the lacrosse vote."

"Will?" I asked.

"Blond guy? On the lacrosse team?"

"Oh, right, that guy. Do you hang out with him a lot?"

"More lately, I guess. He's been hanging around the house a lot." Too afraid to be in his own house, perhaps?

I snapped my fingers like I just remembered something. "Oh, one of your pledges is in my Bio lab. We dissected a pig together. Reek?"

Chad looked confused, then a slightly annoyed look came over his face. "Milo, you mean. I really don't like the nickname thing but the brothers won't stop."

"He's a nice kid."

"Super nice. Really smart. I hope he sticks around." Chad was apparently the master of giving out information that was inherently meaningless. He smiled again, this time more flirty. "Speaking of parties, I can't believe you don't remember meeting me at Charles's house."

"Did we talk?"

He sipped his drink. "I was hitting on you."

"Not hard enough apparently."

"Would I have had a chance?"

"I'm sure you found someone to pair up with."

"I ended up sleeping on the floor with six other people."

I could feel the crackle of heat, a deep itch within me. All this careful living had put a serious dent in my social life, which is to say, getting my fair share of vitamin D. "I slept alone that night." I had an image in my head suddenly. Standing in front of Charles wearing only his shirt. I thought about him reaching out and slowly unbuttoning the buttons, his hands sliding down the exposed skin.

"What a shame," he said, unsmiling.

Suddenly I wanted Chad to fuck me. I wanted his weight to

crush down on me. I wanted him to be bewildered by me, like ancient Greek soldiers coming upon Medusa.

I reached out and snaked my arm around his neck, pulling his mouth down to mine. He smelled like woodsy cologne and was not a bad kisser. We made out and the itch grew worse. His arms were wrapped around me, trapping me, and I rubbed one of my legs against him. I broke our kiss, murmuring at him, "Let's go somewhere."

"Sure," he said. "No one's at the house tonight." We quickly left.

Chad had the largest bedroom on the top-most floor of the SAE house. It was shockingly neat, with a cleanly made bed and organized bookshelves. He closed the door and we started making out right away. One of his big hands was up my shirt. I closed my eyes, throwing my head back, then feeling his mouth on my neck.

I grabbed him by the shoulders and pushed him back into a sitting position on his bed. I took my dress off, realizing I could see a perfect reflection of myself in the dark window behind the head of his bed.

We both took off my bra and I let him take me in with his eyes. I plucked at his shirt and he removed his jacket, his sweater, and finally his T-shirt, revealing muscular shoulders and tan skin. He had some chest fur—not my favorite—but not a lot of it. He pulled me closer, his mouth on mine. I pushed him back, saying, "No shoes on the bed."

He grinned and bent to take off his black shoes, then looked at me expectantly. "Pants," I said. He wriggled out of his jeans and let them fall on the floor. He pulled me closer again and kissed my chest. I eased my panties off and climbed onto the bed, pushing him onto his back. He cupped between my legs and moved in a slow pulsing motion, but it wasn't like I even needed foreplay at that point.

I was nearly pressing him inside me when he stayed me with one hand, laughing. "Hold on a sec, I need a condom."

"I'm on birth control," I said, impatient as he ruffled through his jeans pockets. I could forgive his fastidiousness because he had it on quickly, then was easing me onto him. I gasped and buried my face in his neck.

"Is that okay?" he murmured.

I nipped at his ear, squeezed him, then pushed him onto his back. In the darkness of his window I could see our reflection, like a mirror. My hair looking wild, his hands reaching up to touch me, our bodies moving in unison. I leaned down to kiss him, feeling his teeth behind his lips. I wrapped my fingers around his neck.

Sunlight and birds woke me up. Chad was spooning me, one of his veiny arms over my chest. I yawned, and his stomach growled loudly. He laughed. "I just woke myself up. Breakfast burrito?"

"Sure." I dug into my purse for my phone. There were a few notifications, and someone had texted me a picture. I stared at it, confused. It was of me, sleeping, a striped background behind me. The same pattern of stripes on Chad's pillows. "What the fuck?" I screamed.

Chad, who was hopping into his pants, froze, alarmed. "Is this your idea of a joke?" He pretended to be confused and I threw the phone at his face. He caught it with surprising deftness, then looked at the picture. I watched his expression carefully. He looked genuinely bewildered.

"But that's my…" He looked up at me, horrified. "Chloe, I didn't send this—this isn't even my number."

"Give me your phone," I demanded. Wordlessly, he unlocked it and handed it over. He had not sent a text since last night when we decided where to meet up. I even went back in time and verified. He actually *had* texted Charles about the SAE pledge event—neither of them had lied. I handed it back to him, then hunted for my clothes. Chad was crossing the room to get to me. "Is your door even locked?"

"Why would I lock my door in my own house?" he asked, oblivious. I looked behind him and saw that both his windows were open a few inches. God, the joy of being a Chad and never having to worry about locked doors. The thought of someone sneaking in here while I slept like an idiot...watching me and taking a picture. I pulled my dress on. "The only reasonable explanation I can think of is that one of the guys thought it was funny."

One of the guys. One of the guys with access to the house. I was too angry to speak.

He put his hands on my shoulders—if he had done it with anything but the upmost gentleness, I would have bit his head off praying-mantis-style. "It's *not* funny," he said. "It's really uncool. A total violation of our privacy, and I'm going to have a talk with them."

What if it was Will? Will had been here. Why don't I actually *think* before I do shit? "I'm upset. I'm going home."

His eyes got wider. "I understand. I'm sorry. I hope you don't hold this against me."

"I'll see you around."

36

Andre studied the row of pictures in front of him, resisting the urge to look across the table where the detectives watched him. "Take your time," said Bentley—the nice one.

He wondered if he should just do what Sean had said and pick anyone, lest their focus switch back to him. "I'm sorry," he said. "I don't see him."

Bentley's face fell, and Deever, the other detective, looked annoyed. "That's okay."

"I don't want to say the wrong thing, but I don't see him."

"We can come up with another set," Bentley said.

"Does this have to do with the other guy with the MRI?" Andre asked.

"Do you think it does?" Deever asked.

"Everyone's talking about it. Is there someone on campus killing Adams students or is this a broader thing?"

Bentley jumped suddenly, then began to search frantically through papers and photos on his desk. He shoved a photo in front of Andre's nose. White skin, cheekbones, mussed hair. "Is

this the guy?" he asked at the same exact time as Andre said,
"That's the guy!" Bentley asked him if he was *sure*, really *sure*.

"Positive."

"Wait, I got other pictures." He produced half a dozen, and
the ones in profile only made Andre certain.

"That's the guy I saw."

Bentley put his hands on his hips and looked at Deever with
something like exasperated satisfaction. "It's Kellen."

"Kellen?"

"Kellen!" Andre shouted before he realized he was not supposed to know his name.

Andre hurried across campus, texting as he went. He and
Chloe had been planning on meeting at the library, anyway, to
compare notes. Andre had been working on making a list of
Wyman's former students, narrowing them down to those who
would have been around in the CRD years and might be able
to shed light on the new killings. Chloe had said she was doing
a "deep dive" on the Dufresnes' internet presence.

The library during the daytime was always crowded with students carrying coffees and jostling for table space. Still, every
time Andre took the elevator he kept his hand near his knife.
All of the murders, he reasoned, had happened when the victim was alone. Much like a horror movie there were standard
rules: get caught alone, you die. He hoped the rule about being
the Black guy wasn't true.

Chloe was waiting on the fifth floor, where the dissertations
were stored, in a private study room and was eager to talk about
Kellen being the stranger at the murder scene. "Of course," she
said. "Now it makes sense. Who else would come upon someone bleeding out and a bystander screaming for help and walk
away but a psychopath?" Andre pointed out that Kellen being
present at Michael's death didn't really tell them anything other

than that Kellen was an asshole. "Maybe it gets the police off your back," Chloe said.

"Not sure how you figure. Kellen didn't have any blood on him—it couldn't have been him."

"Are you *sure* he didn't have blood on him?" she pressed. Andre understood that she was suggesting he lie to the police.

"What a terrible party," said a familiar voice. Andre looked up to see Charles entering the room while taking off his coat. Andre shot a look at Chloe, who had apparently invited him. He would have preferred a warning. Forced to pick between two psychopaths who had each warned him against the other, he banked on trusting neither. But at least he had settled into a working relationship with Chloe, who had proven herself reliable. While he didn't trust Charles, he didn't seem murderous. He came off more like a person who was supposed to be attending a polo party but made a wrong turn and ended up at college. Unless, of course, that was all put on.

"Are you going to help, or be an asshole?" Chloe asked.

"Are those two things mutually exclusive?" Charles dropped a greasy paper bag on the table and a puff of white powder emanated from it. He withdrew a bizarre food-like object from the bag. "So, what are these developments you're so excited about?"

"Do you know the girl in the picture I sent you?" Chloe was watching him carefully.

"Never seen her."

"What the hell is that?" Andre asked.

"And why didn't you bring us any?" Chloe added.

"There's a funnel-cake cheeseburger truck outside," Charles said, and Andre watched in horror as he proceeded to add several packets of mayonnaise and relish under the top layer of sugar-encrusted funnel cake. "Who's the girl? Is she in the program?"

Chloe turned her laptop around and activated a PowerPoint presentation that started with the picture of Emma she had taken. "We saw this girl eating dinner with Wyman in an *inti-*

mate restaurant. Emma Dufresne, not to be confused with her twin sister, Megan Dufresne."

Charles paused midbite. "Twins?" Andre got the sense that Charles never took anything seriously, so it was a little satisfying that they finally got his attention.

Chloe clicked to the next slide, which now showed another picture of her from Andre's video. "Here's what I figured out. She's a philosophy major, a junior—just like you, Charles. It's hard to find anything about her because she's not really on the internet. This is her Instagram—notice that she has a bunch of followers but she doesn't follow anyone herself. Here's the kind of stuff she posts."

Andre watched a series of slides breeze by. She was a photographer—and a good one—but the only thing she photographed was insects. High-definition extreme close-up photographs of various insects: a fly with its mirrored eyes, a praying mantis, a bumblebee in midflight. "Those are really good," Andre murmured, unable to help feeling a twinge of jealousy.

"She's placed in several photography contests, all with pictures of insects. She never responds to comments on her Instagram posts."

"Bug girl. Got it," Charles said, his mouth full.

"This is her sister, Megan," Chloe said, switching to a snapshot of a Facebook profile. It was standard fare for the pumpkin spice latte brigade. A post about loving the autumn weather. A cute dog. Some people at a party drinking beer. "She's a junior at American University. There's more stuff about her on the internet than her sister—she used to compete in gymnastics when she was a kid and wrote for her high school newspaper."

"Wait," Andre said, pointing. "Look under 'Relationships.' She doesn't say anything about having a sister, or a family or anything."

"Not everyone fills that out," Charles said. The burger had been consumed with surprising speed. He wiped at his mouth with a napkin, then tilted his chair back, folding his arms across his chest.

Chloe clicked to a new slide, *Lingering Questions*, which had bullet points. "Why do they go to two separate colleges in the same city?" she asked.

"Uh, because they got into two different places?" Charles said, his tone suggesting that Chloe was being stupid.

"Well, there's this thing called poverty that most of the rest have? And most schools have a thing where if you have two siblings around the same age you get a huge discount if they both attend the same school."

Charles shrugged. "Maybe they don't like each other."

"It wouldn't matter," Andre realized. "Because if you come to the program, college is free. So Emma's in the program, but Megan isn't."

"You don't even know if Emma's in the program—" Charles started, but Chloe interrupted him.

"But they're twins," she murmured, standing up and beginning to wander around the room. "They could be fraternal twins who just look a lot alike, or they could be identical."

"Why does that matter?" Andre asked.

She held up a dry erase marker. Charles looked pained. "What if they're a natural experiment? Identical twins, but one is a psychopath—Emma—and the other isn't. That makes Megan the perfect control for Emma. Want to compare brains, or behavior, or whatever? Run Emma against her sister, who has the same genetics and comes from the same family."

It was an intriguing idea. Andre knew enough about psychology to know that the field often relied on twin studies to tease apart the nature versus nurture question, about how much certain traits are heritable versus how much environment can shape a person. "But if they're identical wouldn't they both be psychopaths?"

"Only if we think psychopathy is entirely determined by genetics."

Charles successfully tossed his paper bag into the garbage bin across the room. "Tell you what, if Emma's a junior I may know people who know her. Give me a few days to look into her and I'll report back." Chloe looked at Andre as if trying to say something silently he couldn't quite read. Charles did seem like a guy who knew a bunch of people. And really, he hadn't been much of a help yet, so let him do this one thing.

"Sounds like a plan for now," Andre said. "And regardless of if Emma's in the program, why is Wyman having a private dinner with her?"

"Why's that weird?" Charles asked.

"Are *you* having private dinners with him?" Andre said. "You don't go to dinner at a nice restaurant with your shrink. Or if you do, there's something weird going on."

Chloe sighed. "Andre thinks they could be having an affair." Charles laughed heartily, which got Chloe laughing, and after a moment Andre found their laughter contagious and couldn't stop himself from joining in.

"And now for the fun part of the evening," Chloe said, turning to Andre as she popped to her feet. "I reserved every single dissertation you asked for." She opened the door and wheeled in the library cart just outside their study room.

"What are those?" Charles asked, dismayed at what appeared to be real work.

"Dissertations from former students of Wyman's," Andre said. The fifth floor had hard copies of all dissertations that had been filed at Adams. Andre had reserved all the relevant ones to search for information suggesting links to CRD. Wyman was a lot older than he looked and had had many students—the first thing Andre had done was eliminate anyone from the list who predated the late nineties. Some students were easy to find off academic "family tree" websites because they had gone on to become academics themselves, and some were full-time clinicians.

Andre shoved a stack of dissertations in Charles's direction. "Look for anything about psychopathy, murder or paraphilia."

"Why does it matter what Wyman's students studied years ago?" Charles asked.

"Wyman thinks these killings have something to do with CRD, which means he knows or thinks something we don't know yet. He never published about CRD, but maybe one of his students did. Or Wyman's never published about someone who failed out of the panel study, but maybe one of his students did," Andre said.

Chloe sprawled on the floor on her stomach, and after some theatrical sighing, Charles sat across from Andre at the table, and they flipped through the leather-bound volumes.

As Andre did so, he couldn't help feeling the persistent nagging guilt he felt whenever they did their investigative stuff. How was it that all of his friends seemed to get their work done and still have time for partying, smoking pot, working on their six-packs—both liquid and muscular—and sleeping till 3 p.m. on the weekends? Consistent with his diagnosis, Charles seemed like someone who paid people to write papers for him, or perhaps relied on his frat's test bank, but Chloe, he had learned, had come into college with a bunch of AP credits and never seemed to complain about how much work she had or if she was even able to get it done. He had thought about asking her but hesitated, not wanting to reveal any weakness. *Maybe there's something to this bullet journaling thing*, Andre wondered, flipping pages.

Chloe made a noise—she had found one about psychopathy, but it took her a good ten minutes of looking through it to determine that it contained nothing useful. "You know this is a waste of time, right?" Charles said. He had been paging leisurely through dissertations, so leisurely that Andre realized he would probably have to double-check everything Charles did.

"I don't see you coming up with any solutions," Chloe said, kneeling up now, and rolling her head around to crack her neck.

"I told you I would look into Eleanor—"

"Emma!"

"But I also don't want you doing something ridiculous that gets Wyman in trouble," Charles added.

"You're just lazy and don't want to do any work," Chloe said.

"This isn't the best use of my skill set."

"Skill set," Chloe muttered. She stretched into child's pose, and Charles liberally checked out her ass. "Why don't you make yourself useful and get us some food. I'm starving." Andre shrugged in agreement. Apparently eager to shirk work, Charles put on his coat before he left. "That boy has never had to work a day in his life," Chloe said.

"Go easy on him. He's trying to be helpful." Chloe had an eyebrow raised and was carefully studying him. *Uh-oh.* Why did she have to view Chloe vs Charles as a zero sum game? The more help they had, the better. "You don't know how to work him," Andre said.

Chloe laughed. *"Excuse me?"*

"You pick on him when it's clear all he wants is for everyone to think how great he is. The guy ran for office—he probably lives for people blowing smoke up his ass."

She seemed to contemplate this seriously. "So you think it's better to just play his game?"

"Play his game and let him think he's winning it. And what did you invite him for if you don't want us all to work together?"

"I *do* want us all to work together—he's just really annoying. And I wanted to gauge his reaction when I brought up all the Emma stuff."

"Didn't seem like he knew her at all."

"He was pretty quick to volunteer to find her."

"Does she really seem like someone Charles would hang out with?"

Chloe sighed, then shook her head. "Andre, there's something else you haven't seen." She got up and sat next to him at the table. On her phone was a text—a picture of her sleeping. "Someone took this picture of me in the middle of last night and sent it to me."

"They got into your dorm room?" he asked, sitting straight up.

"No, I was at this guy's house. A frat house."

"He took it?"

"I'm one hundred percent certain he didn't. He's basically a golden retriever and he keeps apologizing about what happened. Blah blah he's going to make SAE take sexual harassment training or blah blah to make it right."

"Wait a minute—do you understand what this means?" Andre exclaimed. "It means they were a few feet away from you and *didn't* kill you." Chloe seemed stunned. "Maybe they don't intend to murder you at all."

She stared at the phone. "Maybe they did—the guy I was with was really big. Maybe they saw him and got scared off?"

"Did you Google the number?"

"Nothing comes up."

"Is there some way you can find out if it was from a real number or a spoofed number?"

"I'm not that tech savvy," she said, opening up her laptop again, "but maybe I can find something on the internet about how to tell."

They worked in companionable silence. Andre flipped through one of the dissertations at random and settled on an acknowledgment page. The author thanked Wyman and the Wyman lab and listed several other names, all of which were already on Andre's list except for one—John Fiola. He pulled open another dissertation and flipped to the acknowledgments. The same students were thanked, including Fiola. Andre checked every single dissertation from the CRD era and found the same student listed in the acknowledgments.

Andre checked the electronic catalog: Fiola had a dissertation entitled "Toward a Greater Understanding of Sexual Violence in Psychopathic Men." He hurried out of the room and to the stacks and double-checked the call number: all the other dissertations had been there, but the one he wanted was missing. Each dissertation had two copies—how could *two copies* have both gone missing? He made a mental note to ask the librarian downstairs as he went back to the study room.

A Google search for "John Fiola DC" yielded results both interesting and disappointing. Tragic Collision Kills Cleveland Park Resident, read the headline from years ago.

John Fiola, a recent recipient of his PhD from John Adams University, was the victim of a tragic drunk driving accident.

"Chloe," he said. He was annoyed to see that she was fiddling around with a dating app. *Can these people take anything seriously?* "Look at this."

Fiola is survived by his fiancée, Mira Wale.

37

What a way to burn a Friday night, spending it with a dweeby RA who was probably trying to get into my pants. But a plan had been formulating in my mind for the endgame with Will. If I found out who was committing the other murders, I'd have the perfect stooge to point a finger at. If only I had been in the psych building when Michael was killed. What if I had gotten there a second earlier and seen who had done it? At this point, I'd already be following them, would have already figured out where they lived and would have been crafting a believable story about them going after Will. Maybe they thought they were hunting me, but I was also hunting them, thinking two steps ahead to their high-profile arrest.

I'd already met with the RA, Trevor Koch, once at the Bean where he marked up my fake CV with a red pen and talked down to me about psychology for twenty minutes. It took all my self-control to plaster a dumb look on my face and keep nodding while I pretended to listen. In reality, I was carefully observing him, collecting all the information I needed. Trevor was gangly and awkward and had zero fashion sense—this was

not a guy who got a lot of attention from girls. He didn't seem
nervous around me but I got the sense that he thought being
condescending was a style of flirting. But most importantly, I
picked up an odor. A particular skunky odor.

A week later, I sent a bubbly text asking if he had a pot
hookup because, being new in town, I didn't have one myself,
hence tonight's activities. I had invited myself over to "hang
out," which of course had to involve a long evening of sitting
around consuming pot with his hookup and having high conversations. Trevor lived in Strayer, one of the smaller dorms
across the quad from me. We were hanging out in his roommate Ray's room, which shared a Jack-and-Jill bathroom with
Trevor's attached room.

Trevor was sprawled perpendicular on Ray's bed, staring up
at the ceiling at the glow-in-the-dark stars that someone had
stuck up there. I was sitting at the edge of the bed, playing with
the lava lamp on the table, the only source of light in the dark
room. Trevor had awkwardly angled his body toward mine, but
not gussied up the balls to actually touch me. Ray and these two
other guys called Mousey and Pete were sitting on the floor in
front of a laptop arguing about some woman and her internet
drama on a forum.

Trevor waved a hand dismissively, then said very slowly, "I
could dox her like *that*," he said, snapping his fingers.

Just then his cell phone made a noise. "Food's here," Trevor
said, getting up and shoving his Converse on. The friend trio
didn't seem to notice; they barely grunted when I said I was
going to use the bathroom.

Once inside the bathroom, I locked the door to Ray's room
and opened the door to Trevor's. I was met with a dark room
accented by the pale blue light, probably from a computer, coming from the little inlet where his bed was. He had a giant table,
possibly stolen from one of the common rooms, filled with
computer equipment, some of which was alive and humming,

some of which was in the process of being dissected. It was ab-
normally cold in his room.

Where would I be, if I was a key? I was betting he wouldn't
keep Wyman's office keys on his person. I used the flashlight
on my cell phone and shone it over the table, looking for a key
ring. A coat was thrown on the floor—I checked the pockets
but found nothing. Didn't he have a proper desk? Maybe it was
where his bed was. I quickly moved to that part of the room but
then froze when I met a sight I didn't know how to interpret.

There was his bed, but the inlet was dominated by his desk,
which had four large, glowing computer monitors. One showed
a girl shoving a dildo into herself. Another showed a girl clip-
ping her toenails. The third showed what looked like someone
asleep in bed. The fourth showed a narrow, neatly made bed
with a lavender, pin-tucked duvet. Two pillows. A chemistry
book. The familiar window just behind the bed. A stuffed whale.
It was *my* bedroom.

"Do you like them?" came a voice.

I jumped without being able to stop myself. Trevor was standing behind me. I could see his room door was open a little—I
hadn't even heard him come in. "I don't understand what I'm
looking at."

"Cam girls," he said. "Top left is a real feed—Natasha in
Ukraine, she's a professional. Actually, all of them are but you."
I was still putting it all together, but a quiet rage was washing
over me. More videos of me floating out there for anyone to
see? Are you kidding me? I needed to be very careful about what
happened next. He grinned, showing small, even teeth. "You
need to pay more attention to what links you click."

My head was in a whirl, trying to remember anything weird.
But who even thinks about all the things they click on and read,
stupid bank notifications popping up on your phone and remind-
ers to fill out some form? Then I remembered—about a week
ago I had gotten a DM on Instagram from some new company

that was recruiting girls to do sponsored posts about their beauty products. I'd received similar offers before, and who doesn't like some flattery and an offer of freebies? I did click on the link absently, while walking between classes, and never thought of it again. And that had happened a few days after I met Trevor.

"You're smarter than you look," he said. "But I figured if I appealed to your vanity..."

Some instinct told me to stay calm. "Why would you do this?"

"I know who you are, Chloe."

Oh, no. I had been banking on the fact that I had never seen him in the office before—I had assumed the RAs wouldn't have a picture of me or something on file. I'd made too many assumptions. I don't have a lot of flaws, but a total lack of humility is one of them.

"As soon as you came into the office snooping around for information, you gave yourself away."

This disgusting perv—he'd been playing with me this whole time. I wanted to gouge his eyes out, but all I could think about is what he might have seen on my webcam. Me getting dressed. Me hooking up. Chad had been over for a "study" date. I had done tequila shots with Billy the Crew one night when I was bored. But most critically: *Had I done anything associated with my Will plan in front of the camera?* I hadn't in the past week, and I didn't use my computer at an angle you could see from the webcam. "Obviously, you're going to get fired for this," I said, resigned, not even sure if he cared.

He cawed with laughter, then put his hand on my shoulder in a weird, affected way. "Oh, honey, you still think I'm an RA?"

He was in the program. He knew what I was the second I showed up trying to get an in with the office. "Why were you on one of Wyman's computers?" He had seemed so at home there—exactly the body language of someone in a workplace.

"Waiting for Elena. I was seeing if they'd ever gotten any better at passwords."

I turned back to the cams, folding my arms across my chest as I looked at the screens, putting on a posture like I was more annoyed than enraged. I had to choose my next steps wisely. Trevor was the seventh student in the program. Trevor might be the killer. He was certainly clever and perverse enough. How out of it were his fellow trolls in the other room? Would they hear if I screamed? I had my wasp spray—my hand edged down to it. "I should be charging you for the free show," I said mildly.

"Ha ha. A girl like you could make some money."

"Are you the only one who has this, or did you make it public?"

"I didn't share it."

I turned to face him, doing a polite golf clap. "All right, I give it to you. You won." He grinned, his eyes sparkling in a way I had never seen before—he had always seemed somewhat dull and phlegmatic. "Here's the thing, though," I said in a smooth, friendly tone, gesturing to the monitors. "I don't like this. I'm not sure I believe that you didn't share it, or record any—" He tried to protest but I steamrolled over him. "And you know, in today's day and age, hacking into a girl's webcam so you can jerk off to her, well, it just doesn't sit right. I mean, I could get you kicked out of school." I examined my nails. "Or maybe a few well-placed posts on social media could go viral and then nobody could ever Google your name without the story coming up. Trust me, I would see to that."

He looked a little alarmed. "I'll cut the feed right now!" he said, holding up his hands innocently. He leaned over his keyboard and did a series of rapid things—the feed cut out. But what did that even mean? For all I knew he could get straight back into it. "I didn't save anything, I promise."

"Like a promise from a psychopath even means anything?"

"Listen, I'll do you a favor—you need to take internet security seriously. Get yourself a good password manager—use it the right way and even I can't get into your stuff." He proceeded to lecture me about technology, while I stared at him, stunned. He had gone from sinister to good-natured—it was almost like he thought my discovery of him creeping on me was an icebreaker to a new friendship, or worse, something more. I was spiritually vomiting.

I sighed. "I'm very upset, Trevor."

He blinked a few times rapidly. "I've seen you around campus. I know the sort of people you hang out with." What the hell did that mean? "I'll do you a solid." He hunched over his keyboard again. He dug around for a while before he found something—a folder entitled simply *cunt*. He was emailing something to me—to my real school address, which was in my name.

"You're crazy if you think I'd actually open an attachment from you."

He put his hands in his pockets. "That folder contains some information about someone you really need to see. I like you, Chloe. Most girls are boring but you aren't. You're like me." The wasp spray was tempting me, but I needed to pay attention to his every microexpression. "You need to be careful about the company you keep," Trevor said.

I fled from Trevor's dorm like a bat out of neckbeard hell. I was so mad my ears were hot. I was holding my phone, desperate to know what was in that file, but of course I wasn't going to open it. I didn't even want to open my email app just in case my phone would automatically download the file. Trevor was a creep and a liar—but he knew just where to get me, that I would be too curious to not open it.

I felt an urge to text Andre—he had proven insanely reliable for a psychopath, doing tons of legwork about Wyman's history and everything, but I had to remind myself that he had done all that to save his own ass, not mine. No, I would deal with this alone.

Strayer was kitty-corner to the library, where one of the

twenty-four-hour computer labs were. Once I signed into my email I stared at the attachment, dying of curiosity, still angry. I dragged the folder onto the desktop to save it, then quickly signed out of my email.

I looked around, assuring that I had privacy, then clicked on the *cunt* file.

It consisted of a single PDF called "PatientFile34522." I recognized the first page—it was the same intake form I had filled out when I signed up for the program, but my eyes froze on the first line. *Portmont, Charles Andrew.* My heart started beating hard.

Why would Trevor have this? The document was about thirty pages and was cut off in the middle of a sentence. After a couple pages of generic stuff, there were what looked like clinical notes initialed LW or ET. Those first few pages were not surprising. Charles's poor little rich boy background, getting into trouble as a kid and being sent to one boarding school after another. Your father's an asshole? The huge empty spaces of all your vacation homes don't provide any comfort? Blah blah blah.

I scanned until a few words popped out at me.

Working with Charles continues to be a struggle. He continues to display high levels of sadism, which hasn't changed since I began seeing him. The pleasure he takes in causing others' pain dates back to his childhood. He expresses no remorse for any wrongdoing or criminal activity. For the second time this month, he has talked at length about the sexual desire he associates with thoughts of killing and maiming young women. Has talked about dreams of having sex with dead bodies. I've had to let another RA go. Have thought about going to the police about Daisy but am frightened of the consequences. (Father is very powerful.)

This had to be fake. Trevor playing a game. Then again, he had seemed genuinely worried that I would try to get him kicked out of school. And why would he just happen to have a fake file about Charles on his computer? That awkward way he had touched my shoulder... I think Trevor Liked me—like with a capital *L*—and maybe he had seen me talking to Charles and, in his own fucked-up way, worried about me or was jealous? Some of the stuff in the file I knew to be true: Dr. Wyman's signature looked real, and whoever wrote the notes accurately described Charles's charm, his laziness, and his quick way of going from one mood to the next. Both boys were terrible, but which one was worse?

Wait, who was Daisy—an RA? I quickly opened Google and searched "Daisy Adams University," but with low expectations. The first two listings were duds, but then there it was, an article from the *Daily Owl*. Sophomore Suicide Raises Questions About Student Health.

Apparently, last year a student named Daisy Crosby jumped off the top of the Math Sciences Tower—which everyone called Suicide Tower—to her death. The article included a quote from her voice instructor about how such a beautiful talent was wasted. She was a voice major, which would put her in Albertson Hall all the time—exactly where Charles frequented.

Maybe it had been obvious all along. Even his frat brothers literally called him "Terrible Charles." I had to face the fact that I had a significant bias about Charles and it had colored my decisions. From the moment I heard about the killings—from *him* no less—I had not for a second seriously considered that Charles could be responsible. Why—because he had helped me back in Fort Hunt? Maybe I liked to think he helped me because secretly he wanted me, but maybe it really *was* in self-interest—maybe the last thing he needed was people getting assaulted on his property because that's where he buries his bodies.

Ted Bundy murdered by wearing a fake cast and asking women to help him, and they never thought he was sketchy because he was supposedly handsome and charming. People, including his girlfriend at the time, and his friend, crime writer Ann Rule, suspected him, but also questioned their suspicions because they simply *couldn't* believe it was him. Despite it being in front of their faces the whole time.

As I headed home, it occurred to me with sudden clarity—the sad thing about poor, beautiful Terrible Charlie Bear. Once I took care of Will, I would take care of Charles, and this time I wasn't going to have any blinders on.

38

Charles opened his eyes in the dim light, making out the fuzzy hexagonal pattern of the tile in Kristen's bathroom. His vision was terrible without his contacts, but he knew that the white pill lying at the base of the toilet was an Excedrin. The last thing he remembered was Kristen curling up beside him as they fell asleep, then waking up a few hours later with terrible waves of migraine pain.

He got up and moved toward the bedroom, still feeling dull pain in the back of his head. But then he froze. Was he seeing things, or was there a dark figure in the bedroom? Sometimes the migraines affected his sight, but this typically took the form of tunnel vision. The bedroom was too dark to see clearly, but there—wasn't there something even darker at the center? Standing, hovering over the bed as if peering down. Right over Kristen.

Fuck. His gun was in the nightstand—all of two feet away from the intruder and halfway across the room. Charles reached out half-blindly, his hand finding a vase. *I might hit her*, he warned himself, but there was no time to waste—the shadow, the *thing*, was now leaning over his girlfriend. Charles launched the vase across the room—then came a thud, a grunt, glass breaking, a scream. The figure moved toward the window, and Charles darted to the nightstand as Kristen screamed again. He could barely make out the dark shape crawling out the window but he fired the Glock anyway, each pull of the trigger providing a flash of light. He could just make out the shape of an arm right before it disappeared. He moved closer to the window, then fired out of it through the broken glass, firing somewhat blindly into the street. Kristen was still screaming but he blocked her out, then used the butt of the gun to break the rest of the glass out of the window so he could stick his head out. Why did his vision have to be so bad? He could make out no shape moving away; there was no one out on the street, just a taxicab heading north.

He leaned back, realizing that he was holding his breath. His ears were ringing. He turned the lights on and fumbled for his glasses on the nightstand. Kristen was hugging her knees to her chest, her eyes huge, blankets pulled up around her protectively. "Charles, there was something *here*."

He examined the wall surrounding the window. Luckily, he hadn't shot the wall. "I'm calling 911. When they come, don't tell them I fired a gun. It's my dad's, it's legal, but I could get in trouble." The myriad gun laws in the city were hard to follow, in between gun control legislation that got passed and various court cases and acts of Congress that prevented that legislation from actually being enacted because of DC's lack of local sovereignty. He dialed 911, then with the phone to his ear gathered all the spent shells, then washed his hands.

He sat on the bed with Kristen as they waited—she was still shaking—and held her. He felt a heat of hatred so intense he couldn't hear anything. Even with all the fallout from what had happened last year with Daisy, Charles's cyberattacker had never figured out where Kristen lived. Kristen's family, like many wealthy people, valued privacy, and when they did things like buy houses for their daughters, they did it through companies that could shield the owner from public records. Last year, the harassment had never come to physical violence. One thing he did not know was if that shadowy figure had been looking for Kristen, or for *him*.

The police arrived and took statements. Charles couldn't wait for them to leave. Only then did Kristen call her parents as Charles searched for some plastic and tape to seal the window. It didn't keep the cold air out and certainly wouldn't keep a person out. "Thank God Charles was here—I'm so freaked out," Kristen said into the phone. "A burglar, I don't know. It's just, with those *murders* here…"

She handed him the phone and, sounding as calmly as he could, he reassured her parents, who were justifiably alarmed. Perfect boyfriend needed to be reliable and steady, an asset rather than a liability to their daughter. He disconnected, then took her head in his hands. "Listen. I'm never going to let anyone do anything to you."

"I don't even feel safe in my own house!"

"Let's go to my place—it's on the sixth floor and security's good." She looked doubtful. "We can always stay at Fort Hunt—no one can get you there. The driver can take us back and forth." He helped her pack—Kristen was not the sort of person that was good at waking up in the middle of the night. He opened the medicine cabinet to get his Excedrin and her prescription, then found himself staring at the little orange bottle. It was a new one, the one he had picked up for her a couple days ago on his way to meet Andre and Chloe at the library. He hadn't thought of it at the time, but it now seemed salient. The prescription bottle—with her address printed on it—had been in his messenger bag, and he had left it behind for an hour. Plenty of time for Chloe to snoop through.

39

Day 11

My smashed-up webcams were in the garbage, which meant that I could safely dress for my "date." It was 10 p.m., and Will was expecting a blonde girl named Daniella who wears patent leather pants and has a low bar for men. I was not wearing patent leather pants, but jeans with a deep enough pocket to hold my switchblade. I had specifically picked our meeting place, a pseudo dive bar called Ivy and Coney because it was sparsely populated on Thursday nights.

I stood in the entrance, taking in the disinterested hipster bartender and two guys enamored with their beers in the corner. Will sat alone at a high-top watching basketball, chewing with his mouth open. I slipped onto one of the stools next to him, withdrawing my knife but hiding it beneath the flowy sleeve of my batwing shirt. I pressed the blade into his inner thigh, the metal digging into his jeans but not cutting through.

His eyes went huge. I could see the realization that he had been tricked flow onto his stupid face.

"Let's stop playing hide-and-seek. You have until October 23 to give me the video. I know you have it."

"You're a fucking psycho." He swallowed. His mouth must have been dry because I could hear it.

"Yes." I withdrew the knife a little, taking my phone out with my other hand.

He leaned forward and whispered, "I could punch your little head across this room."

"You could. Will you, though? In front of everyone? Do you know what's going to happen to you if I don't get it on the twenty-third?" I held up my phone where Snapchat was open.

"Why the fuck are you obsessed with the twenty-third?" I ignored him, but once he saw my phone, he frowned, clearly thrown off. I flicked my finger down the screen so he could see the hundreds of lines of messages. The heart emojis and the *xoxo I love you*'s. "You've…you've been talking to my brother?"

"Davey's not very savvy for a ninth grader. Davey is in love with a girl he met online. See how easy it is? Do you know what's going to happen to little Davey on the twenty-third if I don't have my video?" His eyes got huge. I stared back at him without blinking.

"He's just a *kid*. He's my kid *brother*. What are you—?"

"Did you think I forgot Brett?" There was an involuntary jerk as Will realized what I was saying. Brett, the all-American friend who held Will's phone that night and filmed when he could have been saving me. Here's the sad, cold truth, Friends and Neighbors. No one is ever going to save you. "Poor Brett— too *parochial* to go anywhere but Rutgers. But convenient for me, him being a local and all." I tilted my head. "Tragic thing, that car accident over Thanksgiving weekend. Was he driving drunk? Well, you can't perform an autopsy on a body that burned. He was one crispy critter."

"You're. Fucking. Insane."

"I accept myself for who I am." I grabbed his chin gently with my thumb and forefinger. "October 23. Do. You. Understand?"

He blinked. "Yes."

40

How much do you feel each of the following emotions? Charles's watch asked him as he jogged down the street. Kristen was safely at Fort Hunt and the driver had taken him back to campus as soon as she felt okay with him leaving. Blindly angry was all he felt.

Chloe had gotten into Kristen's house. The point of her home invasion, he had no idea. He had been too distracted with ridiculous theories about a cyberattacker when Chloe had likely been the culprit all along. Chloe had probably made up everything about Will—maybe what Charles had walked in on was a murder in progress. He had never bothered to ask Will his side of the story.

He skipped the mood log, knowing that if he responded there would be some record of him behaving badly. He knew from two years of therapy with Wyman that when he got into moods like this, the best thing for him to do was to go somewhere quiet and sit on his hands. To bite back that part of himself that was too impulsive to be reasonable.

Instead, his pace to Will's house was rapid. But he stood at the doorstep knocking for five minutes before he realized Will wasn't home. He headed for the SAE house, but there no one had seen him. After a quick and fruitless search, Charles flopped on the couch, completely ignoring the other brothers but taking advantage of their bong. *Calm down*, he told himself. He couldn't think straight when he got like this. Chad stood in the doorway of the kitchen, eating Icelandic yogurt, talking to someone on the phone. *What would Chad do?* Charles wondered.

Chad, he imagined, did not get tangled into situations like this because he probably had an internal default that told him what to do, the *right* thing to do. He didn't get distracted by hot girls and their lies and games.

Will came in about ten minutes later, looking flushed. He headed to the kitchen—probably to get a beer—but Charles made a come-over-here gesture that did not make a response seem optional, and he pulled Will into one of the filthy bedrooms.

Charles wasted no time. "What do you know about Chloe?"

"Chloe?" The bovine way Will had said it. Thick with the lie of pretending the name was unfamiliar. Underneath was a hint of alarm.

"Chloe Sevre."

"Uh…"

"Has she been harassing you?"

Will gave a dumb little laugh. "Harassing?"

"Someone broke into Kristen's house last night—I think it was her." Will's eyes got wide. "What's the video she's looking for?" he tried. "I already know about it, so stop pretending," Charles said impatiently.

"Okay, this bitch is *crazy*. She's totally stalking me. She broke into my locker and did something to my phone—she broke into my house. I should go to the police!"

"What's on the video?" Charles repeated.

"We, you know, hooked up and stuff and *she* wanted to make a video so we did. She's batshit!"

"Then why's she stalking you?"

"Because I dumped her! She's *crazy* and now she won't leave me alone!"

"You met her at Adams?"

"No, we went to high school together, but I was a couple years ahead of her. I'm starting to think she *followed* me here or something—you know how fucked up that is?"

Charles felt a sinking sensation. "So you were, what, a senior and she was a sophomore?"

A muscle by Will's mouth twitched. "Yeah."

He's lying, Charles realized, the thought freezing the rush of angry emotions. Merrifield Teacher Accused of Sex with Students—Charles remembered the title of the article. Will didn't go to the same high school. Charles knew because his freshman year Will talked constantly about how his high school lacrosse team—at *Cloverfield*—had gone to state. The indignation on his face was entirely different from the look on Chloe's face when she had swung that geode—raw rage. Chloe's emotion had been visceral, Will's defensive.

If he was innocent, Will had every right to go to the police if someone broke into his house—just as Charles had. But what would make him not want to? *He did it*, Charles realized. *He totally did it.* "So now she's...?"

"I don't know," Will said, running a hand through his unruly hair. "She thinks I have the sex tape or something, and she's totally obsessed with me. The thing is, I don't even have that phone anymore—*I can't find it.*"

A sex tape. He thought it was a sex tape. Charles was glad that his face wasn't particularly expressive. "You'd better find the video. I don't think she's going to stop till she gets it."

Will shrank back. Charles abandoned him to pace around the front yard of the house, wondering how many guys just like Will he had looked in the face without even realizing it. If the video existed, Charles understood why Chloe would want to be in sole possession of it—any idiot could. And even with Will and the specter of his video hovering over her, Chloe with all her PowerPoints and whatnot had certainly done more than Charles had to track down the killer. Meanwhile, he had been withholding information that might have helped just because he didn't trust her. And while he was dicking around, the killer had gotten close enough to him to get into Kristen's bedroom. *I need to talk to her,* he realized, *and we can sort this all out together.*

41

Day 10

I peered through my peephole when someone knocked, seeing a distorted image of Charles wearing a hunter-green sweater. What was he doing here? And for fuck's sake, *no one in this dorm takes security seriously*! Or maybe he charmed his way in. I had just finished switching all my passwords over to a new—and expensive—password manager and had been working on finalizing my plans for Phase Four. I hadn't yet decided exactly how I was going to dispose of Charles, only that I didn't want to handle him and Will at the same time. Both were fit and bigger than me. But I knew one thing for sure—I needed Charles out of my way for the next two weeks.

He knocked again, but this time I was ready. I swung the door open and zapped him with the stun gun. He gave a cry and fell. People were doing power hour down the hallway, so no one noticed, not even when I grabbed him by the belt and shirt and dragged his still-shaking body inside my room. I nudged the door shut with my foot and locked it. Yessica wouldn't be home for another three hours. He was incapacitated for now, and we were alone.

Should I just get rid of him now? I could drag him to the window and push him out—the fall down would probably kill him. Then again, actually getting his body out the window might be hard. Maybe if I shocked him over and over with the stun gun he would die? I knew he got migraines—maybe I could just tell people he came over and had a seizure or something. I contemplated the baseball bat I had gotten from a sidewalk sale.

"Ch-Chloe!"

"Shut up! I know who you are." I put the stun gun in his face and made it emit its satisfying snapping noise. "You've done a good job making it seem like it was never you, but I've had an awakening. You just *happened* to be the person with Elena who found Kellen's body? You were probably waiting for her to show up so you could gloat!"

"G-gloat? No, I—"

"Party's over." I tapped the ground with the baseball bat. "It'd be a shame wrecking that beautiful face of yours."

"Wait—"

"I know everything about you—"

"Wait, wait. Do whatever you want to me, just let me ask you a question." I made an impatient gesture. "Where did you go to high school?"

"Merrifield High. Why?"

"Will went to Merrifield, right?"

"No, he went to Cloverfield."

"Was there a scandal with you being involved with a teacher?"

"Alexei, yes."

He closed his eyes and breathed more slowly. I wondered if I had seriously injured him, but then he looked straight into my eyes with a look I couldn't read, something soft around the edges for the first time. "You never lied to me once, have you?" he asked, sounding amazed.

"I'm not a liar like you! I know everything now, about Daisy and how you killed her."

He looked alarmed, trying to sit up, but apparently it still hurt where I shocked him. "That's not what happened. I didn't kill her."

I gently tapped his forehead with the baseball bat. "I got into your files from Wyman's office. I know exactly how perverted your brain is."

"And the file said I killed Daisy?" he seemed genuinely puzzled rather than alarmed.

"More or less."

"Can I see it?"

This torture session wasn't going how I planned. I was annoyed—he should have been afraid of me. I opened the file and handed him my laptop, hovering near him with my weapons. His eyes moved quickly down the page, his mouth open. Suddenly he hissed like the snake he was. "Chloe, did you *read* all of this?"

"I skimmed. Pretty sickening stuff."

He looked at me, exasperated. "Here, under *Sexual proclivities*. 'Subject possesses a wide variety of perverse, disturbing sexual drives, both in behavior and in the pornography he watches for several hours a day. He admits to indulging in sexual acts with animals on his family's estate growing up. The list included the family dog, stray cats, sheep, even hermit crabs.' Really, Chloe?"

"Hermit crabs!"

"We've never had a dog. My dad hates them." He closed the laptop, looking at me thoughtfully. "Where did you get this file?" I remained silent. "Was it from someone who's really good with computers?"

"Someone. He's looking out for me."

"He's in the program," Charles said, tapping the laptop.

How could he possibly have figured this out with so little information? Charles raised his eyebrows. "Am I wrong?" He struggled to get into a sitting position. "I met Daisy last year in the music department. She was a really pretty girl. She mentioned once that sometimes a guy would creep on her Instagram and like all her pictures and see secret messages directed at him. You know, if she takes a picture of a latte with a heart in it, it's really a message to him."

"Oh. One of those."

"Daisy and I slept together. We—"

"You cheated on Kristen?"

He looked weary. "We survived it. Someone must have been really attached to her, because he attacked us both in every way he could. All my accounts got hijacked, my utilities shut off. Credit cards got taken out in my name. Child pornography sent to my email."

"That seems extreme."

"That's nothing compared to what he did to Daisy—all of the above plus more. He must have spent hours reading through her emails and texts to come up with every snarky thing she ever said about anyone, so he could send it to her friends and alienate them. He posted her phone number and address on all these personal ads for women seeking casual sex. It drove her crazy."

"Did she report him?"

"She went to the police, but she couldn't pinpoint who was doing it—neither could I. They said, 'If someone's harassing you online, why don't you get offline? What did you ever take a nude picture of yourself for?' The police both didn't have the know-how and didn't care."

"How did you get him to stop, then?"

"I paid him. I should have been more careful—I should have been specific and said to leave both of us alone. I didn't realize that he kept on with her. She was a sensitive person—she couldn't take it. She was the second suicide off Suicide Tower last year. The tower in the Math building—people have jumped off it before."

What a dumb name—Daisy. That sounds exactly like someone who would kill themselves instead of carefully plotting a way to destroy their enemies. And I was almost disappointed in Charles in opting for the easy way out, but I suppose as a rich boy he doesn't know any better. He's never had to scrape his way through the world.

"And how am I supposed to know that literally everything you just said isn't a lie?"

He made a hold-on gesture, scrolling through his phone. When he handed it to me I could see email after email of him trying to deal with the aftermath of the cyberattack last year. Even personal emails to Kristen. A complaint he had filed with the police. He was telling the truth.

"I'm guessing," Charles said, now struggling to his feet. I still stood in a defensive position. "That whoever gave you that file is the same person who attacked me."

"Why would he have a fake file on you?"

"Maybe he got the real file and made up some fake stuff with the intention of publishing it somewhere, or maybe giving it to Kristen. That's how I know he's in the program."

"Huh?"

"This guy attacked me in every way possible *except* exposing that I'm a diagnosed psychopath in this special program for psychopaths. He was covering his own ass." Charles was watching me carefully. "Does the person I described sound like the person who gave you this file?"

Goddamn it. Charles was right again.

"I went and talked to Will," Charles said. "I directly asked him about what happened with you and I could tell he was lying. Not even lying particularly well—it's like he's convinced himself he's in the right. I trust you, Chloe. Now can you trust me? Because if you can, I can tell you everything."

What *else* wasn't he telling me? "Okay."

"No, I want to hear you say that you think that file's fake."

"It's fake—all right? The guy is a loser named Trevor. He pretended to be an RA in the program and I fell for it. Meanwhile, he hacked my webcams and has been creeping on me. He flat out told me he's in the program—it's like he wants to be buddies now."

Charles looked alarmed. "Then Trevor is extremely dangerous. Someone broke into Kristen's house—I'm sorry, I thought it was you, but now I know it's him."

Trevor had serious skills. He was smart enough to fool me, and this alone made me suspect him more than the other psychopath in the program, Emma, who I knew so little about, anyhow. I didn't know why he was doing it—maybe he was a serial killer fanatic or something, but who cared. The most important thing was that no one could know for sure who the killer was and have them locked up before I could kill Will. Ideally, I would have an opportunity to plant some evidence. "What about the twins?"

Charles shook his head and wandered out of my room into the common area, his hands shoved into his pockets. "Um, it's not the twins."

"What makes you so sure?" I asked, suspicious, following him.

"Well, I kind of lied. I know Emma—we're sort of friends because of the program, inasmuch as a person can be friends with her. I just didn't want to tell you about her."

"You've known her all along?!"

"I didn't trust you! I was protecting her!"

"You're *sure* it's not her?"

"I mean, ninety-nine percent. I don't know much about her sister, but I can see what I can find out about her. I keep trying to make plans with Emma but she's super weird and not easy to get ahold of."

"So we have a list of all seven students, then," I mused, turning the information over in my head.

Charles chewed on his lower lip. "Let's go with the most obvious thing—we already know Trevor's sadistic. He managed to figure out that you and I are in the program. He's crazy good with computers—he probably got into that experiment room and killed Michael, and maybe messed with the MRI somehow. We have to find proof about Trevor."

I went to the windows and watched students cutting across the brick pathways of the quad. "Trevor doesn't realize that I think he's disgusting. I could get close to him." And be in control of any information I found out...

"That's not a good idea—he's dangerous. He was hovering over Kristen while she was sleeping."

Apparently, he has a thing for sleeping girls. "Just because Trevor is a creep doesn't mean he's a murderer."

"It would probably be to your benefit to have a healthy fear of him."

"I'm not afraid."

"Uh-oh, is there another geode in your pocket?"

I laughed. "I can become friends with him. Maybe do a more thorough snoop of his dorm room."

"No," he said, suddenly vehement.

"Why not?" I said, edging closer to him. I had to admit I was relieved it wasn't Charles, after all. He trusted me—it gave me a little leeway to almost trust him.

"Because you're attractive—if he takes a liking to you, I don't know what he'll do."

"So you think I'm attractive?" I teased.

Charles sighed. "Why do I get the sense that you're going to do whatever you want to do regardless of what I say?"

"Bingo," I whispered, touching the tip of my index finger to his nose.

"We need to plan. Emma likes me—I might be able to get some information out of her, where she was those two nights to rule her out."

"Sounds like a plan."

"Chloe, there's something else we have to consider, but you're not going to like it."

"What?"

"What if it's Will? What if it's been Will all along?"

"What? My Will? *Stupid* Will?"

"You got attacked at Stupid Will's house. Stupid Will has a motive to get rid of you."

"Stupid Will has access to the SAE house," I muttered. Charles looked puzzled, so I showed him the picture someone had texted me. "Someone took a picture of me sleeping at the SAE house."

"Why were you sleeping there?"

"I get tired after fucking."

"Chad, really?"

"What makes you think Will could be a criminal master-mind?"

"We already know that one person on campus is capable of killing people. And we know another person who is capable of—of doing what he did to you. Isn't it improbable that those would be two different people?"

"Then what's his motive for killing anyone else in the program? Will isn't smart enough to do all this. You should see how dumbly he falls into my traps."

"Maybe he falls for them on purpose. Chloe, there's an intersection between these two crazy things, and that intersection is *you*."

I was already impossibly biased against the idea. Did I think that Will murdered two people without leaving behind enough evidence to get caught? The same guy that literally filmed himself committing a crime? Hell no. But maybe it wouldn't hurt to have Charles think this—it could help my endgame.

"I'll think about it. Honestly, I'm too exhausted to do anything right now. I have a French paper and my Bio lab report and all this Wyman stuff, and on top of it I have to deal with Will." I sighed. He did, too.

"You stunned me. With a stun gun *I* bought you."

"It's the risk you run being generous."

"You really thought I was a serial killer," he said, shaking his head.

"What did you expect me to think seeing that file?"

"I don't know—have a little faith?"

"I'm sorry." He made a fake sad face. "I'm sorry!" I said, laughing, putting my hands on his arms. "Can't you forgive me?" I looked up at him beseechingly.

"Never," he murmured, smiling. He hugged me in that same flirty way I had seen him be with other girls but not me. Flirt friends. Totally innocent. I squeezed him with exaggeration, feeling the muscles of his chest, the ribs beneath; my arms then slipped around his waist.

"All is forgiven," I said. "We kiss and make up." I reached up and kissed his cheek. I'm not sure how it happened, if he turned his head or if I did, or we both did, but then his mouth was on mine. His lips were soft. The kiss only lasted a couple seconds, but we paused there, a mere millimeter away from each other. He nudged my face up with a subtle movement of his head and then kissed me, this time his mouth open, our tongues touching, an electric thrill shooting through my body.

Then I heard the sound of a key working its way in the lock of our door. We pulled away just as Yessica came in. She looked at Charles suspiciously.

"Hello," he said, all charm.

She gave me a look any woman could interpret—girl, you should know better.

42

It was so rare that Megan would agree to be in the same room with Emma that Elena had made certain to arrive early so she could see as much of the girls together as she could.

Emma arrived on time, her face expressionless, and hugged her knees to her chest on one of Leonard's chairs. "Hello," she said to both Elena and Leonard. Emma cared little about her appearance—broadly speaking—and this was yet another reason why she was an intriguing addition to the study. Sometimes her hair wasn't clean, and she didn't have the charm and penchant for manipulation that psychopaths typically used to win the admiration of others. This would require actually being interested in other people. It was like she was a ghost in human form; Elena had once imagined that this was how Emma took her remarkable photographs of insects—she could sneak up on them without notice.

Megan came in moments later, her face tight, a scarf wrapped around her neck. It was remarkable how different the twins looked even though they were identical. They had the same facial features, and they were the same height, but that's where the resemblance stopped. Megan dyed her hair auburn and years of competitive gymnastics as a child had altered her physique. She didn't compete anymore, but she always seemed shorter than Emma, broader in the shoulders. Her life consisted of worrying about classes, her boyfriend, and hanging out with her friends. She wanted a normal life, but had to contend with having a bizarre family.

Megan chose the chair that was farthest from her sister.

"Hello, Megan." Leonard closed the door, then sat back down. "We haven't seen you in a while." His casualness grated on Elena's nerves. They had had one of their rare arguments yesterday. Elena thought they should discuss what was happening with each member of the program. She could still see the horrific image of Kellen's body, the ichor syrupy on the floor.

Elena thought it was unconscionable that Wyman wasn't explicitly warning their students about the murders. First Michael, then Kellen. Wyman had assured her that he was working closely with the police and there was no reason to be worried—the police had a significant lead pointing to a local drug dealer. Elena was adamant, but Wyman had wielded a final argument that had convinced her: their students were not average students. Witnessing or being proximate to a murder was just not the same thing to them—any one of them could easily misuse the situation for some personal gain. Maybe for media attention—what if they publicized the program?—maybe for financial gain; it was not a tragedy to them, but something they could *use*. She thought of the way Charles had looked at Kellen's body with interest, rather than terror.

"I imagine you've settled into the school year somewhat already," Leonard said.

Emma didn't say anything. Megan chimed in instead. "Classes are getting more intense. I'm busy with organizing stuff for my sorority."

"Sisters," Emma said. Expressionless, it was impossible to tell if she was somehow kidding. "We had a new sister once."

"She's referring to sixth grade," Megan translated. "This fad where everyone got these heart necklaces. You know, a heart broken in two pieces. One girl wears one half and the other wears the second half."

"Some said 'Best friends.' Megan's said 'Sis' and the other one said 'ters,'" Emma said, more eagerly.

"Maureen Demirez was my best friend that year," Megan said carefully. "We each had half of the necklace."

"They knew each other from gymnastics," Emma said. Megan had legitimately been good up until then, competing in state and regional competitions.

"That was the year I had my injury," Megan said, averting her eyes. She didn't like to talk about the injury at practice that had torn several ligaments. Despite physical therapy and the best sports doctors the family could find, it had ended her competitive career.

"The news said there might be rioting," Emma said abruptly. This wasn't outside the realm of normal for her—because conversations often disinterested her, it wasn't unusual for her to completely hop between topics, playacting what she thought a conversation was.

"Rioting—oh, the protests?" Leonard asked.

Megan was distracted for several minutes before she started talking in earnest. She, like many undergraduates, was anxious about the political climate and constant barrage of bad news on the TV. Just last week, police clashing with protestors had led to dozens of arrests and a fire downtown. This conversation went on, Emma occasionally throwing in a fact she had read. Every time she had a session with both girls, Elena was fascinated at what their contrasting behavior could mean. How on earth Leonard had managed to recruit a pair of identical twins where one was psychopathic and the other wasn't was beyond her. She did know that it had been expensive to recruit them. Megan hadn't even wanted to come to DC, but with a considerable signing bonus for both girls, Emma's free tuition and Leonard "making some calls" at American, they had managed to be convinced. He was cagey about the amount, but Elena's understanding was that it had taken a significant chunk of grant money.

But it would probably be worth it. The field was only on the verge of beginning to understand to what extent psychopathy was heritable. Certain psychiatric disorders—schizophrenia, bipolar disorder—were highly heritable, a fact that had been determined by studies over the years comparing monozygotic twins—those who share one hundred percent of their genes—and fraternal twins. If one identical twin had bipolar disorder, there was about a sixty percent chance that the other would have it, as well. This was what made the Dufresne twins fascinating: Emma had been diagnosed, and Megan, too, had been tested. While Megan was not psychopathic, she had an anxiety disorder and often seemed to bear the brunt of their family's problems. Emma was something to be managed, and while she didn't want to do it, Megan was the closest relationship Emma had. Their parents out in San Diego—the nice house and the Bernese mountain dog—had seemed about as kind and do-gooder as parents got, so what was it that had shaped the twins to be so drastically differently?

When the session ended, Emma scurried from the room, Leonard said his goodbyes and Elena and Megan left at the same time.

Megan lingered by the door. "Something wrong?" Elena asked. She believed she had a better rapport with Megan than Leonard had—it was just easier for two young women to relate to each other.

"I've been thinking a lot about the vault accident lately," she said. They headed down the hallway and started down the stairs together. "It was just a normal practice. I had done that vault a million times—it wasn't even the hard one. Mom brought Emma to practice with her, but I didn't care—she would just sit there and read."

"What happened?"

"I was about to do my vault, about to start running, and I happened to look up and Emma was just *staring* at me. *That's* the vault that tore my ligaments." They stopped on the landing, Megan looking up at Elena with earnest eyes, the exact earnestness someone had on their face when they were about to tell you how they saw a UFO once. "It was like she willed it to happen. She wanted me to get hurt."

"Megan, that's outside the laws of physics," Elena said gently. "Maybe she spooked you—"

"But yeah, it was me who fucked up the vault and ruined my career." Megan hopped down two stairs ahead of her, and Elena wondered if she had offended her. "It's not like I was ever going to make nationals, anyway. But she got what she wanted."

"And what's that?"

Megan barely turned to address her. "For me to never leave her behind."

43

Groaning, Andre opened his eyes. Something smelled. His own T-shirt. He pulled it off—he had definitely vomited last night. He tried to sit up but his body immediately told him not to.

How could you be so stupid? he thought, and the voice he heard in his head was not his own, but Kiara's. He had gotten drunk last night at Marcus's house. He hadn't meant to—he had been incredibly careful about drinking ever since he found out about the murders. What good was the baseball bat under his bed, and the careful traveling across campus, and the triple-checking of dead bolts, if you were just going to stumble down some street, drunk and stupid? But someone had brought two twenty-four-packs of alcoholic root beer from Trader Joe's and it was so sweet you couldn't really tell there was alcohol in it. Andre had done what countless other college freshman do every single day: he had had a good time, got drunk with his friends, and stumbled home with his roommate to have a hangover the next day.

Stupid stupid stupid. You could have been killed. He stumbled out of bed and crawled to the bathroom, vomiting up horrifyingly black liquid. The very sight of it made him more nauseated. Moaning, he flushed the toilet and curled up on the cold bathroom floor, shivering.

"I'm dying," he said quietly. He felt a sudden, intense desire to be home. Not *here* in this weird, dangerous place, but back in NE at his house, in his comfortable room overlooking the back-yard. Mom and Dad downstairs having coffee. He even missed Isaiah forcing Andre's head into his armpit, laughing maniacally. He had always been so bored at home, so bored that he never thought he would miss it.

What a baby. Eighteen and you're homesick? Andre struggled to a sitting position, leaning against the bathtub, and got out his phone. He had a missed call from his dad. His finger hovered over the Call Back button. One button and maybe all this would be over. His parents could whisk in and everything would magically be better. He wasn't sure how, but maybe it would be. Maybe they wouldn't be that mad. He could just leave, tell them that full-time school was too much for him, and once he was away from Adams, the danger would be over. He jumped when his phone rang—it was his father. After a brief greeting his father immediately asked if he had woken him up.

"What? No."

"Oh, you sick? You sound sick?"

"Just, ah, out a little late last night."

"You're not drinking, are you?"

"Of course not. It was an ice cream social." What did his parents think college was, anyway? Study parties and, well, ice cream socials? "I was talking to a girl." That would throw him off.

"Ooohh," he cooed. There was a pause—it sounded like his father had put his hand over the phone to say something to some-one else, probably his mother. The pause seemed an eternity for Andre, who debated finally saying something, something that could end all of this. All it would take was one word, although he wasn't sure which word to start with. "Listen, Pooh, we wanted to let you know that the surgery is scheduled."

"It is?" His father's back surgery had always felt on the horizon. But there were always more appointments to go to, and his father's diligent way of researching the hell out of anything before committing.

"November 3—I'll be back on my feet in time for Thanksgiving."

Andre felt a wave of panic. "That's so soon." His father was the guy tending to patients in the ambulance, not the one on his back. A huge, healthy man with a booming voice, not an unconscious body attached to a bunch of wires and tubes. Even the thought of him in a hospital bed made Andre feel more nauseated.

"It's nothing to worry about. You know what they call it when they remove a disk? A discectomy!"

"Very funny," he said impatiently. "But anesthesia and everything?"

"It's not what you're picturing—they're not going to cut me open. It's minimally invasive. Smaller incision, smaller tools, and two guys at work had this same surgeon."

"I can come home that weekend," he offered quickly. *And no, I will not tell you anything that will stress you out, like that I may or may not be committing fraud to pay my way through college or that there's a serial killer on the loose. Nothing like that at all, I swear.*

"Yeah, Pooh, it'll be good to see you."

So much for the spilling of secrets.

"Dr. Torres?" Andre asked, sticking his head into Elena's office. A few hours and two Pedialytes later, he felt marginally better. "I was finishing a survey and the screen froze."

She got up and followed him down the hallway to the experiment room he had been working in. She leaned over the computer and wiggled the mouse. "Sometimes they're wonky," she said. He sat down beside her.

"I don't know if you heard," Andre said, figuring he might as well try to fish. "I was able to ID the guy I saw the night of the stabbing. It was another student named Kellen Bismarque." Elena frowned, looking at the computer screen, shock making her eyes blank, but she didn't comment on this. Andre opened the package of M&Ms he had been given in another experiment and offered her some. "If you're a regular person, doesn't all this processing of emotions make you tired?"

"Sometimes."

"Dr. Wyman's probably seen a ton of crap in his time," Andre said. Maybe it was the Pedialyte talking, but he was feeling bold. "I was reading somewhere that he was the psychologist on the CRD case back in the day."

"Oh, yeah, but he never talks about it," Elena said, her eyes not leaving the computer as she hit ESC again.

"That must have been crazy."

"That case devastated him. Can you imagine being someone's therapist for two years only to find out they were a serial killer?"

Andre was stunned, glad for the distraction of the computer unfreezing so that Elena couldn't see his face. He had always thought that Wyman had been hired by the police to evaluate Gregory Ripley to see if he was "sane" enough to stand trial. But this detail, while bizarre, made more sense. He treated the guy for years—*that* was why he had fought for him.

He finished the survey as quickly as he could, then bounded down the stairs and outside, pulling his phone out. He and Chloe had for the past week been unsuccessfully trying to contact the former fiancée of John Fiola, but she hadn't responded. Chloe had found her home address and advocated for simply showing up—Andre thought this ill-advised. This tiny morsel of new information was the closest thing they had had to a clue since discovering Emma. Important update, he texted. Let's meet?

She responded a few seconds later, saying she would round up Charles and they could meet at his house. Interesting, Andre realized. Chloe didn't want him to know where she lived but never made it seem like that's what she was doing.

He figured he would have time to pick up a late dinner and stopped at the SAC. He had to cajole a worker to make him a burrito because they were moments from closing. Content, he ate his burrito while searching on his phone for stuff about John Fiola—ancient social media posts on sites he hadn't even heard of before, and an article from the *Daily Owl* that quoted him for a grad school social event.

Andre crumpled up his foil wrapper, but when he went to throw it in the trash he realized something was off. There was no one else in the cafeteria. There always seemed to be students there at any hour, eating or studying across from the huge display of TVs glaring news. He was alone except for the silent babbling of CNN talking about the protests, the smell of floor cleaner suddenly salient. *It's fine, just hurry up*, he told himself as pulled on his book bag. He would go outside and there would be the inevitable crowd of people and he could walk to Charles's house in safety.

He just had his hand on the door when he heard from behind him: "Hey, man."

Don't turn around. But he did, anyway. A few yards away was a big dude—like football big—you could tell even though he was wearing the same oversize Adams sweatshirt that everyone owned. He was holding up a white cord. "I think you dropped your phone charger?" he said. He was smiling, but Andre could only stare back.

Had he even brought his phone charger with him today? He didn't think he had. And millions of people had the same white iPhone charger. He committed himself to trying to memorize what the guy looked like, but he had his hood up. He was white, with brown hair and very straight teeth, and was still holding out the charger.

"Ah, no thanks, man, it's not mine."

The man cocked his head to one side. Was he even an Adams student? Or just someone who slipped into the cafeteria after hours? "You sure?" The bulky sweatshirt—he could be wearing it to conceal something, a weapon. Not that he needed one. The guy looked like he could pop Andre's head off with little effort.

"I'm good," Andre squeaked, and chanced to turn his back to flee from the building into what he hoped was a crowded campus thoroughfare.

Except this time it wasn't. Every now and then the planets aligned and somehow all students were collectively hungover, or too tired to go out, or it was drizzling and they were lazy and just wanted to watch Netflix. Through the windows of the tall academic buildings surrounding him, he could see people inside, but there was no one on the street but a lone homeless person smoking a cigarette. Andre shoved his hands into his pockets and walked quickly, hoping the man wasn't following him. No one was going to stab him in the middle of the street, right?

Why weren't there even any cars on the road? In the distance he heard a persistent siren and realized the police might have blocked nearby roads for a motorcade—that always messed with traffic. It was strange that in a city there were still occasionally places that seemed devoid of people.

It occurred to Andre that the only times he had genuinely been scared for his safety had been times when there weren't people around—not the times when there had been a crazy person on a bus or even just people sitting on the stoop when you could hear gunshots somewhere in the distance. That felt okay because there was always someone who met your eye or made a joke. He chanced what he hoped was a casual half turn around and saw that no one was behind him, at least not that he could see, but there were plenty of dark nooks to hide in between streetlights.

Then he saw a couple exit Anderson Hall ahead of him and begin to walk in the same direction. Relieved, he quickened his pace to catch up with them, but then noticed one of them half turn around and saw him. Then their pace quickened. *I'm not the bad guy here*, he thought with sad irony.

He didn't bother to try to catch up with them and they quickly turned off onto another street. He was only three blocks from Charles's when he sensed in his peripheral vision someone on the other side of the street crossing over to his side, behind him. His heart lurched. He hadn't gotten a good look at them, given the angle, other than the vague notion that they had seemed male. Part of him wanted to turn around and look, but another part of him said that this was a bad idea—walk faster. Andre did so, straining his ears, but he could barely hear anything behind him and his pulse was beating loudly in his ears. He pulled his hand from his pocket and rested it on the hilt of his hunting knife.

This absolutely can't be how I die, he thought. Caught in the horror movie cliché of someone slowly following you, all while on the verge of figuring something out. But there's one thing everyone did wrong in horror movies—even the final girl. They were, for some reason, incapable of logic or running fast without falling down. Still trying to look casual, with his other hand he pulled out his cell phone, pretending to look at it while he used the dark screen as a mirror. He could see no one behind him. They must have turned off.

He heard a noise to his right as he came to a cross street. Andre stopped and turned, his eyes struggling to adjust from the garish yellow glow of the streetlight to what seemed like the impenetrable blackness surrounding a dumpster. Was there something there? Something silently watching him? It was too quiet.

Oh HELL no, he decided, and with no further deliberation he sprinted as fast as he could, faster and with more determination than any idiot in any horror movie, not looking back, not giving himself the time to doubt what his instincts told him. He didn't falter or stop until he had reached the safe bright lights of Charles's lobby. Luckily a woman had reached the door at the same time and he followed her in, but then she hesitated with her fob out in the vestibule before the locked inner doors. "I'm sorry, I can't let you in. You'll have to call your friends if you don't live here."

He started to laugh—it hurt but it was still funny.

44

Here we were in a crisis and Charles was swimming laps. We were supposed to meet Andre soon, and it was critical that I talk to Charles before we met. The Aquatic Center, which housed the indoor pool, was pleasantly warm and humid compared to the cold air outside. Had Charles thought this out? Was it even safe to swim? There were a few people swimming laps, but I identified Charles by his showboat-y freestyle. He kick-turned off the wall, then rippled underwater for a third the length of the pool, headed in my direction. I crouched by the lip of the pool and stuck my hand in front of him as he approached. He stood up, blowing water off his face.

"Who's that?" he asked.

"Can't you see me, dum-dum?"

"Not without my contacts, but that sounds like the dulcet tones of Chloe." He plucked his goggles from his eyes and settled them in his hair.

"Come on. We need to talk before we see Andre."

He waded to the edge of the pool, then pulled himself up. He wore racing-style jammers that came to midthigh but regardless did not leave much to the imagination. He definitely had the build of a swimmer—slender, but bigger in the chest. I took advantage of his temporary blindness to do a thorough visual accounting of nearly every inch of his dripping, creamy skin.

He grabbed a towel and started to dry off. "Give me a minute to change." Charles looked over his shoulder as he approached the men's locker room. "Unless you want to help."

I showed my teeth at him.

He emerged wearing khakis and an Adams sweatshirt. "You should always wear your contacts in case something happens. You'd think you'd learn that after what happened to Kristen," I advised. He held the gym door open for me with sarcastic flamboyance. He always grew sullen when I brought up Kristen.

"What did you want to talk about?" he asked. We headed toward his apartment, where Andre would meet us.

"I've been considering your Will theory, however ridiculous. I'm taking it seriously, but we can't tell Andre about him."

"Why not?"

Because then there's one more person who knows I have a motive to kill him? "Because it's *private*. We'll make something up." As we walked, I prepped mentally—Charles seemed set on Trevor or, more ridiculously, Will being our little hunter, which meant that I had to get Andre to think it was Emma to buy me a few more days. This shouldn't be too difficult because Andre was now seriously considering that the twins were secretly Wyman's love children. Trevor seemed the most likely to me, which meant I had to distract everyone from actually nailing him until after Phase Four of Will.

Andre met us just outside of Charles's apartment, looking sweaty. "What's your problem?" I asked.

"I thought someone was following me."

"Welcome to my day-to-day life," I said as I pulled the door open after Charles unlocked it.

Charles got us some beers and we positioned ourselves on his couch. Apparently, Andre wanted to chug his entire beer before getting to work, which I thought was a little dramatic. "We each have updates," I said. "You start, Andre."

"Let's go back to the beginning with Wyman," Andre said finally. "Almost twenty years ago, he worked on the case doing in-depth interviews with CRD after he was arrested. I couldn't understand what made him argue against the death penalty, which was what Virginia was trying for." I nodded. "But come to find out—and Elena just told me this—that Wyman was actually CRD's therapist for *years* before Ripley got arrested. What if he knew?" Andre said.

"Knew that the guy was killing?" Charles asked.

"What if Ripley was Patient Zero? Wyman's first guinea pig on a method to treat psychopaths. Except things go horribly wrong, and the last thing he wants to do is admit it."

"Psychologists are legally required to report it when a client threatens someone," Charles said. He was already trying to catch a sympathetic eye from me but I didn't look at him. I wasn't sure exactly what I thought of Wyman, but it seemed Charles had a soft spot for him. He was too attached after two years of being coddled in therapy by the man to see the possibility that he wasn't an entirely benign do-gooder.

"They're *supposed* to. But what if Ripley talked about having killing urges and Wyman thought he could develop some process to stop him, that this would be groundbreaking research," Andre said. "Or what if Ripley said stuff and Wyman didn't take him seriously? You know how we all talk big in therapy— I did this, I did that."

Charles frowned. "I don't see how all of this, which happened before we were born, even matters—we're getting hunted *right* now. And we've only got three real suspects." He held up a finger. "Emma, who I know—"

"What do you mean you know Emma?" Andre asked.

"He knows Emma," I said.

"I lied to you," Charles admitted, not sounding contrite. "I didn't trust you guys so when you asked I pretended I didn't know her. Yes, she's in the program—she's a junior. We've…interacted. She's kind of a weird person, but I can't see her being a serial killer."

"We don't know that!" I interrupted. "We haven't accounted for her whereabouts."

"I can work on her, but it's not her," Charles said. "Then we have Trevor, Chloe's little friend."

Andre looked at me, surprised. Miserable, I recounted how I had been fooled by Trevor the "RA," and Charles gave an abbreviated history of the cyberattack, and I got angry all over again. I hated being made a fool of. Andre looked more alarmed as Charles filled him in about the attack at Kristen's house. "Trevor is a person who is sadistic and misogynistic, and has really dangerous capabilities. He's been in the program for two years—maybe Wyman said something that set him off. Psychopaths can get like that—hold grudges forever over some minor infraction," Charles finished, then he fell silent. Then I realized Andre was staring at me. Uh-oh, he was upset about something.

"Chloe tried to stab him and you tried to shoot him," Andre observed. "Still, he got away. Who's the third suspect?" he asked.

Charles resisted looking at me. "There's another student at Adams, a junior named Will Bachman. He's not in the program that we know of, and I don't know what his motive could be, but that doesn't mean there might not be one." Andre looked at me for confirmation, but I stared down at my hands as I picked viciously at a hangnail. "I can't really get into it," Charles said, hesitating like he was reluctant to speak, "because of how I got the information, but basically he's a bad character. He—"

"Bad in what sense?"

"He's in my frat. I know that he committed at least one violent crime when he was young. He lives near where Chloe got attacked. He's talked about Kristen, about how hot she is and he'd move on her if she weren't my girlfriend. He's an athlete, so we know he can move fast."

Andre was still staring at me and I knew why. We had been working more closely together, just the two of us, with me telling him not to trust Charles, and here I was leaving him out of the loop on a bunch of stuff I had figured out with Charles. I needed to get back on his good side.

"Anyhow," Charles said, "I think we should focus our attention on Trevor. I'm thinking of going to the police with the whole story, the hacking from last year, too."

"The police aren't going to help us," I said, looking at Andre, psychically telling him to agree with me. "What are you going to say, that we're all a bunch of psychopaths but we think this other psychopath did it?"

"Yes," Charles said.

"We need to get proof," I said.

"How would you plan on getting proof?"

"The old-fashioned way," I said. "We spy on them, we milk them for information any way we can. I'll take Trevor—he already wants to be friends. You said Emma likes you, so set up a date."

"I can get Will, too," Charles said, gathering up the empty beer bottles. I glanced up at him, telling him with my eyes, *No, you will not. I will handle Will.*

"In the meantime, let's talk about security. Namely, yours sucks if someone was able to crawl through your window," I said.

"You let someone take a picture of you while you were boning Chad!" Charles retorted. "Kristen and I are staying at Fort Hunt. You can't just wander onto the estate, and my dad's guys are there all the time." What a bunch of rich assholes. Here Andre and I were suffering while the two of them were probably drinking mai tais delivered by a butler. "I can give you a gun," he offered Andre suddenly.

"You never offered me a gun!" I yelled.

"I have a couple pistols. If you know how to use one, I can lend one to you," Charles continued, ignoring me.

Andre looked torn. "No… I don't know anything about guns and don't want to be caught with one. I could just stay with my parents."

"And put your family at risk?" he suggested. "You could stay here. I have a second bedroom and the doorman here seriously doesn't let anyone in."

Why was Charles suddenly being so generous to Andre? I narrowed my eyes at him and he smiled at me.

Andre, too, was suspicious, or at least not gullible. "I guess if it comes up…and I need to," he said in the way people do to be polite. He accepted a key chain from Charles that had a fob for the front door and a key on it.

I got up. "Well, fun times, but I have stuff to do." I actually just wanted to get away from them both before they started asking invasive questions about Will.

"Remember what I said about Trevor," Charles said when I was almost to the door.

"You're cute when you're anxious."

"Be careful."

Screw being careful.

45

Day 5

There was an alcove in the Humanities Building where I liked to sit with my computer to do work in between classes—the clock was still ticking for Will. Namely, narrowing down locations for Phase Four, the final phase. One option was somewhere really crowded and chaotic—like the frat house—but this would necessitate some method of murder that might not be reliable, like poisoning, or a single stab-and-run. I needed it to take a while for the body to be found. I wanted a place where I could both kill and hide him, because transporting a body wasn't practical—no car and no amount of yogalates was going to make lugging around one hundred and seventy pounds of dead weight easy.

Rock Creek Park was of course one of the first places I thought of. The park was DC's version of New York's Central Park—1,700-something acres of green stubbornly sitting on prime real estate. While there were various places to do activities there—bike paths, trails, and an equestrian center—there were also expanses of forest. I knew for a fact that Rock Creek might be a good choice because a two-second Google search revealed that many murders had already occurred there. People—mostly women, of course—who went jogging and never came home. It was tempting, but the main problem was that it was fall. I wanted to set Will on fire, but if there were dry leaves everywhere, there could be a massive conflagration, and that would only bring *more* attention, not less.

No, I had to find somewhere equally secluded, but fire-friendly.

I winnowed it down to a construction site and the National Arboretum, which I had just checked out yesterday in person. The arboretum had massive expanses of unoccupied land filled with trails, plant exhibits, and fields of grass dotted with trees. Most interestingly it had a bizarre installation: a careful arrangement of the original twenty-two columns from the Capitol Building, built in the 1800s but eventually moved to the arboretum when they were replaced with more architecturally sound columns. The site looked like the ruins of a Grecian temple, possibly the perfect place for a burnt human sacrifice. I was concerned, though, with how far away it was from campus, and I wasn't sure if it had security guards at night. It probably did because the arboretum also had a collection of bonsai trees that must have been worth a lot of money.

I got an alert for a mood log: it asked me what I was doing, and because there was no option for "scheming" I picked *Studying.* I still had fifteen minutes before class started. I scrolled mindlessly through Instagram before I saw something that made me choke.

It was a post from Chad featuring him holding a banana to his head like it was a phone.

Hey, peeps! Still collecting phones for the Women's Shelter! Any cell phone, any condition. No chargers necessary.

Is that phone low carb? someone commented.

I shoved my stuff in my bag and tore down the hall, drawing stares and not caring, then waited impatiently in the elevator with my phone out, ready to dial Chad. Yes—call, not text! I needed his undivided attention. And I needed to see him before Will saw that post, assuming he was smart enough to figure out what it could possibly mean.

I sprinted down the street toward the SAE house. It was 4:35. Will got out of a poli-sci lecture at 4:45, if he had even gone to class today. At this point, I had just been biding my time—I didn't think I was going to get the video, and was making the final preparations for Will, waiting for the crazy day of protests. Just yesterday the *Post* was saying that Airbnbs all over the city were sold out, rented by protestors for the event.

The front door was open. I burst into the house and two boys playing a video game barely even looked at me. "Chad!"

"In the kitchen!" he called. I ran in there and he was making what looked like a thirty-seven-egg omelet. "So you think you left your phone here?" He was wearing a muscle shirt and a puzzled smile.

"Yes, at the last party." He led me to a room behind the kitchen that held an assortment of broken appliances. There was a huge box in there, halfway filled with cell phones. I began to paw through it.

"What's it look like?" Chad asked, stooping to help me.

"It's an iPhone 4 with a white circular sticker on the back. The bottom right corner is dented in." I would know that phone anywhere—I had memorized every detail of it.

I pawed some more and then—there it was! Still with the white STX lacrosse sticker on it. Will must have left the phone with a bunch of junk when he lived at the house during his first two years. I grabbed it and made sure Chad wouldn't see the sticker. I then leaped at him, throwing my arms around his neck, nearly knocking him over. "You're the best!"

"Am I?" he said, smiling winningly. "Stay for supper. I'm making a frittata."

"Rain check!" I replied, pecking him on the mouth before I ran out the door.

Back in the privacy of my room, my door shut, I shoved the iPhone 4 charger that I had bought online into the phone and waited eagerly for the phone to charge. Luckily that particular model didn't have the fingerprint ID function—otherwise, I would have had to perform minor surgery on Will. Not that I wouldn't be good at it. Impatiently, I stared at the phone until it was charged enough to turn on. I pressed the home button and the familiar icons appeared in front of me. First, I made sure it was on airplane mode. Even though Will had probably deactivated it years ago, you can never play it too safe.

It was not hard to find the video because I knew the date when it was recorded. Did I watch it? As if I needed anything else to fully confirm what lay ahead for Will?

I had the video—it was clearly him and it was clearly me.

There is no statute of limitations for rape in New Jersey. But no, I was never going to endure the slow grind of a court case where people would troll through my Instagram for "scandalous" pictures of me having the nerve to look attractive or have fun with my friends on a night out; where people would question if I was actually traumatized because clearly I'm a slut with straight A's; where the question wouldn't be "What happened to Michelle?" but "Why didn't you…?" Instead, the narrative would be about how I had the nerve to ruin Will's life, his good grades and his lacrosse, and about how every woman is asking for it. Fuck. That. Shit.

The day it happened, I didn't go to the police, or my clueless mom. I stayed at home and decided that, one day, I would kill Will Bachman. It was just a feather of an idea back then, floating, not as solid as it would eventually become. No—that would come after hours of research, experimenting, self-defense classes. Will left for high school and I was left in junior high. Afterward, we went to separate high schools. Will moved through the world for the next five years never thinking about me or what he did. I was going to make sure that those were the last two things he thought of just as he died. Now, with the video, I was ready.

46

Charles stood in the crowded entryway of Ted's Bulletin and looked for Emma, who had texted him that she was already here. The stools at the bar were all taken and a crowd of people clustered to the left of him, waiting in the separate line to make purchases from the bakery at the front. He noticed that Emma was standing outside the restaurant on the other side of the glass. He waved, then observed her glazed stare. She was watching through the glass as a pair of white-capped bakers quickly piped filling onto pastry dough to eventually form homemade Pop-Tarts.

God, what a weirdo, he thought. He stepped toward the window, pasting a smile onto his face and waving. Emma noticed him. She didn't smile back, but walked toward the revolving door and came inside. "There you are!" Charles said cheerfully.

"I was waiting," she said.

He went to the hostess, who asked them what type of table they wanted. "Booth," Charles said immediately. A booth provided some degree of privacy.

They sat across from each other and were handed oversize menus. He peeked above the top of his menu to study her. She looked tired with big circles under her eyes. "Have you been all right?" he asked, putting his menu down.

"What do you mean?"

"You look tired." He leaned forward, smiling ruefully. "Sorry—I know girls hate it when you say that. But...with everything going on."

Emma looked at her menu without saying anything. Charles tried to imagine her wielding a knife. Was it as simple as her hating Kellen or Michael for some minor offense? Or maybe she had had a crush on them? *What if she gets a crush on you?* he could hear the teasing voice of Chloe saying in his head. Charles was fairly certain he was on Emma's good side. While she apparently did not function like most other people and answer texts within a day or two, she did finally respond to him and say she would meet up. Emma was exactly the sort of person who completely ignored social invitations when she felt like it. "They have alcoholic milkshakes here," she said.

"Yes, let's get one," Charles said.

"I'm not twenty-one."

"Don't worry about it," he said.

"That's all I want," she added quietly, putting her menu down.

Charles ordered meat loaf and a Thin Mint milkshake. "It's just... I haven't seen you in a while, and everything's been so crazy."

Emma seemed to be staring behind him where a screen was showing a classic movie in black-and-white. "With those boys dying," she said.

"Yes," he said, trying to prompt her. "I mean, isn't it scary?"

"People die," she said. "And sometimes there's nothing you can do."

"I guess... It can make you feel like everything's out of control, you know?"

"Or it's under the wrong control," she said.

The milkshake came in a tall glass with the remainder in a

giant steel tumbler frosty with condensation. Charles dumped a third of his into the tumbler and pushed it across the table for Emma. Rather than bringing the tumbler up to her mouth she bowed her head, not breaking eye contact with him, and suckled from the straw. Charles thought of a life-size bee feeding upon nectar, its black eyes blank with insect thoughts.

She paused to poke her straw deeper into the tumbler.

"Aren't you scared?" he asked.

"I'm not like you, Charles," she said. He wondered what she meant exactly. That she didn't feel fear, or something else?

"Kellen wasn't a bad guy."

"Is that one of the dead guys? I never met him. Was he a friend?" she asked.

His meat loaf arrived. Charles smoothed down his hair. "Not exactly. He was kind of loud. I prefer people who are a little more introverted."

Emma's eyes dropped to the milkshake.

Charles leaned forward. "You like me, Emma, don't you?" he asked. Her eyes were moving across a constellation of points on the table. She seemed to be struggling to answer. "You didn't answer my text!" he teased.

"I did!"

"Not for five days."

"Was I supposed to respond sooner?"

"I wanted to hang out with you," he said playfully. "You're my only friend like me." Her ears turned pink. He dug into his meat loaf. "Don't you feel like we're kindred souls?" She seemed more pained than pleased by this. "Or is that slot already taken by your sister?"

"I wouldn't say she's a kindred soul."

"I always thought it would be cool to have a twin."

"We shared a womb."

For the love of God, please say something useful! "You must be really close."

"Kind of," she said, stabbing at her shake with her straw. "Not really. She should be nicer. She didn't want to come to DC, but she didn't get into Berkeley and because of me we could both afford college."

"What do you mean?" Charles asked, pretending to be distracted by his mashed potatoes.

"Because she's a control in the study, they cover her college at American, too. She said she's going to take her half of the signing bonus and open a business after we graduate."

"Wyman pays for Megan's college, too?"

"I never told you her name," Emma said, looking at him.

"Yes, you did," Charles said confidently. "Isn't American pretty expensive?"

She shrugged. "It's not free money. She still has to come in to get MRIs to compare her brain to mine or whatever, and for group therapy."

"The two of you? Together?"

"Yes, it's very fun." He couldn't tell if she was joking.

"Well, I haven't decided what to do with my signing bonus," Charles said, having no idea if he even received one, or for what amount it had been. His parents handled all the financial stuff.

"I was thinking of doing a gap year to travel and take photos. Twenty thousand can go pretty far in Asia."

Emma stepped out of the booth to go to the bathroom, leaving her purse behind. Charles casually rooted through it, imagining that if anyone saw him they would think him a boyfriend looking for a spare tissue. There was nothing in there but a pamphlet for an exhibition at the Museum of Women in the Arts and a plastic key chain shaped like a ghost. When she returned he carefully tried to ask her where she had been the nights of the murders. The best he could uncover about her whereabouts the night of Michael's murder was figuring out that she had been in a photography lab. He didn't think he could directly ask about where she was during Kellen's death, too, without arousing her suspicion.

Charles texted Chloe and Andre of his success immediately as he walked out of the restaurant, expecting accolades, but no one answered. He pouted, heading toward Shaw Tavern, where Kristen was having dinner with friends. He had been encouraging her to be with friends as often as possible, which hadn't been hard because she, like many other students, were spooked about the murders, still following every bread crumb about the investigation.

Would Kristen be jealous if he told her he just had dinner with Emma, or would she be proud of him for being kind enough to spend time with a lonely girl? He shoved his hands deep into the pockets of his peacoat, feeling the familiar grip of his Glock. Even though he had already taken the gun, he had asked his father to borrow it the morning after Kristen's break-in. "God, take it, take the shotgun if you want," his father had said, not even looking away from the mirror as he tied a perfect Windsor knot.

Charles paused at a red light, then saw a familiar figure across the street, half a block away. "Chloe!" he called, but she didn't hear him. He jogged to catch up to her. "I texted you—I just met with Emma!"

"Good," she said, sounding distracted, not stopping to talk. She was wearing an oversize book bag. He walked with her.

"Slow down, let's talk."

"I'm in the middle of something."

She had never brushed him off before. She was always posturing in one way or another—this was the first time she seemed genuinely preoccupied.

Will, Charles realized. Maybe Will had finally told her he didn't have the video.

"Tomorrow, then," he said.

"I'm busy."

"Busy with what?"

"*School,*" she said, annoyed. "The *protests.*"

"Since when do you go to protests?" She ignored him. "Did you talk to Will? About the video?" Silence. "Do you want me to press him? I could get him drunk, ask him what he was doing the night of the murders."

"Don't bother," she said flatly.

"You're not going to...*do* something, are you?" he asked.

She was about to turn at the street corner and walk away from him but he reached out, catching her elbow. He half expected a teasing come-on, but also half expected the impatient look she gave him. "Chloe...sometimes you think for a long time that you want something and that you'll be happy when you get it, but usually it doesn't turn out that way."

She sighed. "I don't have time to give you relationship advice, Charles."

47

Day 0

It was time. My plan had been set in motion, but then there had been an unexpected development. Yesterday, Will messaged me on the dating app. I have the phone and will give it to you. Really? That's funny considering THAT I WAS HOLDING HIS OLD PHONE IN MY HAND. That lying little shit. Let me see it, I messaged back, curious as to what he was scheming. He sent back a picture of a generic iPhone 4. Does he really think I'm that stupid?

I told him we would make the exchange tomorrow night, and that I would delete Snapchat off my phone in front of him. He sent back a bunch of question marks asking why we couldn't do it today. (Because Day 1 is too early, dummy!) I said tomorrow at 11 p.m., and that I would message him the exact geocoordinates when the time came, and that if he came with anyone else or told anyone, I would not delete Snapchat and little Davey might get a visit from his online girlfriend.

I streamed the news on my computer as I got ready. Adams had already sent out messages every day this week with security alerts—some of the protests in the lead-in to the big one had gotten violent after dark. The police were out in full force and even yesterday there was a palpable increase in out-of-towners carrying signs. Today, almost every channel showed the clogged streets of downtown DC.

I got dressed in black clothing I had gotten from a thrift store—it smelled as if they hadn't been washed. I slicked my hair back into a ponytail with gel and bobby-pinned the hell out of it, then secured a tight skullcap. I had leather gloves and men's sneakers that were half a size too big. Tucked away in my backpack were two Duralogs, a bottle of lighter fluid, my baggie of hair and DNA, and a couple other treats for Will.

I left behind my smartwatch and set up my laptop to stream Netflix while I was gone—it would do that for a couple hours, and Yessica would be able to hear it through the closed door of my bedroom. Then out the window and down the fire escape I went. I couldn't afford to have the hunter follow me, so I took special care: I darted down alleys, disappeared into buildings, then out different exits, then ducked into a Metro station, less because I needed to go there than because it was a mess of escalators on different levels. Eventually I got into a cab and had them drop me off a ten-minute walk from my desired location, arriving two hours before Will would, and an hour before I would even message him the location. The whole drive over I could hear police sirens and helicopters from local media trying to film the protests.

Ultimately this site beat out the other contender—the arboretum—the moment I saw it in person. The McMillan Sand Filtration Site was built in the early 1900s, back when the city got water from an aqueduct and used sand to filter it instead of chemicals, at least until World War II. Now the massive lot was fenced off and abandoned, the supposed plans to develop the land at a standstill for probably boring reasons.

I waited until there was no traffic, then scaled the chain-link fence. It was lined with green material on the inside, which made the site feel closed off from the rest of the world from the inside. It seemed strangely isolated in the middle of a city where space was at a premium.

The lot was an entire city block of overgrown grass and weeds that were black in the darkness. Giant brick silos that had once held sand stood in a line, some covered in dark ivy, each with an arched entryway cut into the center. I went through one entryway and down a staircase that led to the subterranean cavern where the sand used to filter the water.

When I had first visited, sunlight had beamed down from an opening aboveground, showing off the vaulted ceilings, which curved down into regularly spaced columns. At night, it was as black as a catacomb, the sand cold beneath my sneakers. Belowground, isolated, quiet—it was the perfect place.

I hid my bag behind a column and set to work, spreading the hairs around, and taking the tampon—wet with a little water in a baggie—and rubbing it all over my leather gloves. It didn't matter how careful I was or how much research I did: if you kill someone, they can catch you with a single spot of blood. I had no idea how much of my own DNA could possibly be transferred during this whole thing, and I didn't want to take chances.

When I messaged Will the geocoordinates he said, Okay. But then twenty minutes later, he was confused, standing outside the fence. I messaged him to climb the fence and to head to the underground part through any entrance—he'd be able to see me. I stood behind a column, crouching, and watched as the bright light from his cell phone bounced down the stairs and into the chamber. "What the hell?" I could hear him say—he was facing the wrong direction.

"Over here," I called. I had set a small disposable LED light on the ground. He came toward it, predictably.

"What the hell? Why'd you make me come all the way out here? What is this place?"

"Don't be a baby." That's what he said to me that night.

As soon as he was bending over the LED light I moved, zapping him with the stun gun. He gave a short scream and fell to the ground, shaking. I squatted beside him as he cursed at me, but I kept the gun near his head. "There's something fucking wr-wrong with you! I brought the stupid phone, now leave me alone!" He dug it from his pocket and with some difficulty threw it into the sand.

I pretended to examine the phone, making sure he could see my face. "You know what's funny? I'm pretty sure *this is your phone*," I said, pulling out the real phone.

"If you had it all the time, why the *fuck*—?"

"You dropped it somewhere in the SAE house, you idiot."

"Fine you ha-have your stupid phone. Are you going to leave my brother alone?"

"Once we're done here, I'll delete everything and stop talking to Davey." He looked skeptical. "I promise. I just want you to do one thing for me." I gestured for him to sit, then put the real phone down in front of him, with the video ready to play. "I want you to watch this."

"Wh—" I stunned him again. He screamed and fell over. "Okay, okay!"

I stood behind where he lay on his side in the dark, watching him rather than the video. He didn't say or do anything—he was clearly waiting for it to be over. I looked at his face, realizing that it would be the last time that I, or anyone, would see him alive. He didn't understand the significance of the moment and I couldn't point it out to him. I couldn't give a final villain speech the way they do in movies because it would destroy the element of surprise. There was no background music or camera zooming in. This was real life. In real life, we don't get to edit out the painful parts.

I held the coiled jump rope in one hand and moved closer behind him as the video was a few seconds away from finishing. I looped the jump rope around his neck, shoved him into the sand, putting my foot on his head for leverage. He struggled, bucking, making the mistake that most people make when they're being strangled: they bring their hands to their neck.

If you occlude the carotid artery, the lack of oxygen to the brain can render a person unconscious within ten to fifteen seconds—it's this period of time where they struggle. But once they're unconscious, this doesn't mean they're dead: the heart is still beating, the brain could still recover. There are a number of ways to die from ligature strangulation, or garroting. Cardiac arrhythmia from putting pressure on the carotid artery nerve ganglion. Obstructing the blood flow to the brain via the carotid arteries. Obstructing the jugular veins so the brain can't return venous blood, creating a backup. Forcing pressure on the larynx to restrict air flow to the lung, causing asphyxia. I held the jump rope tight and counted to one hundred just to be sure, my arms and shoulders burning.

I let him go and his head flopped silently into the sand. I would have preferred to check his pulse but didn't want to leave a single Chloe cell on him. I watched him—he wasn't breathing. I had to move quickly. I took his wallet and his phone and put them in my backpack. Next, I lay the two Duralogs on top of him, covered everything with lighter fluid, and lit him up. The state the body would be in would buy me some time. I imagine they would eventually look at dental records. By then, I would have already framed our mystery killer and Will would be the official next victim. I opened his phone (same stupid password) and deleted the dating app just to be on the safe side.

I had a million things to do—and fast—but suddenly it was as if my body balked at the idea of moving. I found myself abruptly, almost violently, sitting down in the sand, my gaze directed at the fire, which was starting to smell.

I had done it. Six years of planning and research all for this. I had succeeded, and Will was dead. I almost couldn't believe it despite the sight in front of me. I had won and he had lost.

I couldn't help thinking about Michelle, the former me, the twelve-year-old me sitting alone in her bedroom the day it happened, the beginning of an idea forming in her head. It was almost as if I could reach into the fire and talk to her through time and tell her, *Yes, I did right by you*, setting her free.

I pulled out Will's phone again and tapped on the video, which was paused on the last frame, an unintelligible blur of darkness. It wouldn't matter because I was about to destroy his phone, but I hit Delete, anyway. It was over—I never had to think of Will Bachman again, at least once I tied up all these loose ends.

With that thought, I was finally able to get up and get moving. Half my murder accessories, including his phone, my burner, and the clothes I was wearing, would end up in the Potomac River, while the other half would get shoved into the garbage at the back of Yum's Chinese restaurant. Speaking of which, it was starting to smell like burnt barbecue.

I left while he was still burning. I had chosen the location wisely, because he could burn for however long without any risk of setting anything on fire or drawing attention with the smoke and smell. I scaled the fence with still-aching arms, listening to the sounds of police sirens downtown. It would take me a while to get to my dump locations. I ate a LUNA Bar and kept moving.

48

The first thing I did when I woke up the next day was to check the *Washington Post* website. Most of it was dominated with coverage of the protests and riots. Even in the Metro section, there was no mention of a mysterious human barbecue. The closest I could do to checking on Will that wouldn't look strange given my internet habits was looking at Chad's and Charles's feeds—nothing about Will going missing.

For all her basicness, Kristen was a good photographer and had posted a picture of Charles standing on a street filled with autumn leaves, smiling. You couldn't tell there was a series of murders going on, or that Charles was secretly meeting with us behind his girlfriend's back to scheme—he just looked handsome and stylish. I felt a pang of something weird and tried to push it away without really thinking about it. I didn't like what he said to me in the street. It's almost like he could tell I was about to do something.

Just then, someone tagged me on Instagram. My mouth went dry when I saw who it was: Pinprick52. It was the same account that had posted the stalker picture of me sitting in French class.

No doubt, the same person who had taken the picture of me sleeping, too. When I saw the picture, I gasped. It was me, from last night, half a block from the Sand Filtration Site, still wearing all my black gear. It must have been after Will but before I dumped everything and changed clothes.

I was followed.

How? I had been so careful.

Whoever they were, they must know what I had done. The picture wasn't close up enough that anyone could tell it was me necessarily. I clicked on the Pinprick52 account and pored over their feed again, looking at their more recent pictures and scrolling backward. That picture of a bench—in the far corner you could make out a bronze bust: one of the statues of John Adams on campus. That bench was right outside Tyler—Andre's dorm. Then the inside of Albertson Hall—I recognized that hall from walking down it so often to get coffee, hoping I might run into Charles using one of the piano rooms. Further back was a picture of a building that seemed vaguely familiar, but I couldn't place. In the background was a bodega, which I quickly looked up on Google maps. The bodega was near the Center for Imaging, where the panel study did its MRI studies—where Kellen had been killed. Further back was a picture of a group of boys leaving the gym. I zoomed in as best I could. There in the back, with his distinctive black cowlick, was Michael Boonark.

I knew what this account was. The Golden State Killer took random trinkets from the houses of people he killed. CRD kept locks of hair. I never understood this—they basically created a dossier of evidence against themselves for the sake of what— pride?

Pinprick52 was documenting their work in real time. Keeping a portfolio. And they had just tagged me. It was an act of aggression. Little did they know, I was the wrong person to target now that I could give them my full attention.

49

"Have you seen Will?"

Charles was so distracted by the girl who had just walked into the frat house that he barely heard Chad, even though he was yelling. The house was filled with a crush of students having a Quiet Riot party. Chad nudged him with his Michelob Ultra and repeated the question. "Will?" Charles repeated. "Did he say he was coming?"

"No," Chad said, frowning. "We were supposed to watch the game yesterday."

Charles shrugged. "You know how flakey he is." He excused himself, his eyes set across the room on the slight brunette standing at the Ping-Pong table talking to another girl.

Not eight hours ago, Charles had been heading to the psych building intending to fish for information about Trevor from Wyman or one of the RAs when he had seen this girl run crying from Wyman's office, brushing past him without seeing him. He feigned concern to Elena, who had told him that the RA, Adelei, had forgotten to lock the lab the night before and Elena had found it open early this morning.

Charles looked around the frat party, spotting Kristen standing outside at the bonfire with her friends. He pushed his way
through the crowd and across the sticky floor. Adelei was by
the table of drinks, chugging some water. Would she recognize
him from the study, though? He had never directly been alone
in a room with her, but had seen her a couple times in the lab.

Charles sidled up next to her. "Hey," he said. She turned and
he smiled at her. "I'm Charles."

"You're that guy." She was drunk. Good—that would make
things easier. Someone in the back of the house was blaring
away on a vuvuzela to shrieking laughter. "President guy," she
continued.

"Yes, I am." She wavered on her feet. "Why don't you sit
down?"

They sat on one of the living room couches. She looked at
him with drunk attraction. "You look familiar," he asked. "Are
you a psych major?"

"Yes!" A flicker crossed her face and her eyes teared.

"What's wrong?" He tilted his head sympathetically.

"I got in trouble at work today. I was supposed to lock up and
I *did* and they think I didn't."

"Maybe you forgot."

"No!" she shouted. "I know I did because I'm OCD. I lock
it and have to touch it five times to make sure."

"Maybe one of the five times you accidentally unlocked it."

"Aha!" She poked his chest. "I have a fail-safe. Part of the
ritual includes walking away and coming back to double-check
it—twice."

Well, that seemed thorough. She probably *had* locked the door.
Then someone else had come in with their own key, or broken in, and accidentally left the door open afterward. "Maybe
someone took your keys," Charles suggested.

"No. I always have them."

"Always?"

"I mean, except at the gym, but I lock them in my locker."

Lockers weren't that hard to open, he reasoned. Adelei's head was bobbing. "Did you drink the green punch?" he asked.

"Yes. No. Is there something in it?"

"Everclear. Grain alcohol."

"Ohhh."

Charles opened his mouth, but then his phone rang, a picture of Darth Vader appearing on his screen. His father calling, probably mad or wanting Charles to appear at some boring event as evidence of good Portmont genes. He sent the call to voicemail and squeezed through the crowded house, hoping for some fresh air and the ability to think outside.

Someone had gotten into the office. If someone got into the office, what exactly would they get access to? Chloe and Andre had been able to get into the office somehow, but had been stymied by the computer. But someone tech savvy, *someone like Trevor*, could easily figure out how to access anything he wanted if he broke in. He could have their addresses, their parents' phone numbers…

Charles's eyes fell upon the black face of his smartwatch. He vaguely recalled when he signed up for the program that location data was only logged when they did a mood log. But that did mean that there was broader location data out there *somewhere*, much in the same way his iPhone creepily knew his favorite locations or where he liked to use certain apps. Michael had been killed while he was alone, and Kellen must have been force-fed buckshot at some opportune time with no one else around. Chloe had been attacked in Will's basement and this same person had known that Charles was sleeping at Kristen's the night they were broken into. Which meant that either this killer had an uncanny knack of knowing exactly when to follow someone for them to be vulnerable, or they literally knew where the panel members were at all times.

Charles immediately began undoing the strap on his watch. He could leave it on a taxicab headed somewhere. He could throw it into the Potomac or plant it on another student. He would have to answer to Wyman and Elena eventually, but he could come up with some excuse.

Just then, he saw Derek teetering across the lawn, holding a forty of Steel Reserve. "Dude! Help me with this!" Charles called to him.

Derek was the tech savvy one at SAE. He said it was easy to turn off location tracking on the watch. Only this turned out to not be exactly true, because the settings had been disabled. Drunk, Derek wobbled into the house and to his computer upstairs to hook the watch up to adjust the settings some other way. Charles watched carefully so he could tell Andre and Chloe how to do the same. He thanked Derek, then headed back toward the front of the house. He sat on the steps, took out his phone, and texted Andre and Chloe about what the RA had told him, and to disable their location tracking, including brief instructions.

Andre responded immediately with, Doing it now! but Chloe didn't respond.

Something tugged at the corner of Charles's mind. He had texted Chloe last night with an invite to the party and she hadn't responded, when normally her response would have been something teasing or to demand a pull-aside to talk about the hunter. Not responding at all wasn't like her. From his position on the stairs, Charles could see Chad sitting on the couch, feeding Adelei some much needed water. Good old Chad, the only person on earth actually attentive enough to notice that Will was missing. Will—when had been the last time Charles had actually seen him? *Chloe, please tell me you didn't do something stupid*, Charles thought.

50

Elena jumped a little when a notification at the bottom of her screen popped up. She quickly clicked on the email and saw that her proposal had been accepted for the European Association for Behavioral and Cognitive Therapies Congress. "Yes!" she whispered to herself, then opened a fresh email to Mai, her fiancée. I got in to EABCT! Partially subsidized trip to Dublin next year?! She was about to click Send when she felt a strange sensation of being watched.

She turned in her chair, then with a small start saw that Trevor was standing in the open doorway of her office. Just lurking there, staring. She felt the hair on the back of her neck stand up. He was dressed in dark clothing and had his thumbs tucked under the straps of his book bag. How long had he been there, just *looking at her*? "Did you need something?" she asked politely.

That was the thing—you had to be polite sometimes when what you really wanted to be was curt. Because if you existed as a woman in the world and were anything but polite you were rude, uppity, a bitch, stuck-up, a cunt, the list went on. Lately her ability to be endlessly patient was wearing thin.

"I have an appointment with Dr. Wyman," Trevor said quietly. Trevor had always unnerved her. She had interacted with plenty of clients who required varying degrees of treatment in her life as a grad student, but Trevor was the only one who genuinely bothered her in a personal way. She had even interviewed violent offenders in prison who seemed more sympathetic.

She smiled shallowly. "He'll be with you shortly," she said. She got up and closed the door as gently but as quickly as she could. Furious, she turned back to her computer and opened a new email.

Leonard,
I thought we'd agreed that I would be getting a heads-up when Trevor would be coming in for sessions. I just found him standing outside my office, and if it's 4:20, I'm guessing he doesn't actually have an appointment with you until 4:30.

She hit Send right away. She texted Mai and worked for two more hours, wanting to make sure that she wouldn't be leaving until well after Trevor was gone. It was dark outside by the time Elena poked her head out of her office. Leonard's door was open and the office was dark. Elena gathered her things and headed outside.

Architecturally, the psychology building was beautiful with its turrets and old windows, but in the darkness of night, bathed by the yellow light of streetlamps, it was creepy. Luckily, Mai was early and soon a Honda Civic turned onto the street and came to a stop. "You won't believe Leonard," Elena said as soon as she closed her door.

"What?" Mai asked, her dark eyes wide. "I got you a celebratory snack," she said, putting a paper bag with an empanada inside it on Elena's lap. A woman after her heart, Mai understood that Elena was always ravenous and sometimes hangry after work, which occasionally spoiled plans to cook a nice meal together.

"I specifically asked Leonard to give me a heads-up any time this one particular client is coming in."

"Oh, the creepy one?"

Trevor had proven himself to be significantly more difficult in sessions with Elena than with Leonard last year, which, much to her secret relief, had led to Leonard deciding that either he would see Trevor alone, or they would see him together. Trevor had spent much of his sessions with Elena smirking, attempting to ask personal questions or trying to impress her with his intelligence about everything. Leonard had explained the change to him in person, and Elena could only hope that it hadn't made Trevor angry somehow. She had caught him lingering once or twice around the office since then. "Yeah. And of course he forgot. I mean, he was really nice when I first brought it up, but he always forgets because he just can't see it."

"Yeah," Mai said. "It's kind of hard to explain your girl spidey sense."

"I mean, hello, it's in *The Gift of Fear*. When I say this person makes me uncomfortable, can you just take me seriously? I said it because I meant it!"

"Did they find out who left the lab unlocked?"

When they had first met at a grad student mixer, Elena's research had been something that made her seem cool to Mai, who liked true crime and never missed an episode of *Dateline*. But reality hit when their relationship became more serious and Mai started asking if Elena's field of study could actually invite danger into their lives.

"One of the RAs. Probably an honest accident, but with everything going on, everyone's on edge. Well, I have news on that front." Elena paused to bite into the empanada, which was a salteña, her favorite.

The sounds of sirens blaring could be heard from down the

street. Mai sighed loudly as two policemen on motorcycles appeared, holding out their arms to stop traffic. When there was a
motorcade the police always arrived suddenly to block off traffic
to make way for the parade of armored sedans and limos—you
were never sure who was inside or how long you'd be waiting.

"We're going to be sitting here awhile." She twisted one hand
into her black fauxhawk, a look Elena could never pull off. Elena
broke the empanada in half and offered it to Mai, who took it
gratefully. "If you have gossip, tell me slow and sensually."

Elena snickered. "It's good news actually," she said. And indeed, it was—hearing it had released an enormous weight off
her shoulders. "A little bird told me that they're close to making an arrest for the two students who got killed."

"Wait, what? What bird?"

"Leonard is friends with one of the detectives. He came to
his office today, and I could sort of hear them talking through
the wall."

"But your office isn't next to his."

"Okay, so I put a cup against my ear and put it to the door,"
Elena admitted.

Mai started laughing. "That actually works?"

"It does. Sort of, anyway. It looks like it was a drug thing and
they're close to making an arrest." What she could not say, but
wanted to, was how tense the past few weeks had been, particularly with Leonard.

Elena thought two students in the program being killed was
too much of a coincidence but Leonard never did—he assumed
that high-risk behavior put people in situations that were inherently dangerous and psychopaths just happened to be attracted
to high-risk behavior. They had had a few conversations about
what the other students in the program should be told, but Leonard always overruled her. If he was going to ignore her concerns, then Elena was absolutely going to eavesdrop on private
conversations with a detective. The confidentiality of the pro-

gram dictated that she couldn't relate everything she knew to her fiancée—who of course didn't know that Michael and Kellen were part of Elena's panel—which had put her in a bind of lying when normally she would never lie to Mai.

"That's a relief," Mai said, her mouth full. They both watched the parade of police cars, sirens blazing, drive by, to be followed by more motorcycles, then sleek, anonymous-looking black cars. Elena smiled, feeling light for the first time in weeks.

It was terrible to have such a blow happen to the program, to not exactly know what had happened and to not entirely feel safe sitting in her office. She could push aside that image of Kellen lying on the floor in his own blood and tell herself that this was the tragic consequence of a series of bad life decisions—exactly as Leonard had said. With the case wrapping up, life would inevitably move on, and everyone could breathe a sigh of relief.

What she could never tell anyone—not Mai or Leonard—especially not now, because she'd be too embarrassed, was the tiny intrusive thought she had had on more than on occasion. Now it felt foolish to even think about it, but there had been a moment two weeks ago when she had been working at her computer, doing data analysis, and a thought popped into her head: *Could it have been Trevor?* She had no evidence to suggest that Trevor could have killed Michael and Kellen, and no evidence that he even knew them. They were both the kind of guys that Trevor would never hang out with—the type of guys he would even hate (although the bar for being hated by Trevor was quite low).

She had idly wondered this based solely off a gut feeling, and now she chastised herself for her prejudice. She was glad she never related her suspicion to Leonard—he might think her unprofessional or hysterical, or lacking in some fundamental respect for her clients. Making the leap from "this person makes me feel uncomfortable" to "this person might be a murderer" was exactly the sort of narrow-minded sentiment that Wyman had spent the past few decades of his life fighting. And here, Leonard's senior-most graduate student was indulging in that exact type of lazy thinking. She was glad she had never admitted this secret thought to anyone, and glad she was about to be proven wrong about thinking the worst of one of her clients.

51

They met at the Shaw Metro stop. Andre wore an ill-fitting blazer—one of Marcus's—in attempt to make him look older. Chloe had more or less copied the exact way that Elena dressed and was sporting a pair of eyeglasses as she frowned at him. "You need better disguises." As they boarded the train, Andre wondered if she had a whole wardrobe of disguises.

It had taken five carefully worded, increasingly longer letters to Mira Wale, the fiancée of Wyman's former, and now dead, student John Fiola, the only one who appeared to have any research connections to CRD. She had not responded to Andre's first Facebook message, nor the second that he and Chloe had painstakingly written, trying to make themselves seem like graduate students from the Wyman lab who desperately needed Fiola's dissertation and unpublished research. Chloe ended up filching some of Wyman's official letterhead and they wrote a formal, physical letter littered with psychology jargon, included a new fake email address, and off it went, later receiving a tepid invitation from Mira.

"Did you, um, do what Charles said?" Andre whispered after

they had settled into plastic seats beside each other. The only other people in the subway car were reading newspapers or looking at their phones. He looked up at Chloe and found her giving him a look of utter disgust—*Of course I did, how dare you even doubt me*, that look said. Andre fiddled with his watch, double-checking that the location tracking was off. "Do you think they could have been using it the whole time? Do you think Elena and all them will notice we turned it off?"

"Tech fails happen all the time," she said, shrugging. "Just play dumb. And don't assume we're safe now—I doubt it's that hard to track any of us even without the watches. We all live on campus. It's not that hard to find out who our friends are, what classes we take, and where we hang out. Think about everything you post on social media. Think about all the times you're walking around—work under the assumption that you could have been followed, because whoever this is, they know what they're doing." As a precaution, they took a series of detours at the Gallery Place Metro station, climbing up stairways and down escalators, hopping onto one train only to change cars and hop off immediately, not wanting to risk being followed.

To Andre, it seemed that every day that passed it felt more and more likely that behind each closed door was someone about to pop out, in every dark car was someone dangerous waiting. He sat in class, trying to pay attention, but wondered if anyone was watching him. Now he slept with the baseball bat in his bed, rather than under it. He didn't know how sustainable it all was because it was increasingly exhausting.

They got off at the Eastern Market stop and headed up the escalator. "You should do most of the talking," Andre said.

Chloe looked up from the map on her phone, her eyes narrowed. Uh-oh. He had suggested this because making up elaborate lies made him nervous and she seemed to do it with aplomb. "People are more helpful when you're white," he said.

He expected her to protest that this wasn't true, but instead she nodded and added, "Also, I'm pretty."

Mira lived in Capitol Hill, on a street filled with yuppies pushing expensive strollers and signs in windows saying Hate Isn't Welcome Here. Andre walked behind Chloe, scanning the street as they went, looking for anyone who seemed to be paying too much attention to them.

Mira's house was a redbrick Victorian with an overgrown garden in the front. Chloe rang the doorbell with no hesitation. There was a long pause—long enough that Andre wondered if Mira forgot their appointment—but then there were shuffling sounds, and the door opened. Mira was an extraordinarily pregnant woman with glossy hair.

"Hello?" she said, sounding skeptical. She stood in the doorway, exactly in the position of someone who could easily slam the door on a salesman.

"I'm Jennifer and this is Brian—Dr. Wyman's graduate students?" Chloe said. She even affected Elena's tone. "Thank you so much for meeting with us. We're fifth years—prospectuses are coming up, and we can't seem to get our hands on John's dissertation anywhere…?"

"So sorry about what happened," Andre added.

Mira leaned on the doorway, rubbing her distended belly. "Your work relates to John's?"

"We're working with one of the same datasets," Chloe said. "That's why we wanted his dissertation—to see if he ran into the same problem of contradictory evidence that we did. There's supposed to be two copies bound at the library but they're both gone."

"Really? That's strange." Her tone was exactly that of someone who didn't really care.

"We were hoping you had a copy?"

Mira made a broad gesture, one that indicated her pregnancy, the wedding band on her finger, the house behind her, which they couldn't see into. "That…was a whole lifetime ago."

"I'm sorry," Chloe said. "We didn't mean to bring it up when you're—you know. Busy and stuff."

She looked like she wanted to be done with them, but then Andre said, "It's just frustrating to think some of John's ideas will never come to fruition. He was brilliant, even as a student."

Mira said, "I'm not saying there *isn't* a copy actually."

"Oh?" Chloe said.

"John and I had a storage unit—his mom paid for it. After he passed away, I was in such a state I just didn't want to deal with anything, really. I had my brother dump a lot of our stuff in there, basically clothes and school stuff and old furniture."

"You still have the unit?"

"His mom never stopped paying for it and I've never drummed up the energy to go clear it out."

Andre had no idea where she was headed but he jumped in. "If you think the dissertation might be in there, what if we cleaned out the unit for you in exchange for having a look?" She seemed skeptical, but intrigued.

"Basically, you've been wanting to pack it up and drop it off at Goodwill, but never have the time—" Chloe gestured to her pregnant belly "—and you don't want to just throw it all out because that's such a waste, am I right?"

"Yeah…there's nothing really of value in there, like IKEA furniture. Actually, you might know students who'd want some of it."

"We can have it cleaned out in a week. I can send you a picture when we're done so you know to close out the account."

"Tell you what…you have a deal."

They had a few hours until it would get dark, so they sprang for a cab to the storage unit facility. There didn't appear to be any sort of office—they could just take the key Mira had given them and head to Unit 345. The lock protested, but then gave, and with a great lurch they managed to get the rusty door to roll upward.

Mira hadn't been exaggerating when she said junk—there was barely room to walk. Boxes, furniture piled up, heaps of clothes on the floor. There was also no overhead light so cell phones would have to suffice.

"Let's triage," Chloe said. "For all we know, the hunter will figure out we came here and burn the whole place down if we try to come back."

We better not have been followed, Andre thought, it suddenly seeming very clear that they were in an isolated location with not even an attendant at the storage facility.

Where would the good stuff be? Not with the clothes or jumbles of furniture. They scoured stacks of boxes on opposite sides of the unit. One looked promising—it contained several books about psychology, but nothing resembling a dissertation. He found several thick binders and, feeling a jolt of excitement, he realized they contained handwritten notes. He crouched on the floor of the unit and flipped through them, but only came across equations he didn't understand. Then a test: Multivariate Statistics Final Exam. "Chloe, this is grad school stuff." She abandoned her box and grabbed the one next to his.

Andre pawed through old textbooks, study guides, a FAFSA form, then pulled another box forward. He paused—behind it was a cheap bookshelf, one shelf bending under the weight of reams of paper and stuffed binders. Two binders were stuck together, and when he pried them apart, he was holding a loose-leaf copy of "Toward a Greater Understanding of Sexual Violence in Psychopathic Men." He held it up, Chloe hissed triumphantly and they stuffed it into his book bag. Andre desperately wanted to plant his ass on the floor and start reading, but they only had about half an hour of daylight left. The last place he wanted to be if the hunter made an appearance was a dark, abandoned storage unit. He hadn't brought his baseball bat; he had worried that Mira would see it. But he did have his knife.

Chloe sat cross-legged on the floor, making three piles. "These look like draft articles, and I think these might be clinic notes. Do those binders look any good?" Andre flipped through one, and the moment he saw the words *sexual deviance*, he erred on the side of caution and shoved it into his bag. He took a liberal approach to taking things, figuring that it was better to take more and sort it out later. Chloe, however, was getting too engrossed, actually reading stuff.

"Come on, it's going to get dark soon," he warned her. His bag was getting too full. Andre unclasped a binder and pulled out the contents, adding it to his collection. The light outside was starting to take on that dusky look of sundown. He began to stuff things into Chloe's bag as she pored over a single notebook. Once that, too, was packed, he was annoyed to see that she hadn't moved at all.

"Chloe. It's getting dark. We gotta go."

"You need to look at this." She handed him a typed list. It consisted of about fifty unfamiliar names with dates and checks or question marks written next to each. *What was this?* Andre wondered, a chill moving up his back. He knew they should get going but he couldn't resist—he pulled up Wikipedia on his phone and looked up CRD, Chloe leaning over his shoulder as he thumbed to the part where the names of all his victims were listed. Or, at least, his official victims.

There was no overlap between the list of names they held and the list of victims. Every date on their sheet of paper was in 2008, two years after CRD had been killed by lethal injection by the state of Virginia. Chloe met his eyes, and he knew she was wondering the same thing: if they had just found a list of fifty or so new victims, murders committed by somebody else after CRD had already been executed.

52

Safe at class, said the text from Kristen.

Good—miss you, Charles responded. Through his car window, he looked into Cathedral Coffee. It was now the sweet spot after lunch but before people would want their afternoon coffee. It had been surprisingly easy to find out where Megan Dufresne worked. She had posted a brief video of her pouring a latte, making a dove shape with the milk, and Charles had Googled coffee shops until he had matched the logo on her apron. Charles called the shop pretending that he had found a lost student ID of someone named Megan and a coworker told him that of course he could stop by to return it, and that Megan could pick it up on Thursday.

Charles entered the coffee shop, which was empty except for some laptop trolls and Megan rearranging pastries with a bored expression. It was bizarre to look at her: she had the same exact facial structure as Emma—perhaps a bit healthier looking, and her auburn hair was stylish. The twins literally looked like before and after makeover pictures. "Hello," he said. Megan looked up but her eyes didn't register the look girls often got where they immediately found him attractive.

"What can I get you?"

"Actually, I was hoping you could help me. You're Megan Dufresne, right?" She looked instantly suspicious but didn't deny it. "I'm a friend of your sister's." She didn't believe him. More specifically, she didn't believe that her sister had friends. "Well, sort of. I'm her TA. I've been worried about her." Her brow furrowed. "She hasn't been at class and she missed our last appointment." Charles had no idea if Emma was actually missing classes. The only thing he could glean from her Instagram from the past week is that she had visited the arboretum and the botanical gardens over by the Capitol, probably to hunt insects to take portraits of.

"Emma doesn't cut classes," Megan said.

"I know—that's why I was worried. Do you think her behavior has been strange lately?"

Megan picked up a rag and began to move it slowly over the counter, even though there was nothing to wipe up. "Strange, how? What class do you TA?"

"Preenlightenment Thought. I noticed—" here he tried to affect a look of discomfort "—I saw some bruising on her arm last month. On the thirteenth actually—I remember specifically because that's my birthday. I didn't think anything of it until she started missing classes later. Maybe something happened to her around then?"

She blinked. "And what business of yours would that be?"

He leaned forward, lowering his voice. "As a teacher, I'm a mandated reporter. If I thought someone was harming her, I would have to report it, or talk to her. I—I should have said something at the time, because I know she doesn't talk to a lot of people. She had sort of opened up to me, you know?" Even her body language had turned defensive—her arms folded across her chest, her legs in a stubborn stance. "She came to my office hours a lot," he added. "She was interested in doing an independent study—"

"On what?"

"Photography as a form of visual ontology. It's not like I could ever see Emma harming anyone, getting into a physical altercation, so I worried that someone might be harming her." This was the whole point of his meeting with Megan, and he uttered it as if it were supposed to be a throwaway thought. He watched Megan's reaction carefully for the confirmation he wanted. That the notion that Emma harming anyone was ridiculous. He would have his confirmation that Emma had nothing to do with any of this, and he could move on to closing in on Trevor.

But instead, Megan looked down at the rag, a furrow in her brow. He had planted a small seed of doubt, one that he didn't think would be viable. She was just there, on the verge of saying something important. "Mr...?"

"Highsmith," he said, pulling the name from nowhere. She looked up, her eyes narrowing a fraction. The suspicion had turned back on.

"Mr. Highsmith, I can check in on my sister, but we're a private family, and there's no need for you to insert yourself."

53

"Help me," Yessica said, looking through her bureau for inspiration for a costume.

"Your fault leaving it till the last minute. We could walk to CVS and rustle something up," I said.

"We can come up with something better. A cat, maybe?"

"You're depressing me. Girls always have the same dumb costumes," I said, rooting through my makeup drawer. "Sexy witch, sexy nurse. Be something original—sexy hurricane!" I said, holding up a wad of fraying cotton balls, thinking of the most recent hurricane, which a few states were still cleaning up from. The look on her face said no. "Too soon?"

"You're weird." She held up a chunky eyeliner and sniffed it. "What are you going as?"

I had sold some textbooks I found in the library to scrounge up the money for my costume. I was going as Clark Kent and had blown most of the money on a Superman bustier. I planned to wear it under a white button-down shirt, half unbuttoned, with my black skirt and my fake eyeglasses. I had a black hat and heels to match, but most importantly, a small messenger bag carrying my essentials: a reporter's notebook, my phone, my stun gun, and switchblade.

"Get your ass in gear!" I admonished as I got dressed. Yessica was still standing there, chewing on a fingernail as she examined her closet. "I have to get there early, but I'll see you at the party."

The Adams Halloween Ball was being held at Fathom Gallery in Logan Circle, close to campus. I wanted to get a lay of the land because even though I had friends going, I was flying solo tonight.

I was tired of this game of cat and mouse, and wanted to be able to confront my attacker face-to-face. I had posted several things on Instagram, making it clear I would be at the ball getting drunk. Trevor might show, or Emma, and I was going to be ready. It could come to a physical fight, or there was my vial of a new liquid solution: a high dose of codeine, dangerous with alcohol, and liable to make you very sleepy if not dead. Maybe Trevor was a master hacker, but he was clearly awkward around girls. I could see him readily accepting a drink from me, planning how he would get me later in the night, oblivious that I was getting him right then.

The Undergraduate Student Association had rented out the whole place, which had three main areas. The DJ was in the main gallery, its glossy wood floors emptied of furniture so people could dance. The brick walls, painted white, had neat lines of framed artwork. Beyond that was an outdoor garden, which had been strung with pumpkin lanterns. On the second floor was a small penthouse where the music wasn't so loud and most of the food was placed.

I took a cat-shaped cheesecake bite and surveyed the exits of each floor. It would be hard for anyone to make a deadly move here; the space wasn't very large and there would be people packed in tight. Then again, it was Halloween, and people would be screaming and walking around in grotesque costumes. How hard would it be to jam a screwdriver into someone's stomach and walk away? People might even see your cooling dead body and think it was a prop.

I noticed on the gallery level that there was a glass staircase leading down to a dimly lit hallway. I went down, pushed open the door, and found a large bathroom, the kind with a dressing area with seating and a marble vanity with fancy towels, lotion, and mouthwash. When I got back upstairs, more people were streaming in.

The party was in full swing half an hour later. Someone had turned on a smoke machine and people sipped punch from sticky cups. Apoorva arrived, dressed as a cat, and Traci, dressed as a box of wine. There was some drama already going on. The boy Traci liked was supposed to be coming with the girl he was hanging out with except Apoorva had heard that they weren't hanging out anymore. We schemed while I kept my eye on the door, examining each new costumed person as they entered.

I nursed a seltzer and did a lap. If I were a killer, I'd be wearing a mask, something that completely covered my face. I took pictures with friends from Bio, making sure to post them immediately. I spotted Chad by a table of food with a couple other SAE brothers. He was dressed in Roman garb and had his hair combed down. "Et tu, Brute?" I said.

"I'm Augustus, not Julius!" he said, exasperated. We laughed. He even had a baby Cupid attached to his calf.

"I like your costume, Supergirl."

"I'm Clark Kent! The real deal, not the Diet Coke version." He gave me a flirty hug, then kept his hand on my back, his expression turning more serious. "I haven't seen you in a while."

"Don't be clingy," I teased. He thought I was still mad about the photo of me sleeping, which he kept apologizing for every time I saw him. I was mad, but not at him—and of course he had no idea of just exactly how busy I was with other activities, such as murdering his frat brother. But Chad would always be grade A in my book because he had found Will's phone and was a decent FWB. I pressed my face to his breastplate. "I've just been so busy with classes."

"So, I'll see you soon?"

"Definitely. Let's have another study date." I pushed my glasses up my nose and gave him an impish look as I slipped past to get some food. A girl nearly spilled a drink on me and apologized in a voice that sounded strangely familiar. *"Reek?"* I asked, incredulous. He was wearing a blond wig and was dressed like a zombie cheerleader, gaunt eyes and makeup to make it look like a chunk had been bitten out of his neck. He nodded. "Damn, you're kind of hot as a girl."

"I know," he said. "It's fun to pretend."

I danced, then frowned when I saw Charles and Kristen making their way in. The last thing I needed was Charles being nosy. I hadn't answered several suspicious texts from him and needed to handle him carefully, now that Will was gone for good. He wasn't wearing any discernible costume and Kristen was dressed like Wonder Woman. I avoided them, heading toward the outdoor garden. Just as I got outside I got a mood log, which I filled out.

Energetic

7

Nervous

1

Sad

1

I peered off the railing of the landing down at the street below. People in costume were crossing the street, yelping as cars beeped at them. I was talking to one of the guys from my floor when I saw movement in my peripheral vision. A robed figure in black moved across the garden. It carried a large scythe, which glinted like it was real. The figure walked strangely— almost as if it were gliding supernaturally. Then I was distracted by another figure: a guy in a suit and tie, but a full horse-head mask. But maybe not a guy—whoever they were didn't have a large frame. There were ghouls and animals and all kinds of costumes with enough makeup or plastic to cover faces entirely.

Without thinking, I impatiently took out my phone and snapped a picture of me looking bored. TFW you're ready to party but the party hasn't started yet. Prick me with a pin and maybe I'll wake up. Come and get me, asshole.

After an hour of fairly uneventful socializing, I wondered if the killer was going to show at all. I headed to the lower floor where the dressing room/bathroom was to freshen up and loosen my bustier, which wasn't exactly comfortable. It was quiet inside and through the door I could hear the boom of music from upstairs and people laughing. I redid my laces, which required some patience and stamina for having my arms curved around my back for an extended period of time.

I exited my stall, then noticed a figure in black standing in the middle of the dressing room in front of the sink. A Day of the Dead skeleton, its face covered in black-and-white face paint, a grim yellow flower perched behind its ear. My hand moved instinctively to my bag.

The skeleton began to dance, moving its body in strange, jerking motions like something out of a Japanese horror movie. "Yessica?"

She broke out into laughter, bending over to put her bone gloves on her skeletal knees. "I scared you, didn't I!" I came closer to the sink to examine her makeup.

"Pretty impressive."

"I found a how-to video," she said as I washed my hands. "I saw your senior boo."

"We chatted. I'll make sure to dance with him."

Yessica bid me adieu and left. I blotted my face with a fancy towel and sampled the blue mouthwash. Just as I was exiting the dressing room, Charles was coming down the stairs. He wore one of the two standard Charles uniforms: a suit with a skinny tie. It was slate gray and pretty unexciting for a costume party. "What are you supposed to be? An endangered species?"

"Huh?" he said.

"Straight white male."

"Very funny," he said, putting his hands in his pockets and contemplating me. "Did you disable—?"

"Of course I did!"

"You've been avoiding me."

"No, I haven't."

He blinked. In the dim lighting there was only a thin band of green around his big pupils. "Chloe…" I knew with absolute certainty he was thinking about Will.

"You met with Emma?" I interrupted. "How'd it go?"

He stared at me for a long moment before he answered. "I asked her to dinner—I get the impression that she might like me." He seemed to be struggling with something. "Emma is weird—it's like she's from another planet. I actually don't know if I walked away with more information. But here's another thing—I tracked down her sister and talked to her."

"Megan?"

"She's a barista over by American. She's protective of Emma, which is strange—"

"—because her social media makes it look like they're not even sisters."

"Right, like Megan's got this embarrassingly weird sister. And I got the impression she was suspicious of *me* because I was asking her about Emma. There's a good chance she might say something to Emma about me. I mean, I gave her a fake name, but if she describes me…"

"Isn't that scary? Knowing that an angry probable serial murderer wants to jump your bones?"

"Fancy that," he said without smiling.

"Well, Andre and I found some documents from Wyman's old student. We're still going through them because I lost an entire day yesterday tailing Trevor."

"Tailing?"

"It was actually pretty funny—he had no idea I was right behind him all day. I went to his dorm, the SAC, to his classes, even a dumb party. One time he almost turned around and caught me! I can't say I found any specific evidence—"

"He could have seen you! You could have gotten yourself killed!"

"How else am I supposed to find clues?"

"Clues? This isn't a game. We could have set up a plan or something where the three of us worked together. You can't get into a situation where he turns around and you're right there. I told you, he's dangerous."

"So am I," I said. Charles sighed, putting up his hands in an expression of frustration.

"He's scrawny and I was armed."

"Why won't you *listen* to me!"

"Because I don't have to listen to anybody," I said. "Besides, why do you care what I do?"

"Is it so weird that I don't want you to get bludgeoned to death? Can you please promise me not to do anything like that again, without the three of us agreeing?"

Oh, I had *done* it.

Charles was mine. Hooked like a little fishy. All I needed to do was keep him swimming the same direction with me, and Will would never be a problem. "Of course not," I said. "We have to be active rather than passive."

"Chloe."

"No. Why don't you want something bad to happen to me?" I asked. "Why can't you just admit it?"

"Admit what?"

I stalked closer to him and pressed my index finger into his chest. "That you care about me."

Charles put his hand over mine. He moved my arm back to my side as if he were moving the limbs on a doll. Then he put his hands in his pockets again as he stared at me. A look over-came his face, one I couldn't read. Someone howled upstairs; I turned my head to glance in that direction. When I turned back at Charles he was still focused on me.

He stepped forward. Suddenly I felt his hand on my waist and he kissed me. Not the way he had in my room, but harder, furious. Some part of me had been waiting forever for him to be like this and I responded naturally, wrapping my arms around his neck, turning my head to the side to let him kiss me more deeply. He pulled me to him, his hands on my ass.

Charles hauled me into the empty dressing room, then pressed me up against the wall beside the door. I locked it, closing my eyes and craning my neck back, feeling his mouth on my throat. I tugged at his tie, pulled him up by the hair so I could kiss him. He jammed against me and I wrapped my legs around him, not breaking our kiss when I heard someone trying to get in, the locked door jiggling. I tried unsuccessfully to stay quiet when he pushed my skirt up farther and I felt his hands on my thighs. I murmured his name. I was tingling everywhere.

He pushed me onto a nearby ottoman and dropped to his knees. He parted my legs and I felt him kiss my inner thigh, just above the knee. He pulled at my underwear so hard that I heard a seam rip. I wriggled and he pulled them off, then grabbed the lower part of my body to pull me closer. He wasted no time—his head bowed and I gasped when I felt his warm mouth directly on me. I closed my eyes momentarily as I felt one of his hands slide down my thigh to my knee, then push upward, changing the angle of my body a little. He made a hum of satisfaction in the back of his throat, the vibration hitting me. I squirmed uncontrollably, burying one of my hands into his hair as his head moved steadily. I stared at the ceiling and gave a helpless little laugh when someone tried the door again. "Charles." I gripped him harder and he picked up his pace. A heady feeling began to overtake me, an orgasm building. He edged right up to it, then, to my frustration, pulled back, planting a demure little kiss on my thigh. I grabbed him by his hair and redirected him, eliciting a little self-satisfied chuckle from him. He delivered quickly and

I came, crying out, a bolt of pleasure shooting from my middle to the rest of my body, making my muscles tense, then shudder. Charles stopped, resting his head on my leg, and we both caught our breath. I felt like a melted candle, soft pliable happy wax.

Charles pulled back, kissing my left knee quickly before he stood up, fixing his tie as he headed toward the sink. Contented, I watched him wash his face and hands, wearing no expression as he performed these rituals. He fixed his hair, which was comically sticking all over the place. He got it into a presentable state with some water. Yes, he needed to look innocent, as if something hadn't happened, because he had to go back to his girlfriend without her knowing what we had done. He was keeping everything a secret from her: the person who hunted us, and now me. I smiled, satisfied.

I was edging my skirt back down as he turned to go. "Wait a few minutes before you leave," he said, then unlocked the door and left. I cleaned myself up, still feeling residual sparks in my body, my fingertips tingling. My glasses had fallen off at some point. I retrieved them and looked at my reflection as I polished the lenses with my shirt.

Put a check by Charles's name, move him to the Chloe column.

I sauntered through the party, examining people, sometimes pushing their masks straight off their faces. I grew bolder with impatience, maybe a little drunk off my postcoital glow. My phone vibrated—a push notification from Instagram. Pinprick52 had uploaded a new post.

It took me a second to realize what it was. A photo of the closed bathroom door from downstairs. *#sluts*.

54

Charles was calling. He had been pointedly avoiding me since our Halloween tryst so I let the phone ring eight times to punish him. I know he's not capable of feeling guilty, and so had concluded that he was frightened of his attraction to me mixed with whatever he had surmised about Will. I had to play this carefully. I put my feet up on my desk, petting my stuffed whale, and assumed a bored tone as I picked up. "You rang, Charlie Bear?"

"Why did you just send me a video of you blowing Chad?" he asked.

I put my feet down. "I didn't!"

"You did. It's from your email."

I woke my laptop up and opened my email but saw no such thing. "When was it sent?"

"About a minute ago... Oh, huh—there's a bunch of people on the To line."

The webcams. Trevor. He *had* recorded. It must have been from one of the nights Chad had come over to "study." I sat in front of my computer and opened a new email, rage filling up my chest. "Read me the names it was sent to." He began to list them. A handful of friends, two of my professors, one TA, and Elena and Dr. Wyman. I muttered out loud as I typed: Please delete the email that appears to have been sent by me two minutes ago. My account has been hacked and the attached file contains malicious malware. Then I sent it.

"Isn't all malware malicious?" Charles said.

"Send me the video. I want to see it."

"Do you think that's safe? It might actually have something encoded in it. I'm running my antivirus software right now. Wait—oh… I think you'd better get over here."

Charles had on a flat expression and was on the phone when he opened the door. "Do I look like I just spent three thousand dollars in a Walmart in Kenosha? Freeze the goddamned account." He hung up and closed the door.

An exclamation point appeared on my watch. I tapped it. *On a scale of 1 to 7, how much of a slut are you?* The screen changed to a dick pic, then another and another. I took my watch off grimly. Charles looked at his, then tilted it to show me. His screen was flashing gay porn.

"Why is he doing this?" I took a seat at Charles's desk in front of his laptop. A media player was open. It was definitely a video from one of my webcams. Chad blissed out with his eyes closed as I tended to him. "That—" My cell rang, and it was Yessica calling.

"Chlo, you need to get on Facebook."

I opened a new tab and went to the site, then felt a new rage come over me. I told Yessica I had to go. Tons of people at Adams joined various Facebook groups that produced memes about college life—the dorms, the cafeteria, the white albino squirrel people spotted on occasion. There was even a group just for our dorm. Posted on every single one I was a member of was a naked picture of me. I recognized it—it was probably pulled from a very old email or my iCloud account.

I hissed and began to type directly under the comment "is this a meme I dont get it."

Hi this is Chloe Sevre. I am not ashamed of my body—I should be charging you bitches for looking. But full disclosure: this picture was taken of me when I was 14 by a 22 year old who then faced criminal charges. bc of my age in the picture, technically it is child pornography which makes disseminating it or even looking at it a crime. I have already contacted campus police, the MPD and the FBI's Cybercrimes Unit. Don't think that they won't come for you byeeeee.

I copied this and posted it on every single other post of the picture.

"Is that true?" Charles asked.

"Not the last part obviously."

I fumed, trying to collect my thoughts. My problem is that sometimes I get so mad I act rashly. "Maybe Trevor actually spotted you when you were following him," Charles said. His tone seemed careful. I went to Instagram to see if that weird account had posted anything about this. I hadn't told Charles or Andre about Pinprick52—I couldn't, not while that picture of me leaving Will was still there. There was a new post but it was hard to tell what it was—a crisscross of shadows, a neon red light.

"He didn't, I swear! Do you think Andre got hacked?"

I texted Andre: Did you get hacked? Development—come to C's place. Charles leaned over my phone and I inhaled his scent while Andre typed back.

Huh? Nobody hacked me. Can't come—in the middle of it, figured out the list

"So, us but not Andre," Charles said. "What list?" He hit the side of his phone as it made noises, then put it down on his desk, frustrated.

"I'll let him explain when he gets here."

"I have a theory."

"Pray tell," I said without looking up as I typed back to Andre. Big Trevor development. What's going on with the list?

"Trevor's been watching you. He's the type of misogynist who is really black-and-white in his thinking. Virgin-whore dichotomy. If he likes a girl, she's pure and good and worthy of him. If she proves herself a whore, which could include any sin from liking another guy to simply existing, then she's a cunt and a slut who brings any harm upon herself to be attacked by the righteous. So maybe he discovered you're not so innocent."

"And since when have I ever marched around like a virgin?"

"Someone tried the door on us at the ball," he said in a low voice, as if Kristen were in the room. "It could have been him. He thinks we're fucking and he got mad."

"What a shame to be attacked for something we've never even done," I said archly. He didn't smile but looked back at me. I sighed, turning back to the computer. "How do we destroy him? I want acid to be involved. I guess the silver lining is that if Elena asks about why our watches aren't geolocated we can blame it on this."

"She hasn't said anything to you, has she?" Charles asked. I shook my head. "I don't think she's noticed yet. I don't know how often they actually look at the data for analysis."

"That might buy us some time."

Charles's phone blooped. "Andre just texted—he says he's coming."

"How about we send our little friend the hunter to take care of Trevor?"

"Unless Trevor is the hunter," Charles said. I could feel him standing behind me suddenly. He reached around me to sign out of Facebook, then clicked on the video to drag it into his trash bin. "You know that actually doesn't delete it," I pointed out. "Maybe you'd like to watch it a few more times."

He opened the trash and clicked on it to delete it for real. "Why would I watch a video when I have access to the real thing?" he said, his face close to my ear. He went back to his chair, crossing his legs and resting an ankle on one knee, shaking his foot. "By the way, you didn't sleep with Chad just because you thought it'd annoy me, did you?"

"Maybe I find Chad sex-worthy."

He snorted. "Chad is objectively terrible by every possible definition."

"Now why would you say a thing like that?"

"General malice?" Charles suggested, a hint of amusement in his eyes.

"Or might you be jealous?"

"God, you're megalomaniacal."

"Duh—I'm a psychopath, get over it. You've been avoiding me."

"No, I haven't—I've been a little busy with the whole, you know, *not getting murdered thing*. And I'm not sure how many times I have to tell you I have a girlfriend."

"And where is this girlfriend right now?"

The look on his face went from playful to cold. "This is me carefully orchestrating her having no idea what's going on so she's safe and she doesn't have to worry. Not that you can conceive of actually caring for another human being, but I do love her."

"And it has nothing to do with the fact that she's fabulously wealthy and all your country club parents can have a big society wedding."

"Fuck you."

"I've never objected to that," I said gleefully. "What were you planning—B school, then working for your dad, getting married at twenty-four and white picket fences with your Stepford wife?"

"Hardly. What do you suggest instead?"

"We could burn down the world."

His eyes were fixed on me, his expression unfathomable. "I'm reporting Trevor to the police for this—if he gets in trouble for real he won't be able to attack anyone else. It's better than nothing."

"Let's hear what Andre's development is before we decide anything."

Charles sighed, looking at another dick pic on his phone, and then stood up, going over to his fridge. He ate Chinese food out of the container, not even offering me any. I took advantage of his rudeness to do some sleuthing in private on the laptop. Trevor had a Twitter account but mostly it was filled with nonsensical but still somehow rude-seeming tweets about computers and Elon Musk.

His most recent tweet, though, posted today, was Fuck the American health care system. Interesting. From my day of stalking I had learned what three of his classes were: Advanced Logic, Comparative Politics, and Economics 125. I quickly logged on to the class websites for each, where professors posted syllabi and assignments, and students would sometimes post messages.

I almost jumped when I saw that Trevor had posted a message early this morning to the entire Logic class, including a picture. Hey, I am going to miss my presentation today. Spent all of yesterday in the hospital and only just got discharged. The picture was ostensibly of his wrist, sporting a plastic medical ID tag from the Washington Hospital Center. This could just be a normal psychopath lie to get out of a presentation, but there had also been the tweet, which might have demonstrated actual anger at the medical bills that were inevitably coming his way. And posting to the entire class to get sympathy and attention, instead of just the professor, was totally something a psychopath would do. He was probably hoping for some sympathy points from the girls in his class.

Everything made sense. Someone attacked Trevor, he ended up in the hospital, got out and, assuming that it was me or Charles who attacked him, exacted his revenge. *It's Emma, then,* I realized. I closed all my windows and shut the laptop. Emma had come pretty close to doing Trevor in, and now we were paying for her attempt.

Andre knocked on the door before letting himself in with the key Charles had given him. "Did you finish the dissertation?" I asked. I hadn't. There was only so much time I could devote to it when I had to follow Trevor for a day and midterms were coming up.

"I did. It's really interesting. I think John might actually have interviewed Ripley himself, but he doesn't specifically say so." Andre picked up on Charles's confused look—we hadn't filled him in about our storage unit adventure.

"Chloe and I found all this stuff in a storage unit that used to belong to one of Wyman's old students. We got his dissertation, and this list, and at first we thought they were all new victims, but then I researched them. Turns out they're all, or were at the time, literary agents," Andre explained.

Andre accepted a beer from Charles with a nod—I didn't like this. They had a buddy-buddy vibe going. "John Fiola was writing a book about the case, which Wyman never did, or any of the detectives who worked on the case. It's pretty weird if you think about how much money a book like that would have made, coming from people directly involved with the case. He wanted a big book deal, and some of the agents were biting. So, I don't know, maybe this is illegal, but I signed up for a Gmail address with Fiola's name and wrote to all of them, some bullshit about me having serious family issues, but now I have time to devote to this project, could you please resend any notes you originally had. Most of them didn't answer, but one did! She just forwarded me the last email she sent him with the attachment—the whole book."

"Send it to us," I said. "We can look through it right now, divide the work between us." Andre nodded and sent the email and then all three of us began to skim. The book was unfinished—about two hundred pages of text plus a chapter outline. When I scrolled down to the original email, it was clear why the book had never been published.

We read your proposal and chapters with a great deal of interest. I imagine you have several agents who are highly motivated to get this story out there. Our concern is with the quality of the writing, which doesn't make this book competitive for a tough market right now. Our proposal would be that you work with a ghostwriter to help tidy it up. We have several we could recommend, and the process would be easy for you. If you're interested, please contact me at the below number and we can chat.

The ghostwriter made sense—John was an awful writer. The pages were filled with purple prose and turns of phrase that were supposed to sound profound.

I skimmed as quickly as I could. John started with CRD's childhood and moved through to when he started killing. I hesitated. Was there any chance at all CRD wasn't actually executed? This almost made sense—he broke out of prison, or got a last-minute pardon from a softie governor, then returned to make Wyman's life a living hell. I did a quick search on Charles's computer. CRD had been put to death by lethal injection in late 2006, a death that had been observed by the prosecutor of the case and members of some of the victim's family.

"Oh my God," Andre said suddenly.

"What?" Charles asked when Andre didn't say anything.

"Sorry, some of this stuff is graphic," he murmured, still reading.

I was at the part where the police had nailed CRD, linking him with DNA evidence. The case was about to go public. My eyes skipped down pages rapidly.

A squeak escaped my mouth.

"What? What?" Andre asked.

"'Between myself, my adviser, and the detectives working the case, we knew the media storm that would erupt once they announced a break in the case. In addition to the named and unnamed victims there were three more victims: Gregory's wife, and their twins.'" I paused for dramatic effect. Charles had his eyebrows raised and Andre comically had his mouth wide open. "'And yet the trauma hadn't ended with CRD behind bars. Marsha—' that's the wife '—committed suicide before the bail hearing. One thing we all agreed upon was that it was in the best interest of the girls to protect their identities.'"

"You think Emma and Megan might be the Rock Creek Killer's kids?" Charles said. "A lot of people have twins."

"They're the right age to be Ripley's kids," I said. I was immediately on the internet, pulling up images of Gregory Ripley to see if there was a resemblance.

"How is that possible? The media would have been all over that. A couple Google searches and you'd have the wife and kids' names," Andre said.

Charles was still skimming the manuscript. "The police helped—they had their names changed immediately and they were sent to live with friends of Marsha's in California."

"Then how'd they end up back here?"

Andre popped to his feet. "It happened like this. They have this idyllic life on the beach, only they start to realize there's something *wrong* with Emma. They call Dr. Wyman and he says she needs treatment."

"Because he was so good treating the dad? Wait a minute," Charles said slowly. "Did you guys get a signing bonus for the panel study?"

"Bonus?"

"You mean beyond tuition?"

"Twenty-thousand dollars," Charles said. Andre and I looked at him like he was crazy. He blinked slowly. "When I went to dinner with Emma she mentioned that both she and her sister each got a twenty-thousand-dollar signing bonus."

"What!"

"I didn't get shit!" I shouted. "You're just telling us this *now*!"

"Well, I didn't remember! I thought we all got one—I don't know, I couldn't remember if I did or not."

"How do you not know about twenty thousand dollars?!" Andre said.

"Portmonts are too busy polishing their monocles!" I yelled, and Andre cawed. He was just as mad as I was.

"Don't you see?" Charles interrupted. "He was willing to pay a premium to get them—and not just because they were twins, but because they were Ripley's twins."

"Isn't it kind of inappropriate to have test subjects you personally know?" Andre wondered.

"This is the piece we've been missing," I interrupted.

Charles still looked doubtful. "Okay, maybe they're Ripley's kids, but I'm supposed to believe Emma's a serial killer just because her dad was? You haven't met her. She's...she's..."

"It makes sense," Andre said. "It's the twenty-year anniversary of when CRD started killing, which is fucked up because it's also the year the twins were probably born. Maybe she wanted to make her own mark. Wyman knows the family, so he's desperate, thinks he can stop her, but he's gotten too attached to be objective. He's having dinner with her! She's supposed to be a patient, not a family friend!"

"Or maybe it's Megan," I suggested. I didn't need the two of them watching Emma like hawks, not when I had final chess pieces to move. It was Emma. She explained the CRD connection. She attacked Trevor, who then thought it was me or

Charles because he didn't know about Emma. And she has a crush on Charles, so maybe she got mad that I hooked up with him and sent the #slut message on Instagram. What I needed was for Charles and Andre to run in circles for a few days so I could take care of one more thing. It would require getting Emma down to the Sand Filtration Site to at least put her in the same location as Will.

I didn't exactly understand why she wanted to kill people in the program—maybe she was mad at Wyman or something—but if the murders were just Michael, Kellen, and Will, I could still make it seem like she was just targeting Adams students because they were convenient. And all male, for that matter—maybe I could work that angle.

"Megan's the normal one," Charles said.

"Who's to say what's normal?" I said. "It's the perfect crime, really. Go around killing people, and when someone fingers you, you say, *Do you really think it's me? Are you sure it wasn't my identical twin who's a diagnosed psychopath?*"

"Oh my God, it is perfect!" Andre shouted. "And if they found DNA, they wouldn't be able to prove which twin it belonged to, so Emma ends up behind bars."

I knew this wasn't really how twin DNA worked—there was still the issue of random mutations that would be different between them, but luckily neither of them had taken advanced biology.

"We need to take action, get enough evidence to stop them," I said. "Let's divide the work. I'll tail Emma. Charles, you see if you can find out where Megan lives, and Andre, you tail Trevor." Andre looked disappointed—he had broken the CRD part of the case and clearly wanted to claim Emma for his own. I made my eyes big and detailed how Trevor had a creepy fixation on me. As Andre's face grew softer, Charles, standing behind him, smirked.

"What about that Will guy?" Andre asked.

"Charles will keep an eye on him. They're in the same frat." Andre finally nodded in agreement—he was shockingly easygoing for a psychopath. But at this point I had already figured out that Andre's agreeableness—unusual for one of us—was all part of his act to get people to like him. It went along with his dimples just fine and would probably work well until he started to look a little older.

Charles peered at me. He knew I was up to something, and the last thing I needed was for him to corner me. I stood up. "Everyone be on high alert." I was in a hurry to leave, half expecting Charles to stop me to probe me further about Emma or Will.

To my surprise, he said nothing. I didn't like the two of them hanging out without me, but now that I had finally narrowed down who the hunter was, there were a lot of things on my to-do list.

55

"Should we come up with a game plan?" Andre asked, not looking up from his phone where he was still skimming Fiola's book. He felt out of place being alone with Charles in his fancy apartment without Chloe there as a buffer.

"Yes." Charles sat at his piano, resting his beer bottle next to him. Andre wondered what the hell kind of college student actually had a piano. He began to play it, a disturbing, intense piece that brought to mind goblins and ghouls.

"Do you know any music that's less horrifying?"

He laughed and stopped playing. "Not a fan of Liszt…? Can I ask you a question?" Charles said. Andre looked up. "How long have you been faking your diagnosis?" He said it almost conversationally.

Andre froze, his stomach lurching. "What?"

"Come on, you can tell me." Charles wore the benign, friendly expression of someone about to sell you a subprime mortgage. "I'm dying of curiosity."

"Why would you even think that?" Charles didn't answer, just looked back at him. You could confuse him for a nice guy, couldn't you? A guy with a sweet apartment who played the piano, who tried to be the voice of reason in their trio. It was hard to reconcile the friendly, open way he was looking at Andre with the fact of what he was. Andre's face cycled through a few expressions—a *haha, you're too funny* expression, a *what the hell* expression. He knew he was about to be threatened in some way, but some tiny part of him, after all this time and all he had gotten away with, felt a tiny bit of relief. Relief at finally being caught.

Charles smiled. "It's the way you act, the way you respond to things. I first noticed it when you were disgusted by that funnel-cake cheeseburger."

"What!"

"I don't feel disgust," Charles replied. "My girlfriend makes it a habit to sniff through the stuff in my fridge because I don't interpret the smell of spoiled food as something dangerous." Stunned, Andre struggled to think of something, maybe a joke, that would distract him. "Also, you just seemed pretty alarmed when I accused you of faking."

"So?"

"So, you catch someone like me or Chloe in a lie and we're lying in the next breath so well we almost believe it ourselves."

"You *seem* normal. Not like Chloe."

"I'm not," Charles said flatly. "I've spent two decades curating an image of normalcy."

Andre took a sip of beer, letting the nearly salty IPA sit in the back of his throat before swallowing. There was something exciting about the truth floating close to the surface, bumping its head up for oxygen. "If I *were* to say something…would you tell anyone?"

"Why would I?"

"Because you lack a conscience?"

"But my lack of conscience is exactly why I *wouldn't* tell," Charles said, his smile practically glittering. He was about to get his way and was probably sensing it. "I'm really curious, so I promise if you tell me I won't tell, because I want to know."

"You won't tell anyone? Not even Chloe?"

"She's hardly my confidante."

Andre played with his label. "I just filled out the application as a joke, but I never thought it would actually go anywhere… And then it sort of took off on its own and started snowballing."

"What? What did you do exactly?"

"The backstory is that when I was thirteen I got diagnosed with Conduct Disorder."

"Oh, I got that, too. I think I was nine, though."

Andre nodded. "I didn't think about it at the time—I mean, I was a kid, but later I read about it and basically thought it was a bunch of bullshit. My family was just in a bad place—of course I acted out. So did my brother, and I always did what he did."

"What do you mean *bad place*?" Charles leaned forward, and if you didn't know what he really was you could mistake him for an inquisitive, empathetic person. Charles was good, Andre thought. Much better than Chloe at faking it. Was this what prompted the outpouring of words, or was it exhaustion, the weight finally being lifted off his shoulders?

"My sister died really suddenly. She was the oldest. It wasn't even like she was sick or something. She just had an asthma attack."

"She died of an asthma attack?"

"It happens," Andre said, his voice clipped. "They called an ambulance and it took over forty minutes to get there."

"DC efficiency."

"Welcome to Northeast. Shit happened in our neighborhood— burglaries, sometimes a shooting. But this was different. It was like it broke everyone. My brother was in the same high school as her at the time. A pretty good student and really good at track. Sprinting and hurdles. Planned to go to college, but then he stopped caring. Didn't go to class. Started hanging out with what my mom called the 'bad elements' in the neighborhood. I was with him sometimes. Or just cutting class."

"So they diagnosed you with Conduct Disorder?"

Andre nodded. "I don't think I have it, to be honest, but it ended up working in my favor. When I was fifteen, I got in serious trouble. Some friends of mine broke into a place—I wasn't there with them, but I drove them away in someone's car right after it happened, but then they got caught. I got put on probation and had to switch to this special school. It was like a transitional school for kids with behavior problems, and some of them were coming straight out of juvenile detention." Andre shook his head. "Some of those guys. It hit me—I didn't want to end up like them. It made me realize how hard my parents worked to take care of us, what I was doing to them on top of all the suffering they were already feeling. Anyhow, the school counselor told me that this program at Adams was interested in me."

"Dr. Wyman?"

Andre nodded. "I started reading about psychopathy. Most of the people with Conduct Disorder end up getting diagnosed with Antisocial and that's basically the same as being a psychopath... I thought, hey, maybe I could make them think I had it for real. I didn't expect it would work, but then when it *did*, and my parents found out about the free financial aid, by then it was too late."

"But how did you get past the screening interviews and all that diagnostic stuff?" Charles seemed delighted by the tale of subterfuge. Andre felt a rash of strange pride.

"I looked up stuff on the internet. Most of the diagnostic surveys are self-report. I just answered the way I knew I was supposed to, based on what I read in books."

"What about the phone interviews?"

"I got my brother and his friend to pretend to be my parents."

Charles gave a short laugh. "So your parents don't know?"

Andre wagged his head uncomfortably. "Not really. I sort of

told my mom it was a special academic scholarship. The next thing I know, here I am."

Charles held up his beer, as if toasting. "Minus the deranged serial killer, it's not a bad deal."

"Was I that obvious?"

"I don't know. Seems like Wyman and Elena are fooled."

"You promise you won't tell Chloe?"

"Why would I? And she's too self-absorbed to notice herself." Andre was relieved, but then Charles smiled, leaning back on the piano with his elbows, eliciting low and high discordant notes. His smile was a little too wide. "Why would I tell anyone your secret?"

This, Andre realized, was what Charles was about. The offer to let him use his apartment wasn't altruistic—it was some way of exerting power. This information was power. Charles didn't personally care about the scheme—he seemed to think that bilking Wyman out of grant money was funny. But he just liked to have that little piece of control. *Don't trust these people for a second*, Andre thought.

56

I knew I should be more patient like Charles, but now that I finally knew who was hunting me, I wanted to hit her head-on like a semi.

Emma was to be taken seriously; this was a girl who, either by subterfuge or physical force, had made Kellen drink buckshot, had stabbed a man and bounced out the window before Andre could even spot her, and had broken into Kristen's house. She had followed me the night Will was killed even though I took every precaution.

I opened Instagram on my phone and went to Pinprick52's account. I DMed, We need to talk. I stared at my phone, expecting an answer back right away. The little green bubble by her name indicated that she was active.

The longer I waited, the more enraged I became. Who was she not to answer me, when I knew she was online?? I waited ten seconds, then huffed my way to the computer lab in the basement of Albertson Hall, which was nearly deserted. Everyone knew the faster computers were in the newer lab in the library, but the Albertson lab had the added benefit of being stupid enough to allow unlimited printing. I opened my email and printed out the entire document that Andre had gotten—Fiola's shitty book. I then hurried home, stopping briefly in the quad to fill my pockets with dirt.

Luckily, Yessica wasn't there to complain about the mess I was about to make in our common area. I began to beat up the stack of pages, crumping the paper, dog-earring random parts, making them look aged by smearing and wiping them with dirt, spilling some old tea to create a stain. Maybe in person you could tell the aging of the manuscript was fake, but I didn't need it to look that real—I would use a filter. I snapped a picture of the cover, then DMed it to Emma. Then I flipped to the page where the word *twins* appeared the first time and sent that, as well. *Ready to talk now, bitch?* I stared at the green bubble. No answer.

But then—finally: Do you understand that I am going to end you?

Do you understand that I am going to expose you? I wrote.

What even is that—it doesn't mean anything.

It's from a book John Fiola was writing. You know, Wyman's student when YOUR FATHER was going around killing people?

His dissertation?

I thought about the missing copies of Fiola's dissertation. What'd you do—steal all the copies from the library and burn them? If you weren't so lazy you'd know he was also writing a book. And I have the only copy. Of course, this wasn't true, but I needed her to think I was stupid enough to say this. I will make a deal with you.

You have nothing I want. I will end you regardless. You are the absolute worst. Your little barbecue confirmed everything I already thought about you.

My mouth fell open. I wanted to ask her why she hadn't rat-
ted me out to the police, but maybe she wanted to save me for
herself, and I definitely didn't want to admit to any kind of
barbecue.

WTF are you talking about? Here's the deal. You leave me alone,
or I will tell the entire world you are the CRD's daughter. TMZ will
be busting down your door.

You know I could just kill you and take that book, right?

You could try. Or we make a pact. I don't know why you are killing
people and I don't care. But there's no way you can get A or C.
They are both armed to the teeth—C's family are gun nuts and he
hired personal security. I know you cant even get into his building.

Lol, MICHELLE.

lol you would have gotten them already if you could. But I can
hand deliver them to you.

???

A trusts me and C wants to fuck me. I can hand them over like
little sheep. You get your manuscript. Then you leave me alone.
There was a long pause where she didn't say anything. Think
about it, I warned. This is my final offer.
      She didn't answer. I put my phone next to my laptop and tried
to tell myself to calm down. I had an entire French essay to write
and my Bio exam to study for, but I kept Googling "Vietnam
booby traps." But then my phone pinged.

You have a deal.

57

Part one of my plan was in motion. I knew Emma was smart—smart enough to have been getting away with all of this. She was at least somewhat reasonably a match for me—except she had one fatal flaw, which her stupid Instagram account revealed. Pride. She was documenting evidence that could count against her, but she did it, anyway—I guess it matched up with her interest in photography somehow. She was arrogant and assumed she was too smart to get caught. She probably thought I was stupid enough to think that I would hand over the book and she would hand over my life.

She would have no idea what I had up my sleeve. But I would need Charles.

I texted him: We need to come up with a plan. We can't just wait around.

Filling out the paperwork for a restraining order against T and filing tomorrow, Charles responded. He sent me a still from Kristen's webcam—he hacked it more than a month ago.

He did? Too bad Trevor wasn't really the killer: for a split second I thought about how it would be convenient if someone took care of Kristen for me. I pictured myself soothing Charles's broken heart afterward.

Fucking creep, he added. She's somewhere safe now.

What about you?

Have fun, he answered. Gun, sorry, autocorrect. I was going to head over to ft hunt in a bit.

I wondered if I could convince Charles to give me one of his guns. He had already said no, but maybe if he saw me scared and in need of protection he would give in. The dorms are being stricter about security, I wrote. but when people think about security they're never thinking about girls sneaking in. It's how I get away with stuff.

I've noticed, he wrote. Are you at home?

Yes. This murder spree is cramping my style.

Poor thing, he wrote.

Come over, we can scheme this out

He fell silent. I went back to my computer, occasionally glancing over to see if he was going to write something. I sighed, then picked my phone back up.

You've been avoiding me, I wrote.

?? I literally just texted you

We're never going to talk about what happened?

Nothing to talk about.

You're an ass

There was a long pause, then he wrote, What are you up to? which was about as infuriating as infuriating gets. "What are you up to" is pretty much the fuckboi way of cowardly suggesting interest without actually suggesting it.

Studying in bed

Sounds hot.

Could be, I wrote.

Oh?

I had fun the other night

Clearly, he wrote. You came really hard.

I did. You're such a tease

??? he wrote, indignant.

Come over. Yessica isn't here

I can't.

☹ You're no gun.

I'm gun, he insisted.

Send me a pic

Are you kidding? I could never run for Congress, he said.

I laughed. You could literally be a rapist and still get into congress lol.

Lol, he wrote.

Send something tame then.

There was a pause on his end. I shifted on my bed, excited. Then a selfie popped up in the chat box. He had his shirt off, revealing his smooth unblemished skin, the indentation of muscles. He was built the way I liked—not too beefy but definitely someone who went to the gym. He might have been naked, but the picture was cut off at his narrow hips, a thin blur of dark hair leading down from his navel. Your turn, he said immediately.

Not so prudish I stripped to my black lace bra and underwear and repositioned my phone until I could snap a picture good enough. Lips parted slightly, looking directly at the camera.

God you're fucking sexy, he wrote.

I can come over there, I suggested.

Not safe, he wrote.

Then bring your gun and come here, I said. I won't lay a hand on you and we should talk. Seriously, has there ever been a bigger load of BS than "We'll just talk"? Maybe "Just the tip."

There was an excruciatingly long pause. Ok, he wrote.

"Yes!" I shouted into my empty room. Come up the fire escape, I said. No one will see you.

He didn't respond, maybe not wanting to acknowledge that technically he was sneaking around. I circled my room, picking up dirty clothes and shoving them under my bed. I ran to the bathroom and freshened up, brushing my hair and spritzing perfume. I ripped my sheets off and replaced them with fresh ones, shoving the used ones under the bed, as well.

By the time I heard the reverberations of someone climbing the fire escape, I was cozy under my sheets, hair neatly arrayed, pretending to read a paperback of *Infinite Jest*. Charles rapped on the windowpane with his fingertips. I lifted the latch I had installed and he edged the old window up with a scraping noise. He crawled in somewhat gracelessly, walking on his hands for a few feet before the rest of his body fell in. We both laughed. I stayed under the sheets but moved over, and he lay beside me. I was on my side and he was on his back. "We need a plan," I whispered.

"What about evidence gathering?"

"I'm zeroing in on the killer, but I need your help. I need to get them to a certain location at a certain time."

"What location?"

"The McMillan Sand Filtration Site. It's this abandoned construction site."

"Why *there* in particular?"

"I just need to tie up some loose ends," I said, playing with his hair.

"What loose ends?" he asked, turning and looking directly at me. In the dim light his pupils were huge.

"This and that," I teased.

"Chloe...where's Will? I haven't seen him in more than a week."

"What am I—his keeper?"

He picked his head up off the pillow. "Did you...do something? At the sand place—is that where you did it?" I laced my hands over my bare stomach and said nothing. "I won't tell anyone," he whispered.

"Good, because there's nothing to tell. Will was a piece of shit and he deserved what he got."

"I know he's bad... Do you think—do you think he did it more than once?"

"Does that fucking matter?" I snapped.

Charles held up his hands innocently. "I don't know. So, your plan is that we get Trevor or Emma there and, what—make it look like they're responsible for Will?"

"Maybe." I beseeched him with big eyes. "They could overpower me—you're the only person I can ask for help."

"What about Andre?"

"I don't trust Andre."

"Racist!"

I snorted. "Not because he's Black—Andre's a one-hundred-percent psychopath. He puts on this totally wide-eyed earnest act all the time, and people like you fall for it." That, and there was certain information Andre could never know about me, stuff that Charles already knew.

"What do you want me to do?"

"I haven't completely figured it out." I had, actually. Charles, Andre, and the manuscript were my bait. She wouldn't expect us to be working together, and between the two of us and any firepower Charles had, we could overpower her. "I need physical backup Saturday night. I haven't worked out all the logistics but I need you there with your gun. We might need to go early to set up traps."

Charles shook his head. "You have a plan for everything, don't you?" It was as good as a promise. I squeezed his arm reassuringly, putting my head back down on him.

"What am I going to do with you?" he murmured, playing with my hair.

"Anything you want," I offered.

He shook his head, exhaling with frustrated humor. "I shouldn't even be here," he said, more to himself than to me. He turned to look at me, his face right next to mine on the pillow. "Do you know why I like being with Kristen?" he whispered. "Besides who she is. I like how normal we are together."

"Is that a good reason to be with someone?"

"Do you have any idea what I felt when they broke into her house?"

"I'm not denying that you think you love her."

"What, then?"

"I'm just saying that she'll never understand you. The darker parts of you. That there's an empty vessel under the mask."

"What's that supposed to mean?"

"No one could ever love that vessel but someone else just like you."

I couldn't read the expression on his face. "Sometimes it's exhausting to act all the time."

I wriggled closer to him and pet his hair. He didn't have any product in it the way he had the night of the Halloween Ball. It was soft, strands of blond mixed in with brown. He swallowed, the action making his Adam's apple bob. "What if we just made out a little—does that count?" he whispered.

I shook my head, crossing the space between us. We kissed, my white bedsheets forming a protective barrier between us. Above the sheet his hand smoothed down my back, stopped at my waist, then pulled me closer. We moved without any sense of urgency but the aching tension still built in me. I felt his lips on my throat. Something hard poked at me and it took me a split second to realize that it was his gun, tucked under the waistband of his pants. He shifted on top of me, pinning my arms above my head by the wrists, and I squirmed under his weight, wanting to touch him everywhere.

"Charles," I whispered.

He pulled back a little, looking at me. With our faces only a couple inches apart, I could tell he was not wearing his contacts. Suddenly he cringed. "You smell like oranges," he whispered.

"Huh?"

He blinked rapidly. "Burned oranges." He got off me then, sitting on the edge of the bed to dig something out of his pocket, then stood up abruptly as he put something in his mouth. "Do you have any Coke?"

"Excuse me?!" I near shouted.

He dry swallowed. "I'm having an aura. It means I'm about to have a migraine. Do you have anything with caffeine?" He was already edging toward the window. I dug a room-temperature can of energy drink out of my bag and he downed half of it. "I have to go lie down."

"Lie down here—we're not done talking."

"I'll see you, Chloe." He was already climbing back onto the fire escape. He was probably just chickening out, thinking that his migraine was punishment for cheating on his precious Kristen.

"You'll back me, won't you?" I called after him, but he was already making his way down the steps.

"I already said I would," he called back.

58

Charles opened his eyes, the numbers of his digital clock bleary in front of him. The pristine lawn of the Fort Hunt house was completely bare of fallen leaves, misted over by dew. He put the news on the radio—he had been listening regularly, wondering if he would hear something about a certain missing college student.

He headed downstairs, walking by his father's office, where he was on the phone with someone. Charles made two Bloody Marys in the kitchen and then carried them into his father's office. He was still on the phone, looking at his son with raised eyebrows as Charles set a drink down in front of him. A champion drinker, he had high standards. He took a sip as he ended the call, nodding his approval as he leaned back lazily. It was Thursday, but he was in Weekend Dad mode—a rare good mood. "I was back in Texas last week and ordered one of these. Guy brings it out with a *fried shrimp* stuck on the rim."

Charles laughed his disapproval, then sipped his own drink. The salty spice calmed him. Away in Fort Hunt, they were safe. Kristen was away from all that threatened her, and he didn't have to think about the whole mess. Why *not* sit around and have a few drinks? Why not blow off midterms?

The elder Portmont stood up, taking a bigger gulp. "I'm headed to London in about six—do you and Kristen want a ride?"

Hop in the jet and off to London. Stay in a nice hotel and catch a few shows while his father had meetings with oil execs. Across the Atlantic, Trevor could never reach him. Why not? He didn't have to help Chloe with whatever nonsense she was up to. But still, the problem wasn't going to go away on its own, and Chloe would probably make it worse without him—it's not like Andre would be able to stop her once she had her mind set. While he found Emma strange, he trusted his own judgment about her. Did he trust Chloe to be the fair arbiter of what would be reasonable evidence that Emma was dangerous? Of course not. "I would, but we have midterms." His father nodded his approval and Charles, hearing Kristen and his mother emerge from the far side of the house, went out to find them.

Kristen, sweaty from a private yoga lesson, headed up the stairs. "Come here!" he called. She laughed and ran, saying she had to shower. He caught up with her in the bedroom and, laughing, they undressed each other, pausing in between articles of clothing to kiss. They had sex in the shower, Kristen yelping when he turned the water cold so they could feel the contrast against the heat of their own bodies. Afterward they lay on the marble floor of the bathroom, wrapped in fluffy towels. "Why don't we blow off midterms and go to London with my dad?"

Kristen perched on one elbow and raised an eyebrow. "Because someone actually has a good GPA right now and doesn't want to blow it because he worked so hard." Charles sighed. "Come on. You just have the poli-sci one, then we can go to dinner as a reward."

"It's at six," he said, glancing at his smartwatch. "Who the hell schedules a midterm for 6 p.m.? What about you?"

"My last two are take-home essays, so I can stay here and work on them."

He cuddled her, tucking her head under his chin. He had told her some of it last night. Not everything, of course—that the murders were connected, or anything about Chloe. But the stuff about Trevor hacking her webcam and the restraining order he had filed. He could tell that she was upset—freaked out by it—but that she forced herself to not appear so. Because she knew that if she got upset, he might take it out on Trevor and make it worse. "We'll do our midterms," he said, "and in a few days this'll all be over."

Charles cracked his knuckles, looking down at his own hand-writing in the blue book on the desk in front of him. About a third of the class had already finished, turned their exams in, and left. This made him immediately want to get up and do the same, even though he hadn't finished. He forced himself to remain and made himself go over every test question. Like a good boy.

When he finally finished he headed down the stairs of the Arts and Sciences Building and outside. Some students huddled around a food truck that sold coffee and organic donuts. Charles looked at his watch—it was almost nine. He took out his phone to text Kristen, but froze when he saw a text from Chloe.

ive caught our prey, all tied up and ready for fun. Then a champagne emoji and a pin indicating her location.

"Shit," Charles muttered. Who did she have tied up? Trevor? Emma? What was the plan even? And weren't they supposed to do it on Saturday? Why did she have to jump the gun about everything? What if she went too far—or already had? He pictured Emma tied to a stake, Chloe prancing around her with a lit torch. Or maybe she had settled on Trevor—and while he was an asshole, doing something rash wasn't in anyone's best interest.

He hailed a cab and was about to tell the location to the driver when it occurred to him that this might be incriminating, depending on what Chloe was up to. Instead, he told the driver to take him to Children's Hospital, which was fairly close to where the pin had been.

He paid in cash, and then jogged east, away from the hospital and onto 1st Avenue, which had little traffic. This must be the sand filtration place, but he had no idea of what exactly it was—he had half assumed it was some warehouse taken over by hipsters.

He paused outside a high chain-link fence, squinting at his phone, realizing that the little red flag was still east of where he was. He scaled the fence, then dropped down. Some of the streetlight was blocked by the fence—he could make out overgrown weeds and some structures, but he had no idea of what he was looking at. Even with his contacts in, he didn't have good night vision. "Hello?" he called.

He weaved between mounds of dirt and discarded machine parts. There was an opening leading into pitch-blackness, but he thought he saw an artificial glow deep within it. A cave? No, a concrete stairwell leading down. "Chloe?" he called.

"...here!" he thought he could hear. Feeling with his hands, he headed into the darkness. He could see the bright light of an LED light bobbing ahead of him, maybe fifteen or twenty yards. His feet strangely sank beneath his shoes—sand? What was this place? "What have you done?"

"What do you mean?" she said, only her voice sounded strange.

Charles spun around, trying to see where she was. He stepped forward, then tripped into a sticky mess of firewood, almost falling before he braced himself with his hands. No...it wasn't firewood. It smelled like the leavings of an old barbecue. Burned fat and sticky soot, something hard beneath his hand. Bone?

He sat back on his heels, pulling his phone out and turning it on to shine a light down. The blast of light was so garish and bright that he almost couldn't make it out. But there it was—a charred skull and a collarbone, crisped meat still clinging on. He turned the phone off, laying it down into the sand. She had done it, after all, hadn't she. He could feel her behind him. "Is that what I think it is?" he asked quietly, not sure how he felt.

"Yes," she said.

He turned, but then felt something smash into his head.

59

With all my spying on Emma, I was behind in my schoolwork, and I wasn't going to let this bitch destroy my 4.0. I had reluctantly turned down the girls, who had decided to go someplace downtown for a three-course dessert, which is the best kind of dessert.

After I finished my French take-home, my reward was getting to do some Emma planning. I had to orchestrate everything perfectly. I helped myself to some of Yessica's trail mix and opened a new browser.

I opened Pinprick52's Instagram for inspiration. I hadn't seen the most recent post: a picture of a statue of a muscular dude with a sword holding up a tablet that said LEX on it. A quick Google search revealed that not only was it a statue that sat out front of the Supreme Court, but Emma had simply caged it off the internet rather than taking it herself. She was sending a message.

Frustrated, I moved backward in time through her posts, looking for clues I hadn't noticed before. Ultimately, it didn't matter why she was doing what she was doing, but knowing her motivation would help me anticipate her moves.

Some of her posts were pictures of places on campus I rec-ognized, but some were too bleary to see what they were. The first post was in July of this year of a cross street somewhere in DC. I tried a different tack: the only way I could see what she had favorited was to be a follower. I hadn't done this already be-cause I was afraid of making more connections between me and the account and the photo of me leaving McMillan. But at this point we had already talked to each other via DM. Which meant that eventually I would have to make the ultimate sacrifice: I would have to delete my Instagram account. But first, I would have to get my hands on her phone, the way I did with Will's.

I followed her account and tapped to look at favorites—then gasped. There was only one favorite. It was of a picture of a girl about our age. A Black girl with a huge smile and long eye-lashes, her hair in an incredibly tight ponytail. I didn't recog-nize her but I instantly made a deduction about what was going on. I shot off a text to Charles and Andre immediately, without thinking. IS THERE AN EIGHTH STUDENT IN THE PROGRAM!?!! DO YOU KNOW THIS GIRL??!!!!

But we all know that a watched cell phone never texts back. It took two whole minutes before Andre got back to me. That's Simone Biles, he responded.

He knows her! is she a senior??

Simone Biles does not go to Adams!! She's an Olympic gold gymnast—won a bunch of national championships. Y do u ask?

It hit me like a bat to the side of the head.

The killer wasn't Emma, it was Megan.

She had favorited from the wrong. fucking. account. Her Pin-prick murder account instead of her normal innocuous basic-ass bitch account.

You guys it's not emma it's megan! She was a gymnast-posts about it all the time on her real account. But as soon as I sent the text to Andre and Charles I regretted it. I had been so proud of my deduction that it hadn't occurred to me to withhold it from Andre, who I wasn't planning on having at my final set piece. Okay—whatever, move on to plan B, whatever that was.

Charles was typing: I know. I figured it out already. Come to the sand filtration site—I've got her.

Fucking Charles! How had he figured it out *before me* and why the hell did he have to blab about it to Andre? Now I'd have to figure out a series of lies for a plausible explanation about a certain burnt offering.

I couldn't get there fast enough, pausing only to grab my stun gun and my hoodie. I sprinted out of the dorm, feeling the blast of cold air through my yoga pants, which were not made for cold weather. I ran down the street, desperately looking for a cab while also calling a Lyft. The cab came faster, but the driver seemed annoyed that I kept getting impatient with him. The police had blocked off some roads because of the destruction left from rioting and we had to take two detours.

Then I was back out in the cold, my eyes adjusting to the dark as I scaled the fence outside of the McMillan site. I knew he would be where Will was. Just as I was running down the stairs to the cold innards of the inner cavern, I saw a bright light midway across the cavern, unless my orientation was wrong, right about where I had left Will's body.

"Charles?"

Something smashed into my head, and my vision flashed bright white before it went to black.

60

Come to the sand filtration site—I've got her, Andre read. His cell reception was spotty—dotting in and out as the subway car made its way east on the Red Line.

First the ridiculous question about Simone Biles, then the realization that Megan was allegedly the murderer they sought, and now Charles's claim: I've got her. *Got her for what?* Andre wondered, feeling abruptly nauseated.

Not quite knowing what to do, he got off at Union Station and for a moment stood paralyzed in the train station. Of course Chloe assumed she was right, and Charles had quickly bought her solution, but what if they were wrong? Would they...do something to Megan—or Emma, whoever it was? "I've got her," not "The police got her," or "They took her in for questioning." He pictured the girl tied up in a dark place somewhere, Chloe and Charles circling with various instruments of torture.

Andre paced through the main hall of the train station, oblivious to the people he was bumping into. Sand filtration—did he mean McMillan? A creepy, abandoned place in the middle of nowhere? It was the perfect place to do something, *something ter-*

rible, without anyone ever finding out. In all his self-interested research on psychopaths, he had seen the same thing over and over again: they could be rash, callous, devoid of empathy for others' pain, and if you crossed them, they could hold a serious and even deadly grudge.

Dazed, Andre stared at his cell phone as the realization had hit him. He had been so focused on his own series of lies that he had so easily fallen under the spell of Chloe and Charles. Sure, he occasionally saw that they were different than him, but he had been pulled in by Chloe and her jokes, her single-minded focus on finding the killer, Charles and his sheen of glamour.

He had thought of their trio as a strange Scooby-Doo gang thrown together and had forgotten that the moral compass guiding each of them was radically different. What did he think was going to happen if they had arrived at a conclusion—something *responsible*? Something very, very bad could be about to happen, possibly to an innocent person, possibly followed by Chloe and Charles moving nonchalantly on, assuming that Andre would be okay with whatever half-assed vigilante justice had just occurred.

Andre cursed quietly to himself, bringing his hands to the sides of his head and squeezing. He was the only one who knew what was going on. The only one who could stop them. His hands fumbled for his phone as he began to run toward the main exit where the line of cabs waited as he gamed out what he should do.

61

I could hear someone moaning. I was cold, my body shaking with chills. My throat ached and my head was throbbing. I opened my eyes, realizing that it was me who was moaning. I felt cold sand between my fingers. I closed my eyes, drifting, light-headed. Did Charles and I go to the beach?

"Not everyone is here yet," I heard a voice say. A female voice.

I passed out again.

The next time I came to, I felt something gnawing on me. My arms hurt and were starting to feel numb in the shoulders. It took me a moment to realize that my arms were pinned behind my back, bound at the wrists as I lay on my side. I blinked into the darkness. What I saw was confusing.

It was very dark, but my eyes had had a chance to adjust. A bright camping lantern was about ten feet away from me. Behind that, I could make out a slumped figure—Andre. He was sitting with his back up against a concrete column, his hands held in his lap in a strange way. To the right was a pale, wriggling blob that I couldn't make out because it was directly beyond the lantern.

There was something gnawing at my wrists again. Chewing on my restraints. I had a sudden memory of *The Pit and the Pendulum* and thought about rats. The rat chewed, occasionally catching nips of my skin. I tensed my arms, pulling, and the restraints snapped quietly. I rolled to my other side just in time to see Charles spitting plastic out of his mouth. There was dried blood on his forehead and his mussed hair was sticky and black with it. But his eyes were alert. He spoke quickly, barely above a whisper. "Run. *Now.* She's coming back."

The muscles in my legs were about to spring to action, but it was too late. I saw a shadow cast by the lantern. A figure moving forward. Megan, dressed all in black, her hair back into a ponytail. Behind her was Andre. Charles was lying on the ground beside me—the only person who apparently had the honor of both their arms and legs being bound. Trevor was sitting cross-legged, looking strangely relaxed, staring to his right directly at Emma.

Megan sauntered over. "It's almost time for our little party."

"Party?" Charles echoed. "I didn't get an invitation." *God, you idiot—now isn't the time for jokes!*

Megan lashed out at him and I cringed as she kicked him, first in the chest, then right in the head. I thought of jumping up to attack her but something made me stop—Andre was looking right at me. Grimly, he shook his head. His hands were bound together but I could recognize the familiar gesture of a finger gun. I looked back at Megan and saw that she held a pistol in her left hand. Charles's pistol—she must have taken it off him. My stun gun was gone—maybe she had that on her, too.

Megan crouched down in front of Charles, who was weakly coughing up blood. Her assault had left him in bad shape, worse off than the rest of us. Trevor and Andre both seemed dazed—maybe she had drugged them or cracked them in the head like me. It was harder to tell with Emma, who was sitting stock-still, a blank, washed-out look on her face. "Are you done?" she said to Charles. "Done being a monster idiot?"

"I thought I'd have another fifty years," he said.

Idiot!

She kicked him again in the chest. I could feel the anger rising off me like heat. God, here I was, perfectly unarmed, when I had practically made it an art these past weeks of always being prepared for an attack.

Charles was curled into a ball, protecting his chest with his bound arms, but he turned a bloody grin in Andre's direction. Andre's eyes were wide and not amused.

"Megan, you can stop," Emma said quietly. "It's not too late. Just because you start something doesn't mean you can't stop."

Megan looked at her with disgust. "No one asked your opinion, mouse. I'm almost done here." A very confused Trevor kept looking from Megan to Emma and back.

I held my breath and edged closer to Megan. She had arranged us so that she had made a circle of captives, with her at the center. Charles was slowly struggling to a sitting position, which must have been hard, given his cringing. He blinked against the bright, fake light of the lantern.

"Ah," Megan purred, "here they come." There were two lights moving across the cavern, coming closer, the bright lights of when people use their phones as flashlights. "You got my message," she said as they approached the group.

Dr. Wyman came closer with his hands up, one holding a cell phone. Elena was behind him, shock blanking out her face.

"Put the phones down," Megan shouted, raising the gun. She held it the wrong way. Sideways, like they do on TV. I don't know a ton about guns, but enough to know that that isn't how people really handle guns if they know what they're doing.

To his credit, Wyman stayed calm and obeyed her, setting his phone facedown. Elena dropped her own phone with a clatter where it landed near Andre. With all eyes on the two psychologists, I took advantage of the distraction and edged closer to Megan. Andre coughed.

"Megan, someone is going to notice all these students are gone and call the police," Wyman said calmly. Oh, stupid Dr. Wyman... I would have lied and said I'd already called the police.

Megan snorted. "Yeah. Because they're not busy with the Lafayette Park protests or anything. Let's face it, no one cares about these five. All of you made it so easy for me." She put the gun down by her hip and an innocent, sweet look came over her face. It was astonishing—as if one face were entirely washed off and replaced with another. "You'd be amazed at the places I can get into."

I tried to edge forward again, but Andre coughed again. I looked at him, annoyed, but he caught my eye and pointedly looked to my left, then back at me, then to my left again. I looked back and saw that about four feet away from me, at the base of one of the columns, an irregular shape broke the smooth architectural line. A broken brick.

"Dr. Wyman, we're going to play one more little psychology game before I kill all of you," Megan chirped.

"I don't think you're thinking straight. You're obviously upset. Why don't you tell me what's going on?" Wyman said.

"What's going on? What's going on is this whole sick enterprise! You think I don't know what a monster my father was? My sister?"

"I'm not like him," Emma said quietly. Megan found her comment so outrageous that it gave me cover to edge a full foot closer to the column and the loose brick.

"Huh!" Megan exclaimed. She pointed the gun directly at Dr. Wyman. "What do you think of that? What did all your tests say? Twenty years of research and all that bullshit just to say that she's just like our dad. Sick. *Wrong* in the head. Not normal like me."

I wondered if Megan was more fucked up than all of us put together.

"It must have been hard thinking about who your father was," Elena said quietly.

"Oh, fuck you! Fuck both of you and your study! Here you are, helping these—these *freaks*—" here she waved the gun at all of us "—when what you should be doing is collecting them all and giving them cyanide."

"Who's your father?" Trevor asked, clueless.

"Gregory Ripley, the CRD Killer," Charles said.

This almost earned him another kick, but Wyman interrupted it. "We believe in human potential," he said. "We believe that people can be taught to make constructive choices, even you. Twenty years ago...some horrendous things happened, and I wanted to create work that would prevent things like that from ever happening again. Megan, you are standing at a crossroads just like he did. Please put down the gun, and let's talk, just you and me."

Megan stared at him, her eyes narrowed, and slowly her eyes moved over to Emma in a way that almost gave me a chill. Emma was frozen on the ground, hugging her knees with her bound arms, looking up at her sister with an expression I couldn't interpret. It wasn't like it was fear—it was like it was resignation. Megan tapped the butt of the gun against her thigh.

"You want to kill your own sister?" Charles said, actually sounding incredulous. His breathing sounded raspy even from where I sat.

"My sister is a monster. I read her journal for years. I always knew there was something wrong with her, like our father, and when she got into this program, I knew for sure. I thought it was a joke at first—why would anyone collect a fucked-up menagerie like this group? I watched her, I watched all of you just to make sure I was being fair. But it turns out, you're sick, you're perverted. I can undo what my father did. The best thing I can do for society is take you out of the population."

"Wait," Trevor said suddenly. "I'm not like them."

Oh, bitch please. The comment was so outrageous that even I had to pause in my inching toward the column.

"I can help you," he added, looking at her almost earnestly.

She was clearly skeptical. "How can *you* help *me*?"

Trevor licked his lips. "I can get into his data files," he said, gesturing to Wyman. "All of them. For years. Every student who's gone through his program. Every student who qualified or even just came close. We...we could make a list together."

You little shit. Wyman and Elena were both staring at him incredulously. Elena gave her boss a little look; it was just a split second but any woman could recognize it. *I told you so*, it said. *I told you about this kid and you didn't listen.* My fingers, numb from the cold, edged their way onto the column behind me, tracing out the outline of the broken brick. I tugged and it gave way, but not entirely.

"What's your game?" I asked loudly. "What did you do over there?" I asked, gesturing with my head in Will's direction. Megan stalked closer to me, smirking. "How many people have you killed? Four? Five? Six? Clearly you're not limiting yourself to just bad guys."

"Bad guys, huh?" she asked, spinning around to face Wyman and Elena. Glad for the distraction, I gave one final tug, and then the chunk of brick was in my right hand, cold and heavy. "You've been playing all these psychological games with us for years, now it's your turn to be in an experiment. I'm going to kill everyone here," she said matter-of-factly. "But if one of you—" here she waved the gun at the pair of psychologists "—is willing to take someone out yourself, I'll let you go free."

Charles perked up, his gaze intent on the scientists. He clearly thought one of them would take the deal. Emma and Trevor were also staring intently, but Andre's face was more emotive: *What the fuck*, his face said. The longest silence went on, Megan waiting for one of them to take the deal. "Megan, we are not doing that. Why don't we go to my office and talk?" Wyman suggested.

"No one wants to talk to you, Do you think any of these freaks actually want to talk to you about their problems?" she asked. I edged closer. In her distraction, she didn't realize I had scooted almost behind her.

"Megan, we are helping these people," Elena said quietly. "No, it's not a population that everyone wants to work with, but that's the whole reason there's so little research about it."

"That's the purpose of science," Wyman chimed in. "To understand things without judging them. I would like to help you, and I won't judge what you've done already if you just put the gun down."

"Name *one* person this program has helped," Megan demanded.

"Me," Charles said suddenly. "I learned to at least resemble a human being. You should try it some time."

"You *terrible* man!" she shouted. I saw her arm move. A flash of light came from the end of the gun, an exploding, popping sound. Charles's body snapped back, falling to the ground. She had shot him. She had shot Charles.

Coldness came over me. It was calm, but it was also a concentrated, white-hot rage. I was too low, though, for the brick, so it was her lower body I sprang at, knocking her down, my teeth sinking into her calf between where her pants ended and her socks began, drawing blood. She screamed and the gun went off, a bright pop of light in the darkness. We scrabbled like two alley cats. I smashed the brick into her head with the sound of a melon bursting, collapsing her nose.

She made a strangled cry. I swung again, finding purchase. There was screaming, I'm not sure whose. I couldn't see anyone else, not Wyman, not Charles, not any of them, just this despicable bitch who I had to end. Someone was shouting my name. I swung again and again, until there was a mass of white lights cutting across the dark cavern in all directions. Shouting. Men in black were appearing like ninjas, blinding me with their lights, shouting.

"Drop the weapon!"

"Down on the ground!"

"Down on the ground now!"

They all shouted at once. I realized suddenly that the lights were trained on *me*. The fancy-looking rifles, too. Blood dripped off my chin. Dazed, I dropped the brick and put my hands above my head, blinking into the lights blindly.

62

"Chloe, come here," Elena said quietly. I obeyed. There were police milling around everywhere, their bright white flashlights arcing across the cavern. The SWAT guys were clustered in what had been the center of our circle of psychopaths. The plainclothes police—I think they were detectives—were starting to block off a large area and push us out of it, telling us not to go anywhere.

Elena withdrew a small packet of Handi Wipes from her purse, and wiped the blood from my mouth and where it had leaked out the sides. Her thin fingers were shaking. "Are you okay?" she whispered.

"Is Charles dead?" The EMTs had come in after SWAT realized I wasn't a threat to anyone—that the real culprit was now Hamburger Helper being photographed by police forensics. They had surrounded Charles immediately like a pack of bees while one lone EMT checked Megan to confirm the obvious—she was dead. There was a lot of shouting and then they carted Charles away on a portable stretcher, a cop grabbing me by the back of the shirt to prevent me from following. Charles had been deathly pale, unmoving. The EMTs had booked it out of here—I had a bad feeling in my stomach.

Elena put her hands on my shoulders and didn't say anything.

Shit. Something just occurred to me. I needed Megan's phone. She either had it on her, because everyone our age is attached to our phones, or if she was smart she left it at home, knowing that the phone could possibly geolocate her to the same place as her intended mass murder. But I had barely taken two steps when two cops appeared, pushing me back toward where Andre was. He was staring, his hand clasped over his mouth and nose, at something a few yards away.

I looked over and saw that several of the police were examining the remains of a certain human barbecue on the ground. I guess it did smell—the cavern was underground, and there was dampness in the air and sand and what was left of Will's body. I would have to make sure to lay down the remainder of my cards carefully when the police questioned me. I trusted that Charles knew better than to say anything, and Andre didn't know anything substantial about Will.

"What—what is that?"

I shrugged. "Another body, I guess."

Andre looked up suddenly and right at me, his hand falling off his face. There was a look I couldn't read in his eyes. I couldn't quite tell what it was, but I knew it wasn't a good one. I feigned some tears. "Honestly, I just want this night to finally be over."

He stared at me. "Right. Right, we all do."

Then all of a sudden the police were ushering the lot of us outside to police SUVs that were waiting. Elena sat next to me during the ride, her thin hand gripping my forearm. "Everything's going to be fine now," I said.

She looked at me, her brow furrowed. They whizzed us away to a police station, then separated us into different rooms, but a nice lady came in to give me some hot tea. I wasn't dressed right and was having residual effects from being left out in the cold for so long.

A door opened and a man came in, smiling in a subdued but friendly way. "Hi there, I'm Detective Bentley," he said. Detective Bentley was DILFy in a *Die Hard* sort of way—I liked him right away. "I've been working this case for the past few months. Do you mind if I ask you a few questions?"

I didn't. It was *very* important that I answer a few questions. Some of what I told him was true—that we knew we were being stalked, that someone tried to get into a bedroom where Charles was, and that we figured out that the twins were the CRD's kids and that the killings appeared to be some form of copycatting. I left out the Instagram part, of course, and embellished a few new details that no one would be able to verify.

"There was one night," I said, starting to shiver again, my teeth clacking. Detective Bentley took off his coat and put it around my shoulders. Bingo. I hugged it around me, smiling gratefully. "I was coming back from the gym and heading to this frat party around nine o'clock and I got the feeling someone was following me."

"Which frat?" Bentley was taking notes.

"SAE, I think? Anyway, I thought I was just being paranoid and went to the party. I was talking to this blond boy—crap, I can't remember his name. We talked for a while, but I got up to go to the bathroom and saw that this girl was *glaring* at me. I didn't think anything of it at the time. I assumed maybe this girl was hooking up with the blond boy, or he was her boyfriend or something, and she got mad. But—" I widened my eyes, filling them with the traumatic tears that I was supposed to be feeling "Mr. Bentley, it was *that girl*—the one who just tried to kill us all!"

"It was the same girl?"

"I'm positive. I remember distinctly, because she *turned* and *looked* at me, like totally evilly! Then she walked off with that boy. It was really weird, though—it was like she was acting like she'd *stolen* him away from me or something. I don't even remember his name."

"Could you describe him? How old? Was he in the fraternity?"

Rambling, I gave him a description of Will that was more or less on point. "I guess that wraps it up... She was crazy in the coconut, and must have figured out that we knew about her dad being CRD."

Suddenly, Bentley put down his tablet and stooped to my level, putting his hands on his knees. "Chloe... I know your moral reasoning is different than regular people, but—"

"Wait, what?"

"We know about the program."

"Who?"

"Some of the police. I do. I've worked with Leonard for years on this program. You seem like a nice girl and Leonard tells me you have very good grades."

"I was a National Merit finalist."

"That's quite an accomplishment! But I want you to think for a second about Emma, and the fact that she probably doesn't want anyone to know who her father is. A lot of people worked hard to keep that a secret because the media would have torn those two little girls into tabloid shreds."

"Were you one of them?"

"It was before my time, but my father was the lead detective on the Ripley case. Everyone fell in love with those little girls."

I snorted. "Everyone had bad judgment, then."

He was undeterred. "Do you think you can keep the part about Emma's dad a secret?"

"I like secrets," I said, hugging his coat around me. "If you tell me one thing." He looked a little skeptical but nodded. "She tricked me—me and Andre and Charles—to get us down here. How did she get everyone else?"

"The same way, actually. She spoofed a text to Charles so

that it looked like it came from you, then she got her hands on Charles's phone. She spoofed Trevor, too, pretending to be a girl looking to hook up." I had to admire that—it was what I would have done, and Trevor *would* go to a weird cavern if he thought he might get some. "But with Emma and the doctors, she just simply asked them to come. I guess they never saw it coming," Bentley said.

I wasn't entirely sure I agreed about Emma. I think there were things Emma didn't want to admit but maybe suspected about her sister.

Andre tried not to stare at Dr. Wyman, who was sitting at the far end of the hallway of the police station, his head in his hands. He looked pallid. Andre had been taken to another part of the building and questioned, then had forensic evidence taken from him, and was now free to go as soon as his ride showed up. He hugged his arms around his chest, still trying to get rid of the chill that had settled into his bones after God-knows-how-long in that underground place. All he wanted to do was be home. Real home, not dorm home. He took out his phone and after considerable thought texted his brother: Long story but I'm at the police station @ Dave Thomas Circle. Can you pick me up? I'll stay at home for a few days. An ellipsis appeared, then a singular Pooh! which was Isaiah's way of saying, *I'm on my way, but I want the whole story and I can roast you over it while we eat some greasy food.* Which was fine by Andre.

He was glad for the few moments alone to try to warm up and think about what he had just seen, which some part of his brain still could not process. It was over. Everything was over. Mystery solved—they'd all go home safe and…happy? Just then, Chloe emerged from a doorway wearing a coat that clearly wasn't hers. He had been separated from everyone else as soon as he had gotten to the police station, and assumed they'd questioned her and also took any forensic evidence. "Don't say any-thing," she whispered to Andre as soon as she slid into a chair right beside him.

He sat straight up. Say anything about what? Was she mad at him? Did she figure out that he had been the one to call the cops on his way to Megan's party—or whatever you wanted to call it—or had she assumed it was Elena or Wyman? Tense, Andre tried to watch her without it being obvious. She didn't seem perturbed; she was swinging her legs and playing Dog Dash on her phone. *You just brained a girl to death*, Andre thought. *I saw pieces of her brain.* "Do you think there are snacks anywhere?" Chloe asked suddenly.

"Probably," Andre said, wishing she would go away. And then she did, practically skipping down the hall. Andre swallowed, his throat so dry it seemed to click. In a little inlet just off the hallway was a table set up with burned-smelling coffee and Sty-rofoam cups. He poured two with hands that were shaking a little and walked down to where Wyman was sitting. Wyman accepted the coffee with a surprised but sad smile that didn't really reach his eyes. He looked like he was physically in pain.

"Are you going to be okay, Dr. Wyman?" Andre asked.

"Sorry, I… It's the strangest sensation of déjà vu. All I ever wanted was for those girls to be protected, to have a normal life."

"You never thought there was something wrong with Megan?"

Wyman exhaled loudly. "When I got the call from Cali-fornia, when they first started to think that Emma might have psychopathy, she was all I could think about—how could I help her? I know my personal relationship with her made it odd for her to take part in the study, but I thought the program might provide a better life for her."

"But, Dr. Wyman…why did you want to help Gregory Rip-ley to begin with?"

He blinked, as if the answer were obvious. "Because he was a profoundly disturbed person—I just didn't know *how* disturbed."

"But when the entire country wanted him executed, why did you testify on his behalf at the sentencing?"

"I'm a Quaker, Andre. I don't believe in the death penalty. A lot of people claim to be opposed to it and the system that perpetuates it, but suddenly those morals disappear with a case like Ripley. I don't believe the state should execute a man, and I don't think any man is beyond redemption. I wanted to help him."

"Do you think he could have been helped? If he'd lived?"

"No, and do you know why not? Because the field of psychology has devoted relatively little time and energy to studying psychopathy. Quakers believe in something called restorative justice. It means when someone does something wrong, you don't take their life or remove them from society, but that person is required to repair the harm they've done."

Andre looked silently at his bitter-tasting coffee. With all his research, Andre knew the arc of Wyman's career, but had never thought of it this way. He felt embarrassed suddenly—Wyman was not some deranged mad scientist, but a man so earnest that it was almost painful to think about. He imagined what it must have felt like for Wyman to have thought he had helped the twins find some semblance of a normal life, only to have this happen, and for it to feel as if it was something he should have been able to see and stop.

Andre struggled for something to say; he wondered if now, in the chaos of everything, it might be a good time to come clean about his diagnosis. When he opened his mouth, though, what popped out was, "Are they going to shut down the program?"

Wyman looked bewildered, then this was almost instantly replaced with a look of sympathy. "No, Andre, I wouldn't worry. It's you guys who were attacked, not the other way around." He patted Andre's back somewhat absently and Andre felt a flush of shame.

Just then, one of the cops reappeared with Emma, swapping her out for Wyman to take him away to a room somewhere.

Emma's expression was blank, guarded. She sat on the bench, perfectly still, the bottom of her shoes resting flat on the floor. If the events of the night had traumatized her, she didn't show it.

"I'm sorry...about your sister," Andre ventured. Since he had plowed through Fiola's book, he had been concentrating on the mystery, on keeping himself safe, and hadn't really paused to think about the fact that there were two girls about his same age who both knew that their father had committed some of the most horrific acts in true-crime history. This was the same man who had fed them as babies, bought them toys for Christmas, and kissed their mother good-night. Their father had been a monster, and their mother had in a way abandoned them, as well. It was more than enough trauma for several lifetimes, let alone one.

Emma turned to face him. Her eyes were a pale shade of hazel, unreadable, and were focused on the wall behind him. "Nothing I ever said to Megan could ever control her."

Andre struggled for something reasonable to say. "It's not your responsibility to control your sister."

"It kind of is," Emma replied. "Because I'm the only one who really knows her. I didn't want her to be that way. She was always smarter than me, always seeing everything as a threat or planning something." She was quiet for a long time. Andre strained to hear the detectives down the hall, but there was the intermittent blasts of radio coming from more than one office. Emma was looking down at her sandy shoes.

She looked up thoughtfully at Andre. "Did you know my father is a trading card?"

"What?"

"They make these cards with different killers on them, like playing cards. People collect them." Then she looked back down at her feet and said no more. Andre still felt the rebuke, even though it couldn't possibly be aimed at him. What kind of people collect such cards?

His ears were burning, and he could think of no defense.

He thought of the pantheon of podcasts, TV shows, and movies about serial killers that he consumed as a form of entertainment. It was all too easy to forget that the people involved were real people and not characters. "I guess I would say there's a line somewhere between wanting to understand something and morbid curiosity," he said finally.

Emma looked up and directly into his eyes for the first time, and she spoke quietly. "There is no line when you're Gregory Ripley's daughter."

Andre's phone vibrated—Isaiah had texted him an eggplant emoji, which presumably meant that he was here. Relieved, he nodded an awkward goodbye to Emma, who only stared at him, and double-checked with the desk officer that he was free to leave.

He walked outside into the chilly air. It was almost three in the morning, and though there was almost no traffic at this hour, the streetlights provided enough light to easily spot Isaiah's car parked illegally, the hazard lights on. He expected to slide into the car, which would inevitably be blasting some awful music, but Isaiah got out, and it wasn't humor and good-natured older-brother ribbing on his face, but concern and anxiety. Then the back door opened and his parents emerged, his father somewhat stiffly because of his bad back. Andre was so exhausted—he had just almost been killed, he was only human—could he help that his eyes watered? They were coming upon him now, glad to see that he was alive, wanting hugs, wanting to know what had happened that he had ended up at the police station. Andre knew that first he would hug them. He would hug them tightly because they were his family and he loved them, and he wanted the comfort and the quiet familiarity of their home, the cup of hot chocolate his mother would make, maybe a piece of toast, before falling asleep in his childhood bed. He would hug them first, and then he would lie to them.

63

The car turned onto Rhode Island, cutting ahead of two people on scooters who barely noticed. Detective Bentley was an
assertive driver. Outside, the sun was shining and people were
texting as if there hadn't almost been a mass murder last night.
Detectives, apparently, didn't drive normal police cars, but ones
that were normal looking but had internal lights and sirens.

After last night's party, they had asked me to come back in
again and answer more questions. I reaffirmed my mysterious
blond boy story, and stuck to everything else. I texted Andre,
who said the police had also questioned him again, and that he
was going to crawl into bed and hibernate for the rest of the
year. I told him it was time to celebrate our newfound freedom.

"Can we put the siren on?" I asked. Bentley shot me an
amused but stern look, then shook his head. "Come on, you
people were two seconds away from shooting me to death!"

"Well, yeah, they saw a girl bludgeoning someone to death."

"What are you complaining about?" I said. "I just solved two
unsolved murders for you."

"Three," he muttered.

"Three?" I made my eyes huge. "So that *was* another body in the sand place? Andre and I thought maybe it was an animal."

"Forget I said anything. You know, there's more than a couple guys on the force who don't exactly feel great that there's a program with a bunch of psychopaths in the city."

"You do realize that someone who was ostensibly as normal as you are was the one who did it?" He shrugged, admitting that I was right. "Get your priorities in order, Detective. The worst I do is kiss boys with girlfriends when we live in a city where a new indictment rolls out every week."

"Fair enough." Bentley arrived at GW Hospital, pulling over the car on 22nd Street to where you couldn't park unless you were a cop, I guess. A couple of GW students peered at us as they crossed the street, heading to the Whole Foods or to classes.

"Stay out of trouble, Miss Chloe," he said.

I looked him dead in the eye. "And what if I don't?"

"Then definitely don't ask for me." We smiled goodbye at each other.

I had just figured out which elevator to take when who did I spot but Kristen Wenner looking tired and washed out, holding a bakery box from Buttercream under her arm. I jogged to make the same elevator as her. "Kristen! It's me, Chloe, from your party."

"Oh, hi," she said, sounding exhausted.

"Is it true? What I heard about Charles?" I whispered. She looked confused, but then I explained, "I'm a volunteer here—we know everything."

"It's true," she whispered. "Poor thing."

"I heard that some crazy girl was stalking people?"

"In as much as Charles can say. Apparently, she was obsessed with half a dozen students on campus—they're still investigating."

"Charles has that star quality—I can see it." The elevator was approaching the sixth floor. "Maybe I can pop in and say hi?" I suggested.

"Oh, do, Chloe!" Kristen said, grabbing ahold of my arm. "I was here all last night and I can only stay for a few minutes. Charles doesn't like being alone. He'll enjoy the company."

Of course Charles had a private room. The TV was on silent and Charles sat up in his hospital bed, watching. His hospital gown wasn't tied all the way so it drooped over one shoulder, showing the bandage just under his collarbone. "I brought a visitor!" Kristen said.

Charles looked at Kristen, then me, then Kristen again, a stoned smile growing over his face. He definitely did not want me fraternizing with Kristen. "Chloe, remember, from your party?" I said sweetly.

"Ohhh," he said.

"I brought you some cookies," Kristen said. She came over to leave them on his tray and kiss him, then she smoothed his hair. "You feeling any better?"

"Tired. I'm on so much drugs right now," he said, sure sounding like it. Kristen stayed for a few minutes, but then apologetically bowed out, saying that I could keep him company for a little while. She left and I wandered to his bedside to take a cookie for myself. I selected the one with the most chocolate chips. "Very funny," he said sourly, but with some humor.

"You should be nicer to people who've saved your life." He edged over on the bed with some difficulty, and I climbed on to lie beside him. "I can't believe we were so dumb," I said. "I never even really considered Megan."

"I was seriously considering her," he replied. "I just thought there was more evidence for other suspects."

"You did not!" I yelled, indignant. "You're just saying that after the fact!"

He laughed. Charles moved the bakery box to his bedside table, and I snuggled closer to him. Under the gauze and antiseptic smell, he still smelled like Charles. "I have a present for you," he whispered.

"For me? For saving your life?"

He reached with some difficulty toward the bedside table where a pitcher of water and some folded clothes lay. From between the clothes he withdrew an iPhone and handed it to me. The home screen was of a gymnast in midaerial. I gasped, snatching it. "How did you get this?" I cried. Shit. It needed a passcode. I tried 1234, then 0000.

"Right when the SWAT guys came, but before the EMTs got to me. I was right next to her body."

"What a fast thinker."

"She had to have known...about Will, right, to bring us all there?"

I didn't answer him, trying more passcodes. On a whim, I typed out the numerical equivalent for B I L E S. Success! I immediately deleted her Instagram account, then put the phone in airplane mode and promptly dropped it into his pitcher of water. I had already deleted my own account—I had done so the second I got to the police station and they let me use the bathroom.

I prodded Charles, realizing that he was dozing off. "Do you think Emma knew all along?"

"I don't know—sometimes I wonder if she did figure out what Megan was doing, but maybe she thought she could talk Megan out of it. Maybe she still feels some kind of loyalty to her," Charles said. "I was so sure it was Trevor."

"It wasn't until I realized he was recovering from some attack at the hospital that I knew it couldn't be him. Megan was hunting him, too."

"He's a piece of shit. He would have happily turned over every person associated with the program just to save his own skin."

"I know," I said. "He's not forgiven. Not in my book. He's made a powerful enemy."

"Save the scheming for another day." He dropped his voice to a whisper. "I forget—I'm lying in bed with a serial killer, technically."

I frowned. "It's not like that." He laughed and in apology put his good arm around me. I lifted my head up momentarily to free my hair. "Charles, you never really thought it was me, did you? That I'm capable of all those awful things?"

"Of course not," he said mildly, but his glazed, stoned eyes were on the TV.

I took hold of his chin and turned his head so he had to look at me. "Tell me the truth, Charlie Bear!"

He smiled too widely, then tucked some hair behind my ear. "Of course I had to *consider* it, but I never *really* thought it was you," he said, his eyes clear and directly focused on me. That's the problem with people like us—we're too good at lying so you never know the truth.

I sighed, tucking my head into his chest, and peered at the TV across the room while I thought about how I was going to destroy Trevor. On the news, a protest was raging somewhere in a country where I didn't recognize the flag they were burning. Then they showed a polar ice shelf melting and falling into the sea. Charles turned his head slightly and kissed my forehead. I'll relax today, and take the day off, I reasoned. There's always time for new schemes tomorrow.

★ ★ ★ ★ ★

ACKNOWLEDGMENTS

The fact that this book exists and the entire business end of it occurred during a global pandemic is a testament to the incredible work and support of so many parties. During one of the darkest periods I've ever experienced, having this book and all these people rooting for it kept me smiling and kept something forever on the horizon to look forward to. In a crazy-emotional year, where it seemed like all the best and worst things were happening at the same time, seeing other people's happiness at this book's success was like a light cutting through the dark.

To my agent, Rebecca Scherer, for picking my humble little manuscript out of the slush pile and having absolute faith that it could be successful. I had total trust in your judgment about how to get this sold despite COVID and you delivered (and delivered and delivered!). I'm proud to be on your shelf. Thanks to the entire team at JRA for all your support to this newbie author.

To my editor at Park Row Books, Laura Brown, for seeing and understanding this novel, asking all the right questions, and pushing it to the next level. I wish you could see fourth-grade me clacking away on a typewriter, college me thumbing through

Writer's Market, thirtysomething me receiving my 300th rejection from an agent—you've made my wildest writerly dreams come true. Thank you to everyone at Park Row who made this book happen: Erika Imranyi, Margaret Marbury, Rachel Bressler, Loriana Sacilotto, Randy Chan, Rachel Haller, Amy Jones, Lindsey Reed, Punam Patel, Quinn Banting, Heather Connor, and Roxanne Jones.

To Liz Foley and Daisy Watt at Harvill Secker for swooping in for the kill to champion this book and bring it to readers over the pond. Mikaela Pedlow, Anna Redman Aylward, and Sophie Painter for working so hard to make this book a success in the UK.

To all the communities and individuals that helped me grow as a writer. To my incredible group of lady writers in DC, in particular to my ride-or-die girls Melissa Silverman and Everdeen Mason—we did it! To the various workshops and their respective teachers who have supported me over the years: the Jenny McKean Moore workshop, Litcamp, the Marlboro Summer Writing Intensive, Breadloaf, VONA, Sewanee, Juniper, Colgate, assorted college writing classes where I too often wrote in present tense, and last but not least the community of writers I went to high school and workshopped with. To all the readers of all the drafts of this book, or any of my books for that matter. To Sgt. Fluffy for MPD and firearms consulting.

To all the people who published my short stories. In particular: Susan and Linda at Glimmer Train, who published my first story; Morgan Parker at Day One for publishing *Twelve Years, Eight-Hundred and Seventy-Two Miles*; Lantz Arroyo, Sarah Lopez, and Nick Hurd at Radix Media for publishing *Guava Summer*—without these significant wins as an emerging writer, I never would have had the confidence to keep going.

To all who contributed to make me who I am today—everyone from my home to my hometown to the French teacher who told me I would go on to do great things even though she did not specify what those things would be. To the public education system and government-funded doctoral program that got me smart. To the people I work with—thanks for humoring me. To DC, the city of my heart. To my readers—I hope this book brought you some joy. To my friends, every last one of you.

penguin.co.uk/vintage

peerless flats

ESTHER FREUD

BLOOMSBURY

First published in 1993 by Hamish Hamilton
This paperback edition published 2008

Copyright © 1993 by Esther Freud

The moral right of the author has been asserted

Bloomsbury Publishing Plc, 36 Soho Square, London W1D 3QY

A CIP catalogue record for this book is available from the British Library

ISBN 978 0 7475 9447 5

10 9 8 7 6 5 4 3 2 1

Typeset by Hewer Text UK Ltd, Edinburgh
Printed in Great Britain by Clays Ltd, St Ives plc

All papers used by Bloomsbury Publishing are natural,
recyclable products made from wood grown in well-managed
forests. The manufacturing processes conform to the
environmental regulations of the country of origin.

www.bloomsbury.com/estherfreud

PEERLESS FLATS

Esther Freud was born in London in 1963. She trained
as an actress before writing her first novel, *Hideous
Kinky*, which was shortlisted for the John Llewellyn
Rhys Prize and was made into a feature film starring
Kate Winslet. She has since written five other novels.
Her books have been translated into thirteen lan-
guages. Her most recent novel was *Love Falls*.

For David

L ISA, HER MOTHER and her brother Max were dogsitting for a woman called Bunny, who owned a house in the Archway. Bunny was away in America and was due back at any time.

Lisa's mother, Marguerite, went to the council when they first arrived in London. The council told her to come back when she was homeless. 'But we are homeless,' Marguerite had said. 'We're just not actually on the streets.' She explained about the dog who was an Alsatian and needed three meals a day.

The council said to come back when she was absolutely homeless. When there was no roof of any kind over her head.

Lisa walked round to see her sister Ruby. Ruby was living two streets away with a boy called Jimmy Bright who dressed like a rockabilly in a white T-shirt and brothel creepers and wore his hair greased into a quiff. Ruby said that most people were terrified of Jimmy Bright. Jimmy despised the human race, with the exception of Ruby. 'He won't mind you either,' she reassured Lisa, 'cos you're me lil' sis.' Ruby's accent had flourished in the two years since she left home and moved to London.

As Lisa walked up to Jimmy's flat, she could see Ruby sitting on the floor in a sea of crumpled clothes. It was a ground-floor flat that opened on to the street with a wall-sized sliding window. It was part of an entire row. Orange brick maisonettes with square, open gardens, and more were being built on the streets on either side. Jimmy didn't have curtains in his flat, and as Lisa approached through the derelict patch of garden, Ruby looked up and caught her eye.

'Hi, babe.' She didn't stir as Lisa slid the door.

'Where's Jimmy?' Lisa half expected him to rise up out of the debris and stop her in her tracks with his razor-sharp tongue.

'Dunno.'

Ruby was wearing a shirt with seven dwarfs all fucking each other on the front. Lisa sat and stared at it and wondered when it would get handed down to her. Everything Ruby had eventually got handed on to Lisa. Ruby was very generous with her things, while Lisa was a hoarder by nature and found it hard to part with almost anything. She had once kept a box of plain chocolates she had won at a raffle, and didn't like, on the top shelf of her cupboard for two years. Eventually they had been discovered and distributed to the family as an after-dinner treat. Lisa pretended to be angry but really she had been relieved.

'How's Mum?' Ruby asked.

'All right.'

Marguerite and Ruby rarely saw each other and when they did, more often than not they argued. Lisa acted as their go-between. It was since Ruby left home, Lisa thought. Or before: since their mother's marriage to Swan Henderson . . . since Max was born . . . since . . . Lisa wasn't sure. She could remember Ruby and her mother getting on, somewhere in the distant past, but hard as she tried she couldn't place the memory.

Lisa had visited Ruby regularly in London while she waited for her sixteenth birthday. 'Don't tell Mum about this,' Ruby always ordered when they parted, and her mother's first question was inevitably, 'So how is Ruby getting along in London?'

Ruby was so unspecific as to what exactly she was to keep quiet about that Lisa never knew how to answer. 'Fine,' she said, and then at night she would lie awake, worrying that if something terrible happened to her sister, it would be her fault for withholding vital information. Now that Lisa was in London herself she understood why Ruby had come back to school for the Christmas Fair, only six months after leaving, talking and swearing like a native East Ender and wearing a T-shirt for a dress and heels so high she couldn't walk down the hill to the pub. There had been no shortage of lifts on offer. Cars Lisa had never seen before swung open their doors.

Ruby was meant to be in London on a History of Art course. By the end of the first term she had already dropped out and was working in a shop that sold bondage trousers and plastic shorts and shirts with one sleeve longer than the other. People were whispering that Ruby was on drugs. That she was having an affair with a Sex Pistol. That it was a sacrilege to cut off that beautiful waist-length hair. Lisa felt immeasurably proud.

Ruby stood up and began searching the floor. 'Bastard,' she said, 'he's taken me fags.'

Lisa had a packet of ten John Player Special in her pocket. She smoked John Player because they had a 'scratch and reveal' lottery in every packet to which she was addicted. She offered Ruby one. Ruby slouched through to the kitchen and smouldered it against the electric ring of the cooker until it caught.

'Mum wondered if you wanted to come round and have supper with us tonight,' Lisa said casually, passing on a message, investing nothing of herself in the request.

'Yeah, I might.' Ruby pulled on her cigarette and changed the subject. 'Jim's old man gets out of the nick next week.'

'Oh.'

'This, you see, is his gaff.'

'Does that mean you'll have to move?'

Ruby sank back down to the floor, her thin, white legs crossing. 'Jimmy says we can all live here, he says his dad's all right. But I'm getting out.'

'You could come and stay at Bunny's,' Lisa said into the silence because she couldn't bear not to, and when Ruby didn't answer she added, 'but then again . . .'

4

'Yeah.' Ruby let her off the hook. 'Anyway, you'll be moving on yourselves soon, won't you?'

'That's true,' and Lisa stretched out a hand for a drag of Ruby's cigarette.

O N THE DAY Bunny returned from America, Lisa's mother went back to the council. Lisa took Max to the park. Max was five and was only really interested in foxes. Foxes were his main subject of conversation.

'Look, there's a red fox in the pond with a fox tail and no ears and it's hungry and I'm going to eat you for my dinner. Are you a fox? I like foxes. I might be a fox when I grow up.'

Lisa tried to focus her mind on what he was saying and even attempted to answer his less obscure questions.

'How long is a fox tail?'

'Hmm, I don't know.'

'Is that fox very bad? Bad fox. Bad fox.'

'Quite bad.'

'Are you a fox?'

Lisa's patience never lasted long. 'No I'm not a fox. PLEASE be quiet.'

'But if a bad fox came out of a hole in the ground in the middle of the night . . .' Max talked very fast with his words close together and his eyes staring straight ahead. It made Lisa feel crazy.

'Shut up.' She shook his narrow shoulders so that his teeth chattered. He continued anyway: 'there's a red f-f-fox and a bl-l-lack f-f-fox and two very big foxes-s-s . . .'

Lisa gave him a final shove so that he fell back on to the grass with a thud. 'Shut up-p-p.'

'Shut up-p-p.' Max mimicked her exact tone and she knew that she was only winning because she was stronger than him. From the day Max learnt to talk he always won with the last word.

Lisa slumped back into the grass. 'I'm sorry.'

Max stared straight ahead with his flat black eyes.

'Would you like to know how to make a deluxe daisy chain?' she asked him.

He rolled over and waited while she reached around her, collecting the longest-stemmed daisies. He had a pale, pointed face with two bright red patches on his cheeks like a child's drawing. His hair fell straight and black over his forehead in exactly the same way as his father's had. Lisa thought how strange it must be for her mother to be reminded daily of Max's father, who at this moment was setting off on a round-the-world sailing trip with a Dutch nursery-school teacher called Trudi.

When they arrived home, Marguerite was waiting impatiently for them. 'They've given us a flat. They tried to put us into bed and breakfast, but then at the last minute they came up with a flat, a temporary flat, until they house us.'

'Bed and breakfast . . .' Lisa murmured mournfully. 'That could have been lovely.' Lisa had always longed to spend the night in a hotel, but to live in one, like a Parisian intellectual . . .

'You don't understand,' Marguerite said, 'it wouldn't be like that.'

PEERLESS FLATS was in Peerless Street and was, as it turned out, just behind the Old Street roundabout. It was a faded 1930s block with stone staircases and bay windows and was hemmed in on every side by tower blocks. The man from the council was waiting. He glanced dubiously at the expectant faces of Marguerite and Lisa as they trailed after him with their plastic carrier bags of clothes.

There were two olive-green doors on either side of each landing. Max ran from door to door head-butting the wood and shouting, 'I am the Foxman, I am the Foxman,' but no one appeared to complain.

The man stopped on the fourth floor and unlocked a door, and for a moment they all stood crowded together in the tiny hall of the flat. The council man showed them wordlessly around. He pushed a door open into the sitting-room. It was oblong and empty, with wooden floorboards and a window with small panes that cut the tower block opposite into squares. There was a bathroom and a narrow kitchen with flowers in orange, brown and yellow on the wallpaper all linked together with hairy green stalks. Max covered his eyes when he saw them. At the end of the kitchen was a toilet in a little room that hung out over the edge of the building.

The man from the council stood in the middle of the kitchen and clicked his tongue between his teeth.

'Where are the bedrooms?' Marguerite asked.

The man widened his eyes as if he hadn't quite caught the gist of the conversation.

'There seem to be some rooms missing,' she said.

The man checked his form. 'You have been allocated a temporary homeless one-bedroom flat.'

'Well, where is it?' Marguerite demanded to know. 'This one bedroom, where is it?' And she kicked open the bathroom door to prove her point.

Lisa gulped. She hated a scene. 'Mum, it's fine.' She felt her ears tensing up and her head filled with a high whine like a dying light-bulb.

The man walked briskly into the sitting-room. 'In council terms this is a one-bedroom flat,' he said, and then noticing Max, swinging viciously from the handle of the toilet door, he softened his tone, 'but I must ask you to remember, this is temporary accommodation and you will be rehoused in the shortest possible space of time.'

He handed Marguerite the keys and left.

They returned the next night in the van loaded up with furniture. Marguerite had driven to the country to collect the things they had left stored in a garage until they had a place of their own. There was an iron bunk bed and the wooden base of a bed that had long since lost its legs. A fridge, a gas cooker and a tall wooden cupboard Marguerite had had for nearly twenty years. They had packed their books into boxes and the rest of the clothes from Bunny's into plastic bags.

As Lisa and Marguerite struggled up the staircase with the bed base between them, Lisa caught sight of something on the first landing, something oddly familiar. Marguerite stopped, jutting the frame into Lisa's side. 'Darling, aren't they yours?' she said, and in a horrible instant Lisa recognized a pair of her knickers. A green and white striped pair, the ones with the elastic gone in the waist. She nearly let the bed slide away from her down the stairs.

'I don't know.' She pushed to go on. 'Mum. Please.'

'But how did they get there?' Marguerite insisted.

At the same moment they both remembered the bags of clothes they had left propped against the wall of their new sitting-room. Marguerite stooped down and hoisted up a smudgy vest of Max's. 'Mum,' Lisa begged, and they began to heave on up.

In silence Lisa passed various grimy items that had once belonged to her. The sleeve of a jumper she had been knitting infrequently since she was twelve. It lay ragged in the crook of the stairs, collecting dust and cigarette ash, and still attached to its ball of wool by a long thread that wound its way down the staircase and out on to the street. Lisa disowned it. She cracked a little pot of blusher with her foot as she continued up.

The door of their flat was unexpectedly shut and locked. Lisa held Max back as they hovered in the doorway and listened. There was not a sound and so they ventured in. Apart from the missing clothes, there was no other sign of a break-in.

'There's a fox swimming in the toilet,' Max shouted from the other end of the kitchen, and when Lisa went to investigate she found that the toilet door was locked. It was locked from the inside. If there is a fox in there, Lisa found herself thinking, he's gone and locked himself in. She felt the skin on her face tighten as the door refused to give. She had a creeping feeling that there was someone holding on to the handle from the other side. Her hand trembled as she unclasped it and backed away.

'Mum.' She wanted to stay calm for Max's sake. Max latched on to a person's fear and his black eyes spun and his voice was louder than was bearable when he screamed.

'Mum . . .' Lisa called, 'I think there might be someone in the toilet.'

Marguerite strode over to prove her wrong. She took hold of the handle and pressed down and pushed up and banged on the door with her fists and called with her face close to the wood. 'Hello. Is someone in there? Hello!' The more she shouted the braver her voice became. It even created a hollowness that echoed back at them through the wood. 'It must just be locked from the inside and someone very small must have climbed out of the window.'

'Someone tiny,' Lisa agreed, thinking of the window, which she remembered as being one square pane of glass. The size of a rabbit hutch. 'Someone rabbit-sized,' she suggested, and stopped herself as rabbits and thieving foxes, borrowed from Max's bubbling brain, began to chase across her mind.

They knocked, as a family, on the door of their neighbour. A young woman answered, pulling her matted wool dressing-gown across her chest as she inspected them through a slice of door.

'We've just moved in at number 52,' Marguerite told her through the crack.

The woman swung open her door. 'Well, hello.' She had a high, Irish voice. 'I'm Frances.' She was as pale as milk with a turned-up nose and skinny, skinny hair. 'Well, there's a hell of a crowd of you.'

Lisa nodded. 'But it won't be for long. They're going to rehouse us as soon as they can.'

The woman smiled encouragingly. 'That's true all right. There's few that is here longer than three years.'

'Three years,' Lisa gasped. 'We were thinking more of three weeks. The man said –'

'Oh the man!' she interrupted. 'Your man said I'd be out of here before the baby came and Brendan was to come over for the birth, but little Brendan is all of six weeks now and I've not heard a word.'

With that, little Brendan, as if hearing himself called, set up a thin wail from the other side of the wall and Frances hurried away to comfort him.

Frances's flat was identical to theirs, with the same layout and overpowering wallpaper. The gas fire in the sitting-room was blasting and the oven door was open, steaming up the hall and kitchen with a heat that made the empty flat feel full. Frances invited them to take a peep at little Brendan, who lay quietly staring at the ceiling with his blue-rinsed eyes that were waiting patiently to change.

Lisa held Max at arm's length. Max hated babies and was liable to shout into their faces. Max only had respect for children older than himself. Unless they had turned into old ladies. Old ladies he took special pains to kick as he passed them in the street.

'Isn't he lovely?' Marguerite cooed, and Frances beamed with pride.

'It's just a great shame his father's not here to see him.' Frances flopped down on to the bed. 'But if he comes over before they offer me a flat, we'll never get a place of our own. It's our only chance.'

'Couldn't he just come over for a visit?' Lisa asked, but Frances stared miserably into the fire and didn't answer. They sat for a moment in silence until the crash of a chair falling in the kitchen roused them. Max had been trying to get at a half-eaten Milky Way on the draining-board.

Frances offered them the use of her toilet. 'Just knock three times,' and she laughed conspiratorially.

She stood on the landing with Brendan in her arms and kept guard while Lisa and Marguerite unloaded the rest of the furniture. They squeezed one half of the bunk bed into the bathroom as a bed for Max, in case he could be induced to go to bed before them, and set up the other half and the wooden base in the sitting-room. Lisa spread the beds with blankets that were as familiar to her as anything she knew.

They had made more homes than she could count feel like home with their unfolding. Frances brought them through cups of pale tea and they stood around chatting and smiling, and all the while straining for sounds of the burglar breaking out of the locked room.

L ISA AND MARGUERITE lay against opposite walls pretending to be asleep and keeping their fear to themselves. The wooden window-frame creaked with every shock of wind and sent waves of possibilities through Lisa's chilled body. She listened so hard she thought her bones might crack. She twisted carefully in her sheets and heard her mother do the same.

Lisa tried to remember when she and her mother had last slept in the same room. Not since she was a child and had slipped out of her own bed, wading through the silk of a black dream to climb in with her mother. Not since her mother had moved upstairs, first herself, then her few possessions, to Swan Henderson's shrine-like room with the king-sized mattress and the roll-top desk where, years later, Ruby had found the love letters addressed to 'Trudi, my sweet'.

Lisa, Ruby and Marguerite had moved in with Swan Henderson as lodgers. They had moved in during the summer holiday when Lisa was nine. For almost a year they had been living in a large house on a bend in the road between one village and the next. It was a bend where cars frequently crashed. It was famous for it.

'We've been living here for ages,' Lisa had said to her mother as spring approached and she watched for the first time as her own daffodil bulbs, planted in the autumn, burst into flower. 'We've been living here for ages and ages. I'm bored,' Lisa tried again to prise a reaction from her mother. Lisa put a moan into her voice, although she wasn't sure how seriously she wanted it to be taken.

'I want to live in a house with my own garden so I can plant a blue rose bush and watch it grow up,' she had complained when they packed up from their last place and moved for the eleventh time in three years; but a part of her liked the excitement and the new people and a different bedroom and a different garden and a different lift to school almost every month.

'It looks like we will be moving,' Lisa's mother said, interrupting her thoughts and taking her by surprise. 'At the end of the summer term.'

'Where to?'

Marguerite didn't know. 'But as always,' she said, 'something is bound to turn up.'

Lisa woke up with a start. The sun was streaming through the uncurtained window and her mother was still asleep with her face to the wall. Lisa's whole body ached and the moment she moved she was reminded of the locked room and the chair they had left jammed against the toilet door.

Max sat cross-legged on the kitchen floor absorbed in a game of Lego. Lisa tiptoed over him. She shifted the chair and tried the handle. Nothing had changed, but in the light of morning the locked door looked less sinister and she tapped at the wood happily with her fingers as she made her way to the bathroom to take a pee in the sink.

Lisa dressed Max and then herself and, taking her brother with her for safety in numbers, she walked out into Peerless Street to find a shop to buy some bread and milk for breakfast. It was Sunday and a strange, empty calm hung over the boarded cafés and the pillared basements of the tower blocks. Peerless Flats itself was still asleep. She kept a hand on Max's shoulder as they wound down the staircase, avoiding the litter of her most personal belongings, and even kicking her green and white striped pants into a narrow corner as they passed. They wandered hazily into Bath Street and through to Ironmonger Row, where they discovered a Turkish baths and a laundry but no shop. They walked slowly back across to City Road and turned in towards the Old Street roundabout. Max was unusually quiet, and stayed by Lisa's side, keeping up with quick padding steps of his plimsolled feet.

'I wonder if anyone except us lives round here,' Lisa said, and Max looked up at her with blank eyes.

There was a row of bus stops at the end of City Road with buses that went to the Angel and Highbury Corner. There was one bus, passing every twenty minutes, according to the timetable, that went up to the Archway and stopped at the end of Bunny's road. Lisa was tempted to wait for it and travel in its warm, red comfort to an area where people lived and shops opened, but she thought of her mother waking up in the empty flat alone with the locked room, and she hurried on around the roundabout, scanning side streets for signs of life and peering into the deserted squares.

Marguerite stirred as she slammed the door. 'Did you get some milk?'

'No.'

'The foxes are dead,' Max explained, and for once Lisa was inclined to agree.

Marguerite, Lisa and Max sat at a greasy table in a restaurant at the top of City Road. It sold kebabs. Skewered, or in bread. It was the only place they could find to get a cup of tea.

Max was very excited and drummed his hands on the table. 'Oh let him have a 7-Up,' Lisa pleaded and Marguerite wearily raised her hand to the waiter and ordered.

Max drained his drink in one furious slurp. He then set about chasing each remaining bubble and destroying it with a shriek and the butt of his straw.

'First thing tomorrow morning,' Marguerite said, 'I'll go down to the office and tell them we have to have a bigger flat. And I'll get them to do something about that door.'

Lisa nodded. She was thinking how she'd be starting college the next day, and her blood rippled hot and cold at the thought.

'And if they won't rehouse us,' Marguerite let her voice trail off, 'we'll just have to think of something else.' Lisa listened absent-mindedly. She was wondering how she'd prepare for her first day without the use of a mirror. 'Something is bound to turn up,' she said and she smiled her mother's own reassuring smile.

L ISA WAS MEETING her father for supper. She was glad to have an excuse for going out and she took the tube into the West End. Lisa rarely saw her father without Ruby. Secretly she thought of him as Ruby's father and felt uncomfortable about seeing him alone, even a little treacherous. After all, it was really only Ruby's tenuous link that bound them together.

They were having dinner in a fish restaurant. Lisa arrived to find her father sitting drinking Pernod with a girl she knew. 'Hello, Dad. Hello, Sarah.' She stood awkwardly at the end of the table.

'Oh, has it been raining?' her father asked, and Lisa looked down at her bedraggled coat and the boats of her shoes and wished she had washed her hair.

The waiter pulled out a chair and tucked Lisa in with a thick white napkin opposite her father. Sarah crinkled up the eye nearest her in a smile. Lisa ordered a Pernod too and picked at the radishes and bread sticks that adorned the table.

'I was just walking along and I saw your father leap out of a taxi,' Sarah laughed, and then added, 'I hope you don't mind, I'm starving.'

Lisa didn't mind. In fact it was nice to have a buffer between her and her father and the inevitable pauses.

Sarah was a year older than Lisa and she had known her on and off since she was seven. They had met at an Easter-egg hunt in Wales in the garden of Sarah's family home, where Lisa had had the great luck to meet up with the owner of a telescope – a man who led her to various eggs nestling in the low branches of trees, on window-ledges and scattered in the grasses of the outer lawn. Lisa had collected so many eggs she couldn't hold them in her arms and a bag had to be found to carry them.

'Are you living in London now?' Lisa asked Sarah, and Sarah said she was working in a clothes shop on the Fulham Road. She stood up to show Lisa a pair of maroon corduroy jodhpurs she had bought there at a discount.

'And how about you?' Sarah asked. 'How long have you been in London?'

'Three weeks.' Lisa felt anxious about having a conversation that didn't include her father. She looked at him from time to time and smiled expansively. 'I'm doing a drama course. At a college in King's Cross. I'm about to start any moment.'

The waiter arrived to take their orders. Lisa's father ordered oysters and so did Sarah, but Lisa couldn't quite bring herself to the challenge and asked for a prawn cocktail. She knew it was a childish and unsophisticated starter but she loved the sweet pink mayonnaise of the dressing, and in a defiant mood she followed it with fish cakes.

Lisa sat at the table and blushed to think how she had suggested only the year before they meet for supper at the Wimpy, Notting Hill Gate. She had seen its red and glass exterior from the top deck of a bus on several visits to London and her longing to go there was overpowering. Brought up in the country on a diet of brown rice and grated carrot, a cheeseburger and chips were her idea of gourmet delight. The Wimpy had in fact turned out to be a success and Lisa even heard her father exclaim over the deliciousness of the hot apple pie spiced with cinnamon, served in little cardboard packets.

Sarah and Lisa's father were discussing the people on the next table. Sarah giggled and pointed out the sharp line of the man's curling, auburn wig. The woman, Lisa's father said, looked as if she had been recently discovered under a large rock. He said it was enough to put him off his oyster. Lisa sweated for them.

'Ruby sends her love,' she attempted to pull the conversation around.

'Oh, how is Ruby? I haven't been able to get hold of her.'

Lisa explained about the flat, and Jimmy Bright's father getting out of jail, but it turned out that Ruby hadn't mentioned Jimmy to their father and he was under the impression she was living with a girlfriend.

'Oh, well maybe she is . . .' Lisa didn't want to betray Ruby's confidence, let alone disagree with her father. 'Well, she probably is by now.'

Lisa drained her Pernod.

'What's Ruby up to, anyway?' Sarah asked.

'Music.' Lisa jumped at the question. 'She's going to be a singer. She's got a friend who says when he can find a band talented enough to play with her . . .' Lisa broke off. She was only repeating what she'd been told. It was strange how much more convincing things sounded in other people's mouths.

'I think I bought her a guitar last Christmas,' her father was saying, and Lisa nodded, knowing he had, and knowing also that it had been stolen or swapped or lent to someone glamorous like Mick Jagger's brother or a roadie from The Clash.

Lisa's father insisted she try an oyster. 'Just swallow it, with a passing bite,' he said.

Lisa swallowed it so fast that she didn't even get a chance to graze it with her teeth and she was left with the sensation of having sea water in her mouth and a pebble on her heart.

'Not quite sure about that,' she said with a grim smile.

Sarah slurped her oysters joyously. 'It's an acquired taste.'

Lisa braced herself for news of Sarah's brother Tom. Lisa had been in love with Tom, among others, ever since she could remember. Once, on a holiday in Wales, they had lain together on a tartan blanket, Tom, Sarah and herself, and she and Tom had held hands and talked about how many children they would have when they were married and what they would call them. She couldn't remember the names they had chosen now, but there were to be three and they had been in complete agreement over every last detail of their upbringing. Lisa could almost see the stars in the black sky, how they had looked that night. Clear and calm and full of promise.

'You know when you stick your finger up your bum?' Tom had asked.

'Yes . . .' Sarah spoke as if she were waiting, and eager, for him to continue.

'Lisa?'

'What?' She unclasped her hand.

'What I just said.'

Lisa refused to be drawn. She stood up and wandered off across the lawn to lean against a box hedge as high as the first floor of the house. She hated conversations like that. She couldn't help herself.

'So how's your brother?' Lisa asked eventually when the waiter had cleared away the plates. 'How's Tom?'

'He's fine.' Sarah looked at her with a sly expression that made her wish she'd kept the question to herself. 'He's learning about farm management in East Anglia. He's living in a cottage on the estate with Lenny. In domestic bliss.'

'Who's Lenny?' Lisa's father asked for her.

'Lenny is a man Tom met at the Marquee. He's black and incredibly good-looking and Tom thought it would be fun to have someone around to keep him company.'

'So what does Lenny do all day when Tom's at work?'

'It's hard to tell,' Sarah laughed. 'The last time I went down there I arrived at four in the afternoon and they were both still asleep. I can't help feeling that Tom probably isn't cut out to be a farmer.

It was only once they were out in the street that Lisa realized how drunk she was. Her head felt as though it was full of cotton wool, and her ears wouldn't pop.

'Which way are you heading?' her father asked her, hailing a taxi.

'Old Street,' she said.

The cab stopped and Lisa's father kissed her very lightly on the forehead. 'Do you mind if I take this? I'm meant to be somewhere.' And he glanced at his watch. He pressed a twenty-pound note into Lisa's hand. 'Will you take the next one?'

Lisa nodded.

'Goodbye. Goodbye, Sarah,' he said and he jumped in.

'Thank you . . . and thank you for supper,' Lisa shouted through the closing door of the cab and she waved at his back in the low back window as he sped away.

Lisa and Sarah walked towards Leicester Square. Lisa weighed up in her mind the quandary of the journey home. If she took the tube, she could avoid breaking into her twenty-pound note. A taxi might be three or four pounds, whereas the tube, especially if she got a half ticket, would only cost her ten pence. Lisa was small anyway and if she bent her knees and looked with wide eyes into the little window – 'half to Old Street please' – she found it never failed.

'If I were to buy some trousers like yours, how much would they be?' she asked Sarah.

'About nineteen pounds.'

'You wouldn't mind, would you? I'd get a different colour.'

'Listen,' Sarah said when they reached the station. 'I'm going to stay with Tom at the weekend. Why don't you come?'

Lisa's heart began to pound. 'All right,' and they kissed each other on both cheeks and said goodbye, separately bracing themselves for the last tube home.

L ISA AND MARGUERITE got up early and, leaving Max asleep in the bathroom, went downstairs to the office. The office was in the basement of Peerless Flats and the caretaker had just arrived and was unlocking the door.

'We have a problem with our flat,' Marguerite told him.

The man looked nervous. 'Which one you in, then?'

'Fifty-two. The toilet door is locked. From the inside.'

'I'll be right up,' he said, 'just give us a moment.'

'And there's something else,' Marguerite grumbled as she retreated.

'What's that, then?'

Lisa sighed and tugged at her mother's arm.

'There aren't any bloody bedrooms, are there?'

The man appeared half an hour later with a bag of tools. He inspected the door and took out a hammer with a rubber top, which he smashed against the wood until the lock snapped and gave. 'Kids,' he said. 'Frigging kids.'

The window was wide open. Lisa stuck out her head and peered down expectantly, thinking she might see a child with the face of a hardened criminal lurking below, but there was nothing in the concrete yard except rubbish thrown from the windows above by people too lazy to use a dustbin.

'Mum,' Lisa said, as she was about to leave for college, 'I'm going to go away for the weekend with Sarah.'

'What weekend?'

'This weekend. On Friday.'

'That's ages away.' Her mother was irritable all of a sudden. 'Why don't you tell me a little nearer the time?' As Lisa opened the door to leave for her first day at college, Marguerite relented. 'I'm sorry, it's only that – it's nothing. Good luck for today.' And she kissed her tenderly on the cheek.

'Bye, Max,' Lisa called, but he just muttered 'Frigging foxes' from the bathroom, where he was dressing himself in a suit of grey, plastic armour.

L ISA WALKED SLOWLY down the long, strip-lit corridor of her college. She was early. As she walked, she rested her hand lightly on the top of her head, twisting her face into an expression of stern concentration as if she were unaware of her own actions, but all the while moving her eyes furtively from side to side to check that she was not being observed. The moment she had stepped through the main doors of the building it seemed to her that the top of her head had begun to open up. She had to keep her hand over it to stop it from catching fire or melting, and when she removed her hand it was as if her scalp were being burnt into by an ice-cube.

Lisa was always early. As hard as she tried to be late or even on time she still found herself arriving before anyone else. It was the thing that set her apart most severely from Ruby and her mother, who were both compulsively un-punctual. In Lisa's last year at school she would ring her mother from a payphone several times during the afternoon to urge her to begin the four-mile drive early enough to collect her on time. It never made much difference. Her mother would arrive in the battered blue van that had once belonged to the local butcher, swerving crazily round the makeshift school roundabout as if to dodge a crowd, long after the car park had cleared and the very last child had been collected. She arrived in such a fluster and armed with so many dramatic and implausible excuses that Lisa could never bring herself to retaliate with more than a moment or two of silence.

Lisa sat in a circle of plastic chairs in the hall where the drama classes were to be held. She rested both hands on her head as if she were purely stretching her arms. She pressed down hard on the bone of her skull to stop the clicking and the whirring in her ears and hoped to God no one would notice. She wondered whether it was the strip-lighting she was allergic to, or just the after-effects of the Pernod. She remembered hearing somewhere that too much Pernod could rot your brain and send you crazy.

There were places for twenty-five students on the Full Time Speech and Drama course. Lisa had auditioned. She had been helped with her pieces by a lady her mother found called Moira Philips who lived in the next village and who at one time had been an actress. Moira Philips was blonde and squeezed tightly into her clothes. She talked in mysterious and casual tones about 'Rep' and 'Equity' and 'up' and 'down' stage. The rumour that Moira's husband had not run off with a Scientology student but fallen and slipped to his death under the wheels of a barely moving train at East Grinstead station, before it was uprooted and sold to the Americans, added, in Lisa's estimation, to her status as a drama teacher, and she paid great attention to everything she said.

Moria Philips advised her to look at a book called *Audition Speeches for Girls* and she helped her choose a piece and 'blocked' it for her. Lisa hoped no one at the audition would ask her the name of the character or what play it was from, as she had taken the book back to the library before memorizing anything more than the lines.

Once everyone who was likely to arrive in the hall for drama arrived, the teacher started on voice exercises.

Lisa had never thought much about her voice before, but now it turned out she had a 'weak R' and certain vowel sounds she pronounced were wrong. Lisa couldn't hear the difference for the life of her. But the worst thing was her accent. When she spoke, the other students laughed and asked her to repeat herself as if she were a foreigner. She remembered Ruby confiding how she had practised for her college canteen, 'I'll 'ave some of them peas please . . . some of them peas . . .' and she resolved to do anything at all in order to fit in.

They stood in a circle and shouted along with the teacher. He was a small man with glasses and nylon trousers who introduced himself as Pete. He didn't fit at all with Lisa's idea of the theatre. 'Wibbly wobbly. Wibbly wobbly,' they repeated after him, stretching their mouths and their eyes and making full use of their lips.

'Bibbly babbly. Bibbly babbly. Moo ma moo ma moo.'

Once they were warmed up he led them in a round of 'Peter Piper picked a peck of pickled peppers. A peck of pickled peppers Peter Piper picked.' They ended on a string of 'Red lorry yellow lorry' and a full five minutes of 'Furious thistle', which was to be enunciated with no spit, whistle or lisp.

The drama teacher wanted the class to improvise. Bev, a short and stocky girl with dreadlocks, was desperate to go to the disco. Her boyfriend was coming round to pick her up in ten minutes. The drama teacher cast Eugene as the boyfriend. Lisa had spoken to Eugene during registration. He worked in the evenings as an usher at the theatre where *Evita* was playing, and his conversation was spiced with references to the show. At every opportunity he would break into a musical number. Lisa waited to see if he would introduce this talent into the improvisation.

Bev strode up and down the makeshift sitting-room. She cursed in full-blown patois. She was furious because at the last minute her mother had asked her to babysit. Janey was her mother. A sixteen-year-old Indian girl with a grave and world-weary expression. Bev was impressively angry. She used such strong language that even Janey was a little taken aback. By the time Eugene arrived to take Bev to the disco, Bev and Janey were rolling around on the floor in what Lisa imagined was a stage fight.

The drama teacher ended the improvisation and announced the start of morning tea break thirty minutes early.

S ARAH'S SHOP was a boutique not far from the Fulham Road cinema. Lisa had managed to keep her twenty-pound note intact by travelling half fare to college and back, and using the luncheon vouchers they handed out to each student to buy her midday meal.

Sarah's trousers were undoubtedly the highlight of the shop's collection. They came in three colours. Maroon, mustard, or a grey-green which reminded Lisa of lichen.

'You've got to have the green ones,' Sarah said. 'To bring out your eyes.'

Lisa kept them on, packing her skirt into her bag with her nightie and her copy of Stanislavsky's *My Life in Art*. They caught the train from Liverpool Street. Sarah had some grass, which she rolled into a joint under the train table. She suggested they smoke it in the ladies' so they'd be in a good mood when they arrived.

Lisa crouched up on the lid of the toilet seat and Sarah leant against the basin.

'Can I ask you a question?' Sarah said, the smoke billowing out of her mouth. Lisa's stomach tightened. Her head began to click with the first bitter inhalation of smoke. 'It's a question from Tom.'

'All right.'

'Tom wants to know . . .' And Sarah began to giggle.

'What?'

But Sarah wouldn't bring herself to tell her. 'He can ask you himself,' she said.

Instead Sarah told her about her cousin Tanya who was still a virgin and ashamed of it and was coming down next weekend in the hope that Lenny would deflower her.

Lisa hated that word 'deflower'. It made her squirm. Sarah looked hard at Lisa through the smoke and Lisa knew what she was wondering. She pulled on the joint and kept the smoke inside her lungs as long as she was able.

Lisa hadn't seen Tom for over a year and he was taller than ever and thinner. His long, grey eyes drooped at the corners. Lisa and Sarah climbed into the front seat of the Land Rover, Sarah shuffling behind so that Lisa had to climb in first and squeeze right in next to Tom. Their legs pressed against each other and the musty oilskin smell of him tingled in her nose. Sarah leant over the seat to talk to Lenny, who was lying stretched out in the back.

'How's it going, Len?' she asked him.

'Not so bad, and you?' Lenny said. Lenny was smoking, and every bit of energy in his body was concentrated in the hand that lowered and raised the cigarette to his mouth.

'Tanya sends her love,' Sarah said, and Tom sent out a peal of cruel laughter that made Sarah twist round to hide the blush that spread over her face.

They were driving out of the small town through flat, green fields dotted with barns and farmhouses and wispy autumn trees.

'So, when are you going to be a famous actress?' Tom jerked his leg against Lisa's.

'I don't know. Never, I expect,' Lisa stammered. Secretly she hoped that she *was* going to be a famous actress, or even an actress of any kind, but after one week of Full Time Speech and Drama she couldn't imagine it.

'Don't be all floppy,' Tom broke in. 'You've got to play the part. You've got to sleep with important people and say "Darling" if you want to get anywhere. Have you got an agent?'

'No,' Lisa said.

'Do you hear that, Lenny?' Tom shouted over his shoulder, and Lenny said, 'Yes, sir.'

Tom's cottage was on a road that led past the gaunt family house of the estate. It was beyond the farm buildings and was surrounded by fields. For Lisa, an air of glamour hung over Tom's house like mist.

It was dark when they arrived. Tom opened the door and flicked on a light. The sitting-room was barely furnished but the floor was so littered with mouldering cups of coffee and dirty plates that it gave the impression of clutter. A stale smell of fried food hung in the air.

Sarah showed Lisa round the house. The kitchen was a bombsite with every piece of cutlery caked in butter or jam and each surface supporting a toppling tower of plates and pans and half-empty cans of baked beans and rice pudding. The cupboards hung open, and proudly empty.

Upstairs there were two bedrooms. An unmade bed in each. Lisa refused to catch Sarah's eye and looked instead into the bathroom, noticing a spray of blood on the wall beside the sink that made her duck back on to the stairs.

'It's great,' Lisa said, as she came back into the sitting-room.

Tom was making a fire with half a packet of fire-lighters and what looked like the remains of a chair. 'How's Ruby?' he asked.

'She's fine . . . she's . . .'

'What?' Tom watched her suspiciously and Lisa wondered whether or not to tell him how Ruby had arrived at Bunny's the night before they moved out with her arm slashed and dripping blood. She had knocked on Lisa's window and, under strict orders not to wake their mother, Lisa had walked with her to the Whittington Hospital where she received a tetanus injection and five stitches. Ruby had made her swear not to tell anyone. At the time Lisa had interpreted 'anyone' as Marguerite and their father, but that was because she didn't know anyone else in London she could tell. Tom, she felt, could only be impressed by the news.

'She got into a bit of a fight last week,' Lisa told him, lighting up a cigarette.

'With who?'

'With a bread knife.' She felt proud of that remark.

At first Ruby told her how she'd been slicing bread when the knife slipped and caught the side of her arm, but later, worn down by painkillers and the long wait in casualty, she had confessed that during an argument with Jimmy she had stabbed at herself in a moment of despair.

'Seven stitches,' Lisa told Tom, and Tom looked suitably impressed.

'You should tell her to come and stay,' he said, and his eyes softened. For a moment Lisa remembered what she had suspected since they were children, that really Tom was in love with Ruby. Something heavy pulled inside her chest and she pushed the thought away. She inhaled deeply. She could feel Tom watching her out of the corner of his eye. It was Tom who had taught her how to smoke. Or at least how to inhale. Before Tom took her in hand, shortly after her thirteenth birthday, she just used to swallow the smoke, gulping it down like a drink and then waiting for a respectable length of time to elapse before letting it out again. This method of smoking invariably resulted in draining the blood from her face and making her feel sick.

'It's interesting how you inhale,' Tom had said to her. She was on holiday with Sarah and Tom's father on the Isle of Man, where all there was to do was smoke cigarettes and read aloud to each other from the *Thirteenth Pan Book of*

Horror. 'You see, whereas you swallow the smoke, I breathe it in.' He hadn't said it in a sneering way and he demonstrated 'inhaling' to Lisa with all the gentleness of an elder brother. They sat by the side of the sea experimenting with smoking styles until Lisa felt so dizzy she almost fell into the waves. Tom had to hold her steady with his hand. It was the summer after that they had named their children on the tartan blanket.

Lisa waited until the last possible moment before going to bed. Sarah had gone up first with a cheerful goodnight and Lenny had followed shortly after. Eventually Tom drained his can of beer, 'I think you're staying in my room,' and with that he disappeared up the stairs.

Lisa changed into her nightie in the bathroom. She brushed her teeth and, as there was no sign of a towel, shook her hands until they were dry. She noticed the blood had been wiped from the wall.

Tom was lying in bed, a long thin shape under the blankets. Lisa slipped in beside him. The moment she touched the sheets she began to shiver.

'Are you cold?' Tom asked, his voice unfriendly from the other side of the bed, and she had to stop her teeth chattering to answer.

There was nothing comfortable about Tom's embrace. When he put his arm around her, bones and the sinews of his long limbs bit into her flesh. They lay still, Lisa's neck resting in the crook of his arm, his hand icy on her shoulder. Lisa stared up at the ceiling. Her mind raced

39

with the beginnings of a conversation. Any conversation. Tom twisted on to his side and reached his long arm swiftly down to the hem of her nightdress. Lisa doubled up and clamped her legs together and gripped his wrist with both hands. She strained with every muscle to pull his hand up above the covers. She turned on his trapped arm and faced him and dragged at his free hand with gritted teeth. Finally his resistance went and she raised his arm up like a trophy and rested it on her shoulder. Lisa's chill had left her. She could feel Tom's hot breath on her face. She folded her arms in front of her, holding them out like breakers against her breasts. Tom kept his hand where she had placed it.

Words Lisa could not get a grasp on burnt in her throat and dissolved. She leant forward and kissed Tom on the side of his mouth. She wanted him to know that she loved him whatever he did. She wanted to tell him that she didn't really care about the sex except she couldn't stand it all being over, as she assumed it would be, and then they weren't due to get the train back to London until Sunday. Lisa released one of her hands and stroked the hair back from his face. His breath came hot and fast, and with no warning his free hand slipped off her shoulder and lunged down the front of her nightdress.

Wordlessly they fought, Lisa tugging at his iron wrists, and all the while rolling away from him with her knees bent up to jab him in the stomach. As she struggled, she caught his smile in the filtered light from the window. 'It's me,' he seemed to be saying, and she relaxed in his arms and grinned stupidly back at him.

'Couldn't we just go to sleep?' She turned and pressed herself warmly into the curve of his body.

'You should have said,' he whispered, touching her ear with his lips, and they lay awake until morning, on guard for each other in the tangle of the bed.

L ISA AND SARAH walked aimlessly along the fenced edges of one field after another.

'Did you sleep well?' Sarah asked. 'Last night?'

Lisa ignored the light in her eye and the stress of her words. 'Yes,' she said. She knew she was treading close to the edge of Sarah's patience.

They walked on in silence.

Tom had had a meeting at midday with the farm manager. He got up at five to twelve, pulled on his clothes and roared away in the Land Rover. Lenny was on a day-trip to London and wasn't due back until the evening.

'Do you think Lenny likes me?' Sarah asked when they'd walked so far in a circle that they could see the back of Tom's cottage three fields away. She sounded as if she had reason to believe he didn't.

'Of course he does,' Lisa said automatically. 'Why shouldn't he?'

Encouraged, Sarah linked her arm. 'And Tom, I know he likes you. He told me.'

Lisa decided against believing her. She couldn't imagine Tom coming that close to a declaration of love. His conversation was almost entirely made up of little cryptic phrases. 'Really?' she said.

Lenny arrived shortly after dark with a gram of heroin. 'H', he called it. Tom shovelled it into four lines with a razorblade and snorted his share into his nose with a rolled-up pound note. The inside of Lisa's head began to shrink and crack and the burning ice that had lifted seeped back into her skull.

Tom smiled at her with his elder-brother eyes. 'It's all right,' he said.

Lisa didn't know you could snort heroin as if it were cocaine. Ruby, she knew, injected it into the veins in her arms. She had tried to get Lisa to share a needle with her but Lisa had lost her nerve at the last minute. Ruby was like Tom. They hated anyone to be left out.

'Come on, Lisa Lu.' Tom crawled across the floor to where she was leaning against the legs of the sofa. 'You won't regret it.'

Lisa's stomach turned bitter and she needed to go to the toilet. 'Is it like . . . like . . .' She could hardly say the word. Tom bent his head down to hers. She lowered her voice. 'It's not at all like . . .' she whispered what was on her mind, 'acid?'

'My God, not at all. It's literally the opposite,' Tom reassured her, pressing the rolled-up note into her hand.

'So you don't hallucinate or anything?' she persisted faintly.

Tom shook his head.

Lisa gave in, and sucked the powder up into her nose, using one nostril and then the other in an imitation of Tom. Tom took the magazine off her lap and patted her leg like a school teacher. He pulled a blanket from the sofa and spread it over the four of them as they lay in a circle in front of the electric fire.

'So when did you take acid?' Tom wanted to know. He sounded annoyed. Tom liked the idea of having introduced Lisa to everything illegal she had ever done.

'About a year ago.'

'What was it like?' Sarah asked.

'All right . . .' and then, admitting a fragment of the truth, she added, 'A bit scary.'

The heroin was beginning to take its effect. Lenny, whose line had been fatter than the others, lay back with his eyelids heavy, and a dark smile on his lips. Tom sank his head on to his chest and was silent. As far as Lisa could tell, it wasn't affecting her, but then the thumping of her heart had subsided and, apart from the occasional click, the inside of her head was as soft and safe as history.

'I had an aunt,' Sarah said, 'who took acid. Someone put it in her drink.'

'Really?' Lisa asked. 'What happened?' A pinpoint of fear was fighting with the milk in her veins.

'She went crazy. She tried to eat a biscuit tin and then she walked to the nearest station and boarded a train. She jumped off just outside Audley End.'

'Was she all right? I mean, did she ever recover?'

'Never, not as far as I know. Tom, did Aunt Bird ever recover?'

'What?'

'From whoever spiked her drink with acid.'

Tom raised his head and looked at her with cat's eyes. 'Never,' he said, and he smiled a thin smile as if he were in some way responsible.

When Lisa woke the next morning she was lying on the floor, her head under the crook of Tom's arm. She scrambled free and stood up. She thought for a minute about what she would do if the others all turned out to have died in the night, but just the very fact of having survived made her feel so cheerful that without even checking on their pulses she went upstairs to the bathroom.

Lisa locked the door and ran herself a bath. She felt thin and white, and when she lay face down in the water the bones in her hips pressed against the bath's bottom and her empty stomach lifted away like the curve of a bowl. She washed her hair and brushed her teeth and put on a clean shirt with her green trousers. She sat outside in the sun. A sense of calm spread over her body. She knew what it was. She had taken heroin and survived and now she would never have to take it again. She had proved herself. Like a Red Indian coming of age and scarring his face with warlike marks. She was sixteen and she had tried every drug she had heard of. She was free to begin her own life.

'Cup of tea?'

A shadow blocked her own private stream of sunlight. It was Sarah.

'Thank you.'

Sarah handed her a mug and slid her back down the wall. She looked over at Lisa and smiled. Lisa caught her smile just as she was raising the drink to her lips and in that instant she remembered the story of the night before. Aunt Bird and the biscuit tin. Trains and parties and drinks spiked with . . . A cold fear froze her arm midway to her lips. Her brain hissed. She set the cup down. A skin was already forming on the tea's milky top. She watched as it hardened and turned a dark rust-brown. She kept her eye fixed on it, expecting to see a tab of 'white lightning' or a 'purple haze' swim to the surface and give itself away.

MARGUERITE AND MAX were cooking pancakes. The tiny flat was filled with the smell of frying batter. Pancakes were something they had inherited from Swan. Grace before meals they had dispensed with, porridge for breakfast they had never mentioned again, but pancakes on a Sunday – that was one of the few things that remained to remind them. Max was sitting up at the table carefully stirring the batter with a wooden spoon. Marguerite was watching over the pan. Lisa stood in the doorway and watched her flip a pancake over.

'How was it?' her mother asked her.

'Fine . . .' She was glad to be home.

Marguerite told her that she'd applied for a teaching job and also that she'd introduced herself to a family of white South Africans waiting to be rehoused. They were politically opposed to the government in their country and they had given up the rolling veld and the mountains and swimming-pools of their land for a one-bedroom flat on Peerless Street. Marguerite had met them in the office during her most recent campaign for a flat with a bed-room.

'They invited us over for a drink sometime.'

'And me too, nowadays,' Max told her, stirring happily.

Marguerite smiled over his head. 'A new word,' she mouthed, 'nowadays,' and she shrugged.

'Anything for a change,' Lisa whispered and she tried to hug Max's bony and resistant shoulders.

They sat in the sitting-room with their plates on their laps and ate the pancakes, piled one on top of the other in a tower, with spoonfuls of honey and the juice of a lemon squeezed between each layer. Lisa felt as if she hadn't eaten for a week. Tom and Lenny only bought McEwan's Export and sweets when they drove into the local town. For breakfast earlier that day they had toasted marshmallows. They had pronged them with forks and held them up against the bars of the electric fire until they sizzled and melted into liquid inside a sweet brown shell. When they were finished, Tom ripped open a bag of jelly babies with such force that they had to be retrieved, one by one, from every corner of the room.

Tom and Lenny had a plan which involved Lisa. They wanted to act as her theatrical agent. Lisa thought it might be better to wait until she had finished her course and then even until after she had trained at an established drama school, especially in view of what had been said about her voice, but Tom said it was never too soon to start putting yourself about. He found a pen and made notes on a pad of paper. Age. Height. Hair. Eyes. Accents.

'Can't you do any accents?'

Lisa couldn't think of one. And then 'Some of them peas please' came into her head, and so as not to seem under-qualified she said Cockney.

'Be prepared for that phone call,' Tom warned her. 'It could happen any time.'

Lisa wasn't sure whether or not to tell him that she didn't actually have a phone. But then it occurred to her that neither did he. She could only assume he must have some grand and alternative plan that he would explain to her eventually.

LISA MET UP with Ruby in a pub in Islington. It was a great dark room with no tables or chairs and music so loud the chords of the guitars thudded in the roof of your mouth. Lisa found her sister lounging against a wall, shoulder to shoulder with Jimmy Bright.

'Watcha, sis,' Jimmy said, and Ruby gave her a hug.

Ruby and Jimmy were both drinking Pils, and Lisa pushed her way through the crowd at the bar to buy another round. 'Same again,' Ruby shouted after her and Jimmy held up his bottle.

Lisa ordered, and watched herself in the low mirror behind the bar. The pupils of her eyes were so distorted by the dimness in the room that they had taken out the light in her eyes. She wouldn't have recognized herself, except she looked a bit like Ruby.

Lisa didn't notice until it was too late that the barman had poured the top half of each bottle into half-pint glasses. She craned to look over at the others. She wouldn't make it back to them in one go, and she knew she didn't have the courage to leave her drink unguarded at the bar. She stared mournfully at the collection of half-filled bottles and glasses. She would take the three bottles and then come back for the glasses, but as she gathered them up, the wide-open mouth of her glass changed her mind and she took two of the bottles and one glass and hoped she'd reach the bar and back again before it came to any harm on the ledge beside Ruby. Having decided which was her drink, she hurried with it, keeping her hand outstretched over the top. She squeezed through the crowd of elbows and arms and thrust the bottles on to the ledge. 'We didn't want glasses,' Ruby grumbled, but Lisa was already slithering away through the crowd, stumbling backwards, to keep an eye, as far as possible, on the golden pool of her lager. She surfaced at the bar, turned and rushed back with her armful of drinks. It occurred to her on her way that she could have poured the beer back into the bottles and then carried all three in one go, using her thumbs and a finger as corks, but now it was too late.

'Cheers,' Jimmy said, raising his bottle, and in the confusion Lisa forgot which glass she'd marked for herself. 'Cheers,' she said, but she didn't drink.

They stood in a row, their backs to the wall, and watched the people come in off the street and squeeze themselves into the crowd at the bar. There was no room for conversation. Lisa relaxed fractionally and took a slug of lager. She regretted it immediately. It tasted bitter. Lisa couldn't help wondering if it tasted more bitter than usual. If it is spiked, she thought, I'll know in twenty minutes. Her stomach contracted. She glanced up at the clock. It was ten-fifteen.

Fifteen, twenty, twenty-five, thirty, thirty-five. If by twenty to eleven her mind hadn't caved in and splintered like a sheet of glass she'd know she was going to be all right. Now that the damage was done the bottle lost its menace and she slugged at it to soothe her anxious wait.

'Another drink?' Jimmy said, heading off for the bar. It was ten-thirty. Her scalp tingled with the new dilemma. 'All right.' Her voice was so small that no one could have heard it, but Jimmy nodded and was gone. Lisa thought she would faint with the exertion of waiting for the heavy hand of the clock to move. Her hands and feet were freezing and her front teeth ached.

'How's it going, sis?' Ruby shouted, inches from her ear.

'Fine,' she yelled back, her eyes stretched out with fear.

'Seen anyone, been anywhere?'

'No,' was all she could manage. 'Not really.'

She leant her head back against the wall. The inside of her skull felt like the brittle webbing of a sack. Moving and cracking and tearing with each swallow.

'Seen anything of the old man?' Ruby asked.

'What?' Lisa didn't know who she meant, and as she glanced around for inspiration she caught sight of the hands of the clock just as they were chugging noiselessly into place. She had been spared. Her shoulders dropped and a sigh hissed like music through her heart.

'I won't be a minute,' she said and, taking her bottle with her, her palm pressed hard against its open top, she went to the ladies' to celebrate. She needed a change of scene and a way of escaping the gaping bottleneck of Jimmy's fresh drink.

'Hello.' A man blocked her way on the steps that led to the floor above. 'I haven't seen you here before.'

'No,' Lisa said. It sounded stupid but she couldn't think what else to say.

'What's your name?' He was from somewhere Lisa couldn't place. Up north, she thought, or America.

'Lisa.'

'I'm Quentin.' He stepped to one side. 'Sorry, were you on your way somewhere?'

Lisa said she was, but she'd changed her mind. 'It was just something to do,' she told him.

Quentin looked at her quizzically.

They walked back down the stairs together. 'Where are you from?' Lisa asked him.

'Belfast.'

Once they were in the comparative light of the pub, Lisa was struck almost speechless by his good looks. She was talking to a film star. He had velvet eyes and a sparkle in his face that shone even in the dim light of the pub. When he smiled, he showed his teeth and his lips formed a bow like a lion's grin.

'What do you do?' she asked him, and he winked and answered, 'Oh, a bit of this and a bit of that.' There was a tone in his voice that made her want to lean against his arm. 'You here on your own?' he asked, and with a quick glance across the bar she said yes. She would have liked to introduce him to the others, but she was scared that Jimmy would bristle into action and turn him into a fool with a flick of his tongue.

Quentin looked at her with added interest. 'You're different,' he said, and she blushed with the thrill of what she hoped was a compliment.

The bell was ringing out closing-time and the grille of the bar dragged down over the insistent heads of the last orderers.

Lisa saw Ruby looking around for her. 'Listen, I'm going to have to go,' she told Quentin, and as she moved away he caught her arm and asked, 'Will I see you again?' Lisa thought for a moment and then said quickly, 'Meet me next Friday at one o'clock outside the King's Cross branch of W. H. Smith's,' and with only enough time to register his surprise she rushed off to catch Ruby and Jimmy as they spilled out on to the street.

Lisa was glad they'd moved to London. She waited breathlessly for the week to pass. She tried to concentrate on college, and practised her voice exercises in the privacy of the toilet. 'Furious thistle, furious thistle, wibbly wobbly bibbly bobbly.' She practised rolling her R's and dropping her accent. She said 'Ta ta Max love' before setting off in the mornings.

One evening Lisa went with Marguerite to see the South Africans who were in fact from Rhodesia, or Zimbabwe as they called it when they remembered. There was a great crowd of them. There were two sisters with pale orange hair. One of them, Heidi, had a baby and it was her and her husband's flat they were all in. The other sister, who had a girl of six, had a flat in another part of the building. All the Rhodesians in London, it seemed, congregated at Heidi's and one Scottish man called Steen. Steen had the same pale orange hair as the sisters but he wasn't related.

Lisa wondered what he was doing there. His eyes were so heavy and of such a dark blue that they bulged out from under his hooded eyelids. You could see the hard-boiled egg of each eye through the thin white skin even when his eyes were lowered. Steen sat in the corner and rolled grass from a tin into a king-sized tobaccoless cigarette. It crackled as he smoked it and the acrid smell of the burning grass got inside the other smell, the sharp smell of piss and baby sick that permeated the room. Instead of covering it, it sent it swirling through the stale air. Lisa felt suddenly cold. Her feet were icy and the skin on her hands was puckered and white. Steen got up. First he walked over to Heidi's husband and offered him the joint, and when he refused it, he came and sat down next to Lisa.

Lisa had promised herself that she wouldn't take any more drugs or even smoke, but here, in this silent room with her new neighbours and her mother looking on, she didn't have the courage to refuse. She took the offering and inhaled deeply, holding the smoke until the count of five so that when she breathed it out it made a thick white plume in the air. Lisa forgot about her feet and even though her head began to crackle there was a reassurance in knowing it was still there. Steen continued to sit next to her and his knees moved gently to the rhythm of the music.

'What is it?' Lisa asked him when the joint was handed back to her.

'Balham home-grown,' he said. 'Do you like it?'

Lisa nodded.

Steen fumbled deep into the pocket of his trousers and pulled out a slippery packet. It was a ball the size of a squashed tomato. It was yellow-green grass wrapped in clingfilm. He handed it to Lisa. He pressed it into her hand. Lisa closed her fingers round the warm and gristly package.

'Thanks,' she said.

Lisa wondered why it was that men always gave her drugs. The men she came across pressed dope into her hands in the same way her father pressed money. She must have a sort of orphan addict look about her. Her mother's boyfriend, after the split from Swan, had brought little packages of red and gold Leb to slip to her on his regular weekendly visits. It didn't make her like him as much as he hoped, but it did make her the most popular girl at school. It also made the separation from Ruby more bearable and she could use it as ammunition to compete against her London excesses.

L ISA DIDN'T BREATHE a word to anyone about Quentin. She kept him a secret, hardly daring to say his name. She didn't mention him to the girls at college, or to Sarah when she called her from the payphone at Old Street station. She only asked if Tom had left a message about auditions for film or theatre parts. She was relieved to find that there was nothing.

'All Tom wanted to know when he rang,' Sarah passed the information on, 'was how to get hold of drugs and . . . where was Ruby?'

Lisa's money ran out and she replaced the receiver with a heavy heart. She took the short cut home. It was a narrow road that cut between two tower blocks and led into an underground car park. There was a ramp at the very end that opened on to Peerless Street. Every time Lisa took this route she promised herself she would never take it again. More than anything, she dreaded walking so close to a tower block. She felt that at any moment someone was liable to fling something from a top-floor window and flatten her as she crawled along below. The smallest thing could kill when dropped from such a height. A pellet of chewing-gum might bore a hole through the top of your head with its accumulated speed. Once, she had heard the echoey shouts of children, and on looking up she had seen two tiny, curly heads smiling miles and miles above. They were hanging at right angles over the edge of the building. 'Derr-brain chicken,' they shouted, and Lisa was so sure they were going to drop a saucepan on her that she backed right up against the wall and waited for their mother to pull them in.

Lisa walked so fast that she cracked the heel of her shoe. It splintered away from the arch of her instep as if refusing to keep up with her ferocious pace. She arrived home in a sweat of frustration and burst into tears. She sobbed and gasped and bent her shoulders, and, through a stream of slimy, welcome tears, thanked God there was no one at home. Lisa ripped off her broken shoe and hurled it across the room. It sailed in an arc across the hall, through the kitchen, and landed with a thud against the toilet door. Lisa limped after it. She picked it up and in a calmer mood studied the hairline crack of the loosened heel.

It wasn't so much the ruined shoe that was the tragedy. It was the fact that she had planned to wear them for her date with Quentin. They were bright green sling-back sandals with a heel so high they made her feel like someone else. She had been wearing them at the pub when Quentin had drawn her into conversation and she didn't want to shock him by turning up at King's Cross nearly three inches shorter than his memory. She had to find Ruby. Ruby, she felt sure, was the only person who could help.

Lisa left a note for her mother and took a bus to the Archway. She knew that officially Ruby wasn't meant to be living with Jimmy Bright, now that his father was out of prison, but she didn't know where else to look. She trudged through the orange-brick housing estate with her shoe in a plastic bag. It was getting dark and it amazed her how few people there were about. She had always imagined London teeming with life. She had pictured it in a continual state of carnival, never taking into account the side streets and dead ends.

Just by looking at Jimmy's flat she knew it was empty. It was dark and there was something abandoned about the great sheet of dirty glass that stretched across the window. Lisa tiptoed through the garden and tapped against the sliding door. Now she was there she hoped that Ruby wouldn't be inside. She dreaded to see her shadow rising up from the floor of that mildewed room. She tapped again. And waited. And as soon as it was safe to leave, she tiptoed back out through the garden and hurried away towards the traffic and the lights of Junction Road.

Lisa took the spiral staircase that led down into the depths of Archway station and jumped on to the first train that pulled in. When Lisa travelled by tube, she always made a special effort to ride in the smoking carriage, even if she had no desire to smoke a cigarette herself. The first time she'd come to London to stay with Ruby she had been more impressed than she could say by the chance meeting of one of Ruby's friends riding on the Bakerloo Line. They had leapt with burning cigarettes into the last carriage of the last train home, and Ruby had slumped down opposite a man in DM boots laced up to his knees. 'Oh, hi, Vic,' she had said as if it were the most normal of occurrences. She didn't even blink at the safety pin he had clipped through his nose. Since then Lisa assumed that if she were going to meet anyone she knew on a train, the smoking carriage was her only hope.

Lisa changed from the Northern to the Metropolitan Line and found herself heading towards Hammersmith. She was going to visit her father. She'd never called on her father unannounced before. Her fist was white and bunched around the handle of her plastic bag. 'If you see an unattended package or bag in this compartment do not panic . . .' She read and reread the compulsive warning printed opposite her on the curve of the wall. 'If you see an unattended package . . .' 'If you, if you see, if you . . .' She began to count out each letter of each word on her fingers. Unattended. She ran it off, from one hand to the next. Package. Seven letters. It took five rounds to let it finally rest at the end of her hand, to let the word trickle off her finger.

Lisa idled along a deserted street behind the closed-in stalls of Hammersmith Market. She wasn't sure exactly what it was her father did, but she knew he was a very busy man. She dreaded disturbing him in the middle of some important business. Lisa's father spent a lot of time talking on the telephone. He had a telephone with no number on it. A telephone that only rang out. He talked to people about

60

horses and the times and towns of races all over England. Sometimes he left his telephone lying unattended on a table top and out of its black and speckled mouth would come a litany of numbers and names that meant nothing to Lisa but that filled the room with an unshakeable suspense.

When Lisa was out with her father he had a tendency to wander off, and she would find him talking through one side of his mouth to men who hovered at the bars of cafés or stood gathering information behind a stall of street-market artichokes. Lisa had once heard a woman whisper that her father was banned from every race course in Great Britain. She had said it with such awe that it made Lisa think of Ruby and the way she was revered at school. Lisa thought of this now as she walked through the dark, leafy streets. She knew the ban must be simply due to her father's invincible eye for a winning horse and the fear he could evoke in each and every bookmaker.

Lisa's father lived in two rooms of a terraced house. It was a small house that was part of a square and there was a miniature playground in the middle. There were swings and a slide and a very muddy sandpit. Lisa was sure she could remember playing in that sandpit when she was a child, and sliding down the slide. Once she mentioned this to her father and he gave her a half-glance and said it was unlikely. She later discovered he hadn't moved to this street until she was ten. It must have been another sandpit she had played in. She regretted having brought up the sandpit or the subject of her childhood. She regretted it so much that sometimes even now she woke in the night with a pain in her stomach and a bitter shameful taste in her mouth.

The light was on in the double room that looked out on to the street. Lisa walked up the stone steps to the front door. The door was covered in graffiti. Smudged-up swear words and splashes of red paint. A board had been nailed over the letter-box and a new double lock shone out of the wooden frame. Lisa remembered that there wasn't a door bell, and now there was no longer a letter-box to clang for attention she assumed she was supposed to shout.

'Dad,' she mouthed feebly into the still air. 'Dad.'

A blind clattered open above and her father's silhouette appeared in the window. She could see him peering out. From twenty feet she sensed his irritation.

'Dad, it's Lisa.' It was too late to run away.

'Oh, hello.' He had both his hands on the window-sill and he was leaning out. 'Do you need something?'

He didn't want to let her in, that was all she could think of. She shouldn't have come. She should never have come. 'Oh, no not really.' Her voice rose up out of a lost part of her. She couldn't remember why she was here.

'Do you need a bit of money?'

And then she remembered. 'It's just I've broken my shoe . . .' and she realized her mistake. Of course he wouldn't know where Ruby was. She was probably out somewhere in the basement of a nightclub and if she brought up her name and her lack of address she might inadvertently be getting her into trouble. 'I suppose if I had a bit of money I could buy another pair . . .' Lisa's voice trailed off as her father slammed down his window. She waited, defeated, on the steps.

Lisa showed him the shoe. It was hard to see the crack by the hazy light of the street lamp.

'Poor you,' her father said. 'Will that be enough?'

Lisa crunched the note in the palm of her hand. 'Thank you.' They shuffled in silence for a moment and then Lisa moved off. 'Thanks so much,' she said.

As soon as she heard his door slam, she began to run. She kept the money in her hand, its cutting edge against her palm, and ran as hard as she could.

L ISA TOOK UP her position by the glass door of W. H. Smith's, the door that led out of the station and on to the street. She had to wait for some time before the giant hands of the St Pancras clock even got to one and struck, and then out of the corner of her eye she watched as the minutes jolted stiffly by. She flicked through a magazine and tried not to look. She didn't want to be surprised by Quentin while studying the time. She wanted to give the impression of a casual, calm and easy-going girl, carefree and a little scatty. She didn't want him to know she was the kind of person who counted the letters of the insides of words and arrived for appointments fifteen minutes early.

Lisa had been concentrating so hard on her breathing, and just exactly how she was going to react to Quentin when he tapped her on the shoulder, that it took her a moment or two to register the chimes of half past one. It took another ten minutes to conclude that Quentin wasn't coming. She folded her magazine and, with a gaping space where all her nerves had been, she wandered into the shop to buy herself some chocolate. It was only then that she saw the other door and the shoulder of a man leaning up against it.

'Quentin?' she ventured, and he turned around and saw her. He had an expression of impatience on his face that took a moment or two to lose. Lisa, having achieved her aim of carefree unpunctuality, let it all go in a moment of panic. 'I was waiting at the other door,' she told him, and Quentin took hold of her hand and led her out of the station.

Quentin was twenty-five and a down-on-his-luck drugs dealer. He was quite taken aback to discover Lisa was only sixteen. She felt him freeze away from her on the park bench where they were sitting. Lisa had expected this. She was used to it. She took out her trump card.

That morning she had released Steen's Balham home-grown from its plastic wrapping and it had expanded into a jungle of stalks and leaves and little seeds, enough to fill a tin tobacco box. She drew this tin out now from the pocket of her coat and without a word flipped up the lid. She slid three Rizla papers from their packet and, under Quentin's watchful eye, rolled them into a perfect joint with smooth white sides and a neat cardboard roach.

Quentin looked anxiously around the park. There was a row of secretaries eating sandwiches on a bench not far away. Lisa struck a match and, cupping the flame in both hands, she set light to the twisted ends of the paper. Tom would be proud to see her now, she thought, and so would Ruby. Quentin was impressed. Not only with Lisa's display but with the quality of the grass.

'Where did you get this stuff?' he asked her.

'Someone gave it to me.' Lisa was regaining power. 'A friend.'

'Some friends you have,' and they both leant back on the bench and let the sweep of the grass roll over them as its heady pull came and went in waves.

Quentin bought cans of lager, which they drank as they walked through the back streets of King's Cross.

'Those girls are probably even younger than you,' Quentin said, as they passed the pale prostitutes lurking on the pavements. They had bare white legs with plasters where their court shoes rubbed, and stripes of blue and pink make-up that refused to mingle with the pallor of their faces. Lisa passed them every day on her way home from college.

They were heading into Holborn. Quentin didn't try to kiss her. He just kept hold of her hand. Lisa liked him all the more for it. He had a strong, warm hand that didn't sweat or hesitate. Lisa hurried along by his side. She was wearing her green sandals, and so far, they were bearing up.

When she had arrived back from the black mistake of her search for Ruby, Max and Marguerite were at home. They had been there all the time, only next door, comforting

Frances, who, Marguerite said, was losing her mind cooped up all day with little Brendan. Lisa had arrived home so numb, she could hardly turn the key in the lock.

'Where have you been?' her mother asked her. Lisa could never lie with any conviction, so she just mumbled and shrugged and sidled into the bathroom. Max was sleeping in his towelling pyjamas, and when she leant down to kiss him he was as still and sweet as a saucer of milk. Lisa had her father's folded note still clutched between her fingers. She looked at it for the first time. She sat on the end of Max's bed and stretched it flat over her knee. It had a 'one' printed on its green face. She turned it over and over, unable to believe what it was telling her. Then she remembered how dark it had been on the steps of her father's house and how, after all, it had been wrong and stupid of her to interrupt his business for something as trivial as a broken shoe. She curled up on the bed next to Max, careful not to brush against his outstretched arm, and listened to the sound of her mother in the kitchen, waiting patiently for her to reappear.

Marguerite helped her mend her shoe with Sellotape and a glue Max used for sticking weapons on to soldiers. If she ran, or walked too fast, she could feel her heel bend, but now as she strode along in the grip of Quentin's steady pace she could only hear a friendly squeak.

'Would you like to see a film?' Quentin asked her. They had been walking in silence for nearly half an hour.

Lisa nodded. The way Quentin said 'film' made her want to go down on her knees to him.

There was an 'X' called *Scum* that had just opened. Quentin said they were lucky to get tickets, but when they went inside, the cinema was almost empty. Lisa supposed it was because it was still the afternoon and most normal people were at work. The film was about a boy's borstal. Quentin said he knew one of the actors in it. It turned out to be a boy who got gang-raped and then committed suicide in his cell because the prison officer wouldn't answer his call. He cut his wrists with a shard of glass. When they found him, he was slumped against the door as if he had been calling for help until the very last moment.

The cinema was freezing. Lisa's feet were so cold she had to take off her shoes and sit with her legs folded under her. She needed to pee for the fourth time since the film began. She jigged around and tried to last out another ten minutes. 'Not again,' Quentin said as she stumbled off down the aisle.

When they walked out into the street it was dark. 'That was fantastic,' Lisa said, even though she had seen most of the film through the slats of her fingers.

Quentin put his hands in his pockets. 'I've got to see a man about . . . something.' Lisa looked at the ground and waited for him to say goodbye. She felt like a piece of sea-weed ready to be washed away. 'North London,' Quentin shuffled his feet. 'D'you want to come?'

Lisa put her arm through his and nuzzled her face against his jacket. She couldn't resist a skip as they walked. This was the beginning of something, she thought, from now on there would be life before Quentin and life after. If they were still together at one o'clock next Friday she would have a little party in her head.

Quentin led Lisa into the pub. It was the pub that she had met him in. She bought him a pint of Guinness and herself a Bloody Mary, because even though she didn't want to stop drinking, she thought she'd better have something more filling than lager. Quentin took his Guinness and wandered off to find his man.

Lisa stood at the bar and looked at herself in the mirror. Tonight she wasn't frightened of anything. She sipped at her drink and abandoned herself to love.

There was a band playing live in a room below the pub and Quentin took her down to listen to the music. Wherever they went, he kept hold of her hand for everyone to see. The man on the door, who was a large, very black man with a shaved head, had some kind of business with Quentin. They couldn't go in to see the band until things were sorted out. Lisa waited for him at the base of the stairs. She drooped against a wall and let her mind wander.

'Here, give us that grass,' Quentin hissed. He was standing pressed close to her and he slipped his hand into her pocket.

Lisa didn't want an argument but she couldn't understand what was going on. 'Why?' She held on to the tin through the thin wool of her coat.

'Just give it, I'll explain later,' Quentin said in such a stern tone that Lisa let her hand go limp. She watched him as he walked back to the bouncer and handed over her tin. She thought she saw a swagger that had not been there before in his retreating shoulders.

'Don't sulk.' Quentin squeezed her hand. 'I'll get you something much better than that.'

'And my tin?'

'Fuck that.'

Lisa felt the words kick in her stomach. It was as if something ugly had been poured down her throat. She wrenched her hand away and crossed her arms underneath her coat, digging her nails into the skin below her armpits.

'Lisa, Lisa, sweetheart.' Quentin pressed her back against the damp wall of the basement. 'Don't be like that, you'll break my heart.'

Lisa knew she should leave, get out, go home, but she felt so tired suddenly and drunk, and her head was full of filings. It was easier to believe what he was saying. 'Lisa, darling,' he murmured as she gave in to him, and with a long sigh, as if he had risked losing something precious, he buried his head in her neck.

Quentin and Lisa stumbled out on to the street. It was midnight. Lisa felt as if days or even weeks had passed since one o'clock at King's Cross station.

Quentin wanted her to come home with him.

'I can't,' she said, 'my mother will be worried.'

Quentin looked puzzled and then a little angry. Lisa hadn't mentioned she lived with her mother. 'Phone her. Tell her you're staying over with a friend.'

70

'I can't,' Lisa said miserably, 'we don't have a phone.' She felt hollow with cigarette smoke and the heel of her shoe was squeaking like a taxi. She wanted Quentin to kiss her and ask when he could see her again.

'Come home with me,' he demanded.

They had walked the length of Upper Street. If Lisa left him now, she could get the last tube home from the Angel.

'I could see you tomorrow?' she ventured.

Quentin didn't speak. The heat had gone out of his hand. He didn't want to see her tomorrow, she knew that. He walked with her into the tube station and they travelled down in silence in the lift.

'Watcha, Quent,' someone called as they walked out on to the narrow platform. It was the actor from *Scum*. The boy who'd been raped. In spite of herself Lisa was relieved to see him alive and looking so cheerful.

'Got any drugs?' The actor nudged Quentin, and then winked and said, 'Nah, only joking.'

The actor was on his way to a party. 'Why don't you come?' And Lisa and Quentin, seeing a way of postponing their differences, took him up on his offer.

Lisa wouldn't have missed this party for the world. It was one thing to have met her first real-life actor, but the party was full of them. There was the main bully from *Scum* and the star of *Quadrophenia*. *Quadrophenia* was the first film Lisa had seen when she arrived in London and she had even toyed with the idea of writing a fan letter to the boy who played Jimmy. She could see him now, fooling about on the dance floor. Thank God, Lisa thought. Thank God I didn't write.

Quentin didn't want to dance. Lisa was so excited she couldn't sit still and she left him sitting alone on a row of chairs. Lisa wasn't a natural dancer. 'Just listen to the bass,' Ruby had told her when she asked for advice, but hard as she tried, Lisa was never sure she knew which one it was.

After three or four self-conscious numbers Lisa went back to find Quentin. He was sitting in the same chair, bent double and sobbing into his hands.

Lisa had never seen a man cry before. She assumed it must be something she'd done. Inadvertently dancing too close to someone on the dance floor or refusing to go home with him. 'I'm sorry.' She was secretly thrilled with the implications of his distress. 'I'm sorry.' She forgave him everything. For stealing her grass and refusing to explain, and not letting her go home when she wanted to. 'Don't cry,' she said and she put her arms around him and kissed the salty side of his face.

Quentin took a long time to come round. His sobs subsided and, just when he'd stopped and shaken his shoulders and taken some air into his lungs, his face collapsed again and he buried his head in his hands. 'Amanda,' he moaned with such despair that it took Lisa a moment to register the other name.

Lisa felt like a fool. Twelve hours with Quentin had wiped her thoughts clean of anyone but him, and she found it hard to accept that all the time Amanda, Amanda, Amanda had been beating in his blood.

Lisa choked back her pride and listened. Amanda was Quentin's girlfriend. They had been living together for over a year and then she had gone to America for the summer to visit a friend. She had written at first and then the letters stopped and there was a long silence in which Quentin convinced himself things couldn't be as bad as they appeared. Eventually he learnt the truth. Amanda wasn't coming back. She was engaged to a Wyoming rancher and they were to be married on Christmas Eve. By the end of this story Quentin was lying with his face in her lap and his arms wrapped around her knees. He was sobbing like a child. Lisa thought she could see people looking over at them as the party began to thin out.

'Come on,' she said tenderly, prising him up, 'let's go home.'

Lisa couldn't find her key. She had to bang on the door for some time before her mother's sleepy footsteps could be heard shuffling over the floorboards.

Marguerite stood there in her nightdress and looked from Quentin to Lisa. 'I thought when you didn't come home, you must have decided to stay the night with a friend,' she said, and Lisa wondered if she'd ever be able to forgive her.

Marguerite shut the door behind them. She didn't comment on Quentin's presence, or introduce herself, but informed them in a matter-of-fact voice, 'It's three-thirty in the morning,' and went back to bed.

Lisa picked Max up like a Christmas lamb and carried him through to the sitting-room, tucking him into her empty bed, without interrupting one long murmur of his dream. Lisa made herself and Quentin mugs of tea with three sugars each and they climbed into the iron bunk in the bathroom. 'Where else am I going to go?' she whispered, when Quentin mouthed that Lisa's mother was lying on the other side of the thin wall, and she turned her face away from him and let her limbs dissolve into an ashen sleep.

'IT MUST BE weeks since I saw or heard of Ruby,' Marguerite said. It was Monday morning and Lisa was leaving for college. She had the door half open. 'Have you seen her?'

'No. Not really.'

'What do you mean, "Not really"?'

'Mum . . .' Lisa protested. Her mother had a habit of introducing new and important subjects just as she was about to leave the house. Sometimes Lisa thought that all their most memorable conversations had taken place with a half-closed door between them.

'Well, you must know where she is living?' Marguerite insisted. Lisa began to edge her way out. She mumbled something unintelligible, even to herself.

'Wait!' Marguerite shrieked, as Lisa inched out of the door. The force of her voice swung Lisa back into the room and just in time to see Marguerite smash her breakfast bowl into the sink. 'Why will no one ever tell me what's going on?' she roared.

Lisa closed the door gently and leant against it, hoping to soak up at least some of her mother's fury.

'I'm sick to death of it,' she screamed, and Lisa hated herself for standing frozen and unable to answer, with only the torments of the arched ears of their neighbours listening in her mind. 'I'm bloody sick to death of it all.' Her mother's voice caved in and her mouth quivered with a rush of tears as she leant over the sink to pick the bits of china from the washing-up.

'Oh Mum, darling . . . please don't cry.' Lisa put her arms around her. 'I'll find Ruby, I promise.'

'It's just that no one ever tells me what's going on.' She was sailing now on a noisy rush of sobs. Lisa stroked her hair. She glanced at the clock. She was going to be late. She longed for the anonymity of the long grey corridors of her college.

'Mum, I've got to go,' and she untwined her arms and went to get a towel to dry her mother's face.

Max was still in his pyjamas. He had made a camp under his bed and was only visible from the knees down. He had started school the week before at a nursery on the other side of Bath Street, where he insisted on wearing his plumed plastic helmet with the visor up. Without it, nothing could entice him through the gates.

'Mum,' Lisa said coaxingly, 'hasn't Max got to be at school in a minute?' and, feeling that she had done everything in her power, she ran at full speed down the ramp between the tower blocks, taking the short cut to the station.

*　　*　　*

76

Dear Dad, Lisa wrote in her afternoon tea break. *Maybe me, you and Ruby could have supper one night? College is going fine. Home life is a bit hellish.* (She felt guilty saying this, but she knew how he loved a hint of intrigue and she hoped to hasten his reply.) *Will you let me know: 52 Peerless Flats. EC1. I hope you're well. Lots of Love, Lisa.*

His reply came by return of post. *Meet me at the Greek at 11.30 next Tuesday eve. I'll try and track down Ruby. Hope those hell gates aren't closing in. Might have a plan. Dad.*

Lisa was so thrilled by this note, written on the back of a betting slip, that she locked it in her treasure chest with her other most precious belongings. Lisa's treasure chest was a wooden box she'd been given for her fourth birthday and was one of the few possessions that had been retained from so many moves and burglaries and changes of address. Apart from her father's letter the most recent addition was a square of lined paper with an address written on it in Quentin's sure hand: 111 Crouch Hill. She silently regretted the ugliness of the word 'crouch'.

Lisa and Quentin had been woken the following morning by Max shouting into Quentin's ear, 'Foxes alarm. Foxes alarm.' Quentin had rolled over and tried burying his head in the covers, but Max wanted a fight. He scrambled down to the end of the bed and bit Quentin's toes and chanted: 'Mr Fox has lost his sox. Mr Fox is stoooopid,' until Quentin did what Max wanted and wrestled with him on the floor of the bathroom. He held him upside down by his feet until he laughed so hard his eyes shone like apple pips and he wriggled out of his trousers.

Quentin dressed while attempting to stave off Max's running assaults. Max used his head as a battering-ram and his arms and legs as creepers. He clung on to Quentin just above the knee and let himself be dragged along like a duster. Lisa watched from the bed as Quentin tore a sheet of paper from a notebook in his jacket pocket, wrote on it, and handed it to her.

'Will I see you next weekend?' he said, as he tried to shake himself free. Lisa felt too sad to answer.

'Goodbye,' she heard her mother's voice drift out from the kitchen as Quentin stood by the front door grappling with Max in an increasingly desperate attempt to extricate himself.

'Goodbye,' he mumbled and Lisa saw him blush a deep crimson just a minute before he freed himself and slipped away.

T HE GREEK was a Greek restaurant in Bayswater. Lisa had been there once before. She had got so drunk on the retsina they served that she had walked into the toilet door and nearly knocked herself out.

Lisa didn't want to be the first to arrive. She wandered in and out of the twenty-four-hour shops on Queensway to gain some time. She flicked through rows of Oxford University T-shirts, and glanced at the postcard tiers of naked women and the Union Jack, avoiding the eyes of the Arab men who watched her with suspicious smiles.

Fashionably late was what Lisa hoped she'd be when she walked into the candlelit basement of the restaurant at nearly quarter to twelve, but neither Ruby nor her father was there. Lisa kept her coat on and waited. She ordered a straight vodka and lit a cigarette, but as she sat waiting at the corner table she was plunged so deep into a quicksand of self-consciousness she found she could hardly lift her hand up to her mouth.

Ruby arrived. 'Dad's just coming.'

'How do you know?' Lisa asked, and Ruby slid her a scowl of incomprehension. 'Because we came together. By taxi.'

Lisa pulled hard on her cigarette to drown out the ringing in her ears. Her mother had once told her that she'd hit a woman for implying that the baby she was carrying, Lisa, unborn, was not her father's child. She didn't have to be told that she was not the only one to suspect it. She wondered if Marguerite had hit her father too. She could see her mother's beautiful freckled arms flailing and her hair sticking to her face as she cried through her nose.

'Hello, Dad,' Lisa said, as her father slid into the seat beside her and kissed her very lightly on the side of the head. They ordered Greek salad with squares of feta cheese, and spinach in pastry, spicy sausage, olives and artichoke hearts just to start.

Lisa told Ruby and her father about life in Peerless Flats. She told them about Max wanting to go out and play as if they still lived in the country, and how he charged round and round the concrete yard of the tower block encased in his suit of armour. Ruby and her father both laughed and Lisa warmed up so much she was able to take off her coat. She told them about Marguerite's campaign for a bigger flat and the regular Monday morning battles with the caretaker.

'I was thinking,' her father said, 'I might be able to get you somewhere else to live.'

Lisa wasn't sure. After all she was the reason her mother had moved to London. She wasn't sure she could desert her.

'It might be easier for them as well,' Ruby said, sensing her uncertainty.

'What sort of thing?' she asked her father.

'I don't know. I'd ask around. Maybe a room in a house. A family I know . . . somewhere central.'

Lisa's mind swelled with images of white terraces and the polished steps of double front doors. She imagined herself wandering through a mahogany-panelled drawing-room into a bedroom with a dressing-table and muslin curtains that swelled in the breeze. Then she remembered Max, and his half-bunk in the bathroom.

'I'll see if I can last out,' she said, and she heaped her plate with warm bread and salad, and glanced up at her father to see if he would forgive her the rejection.

Ruby was in a bad mood. She tried to hide it from her father but she let Lisa know with every stab of her fork. She had abandoned her Cockney accent for this evening, but when their father left the table to talk to one of the waitresses, she reverted back. 'I've been seein' loads of that bastard Tom. In fact a bit too bleedin' much of 'im.'

'But I thought Tom was –'

'Yeah, I know, but he bloody moved to London, didn't he?'

'Is he staying with Sarah?' Lisa asked, wondering why Sarah hadn't mentioned it. Her heart was pounding in uncomfortable stony beats.

'Nah.' Ruby leant over the table to spike a slice of squid. 'He's got a flat in Mayfair.'

'Mayfair!'

'Yeah, he bloody said I could stay there with him, and then when I moved in, it turned out he meant: stay there *with* him. Literally.'

'What do you mean?' Lisa's hands were trembling.

Ruby looked at her and dropped the Cockney. 'Oh, I don't know. He's insisting I sleep in his bed, or he's going to throw me out.'

'Have you not got anywhere else to go?' Lisa was trying to be helpful. 'What about Jimmy?'

'Fuck Jimmy,' but before Ruby could go on, their father returned, sliding into his seat between them.

Lisa wondered momentarily why Ruby didn't ask about Dad's family. The ones with a spare room in their central London house, but she knew why. Ruby wasn't the family type. It was then that she remembered her mother and the reason why she'd asked for supper. She waited until they were out on the street.

'Mum's worried about you,' Lisa said to her as they watched their father disappear in his taxi.

'Really?' Ruby sounded unconvinced.

'Why don't you come round sometime? It's not that bad really.'

'Yeah, I will.'

'Please do,' Lisa pleaded. Ruby shuffled her feet furiously before giving in with a promise. They shared a taxi, stopping first at Mayfair.

'Do you want to come in?' Ruby asked. They were in one of those tiny streets still covered in cobbles where the garages were all converted stables. Lisa looked up at the window with its white light and shook her head. Ruby hugged her. 'Me lil' sis,' she said affectionately. 'I'll see ya soon.'

Lisa watched her as the taxi bumped away. She could hear her calling up at Tom's window. 'Let me in, you bastard, I've lost me bloody key.' She was still standing there when the taxi turned out of the mews and headed east.

LISA WENT TO the pub to look for Quentin on both Friday and Saturday night. She squeezed her way through the crowds, hovered at the bar, and even went down into the basement to see if he was listening to the band. Quentin seemed to have disappeared. She plucked up courage and asked the bouncer if he'd seen him. The bouncer looked down at her and kissed his lips together. He made a sound like a little bird. Lisa waited, but that was all he seemed prepared to say.

Lisa walked home along the high street. She walked fast with a fixed smile on her lips and a preoccupied air as if she were reliving the events of a wonderfully entertaining evening. She had an uneasy feeling she was being watched. When she had to pass the crowd milling about outside the late-night cinema, she was so certain she saw Quentin's brown eyes staring out at her that for a moment she even thought she heard his voice. 'Lisa,' her name rang out, 'Lisa, Lisa,' and, convinced it was the hissing of her own ears, she began to run. She ran with her heart pounding 'Lisa' in her mouth, and as she clattered down the street her name ran with her like a snake. She ran so fast she felt sick and then her weak heel gave way and cracked right off and she was grounded. This time she didn't care. She bent down to slip off the broken shoe and sling it into the gutter. I'll walk home barefoot, she thought, and then the echo of her name caught up with her and an arm slipped around her waist, raising her up from the pavement.

'You can run but you can't hide,' Quentin said in his velvet voice, and with his hand on her shoulder he limped her back towards the cinema.

Lisa didn't like to mention that it was Quentin who seemed to have been hiding. She struggled with a tangled rope of explanations as to why she might have been fleeing demons the length of Upper Street, alone on a Saturday night, and with only one good shoe, but Quentin showed no signs of curiosity. He rejoined the queue and they inched their way forward in silence. Lisa's palm sweated as she tussled with the starts of conversations. She sneaked a look at him. He stood calm and comfortable, his profile perfect and at ease. 'Quentin, what are you thinking?'

Quentin looked at her. He let go of her hand. 'I don't know,' he said, stepping away. 'What are you asking for?'

'I don't know,' Lisa backtracked. He had pulled away from her as if she were a spy, as if by putting her mind to it she could see into his head.

'I was just wondering how you'd been all week,' Lisa tried to save herself, and then with a flicker of rebellion she added, 'I mean, how do you know I even want to see a Marlon Brando triple bill?'

'Well, don't you?' he asked, and Lisa, balancing on one shoe, weighed up the chances of losing him again and sullenly agreed. They sat through *A Streetcar Named Desire* and got about half an hour into *Last Tango in Paris* when Quentin squeezed her hand and said, 'Let's go, I'm knackered.'

Quentin hailed a taxi. '111 Crouch Hill,' he ordered as he held the door for Lisa. There was no discussion and no pause for one. Lisa sat huddled in Quentin's embrace as they climbed higher into the rises of north London. She thought about her mother and how she'd destroyed, one by one, the last excuses of her childhood.

Quentin was disgusted. 'You're not a virgin, are you?'

'No,' Lisa said. 'Of course not.' A high note of outrage made her voice break like a boy's. 'I'm just not in the mood, that's all.'

They lay coldly side by side on Quentin's thin mattress. Lisa could hear Quentin's flat-mate, Paul, giggling and talking through the wall. He had a girl in his room. Paul was a dealer too. He had looked her up and down when they were introduced and something in his look had said, 'You won't last long,' but with sympathy. Lisa thought bitterly of Amanda.

Quentin sighed and snorted. 'If you're going to be like that,' he said, 'at least you can give me a wank.'

Lisa froze with the shame of it.

It's not that I'm a prude, she thought desperately to herself. In her last year at school, a 'prude' and 'frigid' were the worst things you could be. She just wished it could be different. Lisa knew that he was waiting and she reached out and placed her hand on the flat of his belly. He groaned. He was faking. It couldn't be nice. There was too much disgust and uncertainty in her touch. She moved her hand tentatively across his skin and before he could fool her with another moan she drew it quickly away.

Quentin leapt from the bed, pulling the blanket roughly so that she had to cling on to a sheet to keep from being uncovered. He stood naked and angry in the moonlight. She knelt up in her iceberg sheet and watched his erection droop and wither, shrinking into its shell. 'I'm sorry,' she said.

Lisa tried to cry her way out. She pushed her face into the pillow and prayed for the slippery relief of tears. Her eyes were as dry as glass. Even her bones had lost the juice of their marrow and they clicked and cracked when she moved. She felt as dry and brittle as burnt-out coal. When she looked up, Quentin had left the room.

Lisa had a bath the next morning in Quentin's bathroom. She took off her ring, and searched for stray grips in the remains of her hairstyle.

Lisa had woken determined to take Amanda's place. She had peered at the sleeping beauty of Quentin's high forehead and the sweep of his black lashes. She had rested her head on the cushion of his shoulder and hoped he would wake up. She made two cups of tea and brought them back to bed. 'Quent,' she whispered. 'Sweetheart.' She used his own words to lure him. Quentin flung out his arm, just missing her nose, and buried his head in the covers.

Lisa lay in the bath and pondered over strategies. She accepted she would have to sleep with him. Properly. It wouldn't be so bad. She'd done it before and it was never as bad as she made out. She dreaded the shakes it gave her. It made her body jolt uncontrollably like an epileptic. Between each muscle spasm she thought she might die of embarrassment. All she wanted was for him to hold her hand again as if they were the only two people in the world.

Lisa waited so long for Quentin to wake up that she began to feel restless. She helped herself to a bowl of Sugar Puffs in the kitchen and was unable to resist glancing through the various possessions strewn around the room. She came across a photograph of Amanda. She knew it was Amanda because it made her stomach spin. Amanda was beautiful. She had long golden curls and heavy-lidded eyes. She was wearing blue jeans and a soft, yellow padded jacket, and she was leaning against a table as if she had just come in from outside. From tennis or riding. Amanda was not the kind of girl you picked up in a pub. Amanda was the girl at school all the boys wanted to marry.

Lisa found her coat in a heap by the door and her shoes, which were hardly worth bothering with, under a cushion. She was tempted to leave them as a grim reminder for Quentin when he woke, but she couldn't quite bring herself to part with them, and so with her hair still wet, and her feet bare, she tiptoed down the stairs and out into the autumn quiet of Crouch Hill. The moment she slammed the door she remembered her ring in its own pool of water lying on the edge of the bath.

When Lisa arrived home, after a bus journey, a series of ill-chosen trains and the long way round from the station for fear of broken glass, it was early afternoon and Ruby had arrived. She sat at the kitchen table picking nuts and raisins, dry, out of a bowl of muesli. Marguerite sat opposite her with Max on her lap. She glanced up as Lisa came in. 'Where've you been?' Her voice didn't carry the weight of worry Lisa had hoped it would.

'Oh you know . . .' Lisa began.

'Yeah Mum, don't be nosy,' Ruby said, pulling Lisa down on to the edge of her chair.

Ruby had changed colour. The skin on her face was yellow, like an egg hard-boiled in onion, and, as Ruby lifted her head out of her bowl of cereal to squint disapproval at her mother, Lisa could see that she had lost the whites of her eyes.

Lisa glanced startled up at Marguerite. Marguerite was leaning over Max. 'Are you going to help me make pancakes?' she asked. Max hung shyly round her neck and whispered that he would.

Ruby bristled at the word 'pancake'. She thrust her bowl away from her and stood up. Lisa wondered that her mother never connected the cause of Ruby's fury with her own haphazard comments. To Ruby, pancakes stood as black as ink for Swan Henderson. Ruby strode up and down the kitchen. She flung open the fridge door and stared into its uninspiring depths. If it wasn't for the loathing that made it impossible for her to say Swan's name, Ruby might have given her reasons for disdaining to stay even for the mixing of the batter. Ruby slammed the fridge door too hard to stick, and it lunged out again and hung open on its hinges.

'I'm off,' she said, her back bent under the weight of a black leather jacket.

'Nice jacket,' Marguerite said.

'It's Tom's.' Ruby swore as her hand caught in the ripped lining of a sleeve.

Lisa walked her to the bottom of the stairs. 'Are you all right?'

Ruby looked at her, her pupils pinpoints in an oval dish of yellow. 'Yeah, I'm fine.' And then she added with a wince, 'Don't say anything to Mum.'

By the time Lisa reclimbed the stairs, Max was already standing up at the table, a tea towel knotted under his arms, stirring busily away at the pancake mix.

'Ruby looked well, I thought?' Marguerite said.

'Ummm.' It was as near as she could get to what her mother wanted to hear. She bent over Max and tried to hug him. 'Get off,' Max whined. Lisa kissed his cheek. 'Yu-uck,' he squirmed. Lisa laughed and hugged him even tighter, only letting go when he started to scream, 'I hate sloppy kisses, I hate sloppy kisses.' Max rubbed his cheek, flicking batter into his eyes.

'Lisa!' her mother said, and Lisa took a last pretend bite out of his dimpled elbow before going through to the bathroom to wash the layers of grime from her feet.

I T WAS NEARLY two weeks later that Lisa arrived at college to find there was a message for her. The voice teacher, Pete, said she'd have to go up to the head office to collect it. Lisa wanted to know what was in the message and who it was from, but the voice teacher insisted it was confidential. 'Can't you just tell me,' Lisa pleaded, but Pete jutted his chin and said he was only obeying the rules. Lisa stretched her eyes at him. She had been brought up to mistrust anyone who believed in rules.

The head office was on the third floor of the old wing and wasn't open until after lunch. Lisa's fantasies grew with each turn of the stairs. Each flap of swing door brought sweeter and sweeter bids for her and Quentin's reconciliation; each acre of corridor another bend of his knee.

A queue of students waited, wilting up against the wall opposite the door marked 'Head Office'. Lisa joined them. She shuffled her feet and tapped her fingers in a fluttery dance of expectation. She began to imagine her message as a package. A brown-paper package containing her ring and a note with pencil kisses and a time and a place to meet. It occurred to her only a second before she slid through into the dusty light of the office that Quentin had no way of knowing that she was at college, and even if he did, it was unlikely he would know which college she was at.

'Lisa.' The head of department was talking to her. 'Someone has been looking for you.'

Lisa's change of heart was so severe it took her breath away.

'A man was here first thing this morning, asking to see you, demanding even, but as we are unable to give out any personal information concerning our students . . .'

'What did he want?' Lisa asked. There was no paper package.

'He wouldn't say exactly. He wanted to know where you were, where you lived, but of course . . .' The head went on to explain the various laws concerning the security of each and every pupil.

Lisa was too busy shaking off her disappointment to hear what he was saying. She closed her eyes and, as she attempted to focus in on any other men she knew, Max's father disassociated himself from the crowd and stormed up into her brain. Swan had changed his mind, turned his boat around, or dived, and was standing now dripping in the traffic of the King's Cross one-way system. In London to reclaim his family and his only son.

'If he returns what would you like me to tell him?' The head of department was leaning over his desk at her. He had a kind face that had fallen, the rings under his eyes spreading down his cheeks in deep concentric circles.

'Could you tell me what he looked like?' Lisa asked tentatively. The man frowned into his papers as if she had misunderstood everything.

'He was, well, rather bad-tempered, and . . . tall.' He looked at Lisa to let her know he had given her more time than was ever his intention.

'If he comes back I'll be in the hall all afternoon,' she said. 'Tell him to try and find me.'

Lisa sat on her plastic chair and watched as each member of the Full Time Speech and Drama course performed Stanislavsky's 'An Action and Three Activities'. Stanislavsky, or 'Stan', as Denise the American method teacher called him, had a theory of acting that revolved around 'Actions'. Every single thing you did was an Action. Each Action had an Objective, and each Activity you performed related to that Action. Lisa wanted to believe this, but she knew it couldn't possibly be true. As far as she could see, very little she did related to anything at all.

'Does that mean I walk around all day with an Objective?' she asked.

Denise looked at her, frozen, with an arm raised. 'Do you have an Objective?' Her voice was too quiet for comfort. 'You are asking if you have an Objective? Your objective, my dear, is to be an actress.' She let her arm down slowly as if she had been stung in the armpit by Lisa's lack of ambition. 'That is an objective that should be with you always. Every step you take should ring out, "I am an actress."'

Lisa felt humbled. The eyes of the rest of the class were on her.

Eugene performed his three Activities. He walked through an imaginary door and looked around an imaginary room. He walked over and peered into a mirror on the Fourth Wall. The Fourth Wall was Stanislavsky's term for the thin air that divided the actors from the audience. Lisa imagined that when she was sufficiently trained she would actually be able to see the pictures that hung on this wall and look out through the windows that opened off it. Eugene combed his hair and straightened his collar. One. Lisa counted his Activities off on her fingers. Eugene walked over to a chair and picked up his jacket. He pulled it on and buttoned it. Two. Out of the pocket Eugene pulled a piece of paper. He held it up to the light. It had words printed on it in black. It looked like a theatre ticket. Eugene kissed the ticket and put it neatly back in his pocket. With a last look around the room he walked out again through the imaginary door. As soon as he was out, he bounded back in and beamed at the class. 'My Action was to go to a performance of *Evita*.'

'Good,' Denise said, her arms crossed over her chest. 'Eugene, you did good.'

Lisa waited anxiously for her turn. The nearer it got the louder the crackling in her head became. It sounded to her like the badly connected line of a telephone, and sometimes, in frustration, she rapped at her skull with her knuckles as if it were a faulty receiver. Lisa looked up at the strip-lights that ran along the ceiling of the hall. She felt their white heat burning into her. She had heard Heidi, one of the Rhodesian sisters, talking about a man who tested for allergies. Maybe he would say to her, 'No more tomatoes,' and all her troubles would be over.

'Lisa!' Denise shouted as if the whole class were waiting. 'It's your turn.'

Of all the thousands of Activities that must exist in a normal day Lisa was unable to think of one. She peered desperately into her bag for inspiration and saw Max's silver cap gun lying heavily at the bottom.

Lisa strode confidently into the room of Action. She placed her bag on a chair and walked over to the mirror. She nearly crossed her eyes in an attempt to catch a glimpse of her own reflection as she smoothed her hair and took a good long look at herself. One. Lisa rummaged in her bag. She took out a pencil and a piece of paper and scribbled down a note. She didn't write proper words, just made marks on the paper. Lisa folded her note and placed it on the table. Two. She was so pleased with herself she had to stop herself from smiling. Lisa drew the gun out of her bag, raised it to her temple and pulled the trigger. It made a surprisingly loud noise. Lisa fell to the ground and lay still and crumpled for a moment to monitor the effect. There was a cold silence and then the double doors at the end of the hall creaked. Lisa opened one eye and saw Tom craning his neck into the room. He caught sight of her and waved. Lisa stood up, blushing wildly. She looked hopefully at Denise. Denise's face was set against her. 'You are mocking the reality of this situation,' she said. Lisa glanced along the row of students. They were sniggering into their hands.

The door screeched as Tom attempted to slip unnoticed into the room. Lisa kept her eyes on the ground.

'I am appalled.' Denise sauntered over to the table and picked up Lisa's suicide note. She smirked as she glanced over it. 'You see what I'm saying?' And she held it up to illustrate her point.

Tom coughed.

Lisa reeled at the thought that he might come to her rescue and present himself as her theatrical agent, whisking her away in a flurry of abuse, but he stood pale and willowy by the door and waited until Lisa plucked up the courage to excuse herself.

'What are you doing here?' Lisa could hardly look at him.

'It's Ruby . . .' And Lisa realized she must have known it was Ruby all along. She kept her eyes fixed on his shoes. They were blue and ridiculously long. 'She's in hospital.'

Lisa grinned. Just don't step on my blue suede shoes, her brain hummed all by itself. She's in hospital, in hospital. Lisa always grinned when something terrible happened. She hated herself for it. She had grinned when a friend of her mother's was found hanging by a rope in the attic. She had grinned solidly for two hours while she waited for her mother to come home so she could pass on the message. She tried to force Tom's words through her smile as she sang along to Elvis.

'In hospital . . .'

'She wants to see you.'

97

The smile on her lips dropped of its own accord and for the first time since Tom croaked his way into the hall, Lisa believed there was a chance Ruby might still be alive.

'She wants to see you,' Tom said again, and he began to lope off down the corridor.

'Tom, Tom, wait for me.' Lisa ran after him and she grabbed hold of his hand. He leant down to kiss her cheek. His breath smelt of hangovers and lunchtime Guinness, and something in Lisa rose up to meet his kiss with a surge of loneliness. For a moment she thought how, if Ruby did die, she and Tom would be irrevocably united in their grief, they would get married as planned, have their three children, and of course they would call their oldest daughter Ruby.

Lisa slammed down hard on this fantasy. She wanted to punish herself for such sickening thoughts, and in disgust she withdrew her hand from Tom's.

Ruby lay in a high, starched bed in a ward of the Westminster Hospital. The whiteness of the sheets made her yellow face look almost gold and Lisa had to stifle a pang of envy for the glamour of her thin bronze arm.

'She's cold turkey,' Tom had whispered as they entered the ward, and now, as Lisa sat on a stool by Ruby's bed, she tried to decipher what he meant. Brown bread – dead, Eartha Kitt – shit. She assumed cold turkey must be Cockney slang for something, but she couldn't find anything to rhyme with turkey. Murky was all she could come up with. If murky was what Tom meant, Lisa couldn't see why he'd bother to be so mysterious about it.

Ruby had hepatitis and it was the hepatitis that was making her yellow.

'But how did you get it?' Lisa asked, wondering if cold turkey meant contagious.

'Dunno. Dirty gear.' And then, too exhausted to keep up the accent, she whispered in her old voice, 'Do I look awful?'

'No, not at all,' Lisa reassured her. 'Not at all.'

'Does Mum know?'

Lisa frowned slightly at what she knew was coming. 'Not yet.' She was determined to withhold a promise, and Ruby, as if sensing the barricade of her decision, didn't press her. There were flowers by the bed and three bottles of Perrier water. Lisa wondered if her father had already been and gone.

'When did you come in?' Lisa asked.

'Last night.' Ruby rattled out a laugh. 'What happened was that I decided to have an early night for once in my life. When Tom came home he saw me passed out, thought I'd overdosed, and called an ambulance. The next thing I know they're pumping out my stomach.'

Tom got up from his chair on the other side of the bed and walked down to the end of the ward. Lisa looked at the smile on Ruby's exhausted face. She wanted to believe her.

'Anyway, it was lucky really. They said if I hadn't come in, sooner or later I'd have . . .' Ruby's voice strangled up and caught. She slid down the bed so that only her eyelids were visible over the turn of the sheet. Fat, pearly tears oozed out from under them and slid down the side of her face and into her ear. 'I didn't even know I was ill, I mean I knew I was a bit off colour . . .' She tried to laugh, and Lisa pressed the bone of where she hoped her shoulder was.

Before Lisa left, Ruby made her lean close in to the bed so she could whisper in her ear. 'Listen, I've got a favour to ask.'

Lisa nodded.

Ruby gathered up her strength and curled her lip for a London accent. 'Tom's gone all bleedin' holy on me' – she paused while a nurse trundled by – 'and I've got to get hold of some drugs, bad like.' She pinned Lisa with her eye to instill in her the gravity of the situation. 'Just get a bit of smack for me, and I'll never forget it, promise.'

Ruby pulled some money out of her bedside drawer and handed it over. Two twenty-pound notes, crisp and lying in wait. 'Jimmy'll know where to score. He hangs out Thursdays at the Pied Bull.'

Lisa clutched the money. She wished she could ask her to write it all down.

'Oh, and if Jimmy happens to ask,' Ruby added casually, too casually, 'you can mention where I am.'

Lisa hovered at the end of the ward to see if Tom would say his goodbyes and follow her, but as she watched, he stretched himself across the foot of Ruby's bed and showed no sign of moving. The ward sister pushed past her and bore down on him with short, sharp steps.

Lisa intended to tell her mother about Ruby as soon as she got home. She imagined her, furious at not having been the first to know, railing round the kitchen. She saw her elbows shivering on the metal of the draining-board as she cried with her head in her hands. Lisa put off telling her for so long that to come out with the news now, all of a sudden, would be suspicious and inexcusable.

Lisa was distracted for a short time by the conversation over supper. It was dominated by Max. Max described in detail a drawing he had done that day at school. It was a drawing of a fox and he had spent all morning on it. He had made it as big as it would go with zigzag, pointy teeth and a tail that curled up to the roof of the page. Max recreated the shape of it with the pronged end of his fork. Shortly after finishing his picture, just minutes away from home time, another boy, a boy Max hated anyway called Nermil, had taken the fox and, creasing it into a paper aeroplane, had sailed it out of the window and into a puddle. There was nothing Lisa or Marguerite could say to abate his fury. He stabbed at Nermil's name with his fork. He said Nermil was really a gerbil in disguise. He said he was going to kill him.

Lisa ran her fingers through his hair and offered to read him a story. Max flung her hand away and scowled, and then an instant later, sensing his mistake, he crawled on to her lap and said, 'All right, as long as it's a comic.'

Lisa hated comics and Max knew it.

'You're not reading it properly!' he complained every time she missed a bubble or a sound effect.

'Sorry. "Thwack. Splat." Better?'

She kept flicking through to see how far it was to the end.

'Don't do that, it's not fair,' Max whined.

'Lisa!' her mother called through from the washing-up.

Lisa knew the only way out was to start again. 'I'm just going to the phone box,' she called when she had finished, and she slipped out on to the stairs.

Lisa walked up and down Peerless Street. There was a pub at one end into which she was curious to go. She peered through the bottle-base panes of its windows but could see no customers, only a blur of red plush and bar stools and the tottering reflection of the tower blocks. In all those hundreds of flats, she thought, looking up, there must be someone I could get to know.

She was about to turn back into her staircase when Steen appeared as if from nowhere and put his hand on her shoulder. 'How're you doing?'

Lisa hadn't noticed it before, but he was dressed from head to toe in shades of faded orange.

'Fine.' And then she remembered and added, 'Thanks again for that grass.'

Steen stood and stared at her with his eyes moist and bulging. Lisa couldn't think of anything else to say. 'Do you know where the Pied Bull is?' she asked to break the intensity of his gaze, even though she knew very well it was at the Angel.

'What's a pied bull?'

Put like that Lisa didn't really know. Then a thought struck her. Maybe she wouldn't have to go to the Pied Bull after all. She remembered Steen's previous generosity and thought how she might not only save herself a bus fare, but be able to keep some of the crisp forty pounds Ruby had given her. 'You don't by any chance,' she asked him, 'have any heroin I could buy off you?'

Steen swayed slightly. 'You must be joking!' He looked genuinely shocked. He closed his eyes for a moment, and then, giving her a final liquid stare, he walked away down the street.

Marguerite looked up at her. She was kneeling by the bath washing Max with a flannel.

'Ruby's got hepatitis. She's in hospital and she'd like it if you'd visit her,' Lisa said almost in a breath.

'What, now?'

'Well it's probably a bit late now.' Lisa felt as if she were towering above her mother. 'Visiting times . . .'

Marguerite was silent.

'Maybe tomorrow?' Lisa suggested.

Marguerite rubbed hard at the dirt around Max's neck, making him shout and wriggle away from her like a tadpole. Lisa leant against the bathroom door. She was waiting for her mother to react, but for once it seemed she had decided against it.

Lisa wandered through to the sitting-room and sat down on her bed. It was getting late. She toyed with the idea of not going to the Pied Bull. She could tell Ruby that Jimmy hadn't been there, or that he had been there but without any drugs, or that the pub had been raided and closed down. It wasn't so much going to the Pied Bull, but the inevitable conversation with Jimmy Bright that Lisa dreaded. She had never managed to say more than a few words in his presence and even those she had regretted.

'Some of them peas please,' she said now, in an attempt to lose her south-coast voice, and, 'All right, Jim mate? All right?'

Lisa picked up her coat and reached behind her for the handle of the door. 'Listen, I won't be back late,' she mumbled, as if any other details had been previously discussed.

Marguerite looked troubled. 'But don't you have college in the morning, surely?' she asked, knowing she did.

'Yes, but it'll be all right. It's just – look, I'll see you later,' and Lisa wriggled backwards and slipped out on to the stairs.

Marguerite let her go. Lisa knew that her mother regretted the line she had taken with Ruby, ordering her home by eleven, allowing Swan to interrogate her over boyfriends and insisting that she not hitch-hike alone. These attempts at discipline had, she felt, lost her her eldest daughter and, in the wake of Ruby's rebellion, Lisa had inherited a free rein. And anyway, Lisa was sensible. Lisa had been told how sensible she was ever since she could remember. She had even been introduced to people on occasion as the only truly sensible member of her family.

As Lisa walked quickly through the short cut, she thought of Tom and saw his blue shoes hanging off the end of Ruby's bed. In a lazy attempt to push away his image she began to dwell on Quentin, and with a pang she realized she held the perfect excuse for seeing him again. This would not only be her chance for a reconciliation, but she might also be doing him a favour. If he were really as down on his luck as he made out, surely he would appreciate her bringing him some business.

Lisa took the tube to Finsbury Park and waited in the dingy and deserted station for a bus.

'Half, please,' she said, when a bus finally pulled in.

'Half to where, love?' The driver looked at her sceptically.

'Crouch Hill.'

'Yes, Crouch Hill. Crouch Hill where? Top, bottom, halfway up?'

'Halfway up,' Lisa guessed, hoping she wouldn't be thrown off too far from her destination.

'Right, now that we've got that clear.' The driver looked at her. 'How old did you say you were?'

'Thirteen,' Lisa gasped, wide-eyed and with an air of breathy incredulity.

The driver held her stare for a moment and then, whistling through his teeth, punched her out a ticket.

There were three bells by Quentin's front door and Lisa rang them all. No one appeared. She rang them again and waited. As she stood awkwardly on the broken path, she glanced up at his window, slightly open at the top of the house, and saw that a light had been switched on.

That doesn't necessarily mean he's in, she told herself fiercely, arguing against the possibilities. And then, as she watched, she saw a long black shadow sweep across the square of light, move away from the window and vanish. Lisa slunk into the wall, squeezing herself between a row of dustbins, pushing away the thought of Quentin's smile that would settle on his face like a bow as he watched her waiting hopefully. It made the sweat stand out cold on her back. She crept around the side of the house, scrambled out through the hedge, and streaked away over the brow of the hill. The same bus stopped for her on its return journey.

'Finsbury Park,' she said woefully, unable to catch the driver's eye, and he punched her out a half fare anyway.

It was nearly closing time when Lisa walked into the Pied Bull. She clung desperately to the importance of her mission as she had first experienced it. She thought of the fix of Ruby's yellow eye, and the enormity of her task.

Lisa nestled her toes against the edges of her twenty-pound notes, folded for safety one each in the soles of her shoes. The pub was almost empty. She looked around for Jimmy, half hoping not to find him, but he was there, lounging against the jukebox. Lisa walked purposefully over to him.

'Jimmy?' Her voice came out unexpectedly in a high squeak. Jimmy flashed round on her, and for a moment, just before his face softened, she saw the tip of what Ruby had warned her of. His scornful, razor-sharp tongue.

'Watcha, lil' sis,' he said with a laugh. 'Got a message for me, have you?'

Lisa nodded.

'How is she, then, Ruby, the jewel of my life?' Jimmy tapped his foot and broke into a country-and-western croon, 'Oh Ru-ubeey, don't take your love to town.'

Lisa edged a little nearer to him. 'She said you'd be able to sell me –'

'Yeah yeah, all right, great.' Jimmy cut her off, and he clicked his finger at the barman and ordered her a bottle of

Pils. 'Right,' Jimmy hissed into her ear. 'Give us the money.' Lisa stared down at her shoes. Jimmy looked away and sighed a low, hopeless sigh, and Lisa, refusing to be given up on, dropped her bag and, on bending down to retrieve it, slipped her fingers into her shoes and came up triumphantly with the notes.

'All right, drink this, and wait here,' Jimmy said, pushing her glass towards her, and he disappeared through the side door of the pub. Lisa felt a fog settle down over her head. Her left ear hummed as if it had been topped up with water. She stared miserably into the pale round of her beer, scanning its surface for a trace of what she feared, and resolving not to take the risk of drinking it.

It was eleven-fifteen. Lisa took a sip of Pils from the sheer boredom of waiting. At any minute, she thought, the pub would close. She supposed she would have to wait for Jimmy out on the street, and then it occurred to her for the first time that he might not come back. She took a long gulp of lager and regretted it. Now she would not only be waiting for Jimmy but also for the possible disintegration of her brain. She had just condemned herself to twenty minutes of torture, if not a lifetime in a lunatic asylum. She considered ordering an orange juice – Lisa had once been told that the vitamin C in orange juice worked against the hallucinogenic effects of acid – but she decided against it. If her drink was spiked, it would have been the barman, possibly on Jimmy's orders, who had spiked it, and therefore he would be bound to know what she was up to. Apart from anything else acid was expensive and he wasn't likely to let her waste the effects of a good tab. Lisa had another theory that stopped her from ordering orange juice. She was certain that for an under-age drinker to ask for a soft drink would be a sure way to arouse suspicion and bring up the question of whether she should actually be in a pub in the first place.

It was nearly twelve and the Pied Bull showed no sign of closing. Lisa began to worry about her mother. She imagined her waiting up. Listening for every tread on the stairs. She knew from experience that the more she worried about her mother, the less anxious her mother seemed when she did finally appear. But it didn't stop her. Maybe this was what people meant by sensible.

Lisa hovered by the bar, her eyes fixed on the door in an agony of indecision. I'll wait five more minutes, she told herself regularly, and then another five, and the first five after that. She talked herself in and out of giving up on Jimmy, abandoning the money, declaring his treachery to Ruby. But it was at this point in her revolving thoughts that she submerged into the deathbed scene. She saw Ruby's yellow hand reach out to her, pleading for a sign of Jimmy Bright's devotion, her dry lips moving wordlessly, her eyes alight with fever, she saw Ruby sink into the hospital pillow, Ruby, too weak to speak.

Lisa shook herself. She looked up at the clock, into the froth of her empty glass, and around the room at the few remaining people. She glanced, minutely hopeful, towards the door, and with a shock like a punch she saw that it was bolted. She felt herself freezing. Her knees lost their joints and her head shrunk to the size of a tennis ball. The thought of the side door whirred in the pit of her stomach. It loomed larger than life as her only real means of escape. She pulled herself around, expecting to find it vanished, to find the door bricked up or disguised in some way by a row of jukeboxes or a revolving bookcase, but it was still there, unlocked and unmanned, and as she grappled with her dissolving knees, it swung open, and Jimmy Bright strode in.

'Jimmy!' Lisa stumbled towards him.

Jimmy narrowed his eyes. He tilted his head, and motioned for her to follow him outside.

The wind was up and howling round the Angel. They rushed along, their elbows out to fight off the sheets of plastic and the flying cardboard boxes. Jimmy, shaking a clinging newspaper from his foot, dodged into a doorway.

Lisa waited for a lull. 'Have you got it?'

Jimmy winced. He turned to face her. 'Listen, girl, it's up to you. You can either come back tomorrow, or we can give the Old Man a try.'

Lisa gulped. 'Let's try the Old Man,' she said, shaken, but thrilled to be given even the most slender of choices, and she followed Jimmy cheerfully as they skidded on through the swirling litter.

The Old Man was a woman. She was tall and thin and looked about twenty-five. She lived in a basement in a large damp room that smelt faintly of gas. No one spoke. Jimmy handed over the money.

The Old Man curled the notes around her finger, modelling them into a purple paper ring. Eventually she stood up, stretched, and left the room. A dog that had been sleeping in the corner woke up briskly, his ears on end, and trotted after her.

'She likes to take a cut,' Jimmy whispered.

The Old Man reappeared with a white paper packet in a polythene bag, a soup spoon and a syringe. Lisa watched as the Old Man poured powder from the packet into the spoon and melted it over the flame of a candle. When it had melted to a slippery brown treacle, she poured it into the syringe, and, shaking her wrists until her fingers thickened, she pierced a fat vein in the back of her hand. The dog began to bark. The hair along its back stiffened. It snapped and growled and gnashed its teeth at the Old Man.

'Shut up, Hassle.' With her eyes on the needle she smiled a proud half-smile. 'He hates it when I jack up.'

Hassle stretched out his front paws and snarled at the empty syringe. He barked so fiercely that foam bubbled and clung at the corners of his mouth. The Old Man drew the needle out and offered it to Jimmy. Hassle's barking faded to a whine and, with his tail between his legs, he retreated to his basket.

'WHAT TIME do you finish college?' Marguerite asked Lisa over breakfast.

'Five.'

'I'll meet you at Victoria station at half past and we'll go on to the hospital from there.' Marguerite was planning a visit to Ruby and she expected Lisa to go with her. Lisa would have preferred to have gone alone but Marguerite was insistent.

'All right, but please, please don't be late.' Lisa crept into the sitting-room to pack her bag for college. A notebook, Chekhov's *Three Sisters*, her leotard, and Ruby's small white packet of heroin, which she slipped between the loose lining of her satchel.

Lisa sat in the college canteen over lunch with Janey and Eugene. The chip-making machine had stopped working and a furious meeting hosted by the students' union had just broken up. If chips did not reappear on the menu by the following week, the students' union were threatening to set up a picket. Janey and Eugene sat opposite Lisa with a paper plate and five substitute packets of beef, bacon and cheese-and-onion crisps. Lisa had a plate of tinned ravioli. Tinned ravioli was her current favourite food, eclipsing even a cheeseburger. Lisa hadn't grown up with school dinners. For lunch each day she had eaten Marmite sandwiches crumbled at the bottom of a paper bag, an apple and a handful of dried fruit and sunflower seeds. She had only attended the students' union chip-machine meeting out of curiosity and she had been amazed to see so much distress over chips when there was still ravioli available for one and a half luncheon vouchers.

'Was that your boyfriend that came in yesterday?' Janey asked.

It was the first allusion anyone had made to her unsuccessful attempt to impress the method teacher with suicide. Lisa blushed.

'No,' she said. 'No,' she said again and sighed.

'He looked nice.'

'He's sort of my sister's boyfriend.'

'Oh, I see.' Janey leant in closer for an exchange of confidences. 'My sister's got one of those, or at least she did have until she got pregnant and he scarpered.'

'Did she keep the baby?' Lisa asked, assuming she wouldn't have.

'Yeah, Mum and Dad tried to get her to have an abortion, seeing as she was fifteen and everything, but she said she wanted it.' Janey shrugged. 'Takes all kinds. Different strokes for different folks.'

Lisa nodded.

'Are you a feminist?' Janey asked her.

Lisa, never having given the matter much thought, said she thought she probably was.

'Bloody men!' Janey thumped her fist on the table, and Eugene, feeling left out of the conversation, and having turned the last packet of crisps inside out to catch the crumbs, broke into a heartfelt version of 'Don't Cry for Me, Argentina'.

Marguerite was late. Lisa had known all day that she would be, and now, at a quarter to six, it was just a matter of how late she was going to be.

They had arranged to meet by the cartoon cinema at the end of platform 17. Trains to Sussex ran from platform 17, and London, until very recently, had begun and ended for Lisa with this platform and the exotic pull of the cartoons. Lisa looked at the glass-encased posters of Bugs Bunny and Mickey and Minnie Mouse. She had imagined so often what it would be like to sit inside its plush interior and watch Technicolor films throughout a whole day that she couldn't remember whether she had ever actually been inside or not.

She had once been taken to the cinema by a friend of her father's, a girl called Felicity, who had been sent to meet her off the train one Father's Day when her father couldn't make it. Felicity had asked her what she wanted to do and she had said more than anything else she wanted to go to the cinema. She remembered holding Felicity's hand as they stooped to run past the ticket window and slip unnoticed up the red-carpeted stairs. She remembered creeping and falling over the legs of men as they pushed their way to a free seat. But it couldn't have been the cartoon cinema because the film was about a woman with large breasts and long blonde hair who pulled up her petticoats at every opportunity to prove to people that she was in fact a man. The film hadn't been in English and Lisa remembered the subtitles jumping about on the screen. She also remembered that after ten minutes Felicity said it was boring and they had crept out again. Afterwards they had taken photos of themselves in a black-and-white photo booth, all of which Felicity let her keep, and which still occupied a corner of her treasure box. She wondered now what had happened to Felicity.

'Max, would you like me to take you to the cartoon cinema?' she asked, when her mother finally appeared, breathless and full of excuses.

Max stared up at a larger-than-life Pink Panther.

'Yes, but not now.' Marguerite frowned. 'She doesn't mean now.'

'No, another time.' Lisa reached for his free hand. 'Shall I take you another time?'

'All right,' Max said. And he shot at one of Bugs Bunny's ears with an imaginary bow and arrow as they hurried away.

When Lisa, Marguerite and Max arrived at the Westminster Hospital, they found that Ruby had been moved on. She had been sent to a hospital somewhere near Baker Street that specialized in hepatitis.

'You'll be lucky to get there before visiting's over,' the ward sister warned them.

Lisa clutched her bag. 'Come on, let's hurry.' She headed for the stairs. 'Max, if you wait for the lift, we'll be here all night.'

As Lisa shuffled Max through the revolving doors of the main entrance, she saw a familiar shape blurred between the glass partitions. It was Sarah. Lisa stayed in the wheel of the door and caught her in the foyer.

'Ruby's not here,' she told her.

'It's been ages.' Sarah looked at her, curious. 'How are things?'

'It's just that if we don't hurry, we'll miss the end of visiting time.' Lisa could hardly control her agitation. Max and her mother, having followed her back inside, were browsing by the kiosk that sold sweets and newspapers. As she watched, her mother joined a queue of men and women in pyjamas. 'Mum, we really should go . . .' she called.

Sarah looked down at her spray of white carnations. 'I suppose I might as well come with you.'

Sarah was in high spirits. 'What do you think about Tom and Ruby, then?' and she nudged Lisa in the ribs. When Lisa didn't answer, she told her about her cousin Tanya, and how she still hadn't succeeded in losing her virginity. 'No,' Sarah sighed. 'So far no luck. Poor thing.' She looked at Lisa and smiled. Sarah could afford to smile. Sarah had a boyfriend. She had a photograph of him in her wallet that she showed round once they were on the bus.

'He looks very handsome,' Marguerite approved, leaning over to have a look.

'Yes, he does.'

'He looks like wee,' Max hissed from under their seat, giving himself away, as Marguerite was about to pay three full fares.

'And a half,' she added, smiling up at the conductor.

The hospital was behind Lisson Grove. It was white and shaped in parts like a church. It stood in its own garden and made the Westminster, with its solid grey wings, look like a multistorey carpark.

'I'm afraid visiting time is over,' a nurse called out to them as they tried to pass unnoticed through the quiet tiled hall of the main entrance.

'I'm sorry?' Marguerite stopped in her tracks as if unable to believe her ears.

The nurse, patient as a nun, repeated her message.

'But my daughter was only admitted today.' Marguerite strode over to her. 'I think she would appreciate a familiar face, even at this ungodly hour.'

Lisa winced. It had been a mistake to mention God. The nurse's white face hardened. She flicked through her book with quick, decisive fingers.

'Yes, I see. Indeed. Well, you will have to return tomorrow at a more . . . appropriate time.' The nurse shut her book. She was waiting for them to leave.

'Excuse me, Sister.' Sarah lowered her voice in reverence. 'Would it be possible, if it wasn't too inconvenient, for you to take these flowers up to her?'

The nurse softened. She placed a hand on the green stalks of the carnations.

Lisa wondered if she shouldn't ask that her small white package be taken up also. If she had known, she could have had it ready in her hand, or even hidden it among the spray of Sarah's frilly flowers. But now it was too late. It would be impossible to rummage through the lining of her bag without arousing anyone's suspicion. She bit her lip and prayed that Ruby would have the strength to hold out.

Lisa got up early the next morning. She left Marguerite to investigate a one-bedroom flat, which according to Frances was coming free that day on the next staircase, and set off for the hospital.

She found Ruby sitting on a bench in the garden. She was as yellow as ever and seemed to have made some friends. She introduced Lisa to two girls. Marlene, who was West Indian and not yellow but a greenish colour, and a girl called Trish, who was so thin and fragile Lisa wondered that she was able to sit up unaided.

'It's brilliant in here,' Ruby beamed, 'you can get all the gear you want.'

Lisa's face fell. She had Ruby's packet of heroin all ready to present to her.

'You just place an order with Trish's boyfriend and next visiting hour it arrives with the grapes.'

'Oh,' Lisa said.

'Yeah,' Marlene winked, 'we don't half save a lot on syringes.' And the three girls erupted into a fit of giggles. Lisa smiled weakly. She still had a stitch from the last sprint from the station. When they had recovered, Trish and Marlene went off to raid the kitchens. 'There's a whole freezer full of raspberry ripple ice cream.'

'No, ta.' Ruby stayed to talk to Lisa.

'In case I forget' – Lisa took out her packet – 'I'd better give you this.'

Ruby slipped it into the pocket of her dressing-gown without a word. 'Did you see Jimmy?'

Lisa nodded. She tried to keep her face brave.

'Well, what did he say?'

Lisa screwed up her eyes. 'What?'

'What did he say?'

'Nothing.'

'Bastard.' Ruby crossed her arms tight over her chest and scowled. Her wrists stretched out of her hospital gown and revealed the white tissue of the scar that had formed over the self-inflicted gash of the bread knife.

'Jimmy did say' – Lisa spoke slowly as if searching out the memory – '"Ruby, the jewel of my life."'

Ruby tightened her fists.

'He even sang a song about you.'

There was a pause and then Ruby raised her chin. 'Did he? What? He sang a song? About me?'

'Oh Ru-ubeey, don't take your love to town.' Lisa tried to imitate Jimmy Bright's rock-and-roll quaver.

'Oh that old song.' Ruby tossed her head, but she was unable to control the smile that spread over her face like the light behind a Hallowe'en lantern. 'Oh Ru-ubeey, oh Ru-ubeeey, don't take your love to town.'

MARGUERITE HAD MANAGED to secure them a new flat. It was identical to the old one except it had an extra room. She and Max were going to sleep in the bedroom in bunk beds and Lisa was to have the sitting-room all to herself.

Lisa promised she would stay in the flat while her mother went to visit Ruby. Marguerite was terrified it would be taken over by squatters if left vacant for even five minutes.

'Won't you leave Max here with me?' Lisa asked, but Marguerite insisted on taking him with her. 'Ruby never sees her little brother.'

Lisa wondered if it had ever occurred to her that Ruby didn't like children. Max was no exception. When Max was born, Ruby could hardly bring herself to look at him. And now as the years passed, and his resemblance to his father grew, she only ever paid him the slightest and most necessary attention. Lisa, on the other hand, had been so overcome the day they brought Max home that she had given up playing with her dolls. She had donated any doll's clothes that fitted to his tiny wardrobe and the rest had been sent to a jumble sale along with their owners. Max was to have no competition. Soon after, Lisa began to suffer recurring nightmares in which pint-sized Max fell through the window of his bedroom, and Lisa would have to race down the stairs, through the front door and out on to the path to try to catch him before he hit the ground. Lisa always awoke from these dreams convinced they were a sign her brother had been struck down by cot death. She spent a large part of each night holding a mirror in front of his face to check that he was breathing.

Lisa wandered around the empty new flat. The kitchen was covered in the same strangling wallpaper, and the bedroom had squares of lime-green and brown in horizontal stripes. Tulips in boxes. Or tunnels. Lisa found if she looked at them for too long she began to feel dizzy. Only the lavatory was lined in plain woodchip. Lisa sat on the edge of the bath for lack of a chair, and listened to the broken lyrics of a Leonard Cohen song wailing through the floorboards of the flat above.

Ruby stayed at the special hospital week after week. The doctors told her she was not allowed to drink alcohol for at least six months, and she was advised to stay in bed for the best part of the day.

Ruby, Trish and Marlene became firm friends. When Lisa visited, she usually found them in the day-room with their feet up in a cloud of smoke, discussing the latest delivery of drugs. Or when the weather was warm enough, out in the gardens shooting up among the rhododendrons.

Sometimes Lisa bumped into her father arriving with white boxes of cake and mineral water. She told him that they'd moved into a bigger flat and that college was going fine. And he said, 'Ruby does seem to be looking better, don't you think?' Once or twice he and Marguerite passed in the corridor, or one arrived as the other was about to leave. They nodded and made friendly faces at each other, but neither of them ventured to speak.

One Saturday Lisa arrived to find that Trish had died in the night. Ruby sat up straight in her starched bed. Only the palest trace of yellow remained in her face and her hands were bone-white. She clasped them in front of her, digging the nails in so hard they drew blood.

Lisa covered her face with her own hands. She felt sick with dread that she might laugh. She looked out at Ruby through the grille of her fingers.

'I'm sorry.'

She wanted to know the details. To know what had actually happened, but she didn't feel able to ask. She was anxious not to appear morbid.

Lisa sat by Ruby's bed all afternoon. She flicked through magazines and ate some of Ruby's sweets. From time to time she glanced at her sister, sitting sphinx-like against a wall of pillows, staring out through the window on the other side of the ward. Just when visiting time was finally over, Ruby started to itch. She twisted and turned in her bed as if she had fleas.

'He's deserted us,' her eyes were blazing and hateful.

'Who?'

'Trish's bloody boyfriend. You won't see him now for dust.'

'Oh,' Lisa said.

'Listen, on your way out, tell the nurse to bring me a couple of Valium or a sleeping-pill or whatever she can get. Ask the one with the big bum, she's the nicest.'

Lisa kissed Ruby goodbye. 'I'll see you tomorrow,' she said.

Family life became easier once they moved into the bigger flat. They painted it entirely white and resigned themselves to staying there for some time. Lisa even fantasized about having a party. She would invite Tom, and Sarah, and possibly even Quentin. Steen and the Rhodesians would be bound to drop in whether they were invited or not. She could invite Janey from college.

Lisa had become quite friendly with Janey. She had even begun to confide in her. At least she had told her about Quentin. She hadn't particularly wanted to talk about Quentin, but she felt something was expected of her in exchange for learning how Janey had lost her virginity on the pier at Blackpool.

'Do you think,' Lisa asked her, 'that I should go round there? Just turn up and say I've come to collect my ring?'

Janey wasn't sure. 'What? Today?'

'Why not?' Lisa felt full, suddenly, of bravado.

Janey looked at her. She looked her up and down like a man. 'Maybe you should go some other time when you . . . you know, you've made a bit more of an effort.'

Lisa's face fell. She knew Janey was right. Her hair was stringy and she had a ladder in her tights, but she resented her lack of confidence. 'I thought you said you were a feminist,' she mumbled, and added, silent and mistaken, If Quentin really loved me it wouldn't matter what I looked like.

R UBY WAS ALLOWED HOME. The hospital sent letters to both her mother and father informing them of this, and reiterating that Ruby must rest and abstain from alcohol for a further five months.

'Of course you can come to us,' Marguerite told her. 'It'll be a bit cramped, but we'll manage.'

Ruby rolled her eyes. 'I'd prefer to stay here!'

Marguerite looked to Lisa for support.

'It's all right,' Ruby said, kicking off a slipper. 'Dad's found me somewhere.'

Marguerite smiled away her hurt. 'That's wonderful.'

The hospital would have preferred Ruby to have gone to one or other of her parents but Ruby was eighteen, which meant she was over eighteen, and an adult. Ruby's father had a friend whose uncle had recently died. The uncle had been living in a three-bedroom flat in Belgravia, behind the German embassy. This flat was ready for Ruby to move into whenever she wanted.

'Cor blimey!' Ruby said, 'just look at this gaff.'

Lisa unloaded Ruby's bags from the taxi and carried them up the stairs.

'Bugger, bollocks and balls!' Ruby shouted, dancing from room to room.

'Ruby,' Lisa begged her. 'You're meant to be lying down.'

The flat was fully furnished. It had a sitting-room with twin sofas, and chairs and curtains made from matching chintz. The kitchen was enormous and fully equipped with potato-mashers, gravy boats and a well-stocked linen cupboard. The bedrooms were at the back of the flat. They were small, with high, wide beds and lampshades draped in muslin. Each one had a bedside table and a wardrobe. Ruby chose the room with the biggest bed. They didn't mention the uncle. The only sign of his previous existence was a row of smart, black shoes at the back of a cupboard.

Ruby asked her father for a colour television to help her while away the time, and she ordered that the phone be reconnected. After a few luxurious but lonely days she moved Marlene in for company.

Marlene had shaken off the murky pallor of her hepatitis and transformed into a cool, languid beauty of breath-taking sophistication. Marlene had a boyfriend who was out to kill her. She had a photograph of them together that she placed in its silver frame on top of the television, and Ruby, convinced all of a sudden that Jimmy Bright and Tom were both more threatening than they had ever shown themselves to be, made Lisa swear to keep her whereabouts a secret.

When Lisa visited, she had to give the bell three short, coded rings to prove it was her, and then Marlene's almond eyes would appear over the kitchen window-ledge, followed by the sound of her narrow feet treading lightly on the stairs. 'Hello, Lisa?' Her voice came through the locked door, double-checking, before her soft hand turned the key.

Ruby and Marlene only ventured out at night. They didn't begin their preparations until the television closed down, and often it was nearly morning before they were ready to leave the house. Marlene was an expert on make-up. She smoothed Ruby's face with creamy white foundation and patted it with powder that smelt of the secret inside of a handbag. She brushed her curled lashes with mascara until her eyes fluttered like moths, her lips she painted a dark blood-red. Marlene shadowed her own eyes in gold and honey-brown, and outlined her lips in silver. Her fine, high cheekbones she dusted over ivory.

Ruby was no longer a punk. She handed on to Lisa her bondage trousers, her DMs and the Snow White T-shirt with the seven dwarfs. She spent most of the day and night lounging in pyjamas, and when she did get dressed, she wore trailing, see-through layers of crêpe de Chine, and high, strappy heels. When Ruby and Marlene ventured out, it was to travel by taxi to the West End.

MARGUERITE WAS BEGINNING to despair of the council. There was a family of five on the top floor of Peerless Flats that had been living there for four years. Their children spent the evenings sniffing glue on the roof and pissing down the stairwell. Frances had had no news of her permanent accommodation, and little Brendan, still unseen by his father, was nearly five months old. Lisa saw less of her now that they were no longer direct neighbours, but whenever she did, she found Frances on the verge of giving up and going back to Ireland.

Heidi, one of the pale, red-haired Rhodesian sisters, had fallen in love. She had fallen in love with Steen. Heidi's husband moved out on the morning of the day Steen moved in. It was the beginning of the Christmas holidays and Lisa watched from the square-paned window of her bedroom. She felt the whole block cheer as Heidi ran down to help Steen with his bags, her hair wet and brushed straight over her shoulders and her little ginger baby on her arm.

Lisa hadn't spoken to Steen since the day she had shocked him in the street with her talk of hard drugs. She wondered what it was that had stopped him from telling her mother. For weeks she had expected the storm to break, opening the door each evening on a possible typhoon of recriminations only to find Marguerite filling in job application forms, maintaining the same strained air of calm.

Heidi invited them over for a drink. She had transformed her flat into a home for honeymooning. The sour smell was gone and all the dirty dishes and the milk-encrusted baby clothes had been ousted with her husband. There were flowers on the table and the bay window gleamed with the promise of Christmas. Heidi no longer talked about Rhodesia, about the velds and the sunsets and the flocks of wild flamingos. Her eyes sparkled with the possibility of snow and the chance to show her son the lights on Regent Street. Her sister Pam sat across the room, her mouth a thin line of disappointment. It was no fun being homesick on your own. She tugged her gangly, dark-haired daughter on to her knee and hugged her close.

Marguerite joined a housing co-operative. She insisted both Max and Lisa come with her to the first meeting to prove just how badly in need she was of housing. She declared she wasn't going to spend the rest of her life in a bunk bed on Peerless Street.

'Oh Mum,' Lisa said, overcome with guilt, and a twist of dread at the next inevitable move. 'I'll share with Max. I don't mind.'

'Don't be silly,' Marguerite snapped. 'You're a teenager, you need your own space.'

Lisa knew her mother was thinking of Ruby. She was thinking of Ruby and how she had lost her. Lisa wanted to throw her arms around her mother's neck and tell her that she'd never desert her, never leave home, wherever it was, and she mustn't worry or even think about it.

'Of course I'll come to the meeting,' she agreed instead, and she went to try on some of Ruby's newly cast-off clothes.

The New Swift Housing Co-operative was made up mainly of single women and their children. There were a few bearded men in needlecord who took over as soon as the meeting got started. Minutes sheets were distributed. Lisa ran her eye down the long list which included:

Complaints about Jackie

Why is the roof *still* leaking at 199 Huddleston Road

And eventually:

New members

Lisa felt so bored she thought her eyes might drop out and roll away like marbles. She fidgeted and yawned and, without meaning to, turned her minutes sheet into an abstract piece of origami art. The New Swift emblem

130

was a flying bird, a swift in profile. Lisa was disappointed. She had assumed New Swift meant either New people would be housed Swiftly, or at least they would be provided as soon as possible with Swift New houses. Neither of these things seemed likely. By tea break Lisa had resolved to remain forever homeless rather than attend another meeting.

There was a crèche at one end of the room that had been set up by the Co-op for members' children. On arrival Max had barricaded himself into the Wendy house and was busily building armoured personnel carriers out of Lego. Lisa longed for him to stir up a fight or get his finger caught under the wheels of a Thomas the Tank Engine so that she would have an excuse to go to his rescue, but he remained uncharacteristically well-behaved.

The meeting was still several items away from 'New members' when it dragged on into its third hour. Lisa looked at her mother who was brightly following a conversation about positive discrimination in short-life housing, and with a whispered excuse slipped away in the direction of the toilets. In an alcove below the stairs she found a payphone, and she dialled Sarah's number.

Lisa's fingers trembled with relief as the connection clicked and her two-pence piece slid through its slot and dropped into the box.

'Hello?' It was Sarah. She was at home.

'Hello, it's Lisa.'

'Lisa!' There was something breathy about Sarah's voice that made Lisa think she'd been crying. 'Where are you?'

'I'm not sure, somewhere very boring on the 27 bus route.'

'Do you want to come over?' 'Can I come over?' they said together, overlapping and embarrassing themselves. They laughed and Lisa thought she heard a sniff.

Sarah lived at the top of a house in a square in Kensington. The house was owned by a very old lady who was, or had been, a friend of Sarah's parents. When Lisa rang the bell, the door was answered by an equally ancient woman with a fierce look and a bent back. She had to stretch her neck to look up at Lisa.

'Yes?'

'I've come to visit Sarah.'

'Well, you've rung the wrong bell,' and she made to push the door shut. Sarah appeared round the curve of the stairs. 'Don't take any notice of her,' she called. 'Miserable old cow. This is a friend of mine,' she yelled into the woman's ear and, beckoning for Lisa to follow, she raced back upstairs, taking the steps two at a time, falling every now and then and giggling, until she reached the top.

Sarah had two rooms, a sitting-room and a bedroom, with a tiny kitchen on the landing below and a bathroom tucked into the roof.

'It's great.' Lisa sank down on to a sofa.

'It's all right,' Sarah said carelessly, knocking over an ashtray. 'Smoke?' She waved a packet of Rizla papers at her.

Lisa wavered for a moment, her ears ringing out a warning. 'All right.'

Sarah and Lisa sat on the floor and passed a bulging joint of black Moroccan back and forth between them.

'How's Ruby?' Sarah asked.

Lisa, careful not to give too much away and fighting with the first flush of fear as she inhaled, answered, 'Fine. How's Tom?'

Sarah blew a succession of flawed smoke rings into the air. 'Haven't you heard?'

'No.'

She blinked slowly and Lisa, unable to restrain herself, asked, 'Haven't I heard what?'

'We've fallen out. Tom and me. We're not talking.'

Lisa couldn't imagine what would turn Sarah against her brother. What she wouldn't put up with to be on his side. Lisa thought of the time Tom had rolled a joint, especially for Sarah and herself, and watched them as they smoked it. He had encouraged them when they got the giggles, when they raided the larder and fell over on the lawn, only to tell them afterwards that the joint they'd smoked was packed with oregano, Old Holborn and two dried leaves. That might have been the time to turn against Tom, but they hadn't even discussed it. They had kept their embarrassment to themselves and learnt their own private lesson.

'He stopped me from seeing Philip,' Sarah said.

Philip was the man in the photo. The handsome man Marguerite had admired on the bus.

Lisa was amazed. 'How?'

'How what?'

'How did he stop you seeing Philip?' She wondered if Sarah had heard of feminism, but didn't ask in case it was something she had long since given up on.

133

'He turned me against him,' Sarah said. 'He referred to him as "the Chin" and called him a sleaze-ball . . . He gagged on his aftershave and mimicked his voice on the phone, until I, I just sort of went off him.'

'Christ.'

Sarah was rolling another joint. She stopped and looked at Lisa with her eyes screwed up. 'But you must *really* hate Tom.'

'Me?' Lisa flinched. 'Not really.'

'You should.' Sarah struck a match.

Lisa didn't ask why. She didn't want to hear anything she hadn't already guessed at. She held the smoke so long in her lungs it evaporated and she had to lie down on the floor. Microscopic animals were crawling over her eyes and her tongue was thick and white in her mouth. Never again, she promised herself, never again, she vowed, as she continued obediently to inhale. Sarah lay down next to her. She told her about Philip and how in love they had been. How he had bought her a dozen champagne roses and taken her out to dinner on her birthday. How he had kissed her ankles and said they were exquisite. Philip had travelled, and nothing in the whole wide world, he said, was as beautiful as one of Sarah's ankles.

'Couldn't you get back together?' Lisa asked dreamily.

But apparently Philip had been driven into the arms of Sarah's cousin Tanya, and now she had to listen to daily reports of their happiness from various members of her family who still maintained he was a prig.

Lisa started to laugh. She couldn't help herself. The animals had stopped crawling and her heart was as calm and sluggish as a river. She choked and spluttered and cried with laughter until she had to roll on to her stomach to bury her face in the carpet.

'Lisa.' Sarah tugged at her. 'Lisa, come to the shop with me. I need some ice cream.'

Lisa sat up, suddenly starving. 'Cake.'

They bought Arctic Roll, a yellow sponge with an ice-cream centre, and hurried back to the flat. Sarah ran a hot bath. 'So we won't freeze while we're eating it,' she said, and they were so overcome with a fit of laughter they had to crawl up to the bathroom on their hands and knees. They sat in the bath with dinner plates of Arctic Roll and discussed possible plans for revenge.

Sarah was eager to involve Ruby. 'Where's Ruby living?' she asked. And Lisa, her mouth full of ice-cold sponge, shook her head.

'You don't know? Really?'

'Really.'

Sarah believed her. She wasn't supposed to, but she did. The bath water was cooling and the arctic centre of the cake had begun to melt. There was only one towel and Sarah got out first. Lisa had fallen in her estimation. She could feel herself falling. She lay back in the lukewarm water. 'I could try and find out.'

'Hmm.' Sarah was unconvinced.

Lisa slid down between the taps and let her head sink below the surface of the water. She held her breath and thought how she and Ruby had played this game as children. Counting out each other's stamina in bananas, one banana, two banana, practising for the dream of deep-sea diving. They hadn't heard of oxygen masks or snorkels then. Lisa burst back up. 'Ten banana,' she said.

Sarah handed her the wet towel.

Lisa had always been good at keeping secrets. She was so good at it that no one even suspected she had any to keep. She had often found herself having to listen to something she had been holding sacred and to herself for years. Sometimes the secret she had been entrusted with transpired not really to be a secret at all. It was something openly discussed, only in a particular tone of voice. Lisa wondered now if Ruby's Belgravia address was one of those secrets. For all she knew, Sarah was the only person in London who didn't know it. For all she knew, Tom and Jimmy Bright were regular visitors and Marlene's boyfriend had long since been pacified. Lisa shivered and forced herself out of the tepid water. She didn't know why she was bothering to tangle her thoughts up like this when even if she wanted to tell she couldn't. Her throat clammed up like the narrowest neck of a bottle and the words stayed wrapped around her ribs.

'Lisa!' Sarah shouted. 'What are you doing up there?' And Lisa, still dripping, hurried down to join her.

The effects of the black Moroccan had worn off and Sarah was in a sulk. She sat by the gas fire drying her hair and brooding. Lisa made a desperate attempt to win her back. 'I was thinking of having a party.'

Sarah looked up.

'We could invite Tom and work in some revenge.'

Sarah swept the hair back from her face. Her eyes lit up. 'Like what?'

'Like . . . I'm not sure, but we could work something out.'

'Invite Ruby for one thing.'

'Yes.' Lisa wasn't sure.

They planned the party for New Year's Eve. They drew up a list of people.

'I'd have it here,' Sarah said, 'if it wasn't for that old hag downstairs.'

'It's all right,' Lisa assured her. 'My mother will be away then, anyway.'

R UBY HADN'T SPENT a Christmas with her family since
leaving home. This year they were going to some
friends of Marguerite's in Norfolk, and Lisa begged Ruby
to come. Ruby lay stretched out on the sofa with the
television turned down low. She said her whole body ached.
She said she thought she had flu. She said she might come,
maybe, but that Tom had invited her to spend Christmas
with his family in Wales.

'I thought you didn't see Tom any more.'

Ruby shifted uncomfortably on the sofa. 'Shhh.'

Marlene was walking through on her way from the
bathroom to the kitchen, her hair bound up in a towel,
and looking like an Ethiopian princess. When she was safely
out of earshot, Ruby whispered, 'I see him sometimes, when
I can get out.' She sighed. 'Marlene says she gave up
everything and now the least I can do is give up Tom.'

Lisa didn't know what to say, so she told her about
Tom's campaign against Philip. She told the story as bru-
tally as she could, with all sympathy reserved for Sarah.

Ruby just laughed. When she laughed, it made her stomach ache and so she stopped.

'Why don't you come to Wales too?' She squeezed Lisa's hand. 'I wish you would.'

Ruby had given up her East End accent since moving into Belgravia. The longer she was there the more like her neighbours she sounded. She had even started to have her laundry collected and delivered by a private service that starched and folded every item. 'Oh do come,' she said. 'It would be *such* fun if you did.'

'I don't think so.' Lisa pulled her hand away. She wanted to add that she hadn't been invited.

Marlene, still in her towelling turban, reappeared with a bowl of cornflakes and a phial of pink nail polish.

'Lisa wondered if you'd make her up,' Ruby said to cover any talk of Christmas, and Marlene, smiling and setting aside her cereal, began to work an elaborate magic over Lisa's pale face with an assortment of smudgy pastel brushes.

Lisa called Janey to invite her to the party. Janey was so excited she whooped down the phone. She had already promised to babysit her sister's little boy, but she intended to get out of it if it was the last thing she did.

Lisa phoned Sarah regularly to discuss how many packets of Twiglets and Hula Hoops to buy, and how much drink. Neither of them mentioned Christmas. 'Won't there be something special in Wales for New Year?' she asked, worried that Sarah might not be back in time for the party.

But Sarah said, 'Not at all. It's the same dirge the world over.' She was still depressed over Philip.

Sarah had considered inviting Philip, in the hope of luring him away from her cousin, but she was stopped short in her plan by the news that he was taking Tanya to Paris and wouldn't be back until the third of January. 'Well, New Year may not be quite the same dirge in Paris,' she added with a dry laugh.

Lisa was relying on her father to give her some money. Lisa's father didn't celebrate Christmas and wasn't the kind of person to go shopping for presents, but she was certain that as long as she saw him at some point before she went away to Norfolk he would be bound to offer her something.

She called Ruby. Ruby was engaged. Lisa spent so much time in the payphones on the Old Street roundabout that the newsagents where she went for change all knew her. She had a purse full of two-pence pieces that weighed down the pocket of her coat. She redialled Ruby's number.

'Hello?' Ruby's voice was thin and far away.

'Hello, Ruby?'

'Oh Lisa, it's you, could you ring back, I'm waiting for an important call. Do you mind?'

'No, no, of course not,' Lisa said. 'I'll ring back in five minutes.' And her fingers slipped over themselves in her haste to replace the receiver.

It took Lisa another half an hour to get through. When Ruby finally answered, her voice was so faint she could hardly hear her.

'Ruby, are you all right?'

'What? Oh you know, it's just . . .' It was as if she didn't have the strength to go on talking.

'Is Marlene there?' Lisa asked.

'She's gone out.'

It was only eight o'clock. Marlene never went anywhere before midnight.

'Are you sure everything's all right?'

She could hear Ruby hesitating. 'What?' she said eventually.

Lisa wanted to get at her and shake her. 'I'm coming over,' and when Ruby didn't answer, she hung up.

Lisa caught the train to Hyde Park Corner, paid one stop from Green Park, and ran all the way to the narrow street behind the German embassy. She rang the bell, keeping her finger pressed down shrilly, and when no one answered, she remembered, and rang her code of three short rings. 'Ruby!' she shouted through the letter-box. 'Ruby!!'

Marlene's soft voice made her jump on the other side of the door. 'Lisa, is that you?'

Ruby sat on the sofa, bright-eyed and revitalized. 'Hi, Lisa,' she said as if she were surprised to see her, and Lisa, confused and unable to explain the dead weight of panic in her throat, made out she was just passing and could only stay five minutes.

When Lisa changed trains at King's Cross, she walked on to an escalator going the wrong way and was thrown off by the force of its moving steps. As her foot touched down, the step came up and hit her in the soles of the feet so that she lost balance and was thrown to the floor. She couldn't get up. She sat in a huddle in the rush of people and fought the long, angry tears that slipped from her eyes. There had been something personal in the way that iron step had thrown her off. She couldn't get it out of her mind. The coats and bags of a swarm of people brushed over her shoulders. They streamed around her like a line of marching ants, eager not to miss their train. She looked up, and through her tears she caught a woman hesitating, wavering with her conscience, wondering if she should help. Lisa glared. She defied her to approach, and, when the woman backed away and stepped guiltily on to her escalator, Lisa despised her lack of courage and watched her scornfully as she disappeared underground, bodily bit by bit.

Lisa stood up and dusted down her coat. Her hands were shaking and she felt the blood rushing around her head, pumping hot and cold inside her ears. It occurred to her she might be ill. She might have Ruby's flu. Or a late reaction to Max's last month's mumps. This thought consoled her and gave her the strength to descend the three flights of escalator to the Northern Line.

Lisa found her mother at Heidi's, drinking cider with Steen. Max was asleep under a coat.

'Actually, I'm not feeling well,' she said when Steen pressed a glass on her. Marguerite offered to take her back and make her a hot drink.

Steen wouldn't hear of it. 'I make the best hot toddy this side of the border,' and he disappeared into the kitchen.

Lisa cradled the cup in her hands and waited for the drink to cool. She could smell the whisky rising when she blew on it, and with the first sip the bitter taste of lemon stung the inside of her nose. 'It's good,' she said, as all eyes rested on her. It wasn't until something almost unnoticed slipped down her throat that it occurred to her Steen might have added an extra ingredient. 'It's good,' she said again, stretching her eyes with innocence to add, 'What did you put in it?'

'Ah-ha,' Steen winked, and in an exaggerated Scottish accent, 'I'll no be telling my secret recipe.' He laughed quite openly around the room.

Lisa froze. The insides of her stomach turned to water and she set down her drink, hurriedly picking it up again, before rushing to the toilet. She set the cup on the floor where she could see it. She kept her eye on it, hardly daring to blink. She sat on the toilet with her head in her hands. All she could think of was her mother saying, 'I remember when I used to drop acid, it made me want to have a good shit.' Lisa knew her mother wasn't lying when she talked about her youth. She talked about drugs as happily and easily as if it were a walk in the park. She even had a photo of herself on an acid trip, she and Ruby, toddlers, crayoning at the very edge, and Marguerite leaning back on one elbow with stars in her eyes and unearthly strands of white matter swirling around her head.

Lisa joined the others in the sitting-room, her mug, still warm, held against her chest. She sat against a wall, slowly sipping in an attempt to appear normal.

Marguerite came and sat next to her. 'Are you feeling any better?'

Lisa nodded, and then she did something unforgivable, she passed her mother the poisoned cup. 'Have a sip,' she offered, 'it's good.'

Lisa closed her eyes. Every inch of skin on her body was stretched with waiting and she had no way of knowing whether what part of twenty minutes was up or not. Her mother took a gulp and handed back the cup. 'You're letting it get cold,' she scolded.

Lisa watched her mother with terrible sidelong glances. She had lost track of herself and the seething fear dissolved all reason in her brain. She was holding on with her finger nails. Scratching at gravel. Her heartbeats cut into her like flint.

'Shall we go?' Marguerite called to her through thin ice and, with Max still sleeping and wrapped in his coat, they descended Heidi's staircase and climbed their own to their flat on the first floor.

There must have been music playing at Steen's and Heidi's because as soon as they opened the door Lisa's ears filled up with silence. Marguerite put Max to bed and ran herself a bath. Lisa watched her closely for suspicious signs of the hot toddy having taken effect. She followed her around the tiny flat and sat on the edge of her bath while she lay, languid, in the water. 'Are you all right?' she asked, trying to remember if she had ever known her mother before to bathe at midnight. Marguerite squinted at her. The air between them hummed with cold electric waves. 'Are *you* all right?' She turned her head, and Lisa nodded in earnest that she was.

Lisa offered to wash her mother's back so that she could peer round her shoulder to get a glimpse of the secret state of her thoughts. She needed to see into her eyes. Once or twice she caught Marguerite glancing strangely back at her, and she had a thousand explanations for these looks. She could feel the strands of her thoughts twisting round themselves like the steel spokes of a wheel.

Lisa continued to sit on the edge of the bath while her mother stepped dripping from the water, dried herself and pulled a clean, white nightdress over her head. 'Goodnight,' she said, and she closed the door to her and Max's narrow room.

Lisa crawled between the sheets of her own bed and lay awake until the dull shades of the dawn breaking over Peerless Street convinced her she was spared, and she fell into a thankful and exhausted sleep.

T HE DAY BEFORE they were due to go away for Christmas, Marguerite received a letter from a doctor in Harley Street. Lisa watched the colour drain from her mother's face as she read it over breakfast.

Ruby was going in for 'the Cure'. She had been admitted to a drug rehabilitation centre in Ealing.

'But Ruby doesn't have a problem with drugs,' Marguerite gasped, 'they must be mad!'

Lisa continued to spread Marmite thinly over buttered toast. She cut soldiers for Max to dip into his egg.

'Why does no one tell me anything?' Tears of rage sprang from Marguerite's eyes like hard, glass beads. 'I mean all young people experiment, it's normal, there's nothing wrong in it. Is there?'

Lisa shrugged.

Marguerite put her hands up to her face. 'Why will no one tell me what's going on?' she sobbed.

* * *

Ruby was allowed no contact with the outside world until after Christmas. The hospital gave permission to visit on the Saturday before New Year. Lisa wondered if a similar letter had been sent to her father. She wrote him a last-minute Christmas card with the vague intention of alerting him to the facts. *Dear Dad, Happy Christmas*. She couldn't think what else to write. After about an hour of doodling she added, *Love from Lisa*. She ran with it to the post office, where she bought a stamp and posted it before she could change her mind. She was under the impression she had written much more than she had.

She called Sarah from the payphone to warn her the party might have to be cancelled. There was no answer. Lisa wondered who else she should call. She flicked through her address book and realized, a little sadly but with some relief, that the only person she had actually invited was Janey. She was about to call her when she saw Marguerite appear from the sloping mouth of the short cut and head towards the row of phone boxes. She swung open the door of the booth.

'I thought I might find you here.' Marguerite squeezed in beside her. 'I've been thinking, I don't know if we should go to Norfolk.'

'Why not?'

'I just feel so terrible going off with Ruby stuck in that place.'

Lisa knew what she meant. 'But it's not as if we can do anything.' Ruby was not even allowed to receive a card. It was a rule of the hospital, to avoid causing undue distress to those without friends or relations.

Marguerite sighed. She rested her ten pence in its slot and dialled. 'Babs?' The money clattered home.

Lisa slid down the wall of the booth and waited for her to finish. Babs didn't sound as if she was too worried about whether they came for Christmas or not. 'Whatever,' Lisa heard her say. She was an old friend of Marguerite's from the sixties. Someone she had met when she worked as a nude model at the Slade.

'Did you used to model when you were pregnant with me?' Lisa asked as they walked the long way home. Marguerite had left the subject of Christmas open. 'We'll either be there or we won't.'

'What?' She looked at Lisa. 'With Ruby I did, but you . . . Oh I can't remember.' Marguerite had once said that when she was pregnant with Ruby she lived on oysters and champagne, but that throughout her second pregnancy she had survived on a diet of baked beans and porridge. Lisa was never sure what was intended by this particular anecdote, but it made her blanch with guilt when she thought of it.

LISA AND MARGUERITE drove to Ealing in the butcher's van. Max was to spend the day with Frances and little Brendan, well stocked with paper and crayons and without his cap gun. He had to be physically prised out of his armour.

Marguerite rarely used the van now they lived in London. Whenever she did, it either broke down or she became hopelessly lost and unable to trace her way back to the Old Street roundabout. Lisa promised to map-read. She chose a route through the centre of the city, which was a mistake, and then they got caught up in the traffic heading south out of London. They were low on petrol and the engine had begun to overheat. Marguerite swore and accelerated furiously. 'The first person who offers me fifty quid for this wreck can drive it away.'

'Oh Mum,' Lisa moaned as they sped past the hospital turn-off for the second time.

'The Cure' was in a wing of Hanworth Hospital. Hanworth Hospital was a mental hospital and was the kind of place Lisa envisaged in her very darkest moments ending up. It was a large, gloomy, Victorian building in the middle of a field. Lisa took her mother's hand as they walked down a pale green, windowless corridor. The air was thick with the drifting smell of cabbage. They pushed their way through spongy rubber doors, hoping to find an orderly, a nurse, or even a patient, but each green corridor led on to another and another, with never any sign of anyone at all. Eventually they found a staircase and climbed out of what they now realized was the basement. Lisa knew she shouldn't, but she couldn't resist letting her gaze slide sideways, left and right, through the open doors of desperate, lemon-yellow wards. Twisted old men, gnarled up like trees, stood staring into space, or lay like small, ill children on their beds. They traipsed down endless corridors, past whole wards of silence, and then a shout would break out and a struggle and the sounds of hearts pounding and black shoes slipping on the lino.

Lisa's terror ran up and down her arm and trembled in her mother's hand. They walked so close they almost tripped each other up. Eventually they caught sight of a doctor, his white coat flapping as he sped towards them, his body swaying from side to side to keep up with his legs, like a school boy who knows he mustn't run.

'Doctor.' Marguerite tried to flag him down. 'Excuse me.' The doctor, without interrupting his pace, twisted, looked at his watch, shook it at them and, with a mumbled apology, billowed by.

Lisa and Marguerite walked on. There were nurses behind the walls of the wards. Nurses who would be happy to give them directions. They kept to the corridor, defying each other to mention it.

Lisa had a present for Ruby. It was a bracelet of mother-of-pearl that she had bought in the market at Camden Lock. It was the most beautiful thing she had ever seen and she had to wrench away all thoughts of keeping it or even wearing it for one day and wrap it immediately in tissue-paper. It fastened with a silver clasp. Marguerite had a pot of blue hyacinths and a bottle of concentrated apple juice.

Eventually they came out at a stairwell with a large stained-glass window and a signpost to the chapel. A man sat at a desk by double wooden doors. 'We're looking for the Drug Rehabilitation Unit,' Marguerite said, and he looked up and smiled. 'Oh you mean the Cure.' They had to go out through the double doors, along a path and round to the back of the building. They were to follow the signs to Ward 2E.

Ruby was in a bed at the very end of the ward. Lisa recognized her short spiky hair on the pillow even though her face was turned away from them.

'Hello, darling,' Marguerite said, bending down to kiss her.

'Mum!' Ruby struggled to sit up with a glint of real enthusiasm. 'Am I glad to see you.'

Lisa squeezed between them and kissed Ruby on the cheek. Ruby was papery thin and her shoulder was made from the bones of a little bird. 'Happy Christmas,' she said, and she thrust her present on the Ruby's lap. She had been holding it so tightly the wrapping had gone soggy.

'Happy Christmas.' Marguerite moved round to the other side and sat down on the edge of her bed.

'Ow!' Ruby scowled in pain, and pulled her foot away. 'Can't you get a chair to sit on?'

Marguerite leapt up without losing her cheerful expression and looked round wildly for a chair. There were none to be seen.

'Aren't you going to open your presents?' Lisa said in an attempt to regain the moment.

'Yes, open your presents,' Marguerite agreed and she scooped the hyacinth out of its plastic bag. Its blue flower had somehow snapped during the journey and hung now by a strand of thick green stalk. Marguerite didn't seem to notice. She placed it tenderly on the bedside table while Lisa hovered anxiously for Ruby to unwrap her present. 'I hope you like it,' she encouraged, almost unable to endure the suspense. Ruby picked at the Sellotape with unenthusiastic fingers. Lisa had wrapped the bracelet in three layers of different-coloured tissue. She could sense her sister's irritation as she peeled away the paper. Eventually a white glint of pearl showed through and Ruby pulled out the bracelet.

'Oh, I brought you some apple juice,' Marguerite said at the exact moment that Ruby set eyes on the bracelet. 'You just have to mix it with water.'

Ruby put the bracelet to one side and took the heavy bottle.

'Thanks.' She let her arm rest with it alongside her body. 'Thanks.' She kept her fingers tightly round the bottleneck and closed her eyes as if she had been overtaken by exhaustion. Lisa and Marguerite stared down at her. 'I'll go and find some chairs,' Marguerite said, and she tiptoed away. Lisa sat very carefully on the edge of the bed and waited for Ruby to open her eyes. Ruby had the most perfect eyelids. They were shaped like shells with arched eyebrows above and a spray of smart, bright lashes below. Lisa had once taken a photo-booth photograph of herself in their local Woolworth's in an attempt to discover whether or not this particular feature of Ruby's had been duplicated in herself, but the photo had shown a pair of wide, heavy lids, deep-set and shadowy under brows without a hint of an arch.

Marguerite returned with two chairs. They sat side by side at the top of Ruby's bed and waited for her to wake up. After half an hour they decided it was best to leave. Lisa gave a last glance at the mother-of-pearl bracelet nestling in its bed of tissue and considered taking it back. Ruby might not even notice. She hadn't even looked at it. She hadn't even tried it on. She looked down at the arrogant arches of Ruby's eyebrows and felt a wave of bitter rage against her lack of gratitude.

L ISA HAD HIGH hopes for her first New Year in London. She rang Sarah in Wales to tell her about the cancelled party and to ask if she wanted to make an alternative plan, but her money ran out before anything final was agreed upon, and by the time she'd managed to rustle up another ten pence it seemed everyone had gone out or had moved into a part of the house where it was impossible to hear the telephone.

Janey had suggested they have the party anyway. 'Can't your Mum just go into another room?' And Lisa tried to explain to her about Peerless Flats and the bedroom and how there was barely enough space for the bunks.

Up until the very last moment Lisa believed that something fantastic was bound to happen. She, Marguerite and Max spent the whole day playing dominoes and waiting for the rain to stop, and when they eventually had to accept it might fall for ever in sharp grey splinters against their only real window they decided to go out and buy provisions. Lisa stuck a note to the door which said 'Back soon' in case someone were to call while they were out.

The rain was so fierce that halfway to the bus stop they sheltered in a doorway and discussed whether it mightn't be wiser to turn back. 'What about my sponge fingers?' Max demanded from under his carrier-bag hat, and they decided to persevere. There was a supermarket at the Angel where Marguerite said they could buy a treat each as it was New Year's Eve and the last day of the 1970s. Lisa took Max's hand and they wandered up and down the aisles looking for sponge fingers. They found them under 'cake ingredients', and then Max changed his mind and decided he wanted a half-pound packet of marzipan. They found Marguerite by the fruit and vegetables, considering a mound of fresh spinach. 'Oh Mum,' they both whined, and Lisa suggested she get something a little more compatible with marzipan and twenty John Player Special, which was what she had chosen for herself. Marguerite eventually decided on a bottle of cider and a packet of white chocolate buttons.

It was raining so hard when they arrived back at Peerless Street that they could see the drops like bullets bouncing in the road. They jumped over the puddles in the open entrance of the building and raced up to their flat. Marguerite put down the plastic bag of food and rummaged in her pockets. Then she rummaged again, more slowly. 'You haven't got the key, have you?' She looked at Lisa with a defeated face, and Lisa shook her head.

Max kicked the door. 'Let me in!' he yelled, leaving a little wet footprint on the wood. He put his eye to the keyhole. 'Mr Fox,' he called in a persuasive voice, 'can we come in now? I've got some nice things for supper.' Lisa pushed him to one side and tried to pick the lock with a hairgrip she found in her purse. Marguerite had given up. She sat on the top step and opened the chocolate buttons. 'Don't eat them all,' Lisa said and she and Max went and sat next to her to make sure. Once they'd finished the chocolate they opened the cider and Max allowed them each one tiny bite of his marzipan. Lisa scratched her cigarette lottery ticket with a coin and for a single spiralling moment she thought that she'd won. 'Close, very close.' Marguerite consoled her. She'd simply misread the numbers.

Lisa's coat was not waterproof and now the damp of the wool was starting to seep through into her bones. 'We can't stay here all night,' she said.

Max moved closer to her and shivered. 'Why not?' he begged through chattering teeth. 'I'll make a tent and we can sleep in a hammock made out of rats' tails and I'll stand at the entrance to the cave and say, "Who goes there?"'

'Shhh.' Lisa thought she heard a voice echoing up from the stairwell.

'Who goes there?' Max jumped up, brandishing his imaginary sword.

Tom's bedraggled head and shoulders appeared round the twist in the stairs, followed closely by Sarah in a waterproof hat.

'We're having a picnic.' Marguerite shook the cider bottle at them. 'Why don't you join us?'

Tom and Sarah ambled up the stairs. 'Happy New Year,' they said politely and they all exchanged kisses. Max offered Tom a bite of his marzipan, keeping his thumb close to the edge so that he wouldn't take too much. He then commenced to whisper a secret list of all his weapons into Tom's ear. Marguerite asked Sarah about her job in the clothes shop and told her about her own unsuccessful attempts at employment. Lisa took a long swig from the cider bottle and wondered when it would occur to Tom and Sarah that her family were not spending New Year's Eve on the landing on a purely eccentric whim but because they had in fact locked themselves out.

Half an hour later when Sarah asked if she could use the bathroom the truth was discovered.

'It's all right,' Tom said, standing back and breathing through his nose, 'I'll get you in,' and he took a running kick at the door and burst it open with his foot, shattering the lock and cracking away part of the frame.

Max ran into the room with his arms outstretched and spun around like a bat. 'You're brilliant, you're brilliant, will you be my friend?' he screamed.

Tom was so exhausted he had to lie down on the floor. 'Do you think he's going to be all right?' Lisa asked as she tried to hold Max back from using his outstretched body as a trampoline. Marguerite brought him a cup of cider to revive him and Lisa lit him a cigarette and held it to his mouth. His face had gone a deathly tallow-white and his lips were bloodless. There was a part of Lisa that worried he might have stopped breathing and she allowed herself to look into his face with an open reserve of love. Tom recovered and caught her. He smiled slyly and grabbed her wrist as she pulled away. He pulled her down and tried to kiss her. The others had all moved through to the bedroom to inspect Max's collection of fishing flies. 'Do you know where you can find good worms round here?' she heard him asking Sarah.

Lisa knelt over Tom as he smoked. 'Do you care about me?' he asked, his eyes narrow, and Lisa, unable to decide whether or not this was a trick that would be stored and later used against her, didn't answer.

Tom and Sarah were going on to a party they had heard about in a disused fire station in Battersea. They asked Lisa if she wanted to go, but even though she longed to, she felt unable to leave her mother alone in a flat where the door no longer locked or even closed, but hung shakily from one hinge. 'If you want to go, you must,' Marguerite insisted, but behind her smile little flecks of fear swam in her eyes.

Lisa saw Tom and Sarah down to the street. It was still raining but the hail had turned to a fine grey drizzle. Tom kissed her distractedly on the cheek. 'I nearly forgot,' he said. 'Where the fuck has Ruby got to?'

Lisa shuffled her feet and pulled her cardigan up over her head. 'What's that?' she said, as if his voice hadn't carried through the mist of the rain.

'Oh come on, Tom.' Sarah pulled her hat around her ears, 'I'm getting soaked.'

'I've got to find Ruby,' Tom shouted, and Lisa, thinking she might burst into tears, ran back into the arched entrance of Peerless Flats.

F RANCES HAD GIVEN up on the council to find her any-where permanent to live and gone back to her family in Ireland. A single man with paralysis in his left leg moved into her old flat, which, apart from being a scandal as it was on the fourth floor, meant that when Lisa and Marguerite next visited Ruby at Hanworth Hospital, they had to take Max with them.

Ruby was out of bed and dressed uncharacteristically in a Laura Ashley smock with a frill around the bottom. She seemed quite cheerful and took them for tea in the canteen. The canteen was a white wooden building separate from the hospital. They had to walk down a path through the park to get to it. Ruby giggled and told them to watch out for a woman in a red ribbed nylon jumper.

The woman was a few feet ahead of them in the queue and they watched her shuffle forward to order her tea. It was poured for her in a green cup on a saucer, which she clutched with both hands as she inched her way over to the nearest table. Her arms shook so violently as she walked that the tea splashed out in great milky spurts and left a watery trail over the lino. The woman didn't seem to notice but moved on with her eyes wide and fixed on her destination, so that it was only when she arrived that she discovered with a look of vague bewilderment that her cup was empty. Ruby tittered and nudged Lisa in the ribs as the trembling woman promptly rejoined the queue.

Max was very quiet. He stayed close to Marguerite and didn't ask for anything from the counter display of two-fingered Kit-Kats and miniature packets of shortbread. They took their three teas and a glass of flat lemonade and sat at a table by the window. Lisa sipped her tea and watched her mother's reflection in the glass, summoning up the right words to say to Ruby.

'You're looking much better,' she managed eventually, and Ruby smiled and then waved at a woman who was staring over at them and mouthing elaborately, 'Is that your family?' Ruby mouthed back, 'Yes,' and the woman sat down at a table, alone with a mound of biscuits, and began to eat.

'Who's that?' Marguerite asked, and Ruby lowered her voice. 'Christine. She's in the next bed to me.'

Lisa wanted to ask what Christine was doing in Hanworth Hospital. She was middle-aged and heavily made up, with bright blue eyeshadow and a smear of rock-pink lipstick. She looked too old to be a drug addict.

'Why's she in here?' Marguerite asked instead, and Ruby leaned across the table and whispered dramatically, 'She's an alcoholic!'

When Ruby's friend had eaten all her biscuits, she came over to their table. 'Hello, I'm Ruby's friend, nice to see you.' She smiled a big smile that crinkled the end of her nose.

'This is me Mum,' Ruby said, picking up the loop and whine of her south London accent, 'and this is me sister, Lisa.'

'And me,' Max said.

'And this is Christine,' Ruby continued.

'Hello, yes, I'm Christine,' Christine said, and she leant over to Marguerite and said confidentially, 'Oh, you've got a lovely daughter, you really have. What a lovely girl.'

Marguerite blushed and nodded and eventually Christine left them to rejoin the queue.

Ruby was only allowed to be away from her ward for forty minutes at a time, so they left the canteen and walked back through the park. Ruby put her arm through Lisa's and told her about Christine: how Christine was married to a crook who insisted to this day he earned an honest living as a plumber. Christine's husband wouldn't allow her to leave the house or talk to anyone except for him, and so she began to drink until she was drinking so heavily that she needed three bottles of vodka just to see her through the day. Christine thought everything might have been all right if a doctor hadn't prescribed Mandrax to cheer her up and if she hadn't been overcome by the desire to paint the blue carpet in the front room red.

'There's only one thing in her life she's really proud of,' Ruby said.

Lisa couldn't guess what it was.

'She never let her husband see her without makeup. Not in nine years of married life!'

When they arrived back at Ward 2E there was a man sitting on Ruby's bed writing a note.

'Dad!' Ruby ran over to greet him. She almost tripped over a crate of fresh fruit wrapped around with ribbon that was resting up against her bedside table.

'Hello, Dad,' Lisa said and he smiled past her and nervously up at Marguerite. There was an uncomfortable silence and then Max, who had been studying the oranges and lychees and winter raspberries clustered round the centrepiece of pineapple in the giant crate, began in a sudden frenzy to tear open the shiny plastic wrapping.

All three women rushed to his side. Even a passing nurse stopped to comment on the unruliness of his behaviour. 'Max, Max, Max,' they scolded, and then Marguerite added, 'I think it's time we were off.'

Marguerite did a U-turn in the car park and roared out through the hospital gates without bothering to change gear. Lisa had wanted to stay, peeling lychees and gossiping with Ruby, while they lounged with their father in the day-room. She hadn't even had a chance to ask him if he'd received her Christmas card.

'Give us a bit,' she snapped at Max who was sitting in the back of the van, eating a tangerine he had spirited out in the sleeve of his jumper. 'NO,' Max yelled, stuffing the whole remains into his mouth, and he lay down backwards in the spare tyre, and kicked his arms and legs as if it were a rubber ring.

'Brat!' And for a moment Lisa thought of opening the car door and hurling herself out on to the road.

L ISA STARTED BACK at college for the spring term. The Full
Time Speech and Drama course had moved its focus from
Stanislavsky to Brecht, which meant that, whereas last term
the students were encouraged to believe absolutely in everything they did and said, now, when acting, they were asked to
remember that they were in a play, and that they had a duty to
the audience to remind them of this fact. There were techniques that could be used, winking, or talking in asides, or even
giving information on the plot straight out into the front row
without any pretence at mystery or disguise. Lisa felt completely thrown. For her the whole point of acting was the
licence it gave you to become another person, protected by a
stage set and someone else's words, and now Denise the
method teacher, whose main criticism had always been 'I
don't believe it!', began interrupting the action of a scene to
ask what the actors thought was going on in terms of the
play's integral message.

'What type of actress are you going to be, Brechtian or
Stanislavskian?' Janey asked Lisa in the canteen.

Lisa wasn't sure. Really she just wanted to be Julie Christie in *Doctor Zhivago* and wear a fur hat and a tailored coat with buttons down the front. She mentioned this to Janey. Janey rolled her eyes and sniggered, and then told her quite seriously she'd never get into proper drama school if she admitted to those sorts of ambitions. 'It's not fashionable to want to be a film star.'

Lisa made a note of this under Denise's list of books to read:

> *The Good Woman of Setzuan*, Brecht
> *Mother Courage*, Brecht
> and *The Theatre of Revolt*

Lisa had also added *Where the Wild Things Are*, a book about a boy called Max, which she thought she might be able to get from the children's section of the library.

Steen had come round on New Year's Day to fix the broken door. 'Burglars?'

'No, no, just a friend,' Marguerite assured him.

Steen said that really the whole frame of the door needed replacing, but he would try and patch it together for the time being.

Lisa could hardly bear to be in the same room as Steen. The moment she saw him, an electric ringing started up in her ears. She and her mother had never discussed the hot toddy and the strange looks they had exchanged in the bathroom, but since that night Lisa had been almost unable to eat or drink anything that she had not supervised herself, and if for any reason she was distracted from a meal, she preferred to abandon it rather than take the risk that it might have become contaminated in the moment she was forced to look away. Lisa became so thin that her periods stopped, and when she lay in bed at night she could feel her heart beating in her ear. There were days at college when it took all her energy to fight through the crackling and freezing of the inside of her head and to keep the twitching of her eye to a minimum. Sometimes when she turned her head the bones in her neck cracked so loudly that she was surprised the whole class didn't rush over to see whether it was broken, but no one ever mentioned it, and Lisa was so grateful for this that she found herself praying silently at night that she might have the strength to keep up the façade.

Steen mended the door so that it closed and locked, but there was something irrevocably damaged about the catch, which meant it could be opened with a gentle shove of the shoulder, and even though Marguerite reported it to the caretaker, and even demanded several times that it be replaced, nothing was ever done and in a short time, as they continued to mislay their keys, Lisa and Marguerite both found themselves increasingly reliant on the flimsiness of the lock.

IT WAS HALF-TERM and Marguerite decided to go back to the country for a long weekend. Lisa, although she had some days off college, couldn't bring herself to visit the village where she had grown up, knowing how incapable she would be of matching the impact made by Ruby on her triumphant return two years before. She decided to stay in London.

That first night Lisa luxuriated in the emptiness of the flat, relieved to be alone for once with the ringing and twitching she held inside her like a leper. She prepared herself a meal. Rice, and vegetables cooked with a bay leaf and soya sauce, exactly to her mother's own recipe. She moved around the kitchen, humming along to the limited and now familiar collection of Leonard Cohen records played by the man in the flat above.

Lisa laid a place for herself at the table and set down the heaped plate of food, with a small salad in a bowl beside it, and a glass of water at its head. She was about to sit down when she realized how desperately she needed to pee. She leapt up to dash to the toilet before her food had time to cool, but as she moved away her eye was caught by the vulnerable leaves of her salad and the multicoloured vegetables that camouflaged the grains of rice, and, without allowing herself to contemplate the implications of her behaviour, she loaded the dishes on to a tray and carried it through to the toilet, where she positioned it in the doorway in such a way she could keep her eye on it at all times. She had to reach out for the taps to wash her hands and search blindly about for a towel. Eventually Lisa arrived back at the table, where she unloaded her supper. She had to pretend her mother was sitting opposite before she could summon the strength to lift her fork. The saliva in her mouth had curdled white and bitter, giving the fat grains of rice a metallic taste as she chewed them dully together between her teeth.

Lisa put her unfinished meal in the fridge and went through to the sitting-room to watch television. The television was tiny and black and white and had been a present from Frances, who said it was too heavy and awkward to carry back to Ireland. Lisa lay on her bed and turned the dial between each of the three channels. There was nothing on that she wanted to watch but she left it tuned to a modern ballet, in which minuscule black figures flickered about on a background of grey. Lisa's bed, which also served as a sofa, was set against the wall next to the window, over which the curtain had not been drawn as the flat was on the raised first floor and impossible to see into. She sat and stared out into the night and the hazy stars of light from the tower block, and let the music of the ballet carry her away in little jolts. She was thinking how she must get up and jam the door with a chair before she went to sleep, when the dark shape of a man tumbled past her window. It was followed a breath later by a woman's hollow scream soaring up from the basement where the body had landed with a thud. Lisa twisted the dial to cut off the sound of the television, and sat paralysed on the edge of the bed, wondering how it was that the woman had managed to climb down so quickly into the basement. It was possible that she had also fallen, and Lisa had simply failed to notice her as she fluttered by. The woman screamed again, the razor edges of her voice grazing the window and rattling the loose lock of the door. Lisa put on her shoes and a coat, and, leaving the flat door open for a quick re-entry, crept softly down the stairs.

A small crowd of familiar faces hovered on the street. No one spoke above a whisper and there were glints of intrigue and dread in the eyes that she met. Lisa was reminded of the uneasy feeling of her first Guy Fawkes'.

Steen had climbed down past the spikes and spears of the basement railings and was crouching near the woman with a blanket and a string of soothing words. The woman lay, half burying the man with her body, where he had fallen stretched out on his back in the damp and litter of the basement yard.

Lisa saw Heidi standing, smoking, by her staircase. She was wearing a pink padded dressing-gown. 'He fell right past my window,' Lisa told her, and then had to cover her face with both hands to stop the grin that was spreading from taking control of her face.

The inhabitants of Peerless Flats shuffled aimlessly. No one felt they could leave before the ambulance arrived. 'Did he jump?' someone asked in a whisper, and then another voice, incredulous, 'He jumped? Why did he jump?' The man on crutches from the fourth floor who had descended the stairs, despite pyjamas and his disability, told them in an authoritative voice, 'He didn't jump. He was trying to break in.'

'That's no burglar,' Heidi interrupted, 'that's Jim, he lives at number 56, he probably just forgot his key,' and everyone nodded as if this was an explanation they could readily accept.

The ambulance took longer than usual to arrive. Someone had had to run up to the payphone on the Old Street roundabout to dial 999, as not one person in the flats owned a telephone. It was a steadfast show of faith in the temporariness of their accommodation. When the ambulance did arrive, a woman in the basement allowed the men to bring the stretcher in through her bay window, saving them the struggle of hauling his body up to street level by pulley.

Lisa slipped back upstairs. The door to her flat was open and the tiny black figures of the dancers continued to leap and scatter across the screen.

The moment Lisa woke the next morning she regretted not having gone to the country with her mother. She felt so lonely she could hardly bring herself to get out of bed. She considered visiting Ruby. Ruby's hospital was on the outskirts of London, but without a car she didn't know if it was possible to get there. Anyway, the last time they had been to see her, Ruby was so busy she could barely spare the time for a cup of tea. She had a boyfriend in the men's ward on the other side of the hospital, and she had a date with him that afternoon at the AA disco. Ruby told Lisa that her boyfriend was from Liverpool. He was dead handsome, she said, and addicted to a specific brand of cough mixture.

Lisa thought of ringing Sarah. She hadn't seen her since New Year, but the possibility of Tom picking up the phone and demanding to know the whereabouts of Ruby decided her against it. She struggled free of the sheets that had tangled cold and clammy round her feet and went to look out of the window. She half expected to see a man's white outline spreadeagled on the ground below, but the only sign of the night before was the abundance of cigarette butts trodden into the pavement. Janey, Lisa thought. She could ring Janey. And then she remembered Janey was away. She was staying with her gran, who had a caravan near New-haven.

Lisa went through to the kitchen. She opened the fridge, and, overcome with a sudden pang of hunger, took out her icy plate of rice. She had wrapped the food in a sheet of clingfilm and now she swivelled the plate in her hands to check that the sealed edges had not been disturbed. She placed it on the table and turned it slowly round, bracing herself for the moment when she would tear off the wrap-ping and lift a stacked forkful of food into her mouth, but, as she peeled back the edges of the clingfilm, her stomach began to claw and tighten and a wave of fear drove her appetite away. It left her reeling, so that in a moment of despair she lay down on the kitchen floor and let her mouth fill up with tears. 'The worst thing that could happen is that I die,' she said, over and over to herself, but she knew it was not the worst thing that could happen, and even if it was, it was of little comfort.

She continued to lie on the floor. Maybe it was lucky Janey was away in Newhaven. She imagined what she would say if she were to confide in her. She could hear the strain of envy in her voice. 'Just think, you'll be able to use this in your acting!' Despite herself this made Lisa laugh and she scrambled up from the floor and peeled and ate a banana, gulping it down before she had a moment to scare herself off.

Lisa was frantic to come up with someone she could visit. Her father, and a girl called Buzz she had once met at a bus stop, were the only people she could think of. She remembered her father peering at her in the darkness, shifting from foot to foot and waiting for her to go away, and she opted for Buzz. She had had a letter from her some months before saying she was living alone in a Volkswagen van in a field outside Tonbridge. She had invited Lisa to visit. 'Just turn up. Any time.' There was a list of directions. Lisa searched frantically for the letter. Get a train from Charing Cross, she remembered that. She could remember the rhythm of the directions but not the actual words. Get a train from Charing Cross, get off at Tonbridge, walk into the tum te tum – the town centre? the bus station? Get the number something bus, up a hill, across a bridge, get off, climb over a gate and there's the field. Get the number 9 bus? The number 19 bus? The 92? Lisa felt confident the number would reveal itself to her. The train journey might jog it into place. She gave up on her search for the letter and prepared to be away for up to a week. She packed a bag and left a note for her mother.

Tonbridge was in Kent and the train took just under an hour. Lisa spent the entire journey matching buses with numbers until she began to feel sick with the effort. She decided that once she got off the train everything would come back to her. She started to convince herself that she had made this journey before. That she would know her way to the tobacconist and the sweetshop and the park in the centre of town, like a man in a film she had once seen with Greer Garson. The man, who had lost his memory during the war, was astounded to find he knew his way around a sleepy, sepia-coloured village. It emerged that it was the village he had been born in and where his wife, not his fiancée Greer Garson but a plain woman with a bun, still lived.

When Lisa handed in her ticket with a thin crowd of commuters and was squeezed out into the station forecourt, there was nothing in sight that looked even remotely familiar. She stood dolefully on the concrete strip of pavement and wondered which road she should take off the railway bridge that faced her. There wasn't a bus in sight. The people who had travelled with her disappeared into taxis and waiting cars and were sped away. Lisa asked the ticket collector the way to the centre of town, and was pointed wordlessly down the sharp slope of a hill where almost immediately she came upon a bus stop. Her heart leapt as she scanned the timetable, but there were so many buses listed and with such foreign-sounding destinations that she felt sure it couldn't be the right stop. Lisa turned away and continued to walk down the hill, which soon evened out into a straight high street of shops, chemists and bakers and building societies, all closed up for the night. In the distance she could see that the road twisted away out of sight by the side of a tall building. And then she felt sure she remembered. 'Get off the train, go *down* a hill, round a corner, and there will be a bus.' She repeated this to herself over and over as she walked, frightened that these valuable directions would slip away now that she'd finally got a hold of them. But when she reached the point where the road curved, she found she had to cross a wooden bridge over a wide and noisy river, and on the other side, around the corner, there was not a bus, but the ruins of a dimly lit medieval castle that no one, no one at all, could forget to mention.

Lisa turned abruptly and began to walk back the way she'd come. She wanted to stop and ask one of the people hurrying by, holding their coats shut against the light rain, but she didn't know what she could ask. She kept walking until she had walked right out through the other side of the town. She walked past a church with a clock on its tower whose hands shivered as it struck the hour, and along the grass verge of two roundabouts with signs for Hastings, Sevenoaks and Maidstone. The road sloped up in a hill, with high, dark hedges on either side. It was possible this might be the hill Buzz had meant in her letter, but if it was the hill with the field off it, then why would she have told her to catch a bus? The street lights stopped at this point and the hill, with its overgrown hedges, lay shrouded in an eerie night. Lisa traced her way back towards the church. There was a pub on a corner with warm, orange light seeping through its windows. She imagined Buzz sitting inside with a pint of bitter and a table covered with half-ounce packets of Golden Virginia, Rizla papers and cheese-and-onion crisps. She longed to see her smiling, freckled face, and her twinkling eyes clogged almost shut with mascara. She imagined her at a table of men all vying for attention.

Lisa went over to the pub and peered through a window. The glass was knobbled and frosted and gave nothing away. She was about to edge her way through the doors into the lounge bar when a roaring contingent of bikers skidded to a halt in the car park and began to dismount. Lisa flattened herself against the wall of the porch and, as they spiked and steadied their bikes, she slipped away around the side of the pub. Once on the safety of the road, she resumed her walk back into the town centre.

The town was almost utterly deserted now. She stared wistfully into the faces of the occasional passers-by. Mostly young couples wandering aimlessly hand in hand. There was no one scruffy or wild enough to look as if they were a friend of Buzz's. Eventually Lisa found another bus stop and studied the timetable. There was a 209, which sounded hopeful, and a 29, but they had both stopped running shortly before eight. Lisa clutched the return ticket lying deep in the bottom of her pocket, and headed for the station. The last train to London didn't leave until ten to ten and she sat down on a bench to wait. 'Something good has to happen,' she told herself. The more she thought about it the more convinced she became that something good really would have to happen. And she knew what it was going to be. She would meet someone on the train. Someone with whom she could mark this day as the beginning of the rest of her life. Someone to fall in love with. She scrabbled in her bag until she found the mirror that had come as a free gift Sellotaped to a tube of Nivea cream. It was so tiny that she could only see small parts of her face at a time. She inspected her right eye and applied a line of black eyeliner. Ruby, who had recently taken to wearing no makeup whatsoever except a perfect arc of bright red lipstick, said it was seventies and out of date to wear eyeliner. Lisa guiltily applied another smudge of black to her left eye. She had never mastered the art of lipstick. Her lips didn't seem to have a defined beginning or end, and lipstick, unless applied by an expert like Marlene, turned her face into that of a beaten-up fairground clown.

Lisa had to wait for nearly an hour before the London train pulled in. There was no one else waiting to get on apart from a smart woman who had arrived by taxi with less than a minute to spare. Lisa followed her on, attracted by her bustle and the spirit of her late arrival.

Once on the train Lisa was torn between the smoking carriage and the next compartment where the lady had seated herself and was fingering through a slick pile of magazines. There was no one in the smoking carriage except a man in a suit who had fallen asleep with his stomach hanging out of his shirt, and a boy who was listening to a handmade radio and rolling cigarettes from dog-ends that he picked up from the floor.

Lisa went through to the next carriage and sat diagonally opposite the woman. She stared at her own reflection in the glass and pretended to be looking through the window. Eventually she summoned up enough courage to ask the woman, 'Can I look at one of your magazines?' and the shock of her voice made them both jump. The woman looked up without enthusiasm. 'Help yourself,' she said.

As the train rumbled uneventfully through the black night and on into the London suburbs, Lisa had to accept that it was unlikely now anything was going to occur to change this day from the failure that it was.

She kept her head down as she wandered out into the little town of Charing Cross station with its newsagents and its cafés and its resident tramps. She was ashamed to be here again so soon and she resolved to tear up and burn the optimistic note she had left for her mother earlier that day.

LISA SPENT the next few days alone at the flat, living off bowls of muesli that she sieved meticulously in order to examine each raisin, nut and sunflower seed. She stirred it up with water so that she wouldn't have to leave the house even for a pint of milk.

She hoped against hope that someone would break in on her seclusion, but when one night footsteps did stop on the stairs, and a hand rattled the letter-box, shaking the door so that it swayed and buckled on its hinges, Lisa was too ashamed to answer. 'Hello,' she heard Steen's thick voice, 'is anyone in there?' And she buried her face under the covers and held her breath until he went away.

The day Marguerite was due to return, Lisa decided she would have to leave the flat, if only for a short time, or her mother might suspect that there was something wrong. She cleaned and tidied all the rooms, leaving just enough mess to look as if she were alive: an ashtray, a half-drunk cup of tea, a small pile of discarded clothes. She dressed carefully in a red silk dress, which was large and hung in pleats from a belted waist, and put on a pair of white tights to disguise the fragility of her legs. She stood in front of the bathroom mirror and applied pale powdery rouge to her cheeks, remembering Marlene's tricks and makeup hints, and dabbing at her nose, her forehead and her chin to create a rosy glow. She brushed her hair and tied it back behind her ears with a shoelace. She was going to visit Ruby.

She asked the ticket inspector at Old Street for directions, and took a series of trains across London, arriving at the gates of Hanworth Hospital a little before midday.

Ruby was having her lunch. She was lying on her bed, picking the apple crumble from under a thick layer of yellow custard. She offered Lisa a loaded spoon. Lisa closed her eyes and swallowed.

'You're looking great,' Ruby told her.

Lisa shrugged and forced a smile.

Ruby finished up her pudding. Her short hair had grown out of its spikes and lay in soft waves against her head, framing her face so that her eyes shone dark and velvety.

They exchanged the usual family news.

'How's Mum?'

'Fine.'

'Seen Dad?'

'Yes.'

'Max?' Ruby asked, and Lisa began to tell her how he had recently become obsessed with the idea of shark-fishing in Hampstead Ponds and sometimes forgot all about foxes for up to an hour at a time, until she remembered that ultimately it bored Ruby to hear these stories and she switched the subject.

'Ruby . . .' She stretched out on her bed. 'Are you nearly cured?'

'Cured?' Ruby giggled. 'In here? You must be joking! Anyway, it's all right for me, I don't have a problem, it's not as if I were an addict or anything.'

Lisa looked at her hard to glimpse even the faintest shadow of a doubt, but Ruby looked back open-faced.

'So why did you have yourself admitted?' Lisa wanted to know.

Ruby rolled over on the bed, making room for Lisa to crawl up beside her so that her head rested on the same high hospital pillow. 'Promise you won't tell?'

Lisa nodded. She felt like a child again. Ruby's little sister.

'It wasn't the drugs,' she lowered her voice. 'It was Marlene.'

'Oh.' Lisa made a face to show she understood.

'She wouldn't let me out of the house. She said she was in love with me.'

'Oh,' Lisa said again. She tried to imagine Janey, or Sarah, or anyone she knew, saying anything like that to her.

'But do you like it in here?'

Ruby smiled and drew a deep, contented sigh. 'It's not bad.' Then she added ruefully, 'But they're talking about discharging me.'

'When?'

'I don't know. Soon.'

'What will you do?'

Ruby didn't answer.

'You could go back to Belgravia?'

'Yeah, I suppose . . .' Ruby turned on her side to face her. 'Listen, why don't you come and stay there with me?'

Lisa caught her breath. 'Do you mean it?' And then she remembered her mother and the long, laborious meeting she had sat through at the New Swift Housing Co-op, all so she could get a house with three bedrooms to make a home for her and Max. 'I'll have to see,' she said.

Ruby frowned minutely.

'It's just that Mum thinks there's a chance we might get housed and if I'm not there –'

'Don't worry yourself about it,' Ruby interrupted her. 'Anyway, Dad said he might send me away somewhere to recover.'

'Like where?'

'I don't know. Somewhere far from temptation. Kenya or the West Indies, or maybe Argentina.'

Lisa didn't know what to say. 'But what about your boyfriend with the cough mixture?'

'Oh him, he discharged himself, and anyway, I won't be gone for ever.'

Ruby had to meet Christine for some kind of therapeutic activity in another wing of the hospital. 'Sorry,' she said. 'If I'd known you were coming . . .' Ruby walked Lisa out into the grounds and hugged her goodbye. She hugged her very tightly so that a little strangled noise like a sigh came up from inside her chest. 'I keep thinking, since I've been in here, how I used to bully you when we were kids.'

For a horrible moment Lisa thought Ruby might be going to cry. She pulled away so she could see her face. 'I didn't mind, Ruby please don't think about it. I promise, really I promise, I didn't mind.'

Lisa sat in the smoking carriage, chain-smoking John Player Specials and thinking: She didn't bully me, she never bullied me. She thought of Ruby's fiery, uniformed figure racing through the playground, creating waves of anguish in anyone who crossed her, teachers and pupils alike. She smiled to think of Ruby's long, straight hair hanging almost to her waist, and the transfer stickers she liked to wear tattooed across her chest. A friend of their mother's had once reported having seen her on the main road, perched like Loki on the top of a battered pram, while Lisa, struggling and gasping and stretching her arms to reach the pram's high handle, attempted to push her at a befittingly violent pace. What the woman had failed to understand was that it was an honour to push Ruby. An honour she would have defied anyone at all to refuse.

After Ruby left the school, Lisa continued to live on, steeped in the glorious memory of her reign, and when new people arrived in the area, Lisa noted how they treated her with interest and sometimes even made attempts to gain her friendship, but she could never quite forgive them their state of ignorance, and always held them at a distance and even in some small contempt for not knowing, or having ever known, that she was in fact Ruby's little sister.

Lisa was so caught up in her reverie that she changed trains at the wrong station and found herself heading north towards Cockfosters. She jumped out at Finsbury Park, just as the doors were closing, and managed to avoid being rushed on along the Piccadilly Line. She found a map against a wall of the station and began to retrace her route. The map was at a point between two tunnels that led south and north away from the station platforms, and as she stood and calculated the shortest possible journey home, a familiar figure momentarily blotted out the arch of distant light and stepped into the strip-lit gloom of the tunnel. At one glance she knew that it was Quentin. She recognized his swagger and the way he walked with his shoulders back. He sauntered towards her down the gradual underground slope. Lisa continued to stare at the map so hard that it blurred in front of her eyes, and all the time over her right shoulder she could see the dark outline of Quentin as he approached. She heard his breathing as he swayed past, turned the corner and headed in the direction of the trains. 'Quentin,' she called, surprise in her voice, as if she had just seen him, and he turned around and surveyed her calmly as he continued to walk backwards. Lisa ran towards him. She could tell he hadn't recognized her and she took it as a compliment. She smiled up into his face. 'Quentin,' she said, 'it's me. Lisa.' Quentin looked at her for so long, with his brown eyes creased up like a Hollywood photograph and his head tilted a little to one side, that Lisa began to pray for lightning or a sudden fatal heart attack to release her from the mortification of his stare.

Finally he smiled. 'Where the hell have you been?' he said, in a voice pressed down with gentleness, and with an arm around her shoulder he began to walk with her back along the sloping tunnel.

'Weren't you on your way somewhere?' Lisa asked him, but he said nothing. When they got to the concrete ridge which was the stop for the W7 bus he put his arms around her waist and kissed her. He lifted her off the ground and held her hard against him. 'You disappeared,' he said. 'How did you do that?'

Lisa was so happy she felt like lying down to die. She sat next to Quentin on the top deck, at the very front, and let herself be jolted and rattled against him by the movement of the bus. They got off at the top of the hill where they could see the spire and dome of Alexandra Palace on the peak of the next rise, and between them the valley of brick houses with their gardens and hedges and wooden sheds and the streets that wound down into the village of Crouch End. They walked back down the hill to Quentin's house and he kept hold of her hand as they climbed up the three flights of stairs to his flat on the top floor. Lisa sat on the edge of the thin, covered mattress that was Quentin's bed and the only place in the room to sit, and waited for him while he made tea in the kitchen. She arranged the folds of her dress, one by one, so that they covered her legs and hung like shiny red ribbons almost to her feet. She felt her pulse and counted her toes and tried to keep her mind occupied while she waited for him to reappear. It was late afternoon and the sun was setting somewhere over Finsbury Park, throwing a pale and yellow winter light in through the windows of the room.

Quentin reappeared with two mugs of tea. He placed them by the edge of the bed and put a record on the record player. 'D'you like this guy?' he asked her, and Lisa nodded as the first slow beats of an unfamiliar song filled the room. She reached for her tea to hide her ignorance, but before she could bring it to her lips, Quentin was kneeling over her. 'Leave that,' he whispered and he kept his hand on her arm while she replaced the cup. He sank on to the bed and pulled her down with him so that all the carefully arranged pleats of her dress flew into a ruffled mass of silk. Lisa smiled at him. She wanted him to say, 'I love you,' or, 'I've missed you,' or even, 'It's nice seeing you again,' but when she looked into his eyes he just sighed and closed them and, with his hands on her back, he twisted her round so that she lay pressed above him, hard against his chest.

Quentin loosened her belt and slipped open the zip that ran along her left side. He lifted the dress up over her head with one strong sweep of his hands. Lisa lay back in her white tights. She was still unused to the changed appearance of her body and, for the sake of inhibition and the day, she decided she may as well give in to being someone else and allow him to make love to her without a shiver of restraint.

Quentin woke with a start. Lisa had been watching him, propped up on one elbow while he slept. 'Fucking shite,' he said, leaping out of bed. 'What time is it, anyway?'

Lisa didn't know. It was dark and she had been thinking vaguely for some time that she should get up and go home to see her mother and Max who would have returned by now. Quentin rummaged through the discarded clothes strewn across the floor, throwing them into the air as he searched wildly for the clock. 'Jesus God,' he cursed when he found it, 'it's nearly ten. I'll be lucky to get there by closing time.'

Lisa found her dress half buried down the side of the mattress. She pulled it on and stood up in the hope the creases might fall out. Quentin railed around the room looking for his keys, his comb, his cigarettes, his various packets of drugs, and all the while cursing in what Lisa could only assume was a mood of sour regret. She slipped on her shoes, and with her coat over her arm waited dutifully by the door.

Once they were out on the street he took her hand. 'Where are you heading?' he asked.

'Home.'

Quentin nodded. 'I'm going the other way.' He hugged her and she kept her shoulders stiff and straight like Max. 'If you ever feel like calling round' – he looked back up at the windows of his flat – 'don't forget the bells don't work. Just shout' – Lisa softened by way of thanks – 'and I'll be there.' He grinned as if to say: You believe that and you'll believe anything.

'How could you believe me when I told you that I loved you when you know I've been a liar all my life,' Lisa hummed to herself as she walked away. Quentin was waiting at a bus stop on the other side of the road. She could see him under a street lamp, sitting on the wall smoking a cigarette. She waved at him just before the road curved out of sight, but he didn't see her.

Lisa walked on, her mind full of the weight of Quentin's hands. He had stroked her back, running his fingers up the ridge of her spine and cradling the base of her skull in his palm so that her eyes began to soften and she was able to return his kisses without breaking sharply off for air. It was only when he forced himself inside her that she lost the thread of his sweetness, and the domed rooms inside her head filled up with people, leering and scrambling and talking over each other in harsh and whispery voices. All she could do was fight them off and wait for it to be over. She didn't blame Quentin. Afterwards she had lain against his warm back and tried not to wake him with the shaking of her body and the little gasps that rattled out of her ribs when she breathed.

Once Lisa emerged above ground at Old Street round-about, she was filled with such a longing to see her mother that she broke into a run. She ran at top speed to make up for the time lost in taking the long way round. She had intended risking the mournful echo of the short cut, but a sudden stab of happiness had resulted in a decision in favour of her safety.

Lisa could see streams of light spilling out around the warped edges of the door as she sped up the last flight of stairs. Rather than search her pockets for a key, she flapped the letter-box and called in her impatience to be let in.

Marguerite swung open the door. 'Where have you been?' Her eyes were fierce. Her face was flushed with anger. 'I've been sitting here waiting for you since six.' She held the door half closed against her like a shield. 'I was on the verge of calling the police.'

'I'm sorry.' Lisa winced against the loudness of her mother's voice and attempted to slink into the room. 'I'm sorry, I didn't think . . .'

'But it's so unlike you,' Marguerite accused. 'It's just so unlike you to be thoughtless.' She slammed the door shut, and then, remembering, put a finger to her lips. Lisa glanced through into the bedroom where Max was sleeping on the top bunk, his arms and legs flailed out as if he had been drugged mid-bout in a wrestling match. Marguerite walked through to the kitchen and sank down at the table. 'Well, you're home.' And, heaving her voice on to a lighter note, she added, 'Tell me, have you been having a lovely time?'

Lisa took off her coat, revealing the disarray of her mother's red dress. 'Yes,' she said, 'I have.'

Marguerite leant close in to her. She was looking into the very centre of her eyes. 'I'm going to have to ask you something.' She took a breath and swallowed. Lisa looked at the floor. She imagined her mother had decided that this was the moment to explain the facts of life to her. Mum, she wanted to say, don't you think it's a bit late for that? But Marguerite twisted and pulled at her hands. 'Steen seems to think you've been taking drugs, hard drugs. He mentioned something about heroin.' She looked as if she were about to cry.

Lisa was so surprised she laughed out loud. 'Don't be silly!' She shook her head and raised her hands. 'You don't need to worry about me, I promise.' Lisa watched as the visible signs of relief smoothed out the lines around her mother's mouth. 'What does Steen know, anyway?'

Marguerite apologized. 'It wasn't that I believed him, but you can understand that I had to ask.'

'Of course I do,' Lisa said, 'but really, I'm fine.'

Marguerite told Lisa about her time away and all the people who had asked after her, wanting to know how she was getting on at college. She said there wasn't anyone who didn't remark on the extraordinary resemblance between Max and his father. 'As long as it's just physical,' Marguerite smiled. She heated up the vegetable soup that sat on the stove and Lisa ate, keeping her eyes pinned to her mother's face as the lentils and tiny pasta rings she used as stock slipped down her throat.

L ISA WENT AROUND to Heidi to ask for the name and address of the doctor she had mentioned some months ago who tested for allergies. Her mother's interrogation, misguided as it was, had left her with a sense of having narrowly escaped, and she resolved to find herself a cure before it was too late. To cover her tracks, she said it was possible she might be allergic to oysters. Heidi laughed and wrote out the details on a scrap of paper. 'You'll live,' she said, and she continued to scrub at the nappies that had been soaking overnight in the kitchen sink.

Lisa made an appointment to see the doctor, whose surgery was on Baker Street. She attempted to explain her symptoms to him, but he stopped her with a cynical smile, and ordered her to hold out her right arm at an angle. He then placed, one at a time, various small objects in her palm and pushed down heavily on her wrist to check the strength of her resistance. Momentarily he thought she might be suffering from mercury poisoning, and became quite animated as he explained how all the fillings in her teeth would have to be replaced at some great expense to herself, but her arm defied his diagnosis and continued to resist his weight as he pushed down on her wrist. Eventually he was forced to admit that this could not be the case and, after twenty more minutes in which she handled substances ranging from iridium to an Earl Grey tea bag, he informed her that she was allergic to nothing at all except perfume. Something of which she was already aware.

Lisa was so disappointed tears welled up in her eyes as she wrote out her cheque. She was able to draw on some money that she had in a bank account, placed there the previous year as a present from her father. It hurt her to chip away from it. Ruby had taken hers out the same week and spent it on clothes and taxis and edible delicacies from the Harrods Food Hall, but Lisa would have been happy never to disturb her share, leaving it forever safe inside the bank as a calm green reminder of her father.

The doctor packed her cheque away in a small drawer and suggested that her symptoms might be the result of tension. Lisa disagreed. You'd be feeling tense if you'd just paid thirty pounds to be told something you already know, she thought, but she said nothing. The doctor referred her to an acupuncturist and made an appointment for her there and then for the following week.

The acupuncturist was a Mr Bunzl and was unusually tall with the bone structure of an actor born to play Frankenstein. He led Lisa into a partitioned room with a disproportionately high ceiling and told her to remove her clothes.

Without another word he retreated through a flimsy door in the far wall and shut himself out with a faint shudder of the plasterboard. A small heater blew hot air into the draught under the window, and as it was the only heating in the room, Lisa stood in front of it as she undressed. It boiled her legs up to the knee and left the rest of her body quivering with goose bumps. She was in a quandary as to whether or not to remove her vest, regretting miserably that she had not thought to wear her one and only bra. She kept on her knickers and with one arm across her chest climbed on to the high bed that stood alone in the centre of the room. She lay face up under the white cotton cover and waited.

It seemed an eternity before the acupuncturist reappeared. When he did, Lisa said before she could stop herself, 'I hope it's all right I'm not wearing a bra?'

Mr Bunzl looked away and, pushing her question aside with lowered eyebrows, pulled up a chair. He wanted to know the history and precise nature of Lisa's ailment.

Lisa talked as if to the ceiling. She stuck to a strictly physical description of the state of her mind and laid bare the crackling and snapping of her bones. She tried to explain the sensation of cold burning that had descended on her in the strip-lit corridor, and how it was necessary to cover the top of her head with her hand to stop her mind escaping like an icicle. She laughed at her descriptions as she talked, her eyes fixed on the plaster rose in the centre of the ceiling. She laughed to reassure Mr Bunzl that she was not mad. She glanced over to gauge his reaction, but he continued to nod darkly and scribble notes on to a sheet of paper. She omitted to tell him about the violent fear she was seized with and the secret measures to which she would go to save herself from being poisoned. She forgot to mention the slow ebb of her period and the way her throat closed up in panic each time she raised a fork to her mouth.

To Lisa's surprise he didn't stick any needles into her but folded his pad and told her to get dressed. He remained in the room with his face turned to the wall, intent on the scrawl of her case. Lisa dressed quickly. She felt dizzy from having spoken her thoughts aloud in sentences for the first time, and, now that she was safely dressed and out of danger of his needles, a wall of disappointment engulfed her. She had expected her confidence to incite him into action. She had imagined he might stick a needle somewhere in her spine and with a hiss draw the trouble out, leaving her soft and quiet. A child again. But he had done nothing.

Mr Bunzl crossed the room quietly. He bent his knees to avoid towering so much over her and pressed his fingertips together, bringing his hands close up to her face. 'I am pressing the nail of each finger into the tip of the soft pad of the fingers on the other hand.' It was exactly what he was doing and Lisa brought her hands up to match his. 'I want you to do this each morning and each evening for five minutes. It doesn't matter where you press.' Mr Bunzl went on to list all the places in which you could practise pressing the pads of your fingers. 'The bed, the bath, the bus . . . Five minutes with one hand, and then five minutes with the other. This will take away the tension in the head, and all will be well.'

His fee was fifteen pounds and he made an appointment for Lisa to come and see him again in two weeks' time.

'Keep pressing,' he said, holding his hands up at her in a spidery prayer as she left.

Lisa's disappointment had turned to an edge of despair. She dragged her feet as she walked away from the gloom of his surgery. She would follow his daily instructions, she knew, she was too superstitious not to, and even return for her next appointment, but she was unable to believe that the simple pressing of her fingertips would cure her.

LISA HAD BECOME so quiet at college that she suspected she would hardly be missed if she failed to turn up. It was Monday morning and the week started with a class in movement improvisation. It was a class that always succeeded in embarrassing Lisa into virtual immobility.

'What are you? A tree?' the teacher had barked at her on more than one occasion.

Lisa clung to the idea that this, surely, had nothing to do with being a real actress. The kind of actress who toured the country in classic plays that involved wearing bustles and corsets and elaborate hats. She pressed her fingers together and decided to take the morning off. She could visit Ruby and use the hour of the journey to contemplate Quentin and a course of action. She still had the excuse of retrieving her ring. She had seen it in his bathroom, lying forgotten in a soap dish. It was dull and discoloured and, she decided, more valuable where it was.

When Lisa arrived at the hospital, Ruby was about to have her bath. 'I'll smuggle you in,' she said.

First Ruby had to apply for a plug. 'Special privilege,' she winked.

None of the baths in Hanworth Hospital had plugs. Or taps. 'No unsupervised bathing,' Ruby explained, and when Lisa continued to look confused, 'so you can't drown yourself, muggins.' She threw her the cold tap to screw on.

Ruby let the bath fill up to the very top so that when she got in, a layer of water slid off and splashed on to the floor. Lisa sat on a chair and watched her. She couldn't think of a thing to say. 'How's Christine?' she asked at length.

Ruby was lathering her hair. 'Killing for a drink,' and she laughed dementedly and slid her head under the water. When she shot back up, her eyes streaming and her hair sleek and rinsed, Lisa noticed that the row of dark blue scars that ran in dots along her inside arm were beginning to fade. 'Have I got fat?' Ruby asked suspiciously, seeing herself watched, and Lisa denied it vigorously.

Lisa pressed her fingertips together. She wanted to see if Ruby would recognize what it was she was doing. For all she knew, it was a well-known cure. Ruby gave her hair a second wash, sank under the water and said nothing.

When Lisa arrived back at Peerless Street, a man was standing talking to Heidi in the entrance to the flats. As Lisa approached they shook hands and she heard Heidi murmur her congratulations.

'Who was that?' Lisa asked. Heidi lowered her voice, 'It's Jim,' and she nodded in the direction of the basement yard.

'Jim?' She looked up at her window. 'The man who forgot his key? But I thought he –'

'Shh.' Heidi raised her finger to her lips and continued in a stage whisper, 'It's a miracle what people survive.' They stood and watched him as he walked to the end of Peerless Street and disappeared through a side door of the local pub. 'By the way,' Heidi said, 'did you ever see that doctor about the allergy to oysters?'

Lisa froze on the bottom step. 'No, I couldn't be bothered.' And she ran on up the stairs without another word.

For the next two weeks Lisa pressed her fingertips together at every opportunity. She assumed it was better to press too often than not to press often enough, and she listened warily for any changes. Much as she had suspected, there were none.

T HE EVENING BEFORE she was due to go back to see Mr Bunzl, Lisa discovered Tom lounging against a wall in the foyer of her college reading a copy of a weekly magazine. He was very excited. Someone had compiled a list of the ten men they would most like to have a night of passion with and Tom's name featured on it, eighth. Tom thrust the magazine into Lisa's hands. 'Do you know her? Who is she? Where has she been all my life?' he demanded.

The list had been compiled by a girl called Emilia Hilton. She had a mass of bleached hair piled on top of her head like Debbie Harry, but her face was so over-exposed that, apart from two round, bright eyes, she appeared to have no other features. Lisa stared at the girl's name as if she might be able to dredge up some familiarity with her, even though she could have told Tom straight away that she wouldn't know. 'I've got to meet her,' Tom said when she eventually admitted to her ignorance. He stuffed the rolled magazine into the back pocket of his jeans and asked if she wanted to come for a drink.

They walked through the housing estates that stretched away towards King's Cross to where the college pub stood in a paved-over square with two stinking benches and several trees that waved and shivered in their wire encasements. 'I'll come for one drink,' Lisa said, 'but then I'll have to go.' It was Max's sixth birthday and a tea party was being held in his honour. Tom bought himself a pint of Guinness and a Bell's, and insisted Lisa have the same. Lisa obediently drained her whisky but was unable to stomach the froth of the thick and bitter Guinness. Tom obligingly drank it for her and went to the bar to reorder. After the third round he took out the magazine and held it up to the light. He gazed into the startled eyes of the girl whose list he was on. 'I'm in love,' he said in a voice thick with whisky and emotion. 'I'm in love and I've got to find you, if it's the last thing I do,' and he staggered to the bar to put in his order for another round.

Each time Lisa made a move to leave, Tom caught her wrist and forced her back on to the seat beside him. 'Just stay for one more,' he insisted, his grey eyes threatening to overflow. By now there were so many glasses on their table that to attempt to get out from behind it was a daunting prospect.

'I've really got to go,' Lisa mumbled, closing her eyes, and then forcing them open again fast as the spin inside her head began to pick up speed.

'No, no, you can't,' Tom pleaded, and, in an effort to grab hold of her, he tipped Guinness over the outstretched pages of the magazine, so that, as they watched, the face of Tom's dream-girl dissolved into a thin and papery mess.

Tom tried desperately to save the picture by peeling it off in one go, but the weight of the Guinness glued it to the table top and it fell apart in his hands. In a last, desperate attempt to capture even a fraction of the article, Tom succeeded in knocking over the remains of his pint so that the table became a dark sea of matchsticks and cigarette butts, an occasional piece of sodden type floating on its overflowing surface. Lisa looked up to see the barman scowling over at them, and before Tom could topple the whole table as he grabbed at the floating letters of his name, Lisa hoisted him up and, with some difficulty, manoeuvred him towards the door.

'Come and have some tea at our house,' she insisted. And arm in arm they staggered towards the station.

Max's tea party was almost over when they arrived at Peerless Flats. Max was eating chocolate fingers through the visor of his plastic helmet and shouting orders to foxes that hovered in the corners of the room. Marguerite, Heidi and Steen were smoking in the kitchen.

The moment Max saw Tom, he charged him as if he were simply continuing the battle begun on New Year's Eve. Tom threw himself on to the bed to avoid being butted by the hard top of his helmet, and pleaded with Max for mercy. 'I'm feeling a little fragile,' he said, covering his head with his hands and giggling uncontrollably. 'If you don't stop, I'm liable to throw up all over you.' Max roared with delight. He jumped up and down on the bed so that the springs whined and sang and threatened to snap. Tom's long, thin body heaved with the motion. Lisa went through to the kitchen to make coffee.

'I'm sorry I'm so late,' she said.

'It's all right.' Marguerite looked at her proudly and smiled.

'Best years of your life,' Steen said, and he raised his glass.

A low groan of agony rose up from the other room. Tom, clutching his stomach, and closely followed by Max, pushed his way through the kitchen, stumbling over discarded toys and the legs of chairs and fumbling his way blind towards the toilet. Marguerite and Heidi began to laugh. 'Best years of your life,' Steen said again, and Lisa ran the cold tap furiously to drown out the sound of his vomiting.

L ISA LAY UNDER the white sheet on the high bed of Mr
Bunzl's practice. 'It didn't work,' she told him flatly,
when he asked how she was feeling.

Mr Bunzl was astounded. His mammoth hands fluttered
and the heavy bones of his face seemed ready to collapse.
Lisa fixed her eyes on the ceiling and tried to keep her heart
hard against him as she traced the skeletal cracks that rode
across the plaster.

Mr Bunzl stacked her flimsy notes against his knee and
placed them on a chair. 'I am going to use some needles,'
he said in a voice so soothing as to send a chill through the
air. Lisa didn't answer. She was fighting with a lump in
her throat. 'Now breathe in,' Mr Bunzl instructed, 'and
out.'

Lisa felt a tiny sting like the first bite of a bee before the
poison takes effect. She wanted to look down to see the
exact point of the tingling, but the acupuncturist had moved
away from her feet and was instructing her to breathe
slowly in and out while he placed two needles in the top

of her head. She felt nothing but an itching around the jab of each pin.

Mr Bunzl placed six needles in various parts of her body and then stood over her as if he were monitoring the possibilities of an immediate reaction. 'Any pain?' he asked, and Lisa gulped and admitted that there was none.

Whether this was the right answer or not, Lisa wasn't sure, for he then proceeded to busy himself about her prostrate body, placing small lumps of incense on the tip of each needle and setting light to them with a match. Lisa began to smoke like a funeral pyre. She was wreathed in a veil through which she could just make out the retreating figure of Mr Bunzl, side-stepping away from her, until with a click and a shudder of the wall he levered himself out through the partition door.

Lisa walked away from the surgery in a kind of trance. Her eyes felt soft in her head and her mouth was full of lullabies. She stopped at a parade of shops and bought three bunches of sweet white narcissi. She began to run. She ran past the gloomy entrance to the underground station and along a canal that stretched through Maida Vale and led up on to the start of Edgware Road. She leapt, the petals of her flowers flapping, on to the open back of a double-decker bus, and, as she squeezed herself inside and through the throng of people standing, an earlier memory than she had ever known burst in on her. She was running with her mother. They were running for a bus and, as the distances closed in, the grip on her hand tightened and her speed picked up and she was flying, flying out from her mother's arm as the whole world of the city blurred below her feet. She had trodden air with her shoes which were red like the bus, and, just when she thought she would slip out of her shoulder-blade and twist away through the trees, her mother's strong hand had swung her to safety and she had been lost among shopping-bags and the trouser legs of the conductor. She had waited breathless for the world to steady itself and catch her up.

Lisa pushed her way to the front of the bus and stood pressed against the driver's window. She closed her eyes and let her face hang over the honeysuckle centres of her flowers. Mr Bunzl had left her alone while the smoke from the incense thinned and formed itself into delicate plumes that rose in spirals to the ceiling. Lisa didn't know how long she had lain there, but she had become transfixed by the coils of smoke, soft as carded wool, and had forgotten her fury against the wasted weeks of pressing at her fingertips. She had been surprised by the reappearance of the acupuncturist, who moved around her wordlessly drawing out the needles. 'I will see you again in two weeks,' he said and Lisa had written out her cheque without a trace of bile.

Lisa stood her flowers in a glass of water, keeping them in their paper wrapping to give to Ruby on her Saturday visit. Marguerite was unable to go with her as it was the quarterly housing co-operative meeting, at which all new and homeless members were allowed to plead their case. Lisa was on the point of asking if she might take Max along for company, when Max announced from under the table that he had succeeded in making his eyeballs disappear.

'Look,' he screamed, sliding out along the kitchen floor, 'Lisa, see if you can do it too.'

Lisa covered her eyes with her hand.

'Goodbye,' she called, 'good luck,' and, feeling blindly for her coat, she promised to eat the apple her mother had pushed into her pocket.

When Lisa arrived at Ruby's ward, Ruby was not there. Her bed was neatly made and was piled high with her belongings. Lisa squeezed herself between two cardboard boxes and waited. She was tempted to search through a bag to see if Ruby had remembered to pack the mother-of-pearl bracelet that had not been seen or mentioned since Christmas, but instead she drew the apple out of her pocket and inspected it. She turned it over and rubbed it on the sleeve of her coat. It was an English Pippin and not the kind of fruit that ever achieves a shine. There were little weather-beaten creases in its skin which Lisa peered into.

'What are you doing?' Ruby's voice startled her from across the ward.

'Nothing?' Lisa took a bite of the apple to prove she was not afraid.

'I'm leaving today,' Ruby sighed, sitting down beside her and leaning back against her bags.

Lisa nodded. 'That's right. I came to see you off.' She had in fact until this minute completely forgotten the details of her previous visit. Her head began to swim. 'Do you mean leaving, leaving the country? Where did you say you were going? To . . . to . . .?' She took a bite out of her lip in her anxiety.

'Dad's taking me to lunch,' Ruby said calmly. 'Why don't you come?'

Their father arrived wearing a slate-grey trench coat. He had a newspaper rolled up under his arm and he tapped his foot and shifted edgily from side to side. 'I've got a bit of a bet on the two-thirty-five at Sandown Park,' he said. 'Shall we go?' They loaded Ruby's possessions into the boot of the car, a fat and roomy Rover with a severe dent in its left wing.

'What do you fancy?' He glanced into the back where Lisa was still clutching her fading bunch of flowers.

'Lobster,' Ruby said, 'and champagne!' She turned in her seat to watch as the receding mass of Hanworth Hospital twisted out of sight with a bend in the road.

Their father tapped his fingers on the steering-wheel. 'We could, we could,' but he wasn't committing himself.

'A pizza?' Lisa suggested, but he only tapped his tongue against the roof of his mouth.

It transpired he needed to be near a television.

'Why not go to the race course? Watch the horses run from there?' Ruby was not making her suggestion in all innocence, but with bravado and a challenge in her voice. Lisa leant forward so that her face was resting on the back of Ruby's seat. Their father kept his eyes on the road. 'It's an idea,' he mused.

'Is it because you win too often?' Lisa asked him.

Her father swerved into the inside lane to overtake a juggernaut. Lisa and Ruby both grasped the seat. 'Have you ever heard the term "debt of honour"?' He was back in the fast lane and sailing towards ninety.

'We could disguise you,' Ruby broke in. 'I've got clothes in the back.'

Lisa put her arms around her sister's neck and hugged her.

Their father, a thoughtful smile on his face, careered across the dual carriageway and pulled into a lay-by. 'Let's see what you've got,' he said.

Ruby heaved her bags out of the boot and began to rummage through the contents. Lisa ran back and forth catching at garments as they escaped in the tornado of the passing cars. She found a long, sequinned scarf lined with memories of Marlene which their father wrapped around his head and twisted into a turban. 'How do I look?' he asked, and he began to skip across the lay-by from side to side, his hands raised and flat in an Egyptian dance. Cars slowed visibly and Ruby and Lisa rocked on their heels. 'Try this?' Ruby hurled a navy blue beret into the wind and Lisa caught it and handed it over. The beret turned the trench coat into a soldier's uniform and created a sombre and menacing impression. 'All wrong,' they agreed and Ruby continued to rifle. Eventually she found what she was looking for and dragged a white cotton jacket up from the depths of her packing. It looked like a chef's coat with stiff collars and a long split up the back. Their father changed in an instant, throwing his own coat into the back seat of the car and transforming momentarily into Charlie Chaplin before the addition of Ruby's tinted glasses fixed him as an eccentric and mildly sinister Frenchman. Lisa broke the stem of a white narcissus and wove the flower through his buttonhole. 'That's it,' and they piled Ruby's luggage back into the boot.

There was less than twenty minutes before the race was due to start. 'Don't worry, we'll make it,' their father assured them as he sped his car against the traffic. He leapt up pavements, slipped through lights and over-took seamlessly from the inside, provoking a fanfare of disapproval from pedestrians and motorists alike. Once they were on to a clear stretch of road, he reached into the glove compartment and brought out a fat white envelope. He handed it to Ruby. Inside was a map of car parks and a cluster of pink cardboard badges with 'Members' stand' printed across them. 'Didn't think I'd be using these,' he said as he pushed the car through amber lights. The Rover shook and hummed as it reached its limit and the steering-wheel trembled in their father's hand. 'Pin on a badge,' he said, but Lisa was clinging on for her life.

Eventually signs for Sandown Park appeared and the country roads thickened with cars slowing for a parking space. Their father shifted the Rover into the middle of the road, roared along the broken line between the lanes of traffic and slipped through the entrance to the first car park, where within a fraction of his wing mirror he manoeuvred into a free space seconds ahead of a Bentley. The driver hooted violently and two red setters with identical and hostile eyes set up an indignant bark. Lisa, Ruby and their father leapt out and, pinning on their badges, ran away across the field in the direction of the race track.

They crossed the road and were walking through a gate marked 'Members' entrance' when two men in official uniforms closed in on them. 'Excuse me, sir,' one of them said and Lisa hoped that her father would resist using the French accent he had been practising throughout the drive. He looked shiftily out through the blue lenses of Ruby's glasses and failed to answer at all. 'Excuse me, sir, but you must be wearing a tie to go beyond this point.' Their father raised his hands to his throat and a look of amazement crossed his face.

'How extraordinary,' he said in the Queen's most precise English, 'it must have slipped off.' Lisa looked at the clock on the wall of the building opposite. There were three minutes to go. He turned to Ruby and raised his eyebrows above the glasses.

'No,' Ruby said. 'And anyway there isn't time.'

'They have ties for sale in the gift shop,' the second official offered helpfully and before he had finished his sentence their father had disappeared into a white boarded hut. He reappeared seconds later with a shiny maroon tie in a long plastic box. He tore off the wrapping, and holding up the tie as if it were a pass, pushed past the guards who were busy scanning the crowd for similar offenders. Lisa and Ruby followed him at a run.

The horses were prancing and reeling at the starting-post as they found a space high up on the tiered stands and pressed themselves against the rails. It was a startling spring day and the colours of the jockeys' caps spun in the light.

'Number eight,' their father pointed, and Lisa followed his gaze to a beautiful rust-brown horse. A white-and-blue-clad jockey perched in the saddle, leaning along the horse's neck in one last-minute conversation. The horse was Irish, was six years old and was named Balliglasson.

'The going's good and that's what she likes,' their father was saying as a loudspeaker boomed, 'And they're off!'

There were six horses in the race and they all started in a throng, picking up speed as they galloped neck and neck, their hooves flaying wildly and their backs arched. Balliglasson fell behind a little at the first jump and a whole sea of people rose to their feet and growled in low and desperate tones, 'Come on.' Their father remained silent, his eyes fixed on the horse as it began to reclaim lost ground. At the next fence it stretched its front legs and leapt into third place. Ruby gripped Lisa's arm. The loudspeaker was keeping up an urgent commentary. Then a horse fell, throwing its rider, and, picking itself up, raced on alone. It forced the winning horse to one side and Balliglasson seized her chance and roared into the lead. Lisa glanced over at her father. He was as still and white as a statue. Her blood danced in her veins. 'We're going to win, we're going to win,' she sang under her breath, immune to the ferocious grip of Ruby's fingers, numbing her arm just above the elbow. The horses turned into the far straight and raced out of view to anyone without binoculars. Every ear was strained for the commentary, which to Lisa was an unintelligible tumbling of names and numbers with the occasional audible sound of Balliglasson. When the race swept back into sight, three of the horses had fallen behind. A hush fell over the crowd. It was Balliglasson running in a two-horse race with Crimson Creek. They swept over a jump, keeping perfect pace with one another. The voices of the crowd were urgent. 'Come on, come on,' they called, drawing out the sounds between clenched teeth, and the men punched their fists into the air at any sign of hope. Lisa could see the two frantic jockeys raising up their whips as they leapt the final fence and thundered on to the home run. A bell began to ring and the commentary fell over itself with the speed of its recital. 'Go on,' Lisa heard herself murmur, as Balliglasson flew like a leopard towards the finish. Everyone was on their feet yelling and pleading and urging their horse on. Many had their own private messages and the names of the jockeys on their lips. As Lisa watched, her hands clasping the rail, the long stretched neck of Balliglasson glided across the finishing-line a split second before her rival. The race was over. The crowd shook itself silent as if woken from a trance, and some of the men mumbled into their coats and looked around with sheepish and unfocused eyes.

'It'll be a photo finish,' their father said, the colour flooding back into his face. But they knew who had won. Ruby let go of Lisa's arm and they went to hear the final decision on the race-track television.

Lisa, Ruby and their father went for tea to celebrate. They ate slivers of white-bread sandwiches, fruit cake and scones with jam and clotted cream. They had to ask for a second large pot of tea and another jug of boiling water. Their father kept his beret and his glasses on throughout the meal. Full and warm and victorious, they walked back across the field to the Rover, and sailed in a haze of glory towards London.

Their father stopped at a betting-shop near Ladbroke Grove and collected his winnings. He flicked up two fifty-pound notes from the top of a fat pile and slid them out from under their elastic band. He handed them to Ruby. 'Thanks, Dad,' she said.

He gave Lisa the same. 'A hundred pounds!'

'On condition you spend it all today.' Ruby laughed and pinched her.

Their father parked his car, got out and stretched. He removed his disguise and threw it into the back with Ruby's other belongings. 'What are your plans?' he asked.

Ruby fished out her glasses and perched them on top of her head. 'I'll leave everything in the boot,' she said decisively, 'and then you'll *have* to drive me to the airport.'

Their father smiled, said goodbye and retreated up the steps and into his flat. As they walked away, they could see him at the window talking to someone on the telephone.

Ruby suggested they go into the West End and spend as much of their money as they could before closing-time. Lisa had already started to dream of how she might rearrange her treasure box to incorporate the notes, but Ruby was insistent. She hailed a cab. 'South Molton Street,' she ordered grandly, but she remained perched on the edge of her seat.

'Where are you going?' Lisa asked, sliding forward to join her.

Ruby glanced out of the window. 'Dad's got a friend who's going to give me a job.'

'Where?'

'Argentina somewhere.' She smiled and bit sharply at the end of her nail.

'Doing what?'

'I've no idea.'

They were weaving their way into town. Lisa squeezed her sister's hand and tried to imagine what someone like Ruby would do in Argentina. She imagined her in the back yard of a ranch overseeing wild horses, counting out the lengths of time the campanero cowboys could stay on. She smiled to think of the accent Ruby would adopt. 'Will you be all right?' she asked, and when Ruby didn't answer, Lisa rephrased her question. 'Will you be staying on a hacienda?'

'I doubt it.' The taxi was on Oxford Street and Ruby was busy peering into shop windows. 'Let's get out here,' she said, and the taxi pulled up with a screech of brakes. They were across the pavement from the main revolving doors of Selfridges.

Lisa followed Ruby across the rich scented floor of leather goods – wallets and handbags and snakeskin purses – and on into the dizzying world of cosmetics, where the girls smiled coldly out at them from behind their counters. They had only ten minutes before the shop was due to close and they set off at a run for Women's Fashions.

Ruby's style had become somewhat jumbled since her incarceration in Hanworth Hospital. The precision of her earlier code of dress was gone, and even her accent had lost its edge. Occasionally a faint trace of Christine's south London lilt slipped through, and the odd, incongruous Liverpudlian expression, but mostly, today, she sounded like her old forgotten self.

Ruby pushed her way past racks of satin blouses and lambswool, pearl-buttoned cardigans. She ran her fingers through sheaves of flowery dresses and tried on an ankle-length, engine-red coat.

'What are you after?' Lisa asked her. The shop was getting ready to close. Smart, middle-aged manageresses rattled their tills and eyed them with impatience.

'Quick.' Ruby pulled Lisa by the arm, dragging her through a room of polka-dotted party dresses. 'Over here.' And through an arch she caught a glimpse of the shoe department. It was a shoe display so elegant it took her breath away. Shoes, slippers and boots were arranged on shelves of glass like triple-layered trays of cake. There were gold and silver pumps, straight-legged, two-tone riding boots and a centrepiece of stilettos in turquoise and lemon-yellow. Lisa saw a pair of red and blue suede ankle boots set jauntily on a podium. They were laced with ribbon and tied in a wide satin bow. Lisa shook herself free of Ruby's grasp and ran towards them. She knelt down in the thick carpet and, clutching a boot in each hand, began loosening the ribbons. The shop assistant stood over her. 'Do you require assistance, madam?' He was staring haughtily down at her discarded shoe.

'How much are they?' Lisa slipped her foot into place. They were a perfect fit.

The shop assistant averted his eyes. 'Forty-seven pounds and fifty pence.'

'We'll take them,' Ruby said from behind his shoulder.

He jumped imperceptibly and glanced at his watch as if he might just refuse to serve them. 'Cash or account?' he conceded.

'Cash.' Lisa fumbled in her pocket. 'I think I'll keep them on.'

Lisa's old shoes were wrapped in clean white tissue and laid aside in a cardboard box. 'Aren't you going to get anything?' she asked Ruby as the escalator returned them to the perfumed haze of the lower floor.

Ruby held out a slinky, open carrier bag. 'What do you think?' Inside was a minute orange bikini held together with circles of hollow gold.

'For Argentina?' Lisa tried to reappraise her vision of a working holiday. Ruby nodded. 'You never know.'

Ruby had a long-standing arrangement to meet up with Tom. 'I've got a lot of catching up to do.' She rustled the money in her pocket and grinned.

Lisa gripped her arm. She wanted to plead with her to stay away. 'What time is your plane, anyway?'

'Not till tomorrow night. Listen, why don't you come along?'

'What? Where?'

'To Tom's.'

She loosened her hold. 'I couldn't. I mean, it's just . . . I've . . . I'm meant to meet someone.'

Ruby began to move away. 'Well, I'll be seeing you.'

'What shall I tell Mum?'

Ruby was flailing her arms at an approaching taxi. She didn't appear to have heard.

'What shall I tell Mum?' Lisa shouted after her, but Ruby had skipped out into the middle of the road and was negotiating her fare.

Lisa walked down Oxford Street with her eyes fixed on the points of her boots. The red and blue diamonds of their suede toes dazzled her. They made her feet look oversized, as if with one stride they might take her in a giant leap over the moon. It was only now she was outside that she realized how little they went with the rest of her clothes. I'm meant to meet someone, she thought guiltily, examining her lie, and then it occurred to her that this might not be a lie, but a sign that the night destined for her reunion with Quentin had arrived. Over the weeks she had been taking secret bus journeys through Islington, pressing her face to the window as she passed the pub where they had met, and scanning the crowd outside the late-night cinema from the safety of the upper deck. On each occasion she had arrived home without so much as a glimpse of him, but holding steadfastly to the belief that the longer she stayed out of Quentin's way the more he was likely to miss her.

It was still early when she arrived at the pub. She stood almost alone with her back to the bar and sent out quick, shooting glances to check that it wasn't Quentin lounging in an alcove or standing jammed into a corner with a pint of Guinness. She cradled her drink, keeping the fingers of her hand welded over it like a lid. Someone waved at her from the other side of the pub. Her heart leapt and she looked abruptly away. The wave was followed by a whistle. The type of whistle you hear in a park that demands to be obeyed. Lisa began to turn slowly around and away, and as she turned, she glanced into the long, low mirror behind the bar, where she saw, striding towards her with a wide grin and a greased, black curl on his forehead, the jaunty, ice-cool figure of Jimmy Bright.

'Ruby!' he exclaimed. 'Ruby,' and before she had time to correct his mistake, he had clasped her in his arms and was jamming his tongue into her ear.

'Jimmy, get off,' she squirmed, not wanting to create a scene. 'Jimmy, it's me, it's Lisa.'

Jimmy refused to believe her. 'Ruby,' he said, 'you can't fool me. Don't think you can play those damn dirty tricks on me.' He curled his lip at her. 'Who am I?' he demanded, holding her by the shoulders.

Lisa couldn't help smiling at the irony of his question.

'Jimmy,' she answered. 'Jimmy Bright.'

Jimmy leant close in to her. 'Demon Lover,' he crooned, and he tried to take a bite out of her neck. The jukebox was playing 'Little Red Rooster' and he began to waltz her slowly on the spot. Lisa stumbled against his feet.

She tried again. 'I'm Ruby's sister, I'm Lisa, it's an easy mistake to make, people are always getting us mixed up.'

Jimmy continued to hold her close, and they danced on in silence. 'Oh Ru-ubeeey, don't take your love to town,' he sang in the break between records.

'Lisa,' she corrected him.

'Oh Ru-ubeey,' and then he opened his eyes wide. 'Only teasing,' he said, and he let her go. 'See you around, kiddo, and, if you remember, give my regards to Big Bad Sis.' He winked at her, and, as she watched, he walked away across the pub and with both hands in his pockets kicked open the heavy wooden door and sauntered out on to the street.

Lisa gulped down her drink. It was a small measure of vodka without ice or mixers. It made her feel hot and cold and as if she had a right to be there. She looked around more openly now for Quentin, even retracing her steps to the ladies' loo in the hope of invoking the lucky spirit of their first encounter, but, hard as she searched, she knew sooner or later she would have to admit that he was not there.

When Lisa arrived home, the heady smell of a baking cake filled the flat. The kitchen table was spread with a cloth and set for four.

'Who goes there?' Max called out to her from his camp between the bunk beds. 'Enter at your peril,' he snarled as she peered between the drapes and blankets of his cave. She noticed that he had drawn a small army of pencil-thin soldiers on the wall beside his pillow. They had worryingly long noses that could even be snouts, and tall, foxy ears. They were heading into battle with their shields held out in front of them.

Marguerite had cleared herself a space between the supper plates and was writing furiously. She had started an Open University course in the New Year, and at the end of each month a general panic ensued as to whether or not she would be able to complete her essay on time. She would have to study for six years to collect enough credits to get a degree and this, Lisa knew, was her intention.

Marguerite looked up expectantly. 'Where's Ruby?' Her cheeks were flushed.

'Ruby?'

'Ruby,' she insisted. There were flowers on the draining-board and Lisa noticed that her mother had dressed up. She had changed out of her uniform of faded corduroy and hand-knitted jumpers and was wearing a black-beaded dress and makeup, brown eyeshadow with golden specks, and a smudge of cherry lipstick. It didn't suit her. Marguerite stood up and strained her eyes into the dimness of the hall. 'Ruby?'

Lisa blindly followed her gaze.

'Well, where is she?' Marguerite's voice rose and her pad of paper slid off the table. The loose leaves of her notes flew across the floor. 'Where is she?'

'I don't know.' Lisa wanted to run. Something was boiling over on the stove.

'They sent a letter. They said to expect her home.' Marguerite was shouting an inch away from her face. 'Talk to me. Don't just stand there like . . . like some great lummox.' Lisa's head was spinning. Her ears had filled up with a dead weight that made it hard to decipher one word from another. She fought for an answer. The right answer. She could see her mother's eyes tearing into her. She could see that at any moment the hard lines of her face would dissolve into a mesh of tears. Lisa could come up with nothing. She gripped her stomach. She froze in the breath of silence that ensued, and then, as if she had been stabbed, she let out a low, strangled cry.

'What is it?'

Lisa curled over and began to sink towards the floor.

'What is it?' Marguerite was at her side. 'What is it, my darling?' Her voice was gentle now and under control. The animal behind her eyes had fled.

'I've got a pain,' she sobbed, 'a terrible pain.' She allowed herself to sink against her mother, her back bending in an arc of tears.

'Try and tell me where it is.'

Lisa placed her hand across her stomach and pressed. She winced in agony. Now that she put her mind to it there was a pain. A dull, comforting pain that she clung to. Warm tears slipped down her face and fell into her mouth.

Marguerite found a hankie and helped her to bed. 'I'm sorry to draw you into my troubles.' Lisa spluttered and gulped to let her know it was all right. But her mother insisted. 'It's wrong of me. It's wrong, and I'll try not to do it again. I promise.'

Lisa didn't speak. She felt calm and very tired. She lay under the covers with a hot-water bottle pressed against her side and listened while Marguerite read Max his bedtime story.

Lisa stayed in bed the whole of the next day. Max, under orders to keep quiet, tiptoed around her, regaling her with whispered lists of fly hooks, and the weight and size of fish he intended to catch. He told her about Nermil, his favourite enemy, and asked her countless questions about God. Max was learning about God at school. How God was the all-seeing Father. 'Nowadays,' Max said, 'God really gets on my nerves.'

'Why's that?'

Max sighed. 'He keeps watching when I'm on the toilet,' and he kicked his feet grumpily against the edge of her bed.

Marguerite tempted her with tinned soup and grapes. She plied her with slices of cake. 'I had no idea how thin you'd got,' she frowned. 'Just scrape off the burnt bits and it's still delicious. How's the pain?'

Lisa pressed and prodded at her stomach. 'It comes and goes.'

Marguerite swore that first thing Monday morning she would make an appointment for Lisa with the doctor.

Lisa wondered how her mother would find out about Ruby going to Argentina if she wasn't the one to tell her. She worried that her father would forget it was him who was supposed to be driving her to the airport. Ruby would have to leave without her luggage. She would arrive with nothing but her orange bikini and a fifty-pound note. When she started on these thoughts, a pain really did twist inside her stomach and she called out for a drink and a fresh hot-water bottle.

'My poor darling.' Marguerite plumped up her pillows. 'Just lie still, and don't worry about a thing.'

Lisa closed her eyes.

'Lummox,' Max whispered in her ear, and she smiled. Whatever happened now she had an alibi.

When Lisa woke up, it was dark and the door to her room was shut. She could hear voices, gritty and dissenting, lowered in the kitchen. There was a man's voice she didn't recognize. It wasn't the caretaker, or Steen. Lisa crept across the room, opened her door and looked out. She started back. Ruby was there, talking and twisting her fingers, and just behind her, leaning up against the fridge, was her father. He looked small and suspicious and strangely out of place.

Lisa leapt back into bed. 'Mum,' she called out, and she sat up bleary-eyed, as if she had that second woken.

Marguerite tiptoed into the room. 'How are you feeling?'

Lisa hugged her stomach and put on a brave face.

Marguerite sat on the edge of the bed. 'Ruby's going away for a little while.' She switched on a lamp. 'She's come to say goodbye.'

Ruby put her head round the door and smiled. 'Hasta la vista.' She came over and hugged Lisa. 'Dad's going to take you to a specialist.' She lowered her voice. 'They're terribly worried.'

Lisa felt her eyes brim over. She fumbled under her pillow for a handkerchief. 'Will you write?'

'I suppose it's because you're never, ever ill,' Ruby added wistfully.

Their father appeared in the doorway. 'We'd better make a move.' He smiled at Lisa. 'I'll be in touch.'

'I'll be in touch tomorrow,' she heard him tell Marguerite as she opened the front door to them.

'Bye, Mum,' Ruby said, and there was a pause in which Lisa thought she heard her mother sniff. 'Goodbye, Max. And Max,' she called up the stairs, 'adios, bandito.'

Max pelted her with a machine-gun round of friendly fire.

O N THE AFTERNOON of the next day a telegram arrived. It was from Lisa's father and contained what they could only assume were details of a doctor's appointment. MEET GROSVENOR HOTEL 11 A.M. TUESDAY.

Lisa stayed in bed and attempted to catch up on her college work. She was doing a project on ancient Greek theatre and was behind by several weeks. Marguerite brought her own work through from the kitchen to keep her company, she had started with myth, and moved on to music. Lisa flicked through her mother's Open University pamphlets. They were so much clearer than the dusty pile of library books heaped up by her bed. 'What are you doing next?'

Marguerite wasn't sure. She went through to the bedroom and scooped a brown-paper package from under the bed. 'Drama!' She pulled the pamphlets free and let them fall on to Lisa's lap. 'See if there's anything helpful in there.'

There was an entire section on Greek theatre. She sat up in bed and copied happily. She discovered exactly how a fifth-century-BC production of *Oedipus Rex* would have been staged, and that the three actors used to play the parts were the protagonist, the deuteragonist and the tritagonist. She traced illustrations of the reconstructed amphitheatre at Epidaurus, of the *thymele*, the *skene* and the *parados*, and of the masks worn by the players.

Marguerite beamed. 'And who says I'm not a good mother?'

Lisa found a section on the open-air, all-night orgies indulged in by the followers of the god Dionysus and continued to copy.

THE GROSVENOR HOTEL was at the back of Victoria station and, like the cartoon cinema, had been a landmark for Lisa as a child. For many years she had been under the impression, when she looked up at the giant letters of its name, that it was not the Grosvenor but the Gronsovenor Hotel. A tendency towards dyslexia, especially at a distance, often distorted the words that Lisa saw elongated across London, and added to the lasting impression they made on her. 'What's Harry's bristle cream?' she had once asked her father, pointing at a wall-sized advertisement through the open window of a taxi, and he had laughed until the tears ran down his face. 'Harry's bristle cream?' he repeated, his voice hoarse, and he tousled her hair in admiration. She joined in his laughter and her eyes danced. Ruby laughed too and was never again so quick to correct her. 'It's not the Gronsovenor, nitwit,' she had been in the habit of saying, 'it's the Gross Venor!' It was only now Lisa realized with some amusement that it was pronounced with a silent S and they had both been wrong.

Lisa's father was standing on the steps reading the sports pages of a paper. She was surprised to see him there a few minutes before eleven.

'Shall we go?' he asked when he saw her, and he hailed a taxi. 'How are you feeling?'

'It comes and goes,' she told him with a wince. She had managed to convince herself of this. The more she dwelt on it the more strongly she believed in the vivid, stabbing pains that she described.

The doctor was not a specialist, but the doctor of a friend of Lisa's father. The surgery was on the ground floor of a newly painted house five minutes from Victoria. There were magazines piled high on tables between three sofas, and a secretary who sat typing at a desk in the centre of the room.

'Lisa, how nice to meet you,' the doctor smiled, and held the door for her. He ushered her towards a chair. 'And what can I do for you?' He was a small man with a shiny, hairless head.

Lisa didn't know where to start.

'You have been suffering from stomach pains?' he encouraged.

Lisa blinked. She was frightened that if she opened her mouth she might start to cry.

'Apparently they came on quite suddenly, is this right?' He pushed a box of tissues towards her. 'It's all right, everyone feels a bit sorry for themselves when they come to see me.'

Lisa tried to smile and immediately burst into tears. He pushed the box closer and waited for her to stop.

'If you'd like to slip off your things, jump up on the bed, and I'll have a look at you.'

Lisa obediently blew her nose. She lay on the cold, hygenic roll of paper towel and kept her eyes open while the doctor prodded and pressed at her stomach. She watched his face for signs of suspicion. For signs that he might tell on her. Tell her off for wasting his valuable time. Not to mention her father's. 'Ow,' she gasped as her stomach tightened and the doctor pushed his thumb deep in beside her hip bone.

'If you'd like to get dressed.'

Lisa stumbled into her clothes.

'How old are you, my dear?'

'Sixteen.'

'Could you tell me the date of your last period?'

Lisa couldn't remember. 'Ages ago.' She looked at him, startled. 'You don't think I'm pregnant, do you?'

The doctor glanced up, the warmth gone from his eyes. 'Do you have reason to think you might be?'

'No.' Lisa was adamant.

'Well then.' The doctor went to the door and called her father in. 'I don't think there is anything seriously wrong,' he told him, 'but I do think it would be advisable to consult a specialist.'

Lisa felt her cheeks burning with relief.

'I could ask my secretary to make an appointment.'

Lisa and her father both nodded their agreement, and while they waited he paid her bill with cash.

They went for lunch at the fish restaurant in Chinatown where Lisa's father was a regular.

'We could try somewhere else if you'd prefer?'

Lisa assumed he was referring to the Wimpy, Notting Hill, and insisted she was happy where they were.

'You'll be pleased to know,' he told her, 'that oysters are out of season.'

Lisa laughed and studied the menu. She chose corned beef hash with a poached egg. Her father smiled indulgently and ordered salmon.

'How are you getting on with your acting?' he asked.

'All right.'

'It's only that I was thinking, when I was young, and fanatical about horses, the one person I wanted to meet was a famous jockey, Gordon Richards or Lester Piggott.'

'And did you?'

'I did eventually. I hung around so much they gave me a job as a stable-lad.' He paused. 'I had wanted to be a jockey myself.'

Lisa stopped eating. 'Why didn't you?'

'Too tall. I grew too tall. It can happen to anyone. Anyway, I was thinking, presuming you don't know any, that you might like to meet an actor?'

Lisa thought of the boy from *Scum* and the actors she had seen at the party. 'No,' she said. 'I don't know any.'

'There's an actor who drinks at a club I go to. I don't know his name but I get the feeling he's rather well thought of. Quite famous. If you'd like, I could arrange for you to meet him.'

'Could you?' Lisa's imagination exploded at the thought of a possible tea with Dr Who or the Saint. It might even be possible to ask the actor to meet her from college. She tried to picture the faces of the Full Time Speech and Drama course when they saw Marlon Brando waiting for her in the foyer. 'Would you be there too?' she asked, the enormity of the situation sinking in on her, and her father assured her that he would.

It was only when they'd eaten, and there was a silence as they pondered on whether to have pudding or not, that Lisa realized they had sat through an entire lunch without a mention of Ruby. 'I expect Ruby will have arrived in Argentina by now,' she cut in quickly to redress the balance.

Her father ordered fresh raspberries. 'She most certainly should have, unless she hijacked the plane and made a forced landing in New York.'

They both laughed and Lisa asked the waiter for chocolate cake with a double portion of ice cream.

MARGUERITE HAD decided she would accompany Lisa when her appointment with the specialist came round. Lisa sweated in dread at the thought of both her parents sitting, side by side, in the interminable shuffling hush of a hospital waiting-room. She tried to talk her out of it, but Marguerite was adamant.

On the morning of the appointed day a threatening, high-pitched ringing started up in her ears. 'NO.' She shook her head. 'No, it's not a good idea,' and she clutched her stomach and groaned to back up her outburst.

Marguerite rushed to put the kettle on. She stirred honey into camomile tea and, once Lisa was wrapped in blankets and propped up with a pillow, she calmly agreed to stay behind.

The whine in Lisa's ears died. She felt as light as air. She grinned at her mother. 'You mustn't worry about me,' she said, and she added silently to herself with a little skip of her heart, 'I'm all right. I'm all right. I'm going to be all right.'

*   *   *

The hospital was a private hospital and there was not the pale green waiting-room she had anticipated. She was shown into a small room like an office and given a long, cold drink the consistency of milk shake. The doctor watched it travel through her intestine on a television screen.

He looked over at Lisa and raised his eyebrows. He was young and clean-shaven with perfectly manicured nails. 'Do you smoke?' Lisa squirmed, but he didn't wait for an answer. 'Give up. You hear me? You have an extremely sensitive system and any irritant could have devastating effects.'

Lisa pulled down her jumper and came and sat in the spare chair at his desk. She felt giddy with his words and sick with the lead lying at the bottom of her stomach.

'From now on, you will eat three meals a day.' He looked at her sternly, and he began to write out a prescription. She was to mix a sachet of powder with a full glass of water and drink it before each meal. After each meal she was to take a pill. 'Morning, midday and evening.'

Lisa opened her mouth to protest, but the doctor shook the creases out of his trousers and showed her to the door.

'Three meals a day,' she told her father when she eventually found him sprawled across a leather sofa reading a copy of *Country Life*. 'I've heard worse,' he said, and he took her hand and led her out across the sea of carpet.

L ISA SAT IN the canteen with Eugene and Janey. They watched as she tore the top off a sachet of medicine and poured its contents into a plastic beaker. It frothed and fizzed and finally dissolved into a glutinous orange drink, which Lisa proceeded to gulp down. 'I haven't been well,' she told them as she drained her glass. She had to wait five minutes before she could start on her paper plate of ravioli.

'Pete's very impressed with your project,' Janey said. 'I overheard him talking to Denise.'

'Really?' Lisa smiled guiltily.

'He said if your practical comes up to the same standard, you could get an A in your Drama which would mean you were eligible for a full grant to go to drama school. What pieces are you doing?'

'I don't know.'

Janey had chosen hers already. Beatie from *Roots* by Arnold Wesker. And for her classical, Juliet's balcony speech.

'I suppose I could do something from the *Three Sisters*.'

'I'm a seagull, I'm a seagull, no, no, I'm an actress.' Eugene mimicked the exact speech she had in mind with his hand fluttering in mock melodrama across his brow.

Janey's face lit up. 'Listen, we've got time before the next lesson, why don't we walk down to RADA and collect some application forms? You have to apply now if you want to be seen next year. When's your birthday?'

'August.'

'Right, so you'll be seventeen by the time they see you. You can pretend you're eighteen, and by the time you get a place you nearly will be.'

'If I get in.'

'You've got a better chance than I have. At least to them you're not a Paki with a Purley accent. And you've got the chance of a grant.'

Lisa remembered and took her after-meal pill.

'Coming, Eugene?'

'You think I want to waste my time with drama school?' According to Eugene, he had made important contacts during his two-and-a-half years as an usher. 'I shall audition for the top West End shows.' He bared his teeth in a broad, white smile and tapped a double shuffle under the table. His singing followed them as they hurried from the canteen.

RADA was a twenty-minute walk from their college. Janey knew of someone who had been accepted there several years ago, but who had been unable to get a grant.

'From our course?'

'Yes.'

'Accepted at RADA!' Lisa was incredulous.

'And then not to be able to go,' Janey added sorrowfully. 'It depends on what borough you live in. Some boroughs are more stingy than others. I've heard Purley is one of the worst.'

Lisa had often walked into the West End with groups of girls from the Full Time Speech and Drama course. The lunch hour at college had stretched with each term so that often the morning and the afternoon classes were divided by over two hours. The route they took in order to window-shop or browse in the shops on Tottenham Court Road invariably led past the stone façade of RADA. 'Royal Acadamy of Dramatic Art,' they all murmured reverentially as they passed. Until now it had never occurred to Lisa that she might be eligible to apply.

Lisa and Janey pushed open the door and wandered into the hall. There was a wall of gold-tinted glass inscribed with the names of graduating students. Lisa didn't recognize any of them, not having been brought up with television, but Janey pointed and gasped as her eyes travelled down the list.

Lisa looked around hopefully for a real-life student. She expected to see girls in leotards with curling, pre-Raphaelite hair, and men who looked like James Dean, but there was no one about. In fact RADA had finished early for Easter. They found the office and collected an application form each. The application forms came with a suggestion sheet for students preparing speeches. One classical, pre-

236

ferably Shakespeare. One modern. Not exceeding three minutes. At the bottom of the page was an asterisked note. 'Actresses: We would be grateful if applicants could refrain from preparing Beatie from *Roots*, and to see another balcony scene from *Romeo and Juliet* would not be helpful.'

Janey was mortified, and they walked back to college in silence.

That evening as Lisa neared home, passing fearlessly through the short cut to emerge unscathed at the top of the ramp, she saw her mother's anxious face watching out for her from the front window of their flat. Marguerite waved frantically and disappeared from view. Lisa raced across Peerless Street and bumped into her on the pavement.

'Lisa, we've been offered a flat.' She had come out without her shoes.

Lisa shook her head in disbelief.

'We've been offered a council flat. With three bedrooms. Kitchen and sitting-room!'

'And bathroom?'

'And bathroom, of course.' And they hugged each other and ran back up the stairs to their landing. In a spirit of celebration they kicked open the front door without bothering to search their pockets for a key.

The next morning early, Marguerite, Lisa and Max put on their best clothes and went to inspect their new home. It was on the other side of the Old Street roundabout, a little further east towards the City. The flat was a miniature house within a modern block of maisonettes. The doors were painted alternately in olive-green and brown, and the windows were cut in single panes of glass.

'Is this it?' Lisa asked once they were inside.

Marguerite looked sternly at her. 'It's permanent.'

The sitting-room was L-shaped and had a long, sliding window that looked over a graveyard. Outside was a narrow, concrete slip of balcony wide enough to hang a single line of washing.

A permanent home! Lisa thought, and looked over at her mother. Marguerite was rapping at the wall around the gas fire in the hope of locating a hidden flue.

Lisa sighed, and pushed past her. Upstairs there were three square bedrooms with low ceilings and a small, tilting window in each.

Max ran into the bathroom and lay down in the bath. Lisa had told him how, when she was his age, she had spent time pretending to be dead. Max had taken this particular game to heart and practised it whenever he remembered. Lisa, as a child, had lain for what seemed like hours behind a sofa or under a bed, patiently waiting for someone to discover her, but Max, the minute he had closed his eyes, demanded ferociously that all present rush to his aid.

Lisa stood over him now and put her finger to her lips. 'Max, shhh,' she said urgently. He had one eye open and she knew that he could see her.

'Were you worried?' he asked, leaping to his feet.

Lisa lifted him out of the bath. 'The idea,' she told him for the hundredth time, 'is to stay silent for as long as you possibly can. No one should even hear you squeak.'

Max slid rebelliously to the floor. He shot her a scornful, disappointed glance. Lisa supposed that he probably had stayed silent for as long as he possibly could.

Lisa walked back downstairs. The staircase was short and squat with a centre strip just waiting to be carpeted. Inside the kitchen there were matching rows of cupboards, below and above the sink, and new, flecked lino that fitted tightly into every corner. A ventilator hissed shrilly as it spun for air. Lisa found herself thinking nostalgically of Peerless Street, with its draughts and cracks and the temperamental cold tap that dripped for no reason in the middle of the night.

'We are incredibly lucky,' Marguerite told her on the walk home, 'it's practically unheard of to be rehoused so soon.' But they didn't meet each other's eye.

That night Lisa lay in bed and wondered if there was any way in which she would be able to stay on in Peerless Flats. With or without her mother. She ran her hand lovingly over the woodchip paper, and followed the pattern of reflected light where it fell from the window in its nightly grid, distorted on the wall. She listened for the beat of upstairs' music and the familiar creaking of their front door as the wind from the stairwell caught at its loose hinges. She imagined she knew by heart each pair of hurrying feet as they passed each other on the stairs.

Lisa woke with the word 'permanent' stinging in her thoughts. She found her mother already up, puzzling over a letter. 'This is the most extraordinary thing,' and she continued to read. Marguerite shook her head and turned the letter over. 'The most extraordinary thing.'

Lisa tried to take it out of her hands. She could see the New Swift emblem on the letterhead. 'What is it?'

'It seems' – Marguerite let her eyes travel over the sense of the letter – 'that New Swift are finally prepared to offer us somewhere to live.'

There were also two letters for Lisa. One was from Mr Bunzl, asking why she had missed her last appointment. The other was from her father. 'A hot tip for the three-thirty-five Saturday. Ascot. Will you be my guest?' Lisa smiled and folded his letter so it would fit into her treasure box.

She put off going into college and, with Max only too happy to miss another day of school, they slipped sheepishly out on to the street and headed for the bus stop. They saw Heidi folding washing in the bay window of her flat, but they didn't stop to talk. Lisa felt greedy and full of choices. She thought of Frances's soft, despairing voice as she packed up to go home to Ireland, and the family on the top floor who were penalized for pouring the grease from frying-pans out of their kitchen window. It stuck like glue to the side of the building and left a cold, stale smell. They had been waiting over four years to be rehoused.

The New Swift house was on the other side of Archway and they had instructions to collect the key from Russell, a Co-op member who lived near the tube. Russell was one of the earnest, bearded men who presided so laboriously over meetings, and he directed them across the Holloway Road and on through a maze of short, Edwardian terraces intercut with the walls and corners of new, red-brick estates.

'Is it a modern house?' Lisa asked, but Marguerite didn't know.

'The only thing I do know is that it's temporary.' She laughed and shook her head. 'We shouldn't even be considering it.'

The Co-op house was in a cul-de-sac that crossed the railway line at the top of Hornsey Rise. It was a three-storey house with a crack across the ground-floor window and a front garden piled high with rubbish. The next-door house was derelict and boarded up.

Marguerite referred to the letter. 'Yes, this is it,' she sighed. 'And we can live here for anything up to a year and a half.'

Lisa took the key out of her hand and with some difficulty turned it in the lock. Light from a broken window in the back door flooded through the house and caught in the swirling dust dislodged by their arrival. Max ran down the passage beside the stairs, jumped over a hole in the floor-boards and pulled at the handle of the back door. He pulled so hard it came away and he fell over backwards, hitting his head against the wall. 'OW,' he moaned, and Marguerite muttered a regret that she hadn't let him wear his helmet.

The back door was in fact unlocked, and swung open with a twist of the metal pin. Max picked himself up and hurtled out into the sunshine. He was heading for the row of lilac trees that grew in the broken fence between the two back gardens. Lisa caught him just in time and held him by the shoulders. Marguerite came out and joined her, and even Max stopped his struggling and stared. The garden wasn't a garden, but a rubbish dump. It was trampled and rotted and formed into a waist-high plateau of mattresses and faded plastic. Three broken-up cisterns lay half buried. Over the top, glinting in the light, lay a liberal scattering of hypodermic needles.

'Look at those exquisite lilacs,' Marguerite pointed. 'There's a white one, and that purple one there is about to burst into flower.'

'I want to climb a tree,' Max yelled, but they went back inside to explore the house.

The house was light, and dusty, and bore evidence of various ramshackle attempts at redecoration. Several bannisters were bright pink and others had been stripped and polished to their natural state. The wooden floorboards around the edges of the kitchen were painted in black and white squares, as if the lino that had once been there hadn't been quite wide enough.

They trooped into the room at the front of the house. It had a fireplace with an iron grate and was made private by the towering hedge that grew in the front garden. It cast the dark green shadow of a thousand swimming minnows across the walls. From the inside the crack in the glass didn't look so dangerous and the rubbish was out of view below the window-sill. Lisa looked sidelong at her mother.

Upstairs were two large bedrooms with sash windows that stretched from floor to ceiling and a bathroom on the landing below. At each landing the bannisters changed their colour, and as they continued up, Lisa noticed they were speckled with little blobs of shiny paint. Max was the first to arrive at the top of the stairs. 'Reinforcements!' he thundered, as he charged the door to the back bedroom.

'What is it?' Lisa called after him. He had stopped with the door half open and refused to go in.

'Reinforcements for foxes,' he muttered as if his life depended on it, and he started back down the stairs.

Marguerite pushed past them and peered into the room. She caught her breath and then as the seconds passed in silence she let it out with a long hiss between her teeth. 'Look at this.' Lisa stood on tiptoe to see over her shoulder. The smell in the room was thick and bitter and hit her like a gag. She was forced to breathe in through her mouth.

Inside the room was a mattress that looked as if it might have been retrieved from the garden. It was brown and stained and curled up at the corners. In its centre was a dank mound of blanket. Lisa knew what had stopped Max in his tracks. She could feel her own dread of what lay hidden there rising up inside her. She felt Max's fingers tapping the back of her legs.

'Look at those smelly old blankets,' she told him, swallowing her fear, and she thought she understood why it was that women had children. 'Look at those smelly old blankets with nothing inside but air.'

'Yes, it looks like whoever's been living here has certainly moved out,' Marguerite agreed and she strode across the room and threw open the window. A blast of fresh spring air blew through the room and a train rumbled past on the railway line.

'It's a terribly important decision.' Marguerite locked up the house. 'A terribly important decision.'

Lisa bent her head to hide her smile. It was just a matter of time before her mother gave in to the challenge. 'We could hire a skip,' she suggested, 'and wheel the rubbish along the downstairs corridor and out through the front door. If we asked everyone we know to help, it would only take a couple of days.'

'We could keep bees, at the back of the garden.' Marguerite's eyes began to shine. 'I rather fancy being a member of the Inner London Bee-keeping Society.'

Max danced ahead of them. 'Do foxes climb trees?'

'Or we could get a cat.'

'It is possible' – Marguerite was entering into the spirit of adventure – 'the Co-op may let us have it for longer than they say.'

'Anything can happen in a year and a half,' Lisa encouraged. She was thinking about the white branches of the lilac brushing up against the bathroom window. In winter she could make a wood fire in her bedroom, and hang thick velvet curtains to block out the draught. Quentin, who lived just over the hill, might tap his fingers on the glass to wake her in the middle of one night.

Marguerite took her arm. 'But I thought it was what you always wanted. A permanent home.'

'It was.'

Max danced ahead of them in a wild zigzag across the pavement. 'I'll plant an army in the garden,' he yelled joyously.

A NOTE ON THE TYPE

The text of this book is set in Linotype Sabon, named
after the type founder, Jacques Sabon. It was designed
by Jan Tschichold and jointly developed by Linotype,
Monotype and Stempel, in response to a need for a
typeface to be available in identical form for
mechanical hot metal composition and
hand composition using foundry type.

Tschichold based his design for Sabon roman on
a font engraved by Garamond, and Sabon italic
on a font by Granjon. It was first used in 1966
and has proved an enduring modern classic.

B L O O M S B U R Y

Love Falls

'*Love Falls* captures the delicious uncertainty and electrifying beginnings of first love' *Glamour*

It is July, three months after Lara's seventeenth birthday and a week before Charles and Diana's Royal Wedding. When Lara's father, a man she barely knows, invites her to accompany him on holiday, she finds herself in the sun-scorched hillsides of Tuscany, far away from the fumes of London's Holloway Road. There she meets the Willoughby family, rife with illicit alliances and vendettas. The more embroiled she becomes with them, and with the carelessly beautiful Kip, the more Lara is consumed with doubt, curiosity and dread. And so begins her intoxicating journey into self-discovery and across the very fine line between childhood and what lies beyond.

'A vividly rendered portrait of a young girl's journey towards self-discovery and maturity' *Daily Mail*

'Her most subtle and most affecting book yet' *Independent on Sunday*

ISBN 978 0 7475 9319 5/ Paperback / £7.99

BLOOMSBURY

Summer at Gaglow

'A perfectly paced piece of high-calibre storytelling' *Observer*

'Evocative and intriguing' *Elle*

Summer, 1914. It is Emanuel's twenty-first birthday, and eleven-year-old Eva and her sisters are helping transform Gaglow for a glorious party. But their brother's arrival is overshadowed by the talk of war that comes with him from Hamburg, and when he is wrenched from the family to serve his country, Eva knows that nothing will be the same again. Seventy-five years later, with the fall of the Berlin Wall, Sarah's father begins to tell her about Gaglow, the grand East German country estate that will now come back to them. Alternating between Sarah's bohemian life in London and her grandmother's childhood during the First World War, *Summer at Gaglow* unites four generations of an extraordinary family in a tale of loss and love.

'Reading, you become sort of a tourist, delightedly snooping on how these others live . . . Fresh, witty, ironic and touching' *Independent on Sunday*

'Freud's observations are acute . . . and there is delightful, youthful innocence, all the more poignant for its backdrop of war' *Daily Mail*

Published in paperback by Bloomsbury January 2009

ISBN 978 0 7475 9769 8/ Paperback / £7.99

BLOOMSBURY

The Wild

'A beautiful book, savage and tender by turns attending to Esther Freud's still, truthful voice becomes not only a pleasure but a necessity' Jonathan Coe

Nine-year-old Tess has never seen anything like The Wild. An old bakery, converted into a home, it has a fireplace big enough to sit in, a garden with a badminton net and another one for vegetables. And then there's William, its owner. Single father of three, he cooks homemade ravioli, cuts trees down with a chainsaw and plays the guitar. When her mother, Francine, rents two rooms from him, Tess can hardly believe her luck. Her brother Jake, however, proves harder to convince. As the two grown-ups begin to fall for each other, Tess struggles to please the adults as well as win Jake round. But she finds that good intentions don't always bring happiness and that adults are disturbingly capable of making mistakes . . .

'Ranks alongside *Paddy Clarke Ha Ha Ha* as one of the very few great contemporary novels about childhood' William Sutcliffe, *Independent on Sunday*

'She is brilliant – no, more than that, she's probably the best author of her generation – at depicting siblings and their infinite, terrible rivalries . . . exceptional' *Herald*

Published in paperback by Bloomsbury January 2009

ISBN 978 0 7475 9770 4/ Paperback / £7.99

Order your copy:

By phone: 01256 302 699

By email: direct@macmillan.co.uk

Delivery is usually 3-5 working days.
Postage and packaging will be charged.

Online: www.bloomsbury.com/bookshop

Free postage and packaging for orders over £15.

Prices and availability subject to change without notice.

Visit Bloomsbury.com for more about Esther Freud